Alexis de Tocqueville

The State of Society in France

before the Revolution of 1789 - and the causes which led to that event

Alexis de Tocqueville

The State of Society in France
before the Revolution of 1789 - and the causes which led to that event

ISBN/EAN: 9783337230401

Printed in Europe, USA, Canada, Australia, Japan

Cover: Foto ©Andreas Hilbeck / pixelio.de

More available books at **www.hansebooks.com**

THE STATE OF

SOCIETY IN FRANCE

BEFORE THE

REVOLUTION OF 1789

AND THE

CAUSES WHICH LED TO THAT EVENT

By ALEXIS DE TOCQUEVILLE

MEMBER OF THE FRENCH ACADEMY

TRANSLATED BY HENRY REEVE, D.C.L.

THIRD EDITION

LONDON

JOHN MURRAY, ALBEMARLE STREET

1888

CONTENTS.

—◆◇◆—

A 2

SUPPLEMENTARY CHAPTER.

BOOK III.

TRANSLATOR'S PREFACE

An interval of about seventeen years has elapsed since the first publication of this book in France, and of the translation of it, which appeared simultaneously, in England. The English version has not been republished, and has long been out of print. But the work itself has retained a lasting place in the political literature of Europe.

The historical events which have occurred since the date of its first publication have again riveted the attention of every thinking man on the astonishing phenomena of the French Revolution, which has resumed in these later days its mysterious and destructive course ; and a deeper interest than ever seems to attach itself to the first causes of this long series of political and social convulsions, which appear to be as far as ever from their termination.

Nor is this interest confined to the state of France alone ; for at each succeeding period of our contemporary annals the operation and effects of the same causes may be traced in other countries, and the principles which the author of this book discerned with unerring sagacity derive fresh illustrations every day from the course of events both abroad and at home.

For this reason, mainly, this translation is republished at the present time, in the hope that it may be read by men of the younger generation, who were not in being when it first appeared, and that some of those who read it before may be led by the light of passing events to read it again.   For I venture to say that in no other work on the French Revolution has the art of scientific analysis been applied with equal skill to the genesis of these great changes : no other writer has so skilfully traced the continuous operation of the causes, long anterior to the Revolution itself, which have gradually reduced one of the greatest monarchies of Europe to its present condition.

Are we to learn from this stern lesson of experience that the hopes of progress are closely united to the germs of dissolution, and that the great transformation hailed with so much enthusiasm eighty-four years ago was but the prelude of a final catastrophe ; that the nation which was the first to plunge into this new order of things, by the destruction of all that it once loved and revered, is also the first to make manifest its fatal results ; and that the last results of civilisation are no preservative against the decline of empires?   These pages may suggest such reflections, for if the vices and abuses of political society in France before the Revolution were, in some measure, peculiar to herself, the elements of destruction which the Revolution let loose upon the world are common to all civilised nations.

In the present edition, moreover, it appeared to be desirable to make a considerable addition to the volume published in 1856.   At the time of his death in the spring of 1859, M. de Tocqueville had made some progress in the continuation of his work, though his labour advanced very slowly, from the minute and conscientious care with which he conducted his researches and elaborated his thoughts.   Seven chapters of the new volume were, however, found among his papers by his friend and literary executor, M. Gustave de Beaumont, in a state approaching to completeness ; and these posthumous chapters were published in the seventh volume of the collected edition of M. de Tocqueville's works.   They have not before been translated, and they are, I believe, but little known in this country.

These chapters are not inferior, I think, to any of the works of their author in originality and interest ; and they have the merit of bringing down his Survey of the State of France before the Revolution to the very moment which preceded the convocation of the States-General.   I have therefore included these posthumous chapters in the present edition, and they form a Third Book, in addition to the two books of the original volume.

HENRY REEVE.

April 1873.

PRELIMINARY NOTICE.

THE book I now publish is not a history of the French Revolution; that history has been written with too much success for me to attempt to write it again. This volume is a study on the Revolution.

The French people made, in 1789, the greatest effort which was ever attempted by any nation to cut, so to speak, their destiny in halves, and to separate by an abyss that which they had heretofore been from that which they sought to become hereafter. For this purpose they took all sorts of precautions to carry nothing of their past with them into their new condition; they submitted to every species of constraint in order to fashion themselves otherwise than their fathers were; they neglected nothing which could efface their identity.

I have always thought that they had succeeded in this singular attempt much less than was supposed abroad, and less than they had at first supposed themselves. I was convinced that they had unconsciously retained from the former state of society most of the sentiments, the habits, and even the opinions, by means of which they had effected the destruction of that state of things; and that, without intending it, they had used its remains to rebuild the edifice of modern society, insomuch that, fully to understand the Revolution and its work, we must forget for an instant that France which we see before us, and examine in her sepulchre that France which is no more. This is what I have endeavoured to do; but I have had more difficulty than I could have supposed in accomplishing this task.

The first ages of the French Monarchy, the Middle Ages, and the Revival of Letters have each given rise to vast researches and profound disquisitions which have revealed to us not only the events of those periods of history, but the laws, the customs, and the spirit of the Government and the nation in those eras. But no one has yet taken the trouble to investigate the eighteenth century in the same manner and with the same minuteness. We suppose that we are thoroughly conversant with the French society of that date, because we clearly distinguish whatever glittered on its surface; we possess in detail the lives of the most eminent persons of that day, and the ingenuity or the eloquence of criticism has familiarised us with the compositions of the great writers who adorned it. But as for the manner in which public affairs were carried on, the practical working of institutions, the exact relation in which the different classes of society stood to each other, the condition and the feelings of those classes which were as yet neither seen nor heard beneath the prevailing opinions and manners of the country,—all our ideas are confused and often inaccurate.

I have undertaken to reach the core of this state of society under the old monarchy of France, which is still so near us in the lapse of years, but concealed from us by the Revolution.

For this purpose I have not only read over again the celebrated books which the eighteenth century produced, I have also studied a multitude of works less known and less worthy to be known, but which, from the negligence of their composition, disclose, perhaps, even better than more finished productions, the real instincts of the time. I have applied myself to investigate thoroughly all the public documents by which the French may, at the approach of the Revolution, have shown their opinions and their tastes. The regular reports of the meetings of the States, and subsequently of the Provincial Assemblies, have supplied me with a large quantity of evidence. I have especially made great use of the Instructions drawn up by the Three Orders in 1789. These Instructions, which form in the original a long series of manuscript volumes, will remain as the testament of the old society of France, the supreme record of its wishes, the authentic declaration of its last intentions. Such a document is unique in history. Yet this alone has not satisfied me.

In countries in which the Administrative Government is already powerful, there are few opinions, desires, or sorrows—there are few interests or passions—which are not sooner or later stripped bare before it. In the archives of such a Government, not only an exact notion of its procedure may be acquired, but the whole country is exhibited. Any stranger who should have access to all the confidential correspondence of the Home Department and the Prefectures of France would soon know more about the French than they know themselves. In the eighteenth century the administration of the country, as will be seen from this book, was highly centralised, very powerful, prodigiously active. It was incessantly aiding, preventing, permitting. It had much to promise—much to give. Its influence was already felt in a thousand ways, not only on the general conduct of affairs, but on the condition of families and the private life of every individual. Moreover, as this administration was without publicity, men were not afraid to lay bare before its eyes even their most secret infirmities. I have spent a great deal of time in studying what remains of its proceedings, both at Paris and in several provinces.[1]

There, as I expected, I have found the whole structure of the old monarchy still in existence, with its opinions, its passions, its prejudices, and its usages. There every man spoke his mind and disclosed his innermost thoughts. I have thus succeeded in acquiring information on the former state of society, which those who lived in it did not possess, for I had before me that which had never been exposed to them.

As I advanced in these researches I was surprised perpetually to find again in the France of that time many of the characteristic features of the France of our own. I met with a multitude of feelings which I had supposed to be the offspring of the Revolution —a multitude of ideas which I had believed to originate there—a multitude of habits which are attributed to the Revolution alone. Everywhere I found the roots of the existing state of French society deeply imbedded in the old soil. The nearer I came to 1789, the more distinctly I discerned the spirit which had presided over the formation, the birth, and the growth of the Revolution; I gradually saw the whole aspect of the Revolution uncovered before me; already it announced its temperament—its genius—itself. There, too, I found not only the reason of what it was about to perform in its first effort, but still more, perhaps, an intimation of what it was eventually to leave behind it. For the French Revolution has had two totally distinct phases: the first, during which the French seemed eager to abolish everything in the past; the second, when they sought to resume a portion of what they had relinquished. Many of the laws and political practices of the old monarchy thus

---

[1] I have more especially used the archives of some of the great Intendancies, particularly that of Tours, which are very complete and relate to a very extensive district placed in the centre of France, and peopled by a million of inhabitants. My thanks are due to the young and able keeper of these records, M. Grandmaison. Other districts, amongst them that of the Île-de-France, have shown me that business was transacted in the same manner in the greater part of the kingdom

suddenly disappeared in 1789, but they occur again some years later, as some rivers are lost in the earth to burst forth again lower down, and bear the same waters to other shores.

The peculiar object of the work I now submit to the public is to explain why this great Revolution, which was in preparation at the same time over almost the whole continent of Europe, broke out in France sooner than elsewhere; why it sprang spontaneously from the society it was about to destroy; and, lastly, how the old French Monarchy came to fall so completely and so abruptly.

It is not my intention that the work I have commenced should stop short at this point. I hope, if time and my own powers permit it, to follow, through the vicissitudes of this long Revolution, these same Frenchmen with whom I have lived so familiarly under the old monarchy, and whom that state of society had formed—to see them modified and transformed by the course of events, but without changing their nature, and constantly appearing before us with features somewhat different, but ever to be recognised.

With them I shall proceed to review that first epoch of 1789, when the love of equality and that of freedom shared their hearts —when they sought to found not only the institutions of democracy, but the institutions of freedom—not only to destroy privileges, but to acknowledge and to sanction rights: a time of youth, of enthusiasm, of pride, of generous and sincere passion, which, in spite of its errors, will live for ever in the memory of men, and which will still long continue to disturb the slumbers of those who seek to corrupt or to enslave them.

Thus rapidly following the track of this same Revolution, I shall attempt to show by what events, by what faults, by what miscarriages, this same French people was led at last to relinquish its first aim, and, forgetful of freedom, to aspire only to become the equal servants of the World's Master—how a Government, stronger and far more absolute than that which the Revolution had overthrown, grasped and concentrated all the powers of the nation, suppressed the liberties which had been so dearly bought, putting in their place the counterfeit of freedom—calling 'sovereignty of the people' the suffrages of electors who can neither inform themselves nor concert their operations, nor, in fact, choose—calling 'vote of taxes' the assent of mute and enslaved assemblies; and while thus robbing the nation of the right of self-government, of the great securities of law, of freedom of thought, of speech, and of the pen—that is, of all the most precious and the most noble conquests of 1789—still daring to assume that mighty name.

I shall pause at the moment when the Revolution appears to me to have nearly accomplished its work and given birth to the modern society of France. That society will then fall under my observation : I shall endeavour to point out in what it resembles the society which preceded it, in what it differs, what we have lost in this immense displacement of our institutions, what we have gained by it, and, lastly, what may be our future.

A portion of this second work is sketched out, though still unworthy to be offered to the public. Will it be given me to complete it ? Who can say ? The destiny of men is far more obscure than that of nations.

I hope I have written this book without prejudice, but I do not profess to have written it without passion. No Frenchman should speak of his country and think of this time unmoved. I acknowledge that in studying the old society of France in each of its parts I have never entirely lost sight of the society of more recent times. I have sought not only to discover the disease of which the patient died, but also the means by which life might have been preserved. I have imitated that medical analysis which seeks in each expiring organ to catch the laws of life. My object has been to draw a picture strictly accurate, and at the same time instructive. Whenever I have met amongst our progenitors with any of those masculine virtues which we most want and which we least possess—such as a true spirit of independence, a taste for great things, faith in ourselves and in a cause—I have placed them in relief : so, too, when I have found in the laws, the opinions, and the manners of that time traces of some of those vices which after having consumed the former society of France still infest us, I have carefully brought them to the light, in order that, seeing the evil they have done us, it might better be understood what evils they may still engender. To accomplish this object I confess I have not feared to wound either persons, or classes, or opinions, or recollections of the past, however worthy of respect they may be. I have done so often with regret, but always without remorse. May those whom I have thus perhaps offended forgive me in consideration of the honest and disinterested object which I pursue.

Many will perhaps accuse me of showing in this book a very unseasonable love of freedom—a thing for which it is said that no one any longer cares in France.

I shall only beg those who may address to me this reproach to consider that this is no recent inclination of my mind. More than twenty years ago, speaking of another community, I wrote almost textually the following observations.

Amidst the darkness of the future three truths may be clearly discovered. The first is, that all the men of our time are impelled by an unknown force which they may hope to regulate and to check, but not to conquer—a force which sometimes gently moves them, sometimes hurries them along, to the destruction of aristocracy. The second is, that of all the communities in the world those which will always be least able permanently to escape from absolute government are precisely the communities in which aristocracy has ceased to exist, and can never exist again. Lastly, the third is, that despotism nowhere produces more pernicious effects than in these same communities, for more than any other form of government despotism favours the growth of all the vices to which such societies are specially liable, and thus throws an additional weight on that side to which, by their natural inclination, they were already prone.

Men in such countries, being no longer connected together by any ties of caste, of class, of corporation, of family, are but too easily inclined to think of nothing but their private interests, ever too ready to consider themselves only, and to sink into the narrow precincts of self, in which all public virtue is extinguished. Despotism, instead of combating this tendency, renders it irresistible, for it deprives its subjects of every common passion, of every mutual want, of all necessity of combining together, of all occasions of acting together. It immures them in private life: they already tended to separation; despotism isolates them: they were already chilled in their mutual regard; despotism reduces them to ice.

In such societies, in which nothing is stable, every man is incessantly stimulated by the fear of falling and by eagerness to rise; and as money, while it has become the principal mark by which men are classed and distinguished, has acquired an extraordinary mobility, passing without cessation from hand to hand, transforming the condition of persons, raising or lowering that of families, there is scarcely a man who is not compelled to make desperate and continual efforts to retain or to acquire it. The desire to be rich at any cost, the love of business, the passion of lucre, the pursuit of comfort and of material pleasures, are therefore in such communities the prevalent passions. They are easily diffused through all classes, they penetrate even to those classes which had hitherto been most free from them, and would soon enervate and degrade them all, if nothing checked their influence. But it is of the very essence of despotism to favour and extend that influence. These debilitating passions assist its work : they divert and engross the imaginations of men away from public affairs, and cause them to tremble at the bare idea of a revolution. Despotism alone can lend them the secrecy and the shade which put cupidity at its ease, and enable men to make dishonourable gains whilst they brave dishonour. Without despotic government such passions would be strong : with it they are sovereign.

Freedom alone, on the contrary, can effectually counteract in communities of this kind the vices which are natural to them, and restrain them on the declivity along which they glide. For freedom alone can withdraw the members of such a community from the isolation in which the very independence of their condition places them by compelling them to act together. Freedom alone can warm and unite them day by day by the necessity of mutual agreement, of mutual persuasion, and mutual complaisance in the transaction of their common affairs. Freedom alone can tear them from the worship of money, and the petty squabbles of their private interests, to remind them and make them feel that they have a Country above them and about them. Freedom alone can sometimes supersede the love of comfort by more energetic and more exalted passions—can supply ambition with larger objects than the acquisition of riches—can create the light which enables us to see and to judge the vices and the virtues of mankind.

Democratic communities which are not free may be rich, refined, adorned, magnificent, powerful by the weight of their uniform mass; they may contain many private merits—good fathers of families, honest traders, estimable men of property ; nay, many good Christians will be found there, for their country is not of this world, and the glory of their faith is to produce such men amidst the greatest depravity of manners and under the worst government. The Roman Empire in its extreme decay was full of such men. But that which, I am confident, will never be found in such societies is a great citizen, or, above all, a great people ; nay, I do not hesitate to affirm that the common level of the heart and the intellect will never cease to sink as long as equality of conditions and despotic power are combined there.

Thus I thought and thus I wrote twenty years ago. I confess that since that time nothing has occurred in the world to induce me to think or to write otherwise. Having expressed the good opinion I had of Freedom at a time when Freedom was in favour, I may be allowed to persist in that opinion though she be forsaken.

Let it also be considered that even in this I am less at variance with most of my antagonists than perhaps they themselves suppose. Where is the man who, by nature, should have so mean a soul as to prefer dependence on the caprices of one of his fellow-creatures to obedience to laws which he has himself contributed to establish, provided that his nation appear to him to possess the virtues necessary to use freedom aright? There is no such man. Despots themselves do not deny the excellence of freedom, but they wish to keep it all to themselves, and maintain that all other men are utterly unworthy of it. Thus it is not on the opinion which may be entertained of freedom that this difference subsists, but on the greater or the less esteem we may have for mankind; and it may be said with strict accuracy that the taste a man may show for absolute government bears an exact ratio to the contempt he may profess for his countrymen. I pause before I can be converted to that opinion.

I may add, I think, without undue pretensions, that the volume now published is the product of very extended labours. Sometimes a short chapter has cost me more than a year of researches. I might have surcharged my pages with notes, but I have preferred to insert them in a limited number at the end of the volume, with a reference to the pages of the text to which they relate. In these notes the reader will find some illustrations and proofs of what I have advanced. I could largely augment the quantity of them if this book should appear to require it.

STATE OF SOCIETY IN FRANCE

BEFORE THE

REVOLUTION OF 1789.

BOOK I.

CHAPTER I.

OPPOSING JUDGMENTS PASSED ON THE FRENCH REVOLUTION AT
ITS ORIGIN.

NOTHING is better fitted to give a lesson in modesty to philosophers
and statesmen than the history of the French Revolution; for never
were there events more important, longer in ripening, more fully
prepared, or less foreseen.

The great Frederick himself, with all his genius, failed to
perceive what was coming, and was almost in contact with the
event without seeing it. Nay, more, he even acted in the spirit
of the Revolution beforehand, and was in some sort its precursor,
and already its agent; yet he did not recognise its approach, and
when at length it made its appearance, the new and extraordinary
features which were to distinguish its aspect, amidst the countless
crowd of human revolutions, still passed unheeded.

The curiosity of all other countries was on the stretch. Everywhere an indistinct conception arose amongst the nations that a
new period was at hand, and vague hopes were excited of great
changes and reforms; but no one as yet had any suspicion of what
the Revolution was really to become. Princes and their ministers
lacked even the confused presentiment by which the masses were
agitated; they beheld in the Revolution only one of those periodical disorders to which the constitutions of all nations are subject,
and of which the only result is to open fresh paths for the policy

B

of their neighbours.   Even when they did chance to express a true opinion on the events before them, they did so unconsciously. Thus the principal sovereigns of Germany assembled at Pillnitz in 1791, proclaimed indeed that the danger which threatened royalty in France was common to all the established powers of Europe, and that all were threatened by the same peril; but in fact they believed nothing of the kind.   The secret records of the period prove that they held this language only as a specious pretext to cover their real designs, or at least to colour them in the eyes of the multitude.

As for themselves, they were convinced that the French Revolution was an accident merely local and temporary, which they had only to turn to good account.   With this notion they laid plans, made preparations, and contracted secret alliances; they quarrelled among themselves for the division of their anticipated spoils; split into factions, entered into combinations, and were prepared for almost every event, except that which was impending.

The English indeed, taught by their own history and enlightened by the long practice of political freedom, perceived dimly, as through a thick veil, the approaching spectre of a great revolution; but they were unable to distinguish its real shape, and the influence it was so soon to exercise upon the destinies of the world and upon their own was unforeseen.   Arthur Young, who travelled over France just as the Revolution was on the point of breaking out, and who regarded it as imminent, so entirely mistook its real character, that he thought it was a question whether it would not increase existing privileges.   ‘As for the nobility and clergy,’ says he, ‘if this Revolution were to make them still more preponderant, I think it would do more harm than good.’

Burke, whose genius was illuminated by the hatred with which the Revolution inspired him from its birth, Burke himself hesitated, for a moment uncertain, at the sight.   His first prediction was that France would be enervated, and almost annihilated by it. ‘France is, at this time, in a political light, to be considered as expunged out of the system of Europe; whether she could ever appear in it again as a leading power, was not easy to determine; but at present he considered France as not politically existing; and, most assuredly, it would take up much time to restore her to her former active existence.   *Gallos quoque in bellis floruisse audivimus*, might possibly be the language of the rising generation.’ [1]

The judgment of those on the spot was not less erroneous than that of distant observers.   On the eve of the outbreak of the

[1] Burke’s speech on the Army estimates, 1790.

Revolution, men in France had no distinct notion of what it would do. Amidst the numerous instructions to the delegates of the States General I have found but two which manifest some degree of apprehension of the people. The fears expressed all relate to the preponderance likely to be retained by royalty, or the Court, as it was still called. The weakness and the short duration of the States General were a source of anxiety, and fears were entertained that they might be subjected to violence. The nobility were especially agitated by these fears. Several of their instructions provide, ' The Swiss troops shall take an oath never to bear arms against the citizens, not even in case of riot or revolt.' Only let the States General be free, and all abuses would easily be destroyed; the reform to be made was immense, but easy.

Meanwhile the Revolution pursued its course. By degrees the head of the monster became visible, its strange and terrible aspect was disclosed; after destroying political institutions it abolished civil institutions also; after changing the laws it changed the manners, the customs, and even the language of France; after overthrowing the fabric of government it shook the foundations of society, and rose against the Almighty himself. The Revolution soon overflowed the boundaries of France with a vehemence hitherto unknown, with new tactics, with sanguinary doctrines, with *armed opinions*—to use the words of Pitt—with an inconceivable force which struck down the barriers of empires, shattered the crowns of Europe, trampled on its people, though, strange to say, it won them to its cause; and, as all these things came to pass, the judgment of the world changed. That which at first had seemed to the princes and statesmen of Europe to be one of the accidents common in the life of a nation, now appeared to them an event so unprecedented, so contrary to all that had ever happened in the world, and, at the same time, so wide-spread, so monstrous, and so incomprehensible, that the human mind was lost in amazement at the spectacle. Some believed that this unknown power, which nothing seemed to foster or to destroy, which no one was able to check, and which could not check itself, must drive all human society to its final and complete dissolution. Many looked upon it as the visible action of the devil upon earth. ' The French Revolution has a Satanic character,' says M. de Maistre, as early as 1797. Others, on the contrary, perceived in it a beneficent design of Providence to change the face not only of France but of the world, and to create, as it were, a new era of mankind. In many writers of that time may be seen somewhat of the religious terror which Salvian felt at the incursion of the Barbarians. Burke, reverting to his first impressions, exclaimed, 'Deprived of the old government, deprived in a manner of all government, France, fallen as a monarchy, to common speculators, might have appeared more likely to be an object of pity or insult, according to the disposition of the circumjacent powers, than to be the scourge and terror of them all; but out of the tomb of the murdered monarchy in France has arisen a vast, tremendous, unformed spectre, in a far more terrific guise than any which ever yet have overpowered the imagination, and subdued the fortitude of man. Going straight forward to its end unappalled by peril, unchecked by remorse, despising all common maxims and all common means, that hideous phantom overpowered those who could not believe it was possible she could at all exist,' etc.[1]

And was the event really as extraordinary as it appeared to those who lived at the time when it took place? Was it so unprecedented, so utterly subversive, so pregnant with new forms and ideas as they imagined it to be? What was the real meaning, the real character—what have been the permanent effects of this strange and terrible Revolution? What did it, in reality, destroy, and what has it created?

The proper moment for examining and deciding these questions seems now to have arrived, and we are now standing at the precise point whence this vast phenomenon may best be viewed and judged. We are far enough removed from the Revolution to be but slightly touched by the passions which blinded those who brought it about, and we are near enough to it to enter into the spirit which caused these things to happen. Ere long this will have become more difficult; for as all great revolutions, when successful, sweep away the causes which engendered them, their very success serves to render them unintelligible to later generations.

[1] Letters on a Regicide Peace.

CHAPTER II.

THE FUNDAMENTAL AND FINAL OBJECT OF THE REVOLUTION WAS NOT,
AS HAS BEEN SUPPOSED, THE DESTRUCTION OF RELIGIOUS AUTHORITY
AND THE WEAKENING OF POLITICAL POWER.

ONE of the first acts of the French Revolution was to attack the
Church; and amongst all the passions born of the Revolution the
first to be excited and the last to be allayed were the passions
hostile to religion. Even when the enthusiasm for liberty had
vanished, and tranquillity had been purchased at the price of
servitude, the nation still revolted against religious authority.
Napoleon, who had succeeded in subduing the liberal spirit of the
French Revolution, made vain efforts to restrain its antichristian
spirit; and even in our own time we have seen men who thought
to atone for their servility towards the meanest agents of political
power by insolence towards God, and who whilst they abandoned
all that was most free, most noble, and most lofty in the doctrines
of the Revolution, flattered themselves that they still remained true
to its spirit by remaining irreligious.

Nevertheless it is easy now to convince ourselves that the war
waged against religions was but one incident of this great Revolution,
a feature striking indeed but transient in its aspect, a passing result
of the ideas, the passions, and special events which preceded and
prepared it, and not an integral part of its genius.

The philosophy of the eighteenth century has rightly been
looked upon as one of the chief causes of the Revolution, and it is
quite true that this philosophy was profoundly irreligious. But
we must be careful to observe that it contains two distinct and
separable parts.

One of these relates to all the new or newly revived opinions
concerning the condition of society, and the principles of civil and
political laws, such, for instance, as the natural equality of mankind,
and the abolition of all privileges of caste, of class, of profession,
which is the consequence of that equality; the sovereignty of the
people, the omnipotence of social power, the uniformity of laws.
All these doctrines were not only causes of the French Revolution,

they were its very substance: of all its effects they are the most fundamental, the most lasting, and the most true, as far as time is concerned. —)/(nti-clergy

In the other part of their doctrines the philosophers of the eighteenth century attacked the Church with the utmost fury; they fell foul of her clergy, her hierarchy, her institutions, her dogmas; and, in order more surely to overthrow them, they endeavoured to tear up the very foundations of Christianity. But as this part of the philosophy of the eighteenth century arose out of the very abuses which the Revolution destroyed, it necessarily disappeared together with them, and was as it were buried beneath its own triumph. I will add but one word to make myself more fully understood, as I shall return hereafter to this important subject: it was in the character of a political institution, far more than in that of a religious doctrine, that Christianity had inspired such fierce hatreds; it was not so much because the priests assumed authority over the concerns of the next world, as because they were landowners, landlords, tithe-owners, and administrators in this world; not because the Church was unable to find a place in the new society which was about to be constituted, but because she filled the strongest and most privileged place in the old state of society which was doomed to destruction.

Observe how the progress of time has made and still makes this truth more and more palpable day by day. In the same measure that the political effects of the Revolution have become more firmly established, its irreligious results have been annihilated; in the same measure that all the old political institutions which the Revolution attacked have been entirely destroyed—that the powers, the influences, and the classes which were the objects of its especial hostility have been irrevocably crushed, until even the hatred they inspired has begun to lose its intensity—in the same measure, in short, as the clergy has separated itself more and more from all that formerly fell with it, we have seen the power of the Church gradually regain and re-establish its ascendency over the minds of men.

Neither must it be supposed that this phenomenon is peculiar to France; there is hardly any Christian church in Europe that has not recovered vitality since the French Revolution.

It is a great mistake to suppose that the democratic state of society is necessarily hostile to religion: nothing in Christianity, or even in Catholicism, is absolutely opposed to the spirit of this form of society, and many things in democracy are extremely favourable to it. Moreover, the experience of all ages has shown that the most living root of religious belief has ever been planted in the heart of the people. All the religions which have perished lingered longest in that abode, and it would be strange indeed if institutions which tend to give power to the ideas and passions of the people were, as a permanent and inevitable result, to lead the minds of men towards impiety.

What has just been said of religious, may be predicated even more strongly of social, authority.

When the Revolution overthrew at once all the institutions and all the customs which up to that time had maintained certain gradations in society, and kept men within certain bounds, it seemed as if the result would be the total destruction not only of one particular order of society, but of all order: not only of this or that form of government, but of all social authority; and its nature was judged to be essentially anarchical. Nevertheless, I maintain that this too was true only in appearance.

Within a year from the beginning of the revolution, Mirabeau wrote secretly to the King: ' Compare the new state of things with the old rule; there is the ground for comfort and hope. One part of the acts of the National Assembly, and that the more considerable part, is evidently favourable to monarchical government. Is it nothing to be without parliaments? without the *pays d'état*? without a body of clergy? without a privileged class? without a nobility? The idea of forming a single class of all the citizens would have pleased Richelieu; this equality of the surface facilitates the exercise of power. Several successive reigns of an absolute monarchy would not have done as much for the royal authority as this one year of revolution.' Such was the view of the Revolution taken by a man capable of guiding it. →Rid of all tradition

As the object of the French Revolution was not only to change an ancient form of government, but also to abolish an ancient state of society, it had to attack at once every established authority, to destroy every recognised influence, to efface all traditions, to create new manners and customs, and, as it were, to purge the human mind of all the ideas upon which respect and obedience had hitherto been based. Thence arose its singularly anarchical character.

But, clear away the ruins, and you behold an immense central power, which has attracted and absorbed into unity all the fractions of authority and influence which had formerly been dispersed amongst a host of secondary powers, orders, classes, professions, families and individuals, and which were disseminated throughout the whole fabric of society. The world had not seen such a power

since the fall of the Roman Empire. This power was created by
the Revolution, or rather it arose spontaneously out of the ruins
which the Revolution had left. The governments which it founded
are more perishable, it is true, but a hundred times more powerful than any of those which it overthrew; we shall see hereafter that their fragility and their power were owing to the same
causes.

It was this simple, regular, and imposing form of power
which Mirabeau perceived through the dust and rubbish of ancient,
half-demolished institutions. This object, in spite of its greatness,
was still invisible to the eyes of the many, but time has gradually
unveiled it to all eyes. At the present moment it especially attracts
the attention of rulers : it is looked upon with admiration and envy
not only by those whom the Revolution has created, but by those who
are the most alien and the most hostile to it; all endeavour, within
their own dominions, to destroy immunities and to abolish privileges.
They confound ranks, they equalise classes, they supersede the
aristocracy by public functionaries, local franchises by uniform
enactments, and the diversities of authority by the unity of a
Central Government. They labour at this revolutionary task with
unwearied industry, and when they meet with occasional obstacles,
they do not scruple to copy the measures as well as the maxims of
the Revolution. They have even stirred up the poor against the
rich, the middle classes against the nobility, the peasants against
their feudal lords. The French Revolution has been at once their
curse and their instructor.

CHAPTER III.

SHOWING THAT THE FRENCH REVOLUTION WAS A POLITICAL REVOLU-
TION WHICH FOLLOWED THE COURSE OF RELIGIOUS REVOLUTIONS,
AND FOR WHAT REASONS.

ALL mere civil and political revolutions have had some country for
their birth-place, and have remained circumscribed within its limits.
The French Revolution, however, had no territorial boundary—far
from it; one of its effects has been to efface as it were all ancient
frontiers from the map of Europe.   It united or it divided mankind
in spite of laws, traditions, characters, and languages, turning fellow-
countrymen into enemies, and foreigners into brothers; or rather,
it formed an intellectual country common to men of every nation,
but independent of all separate nationalities.

We should search all the annals of history in vain for a political
revolution of the same character; that character is only to be
found in certain religious revolutions.   And accordingly it is to
them that the French Revolution must be compared, if any light is
to be thrown upon it by analogy.

Schiller remarks, with truth, in his 'History of the Thirty
Years' War,' that the great Reformation of the sixteenth century
had the effect of bringing together nations which scarcely knew
each other, and of closely uniting them by new sympathies.   Thus
it was that Frenchmen warred against Frenchmen, while English-
men came to their assistance; men born on the most distant shores
of the Baltic penetrated into the very heart of Germany in order
to defend Germans of whose existence they had never heard until
then.   International wars assumed something of the character of
civil wars, whilst in every civil war foreigners were engaged.   The
former interests of every nation were forgotten in behalf of new
interests; territorial questions were succeeded by questions of
principle.   The rules of diplomacy were involved in inextricable
confusion, greatly to the horror and amazement of the politicians
of the time.   The very same thing happened in Europe after 1789.

The French Revolution was then a political revolution, which
in its operation and its aspect resembled a religious one.   It had
every peculiar and characteristic feature of a religious movement;

it not only spread to foreign countries, but it was carried thither
by preaching and by propaganda. It is impossible to conceive a
stranger spectacle than that of a political revolution which inspires
proselytism, which its adherents preach to foreigners with as much
ardour and passion as they have shown in enacting it at home. Of
all the new and strange things displayed to the world by the
French Revolution, this assuredly is the newest. On penetrating
deeper into this matter, we shall most likely discover that this
similarity of effects must be produced by a latent similarity of causes.

The general character of most religions is, that they deal with
man by himself, without taking into consideration whatever the
laws, the traditions, and the customs of each country may have
added to his original nature. Their principal aim is to regulate
the relations of man towards God, and the rights and duties of men
towards each other, independently of the various forms of society.
The rules of conduct which they inculcate apply less to the man of
any particular country or period than to man as a son, a father, a
servant, a master, or a neighbour. Being thus based on human
nature itself, they are applicable to all men, and at all times, and in
all places. It is owing to this cause that religious revolutions have
so often spread over such vast spheres of action, and have seldom
been confined, like political revolutions, to the territory of a single
nation, or even of a single race. If we investigate this subject still
more closely, we shall find that the more any religion has possessed
the abstract and general character to which I refer, the wider has
it spread, in spite of all differences of laws, of climate, and of races.

The pagan religions of antiquity, which were all more or less
bound up with the political constitution or the social condition of
each nation, and which displayed even in their dogmas a certain
national, and even municipal, character, seldom spread beyond
their own territorial limits. They sometimes engendered intolerance and persecution, but proselytism was to them unknown.
Accordingly there were no great religious revolutions in Western
Europe previous to the introduction of Christianity, which easily
broke through barriers that had been insurmountable to the pagan
religions, and rapidly conquered a large portion of the human race.
It is no disrespect to this holy religion to say, that it partly owed
its triumph to the fact that it was more free than any other faith
from everything peculiar to any one nation, form of government,
social condition, period, or race.

The French Revolution proceeded, as far as this world is concerned, in precisely the same manner that religious revolutions
proceed with regard to the next; it looked upon the citizen in the

CHAP. III. UNIVERSAL CHARACTER 11

→ interests of the individual

abstract, irrespective of any particular society, just as most religions look upon man in general independently of time or country. It did not endeavour merely to define what were the especial rights of a French citizen, but what were the universal duties and rights of all men in political matters. It was by thus recurring to that which was least peculiar and, we might almost say, most *natural* in the principles of society and of government that the French Revolution was rendered intelligible to all men, and could be imitated in a hundred different places.

As it affected to tend more towards the regeneration of mankind than even towards the reform of France, it roused passions such as the most violent political revolutions had never before excited. It inspired a spirit of proselytism and created the propaganda. This gave to it that aspect of a religious revolution which so terrified its contemporaries, or rather, we should say, it became a kind of new religion in itself—a religion, imperfect it is true, without a God, without a worship, without a future life, but which nevertheless, like Islam, poured forth its soldiers, its apostles, and its martyrs over the face of the earth.

It must not, however, be imagined that the mode of operation pursued by the French Revolution was altogether without precedent, or that all the ideas which it developed were entirely new. In every age, even in the depths of the Middle Ages, there had been agitators who invoked the universal laws of human society in order to subvert particular customs, and who have attempted to oppose the constitutions of their own countries with weapons borrowed from the natural rights of mankind. But all these attempts had failed; the firebrand which ignited Europe in the eighteenth century had been easily extinguished in the fifteenth. Revolutions are not to be produced by arguments of this nature until certain changes have already been effected in the condition, the habits, and the manners of a nation, by which the minds of men are prepared to undergo a change.

There are periods in which men differ so completely from each other, that the notion of a single law applicable to all is entirely incomprehensible to them. There are others in which it is sufficient to show to them from afar off the indistinct image of such a law in order to make them recognise it at once, and hasten to adopt it.

The most extraordinary phenomenon is not so much that the French Revolution should have pursued the course it did, and have developed the ideas to which it gave rise, but that so many nations should have reached a point at which such a course could be effectually employed and such maxims be readily admitted.

CHAPTER IV.

SHOWING THAT NEARLY THE WHOLE OF EUROPE HAD HAD PRE-
CISELY THE SAME INSTITUTIONS, AND THAT THESE INSTITUTIONS
WERE EVERYWHERE FALLING TO PIECES.

THE tribes which overthrew the Roman Empire, and which in the
end formed all the modern nations of Europe, differed among each
other in race, in country, and in language; they only resembled
each other in barbarism. Once established in the dominions of the
empire they engaged in a long and fierce struggle, and when at
length they had gained a firm footing they found themselves
divided by the very ruins they had made. Civilisation was almost
extinct, public order at an end, the relations between man and
man had become difficult and dangerous, and the great body of
European society was broken up into thousands of small distinct
and hostile societies, each of which lived apart from the rest.
Nevertheless certain uniform laws arose all at once out of the
midst of this incoherent mass.

These institutions were not copied from the Roman legislation;[1]
indeed they were so much opposed to it that recourse was had to
the Roman law to alter and abolish them. They have certain
original characteristics which distinguish them from all other laws
invented by mankind. They corresponded to each other in all their
parts, and, taken together, they formed a body of law so compact
that the articles of our modern codes are not more perfectly co-
herent; they were skilfully framed laws intended for a half-savage
state of society.

It is not my purpose to inquire how such a system of legislation
could have arisen, spread, and become general throughout Europe.
But it is certain that in the Middle Ages it existed more or less in
every European nation, and that in many it prevailed to the exclu-
sion of every other.

I have had occasion to study the political institutions of the
Middle Ages in France, in England, and in Germany, and the
further I proceeded in my labours the more was I astonished at

---

[1] See Note. I., on the Power of the Roman Law in Germany.

the prodigious similarity which existed amongst all these various
sets of laws ; and the more did I wonder how nations so different,
and having so little intercourse, could have contrived laws so much
alike. Not but they continually and almost immeasurably differ
in their details and in different countries, but the basis is invariably the same. If I discovered a political institution, a law, a fixed
authority, in the ancient Germanic legislation, I was sure, on
searching further, to find something exactly analogous to it in
France and in England. Each of these three nations helped me
more fully to understand the others.

In all three the government was carried on according to the
same maxims, political assemblies were formed out of the same
elements, and invested with the same powers. Society was divided
in the same manner, and the same gradation of classes subsisted in
each ; in all three the position of the nobles, their privileges, their
characteristics, and their disposition were identical ; as men they
were not distinguishable, but rather, properly speaking, the same
men in every place.

The municipal constitutions were alike; the rural districts were
governed in the same manner. The condition of the peasantry
differed but little ; the land was owned, occupied, and tilled after
the same fashion, and the cultivators were subjected to the same
burthens. From the confines of Poland to the Irish Channel, the
Lord's estate, the manorial courts, the fiefs, the quit-rents, feudal
service, feudal rights, and the corporations or trading guilds, were
all alike. Sometimes the very names were the same; and what
is still more remarkable, the same spirit breathes in all these analogous institutions. I think I may venture to affirm, that in the
fourteenth century the social, political, administrative, judicial,
economical, and literary institutions of Europe were more nearly
akin to each other than they are at the present time, when civilisation appears to have opened all the channels of communication,
and to have levelled every obstacle.

It is no part of my scheme to relate how this ancient constitution of Europe gradually became wasted and decayed ; it is sufficient to remark that in the eighteenth century it was everywhere
falling into ruin.[1] On the whole, its decline was less marked in
the east than in the west of the continent ; but on all sides old age
and decrepitude were visible.

The progress of this gradual decay of the institutions of the
Middle Ages may be followed in the archives of the different
nations. It is well known that each manor kept rolls called

---

[1] See Note II., on the passage from Feudal to Democratic Monarchy.

terriers, in which from century to century were recorded the limits of fiefs and the quit-rents, the dues, the services to be rendered, and the local customs. I have seen rolls of the thirteenth and fourteenth centuries which are masterpieces of method, perspicuity, concision, and acuteness. The further we advance towards modern times the more obscure, ill-digested, defective, and confused do they become, in spite of the general progress of enlightenment. It seems as if political society became barbarous, while civil society advances towards civilisation.

Even in Germany, where the ancient constitution of Europe had preserved many more of its primitive features than in France, some of the institutions which it had created were already completely destroyed. But we shall not be so well able to appreciate the ravages of time when we take into account what was gone, as when we examine the condition of what was left.

The municipal institutions which in the thirteenth and fourteenth centuries had raised the chief towns of Germany into rich and enlightened small republics, still existed in the eighteenth; but they were a mere semblance of the past. Their ancient traditions seemed to continue in force; the magistrates appointed by them bore the same titles and seemed to perform the same functions; but the activity, the energy, the municipal patriotism, the manly and prolific virtues which they formerly inspired, had disappeared. These ancient institutions appeared to have collapsed without losing the form that distinguished them.[1]

All the powers of the Middle Ages which where still in existence seemed to be affected by the same disease; all showed symptoms of the same languor and decay. Nay more, whatever was mixed up with the constitution of that time, and had retained a strong impression of it, even without absolutely belonging to those institutions, at once lost its vitality. Thus it was that the aristocracy was seized with senile debility; even political freedom, which had filled the preceding centuries with its achievements, seemed stricken with impotency wherever it preserved the peculiar characteristics impressed upon it by the Middle Ages. Wherever the Provincial Assemblies had maintained their ancient constitution unchanged, they checked instead of furthering the progress of civilisation; they seemed insensible and impervious to the new spirit of the times. Accordingly the hearts of the people turned from them towards their sovereigns. The antiquity of these institutions had not made them venerable: on the contrary, the older they grew the more they fell into discredit; and, strangely enough,

[1] See Note III., on the Decay of the Free Towns of Germany.

they inspired more and more hatred in proportion as their decay rendered them less capable of mischief. 'The actual state of things,' said a German writer, who was a friend and contemporary of the period anterior to the French Revolution, 'seems to have become generally offensive to all, and sometimes contemptible. It is strange to see with what disfavour men now look upon all that is old. New impressions creep into the bosom of our families and disturb their peace. Our very housewives will no longer endure their ancient furniture.' Nevertheless, at this time Germany, as well as France, enjoyed a high state of social activity and constantly increasing prosperity. But it must be borne in mind that all the elements of life, activity and production, were new, and not only new, but antagonistic to the past.

Royalty no longer had anything in common with the royalty of the Middle Ages, it enjoyed other prerogatives, occupied a different place, was imbued with a different spirit, and inspired different sentiments; the administration of the State spread in all directions upon the ruins of local authorities; the organised array of public officers superseded more and more the government of the nobles. All these new powers employed methods and followed maxims which the men of the Middle Ages had either not known or had condemned; and, indeed, they belong to a state of society of which those men could have formed no idea.

In England, where, at the first glance, the ancient constitution of Europe might still seem in full vigour, the case is the same. Setting aside the ancient names and the old forms, in England the feudal system was substantially abolished in the seventeenth century; all classes of society began to intermingle, the pretensions of birth were effaced, the aristocracy was thrown open, wealth was becoming power, equality was established before the law, public employments were open to all, the press became free, the debates of Parliament public; every one of them new principles, unknown to the society of the Middle Ages. It is precisely these new elements, gradually and skilfully incorporated with the ancient constitution of England, which have revived without endangering it, and filled it with new life and vigour without destroying the ancient forms. In the seventeenth century England was already quite a modern nation, which had still preserved, and, as it were, embalmed some of the relics of the Middle Ages.

This rapid view of the state of things beyond the boundaries of France was essential to the comprehension of what is about to follow; for no one who has seen and studied France only, can ever— I venture to affirm—understand anything of the French Revolution.

CHAPTER V.

WHAT WAS THE PECULIAR SCOPE OF THE FRENCH REVOLUTION.

THE preceding pages have had no other purpose than to throw some light on the subject in hand, and to facilitate the solution of the questions which I laid down in the beginning, namely, what was the real object of the Revolution? What was its peculiar character? For what precise reason it was made, and what did it effect?

The Revolution was not made, as some have supposed, in order to destroy the authority of religious belief. In spite of appearances, it was essentially a social and political Revolution; and within the circle of social and political institutions it did not tend to perpetuate and give stability to disorder, or (as one of its chief adversaries had said) to methodise anarchy; but rather to increase the power and the rights of public authority. It was not destined (as others have believed) to change the whole character which civilisation had previously assumed, to check its progress, or even essentially to alter any of the fundamental laws upon which human society in Western Europe is based. If we divest it of all the accidental circumstances which altered its aspect in different countries and at various times, and consider only the Revolution itself, we shall clearly perceive that its only effect has been to abolish those political institutions which during several centuries had been in force among the greater part of the European nations, and which are usually designated as feudal institutions, in order to substitute a more uniform and simple state of society and politics, based upon an equality of social condition.

This was quite sufficient to constitute an immense revolution, for not only were these ancient institutions mixed up and interwoven with almost all the religious and political laws of Europe, but they had also given rise to a crowd of ideas, sentiments, habits, and manners which clung around them. Nothing less than a frightful convulsion could suddenly destroy and expel from the social body a part to which all its organs adhered. This made the Revolution appear even greater than it really was; it seemed to destroy everything, for what it did destroy was bound up with, and formed, as it were, one flesh with everything in the social body.

However radical the Revolution may have been, its innovations were, in fact, much less than has been commonly supposed, as I shall show hereafter. What may truly be said is, that it entirely destroyed, or is still destroying (for it is not at an end), every part of the ancient state of society that owed its origin to aristocratic and feudal institutions—everything in any way connected with those institutions, or in any degree, however slight, imbued with their spirit. It spared no part of the old world, save such as had always been foreign to those institutions, or could exist apart from them. Least of all was the Revolution a fortuitous event. It took the world by surprise, it is true, but it was not the less the completion of a long process, the sudden and violent termination of a work which had successively passed before the eyes of ten generations. If it had not taken place, the old social structure would equally have fallen sooner in one place and later in another —only it would have crumbled away by degrees instead of falling with a crash. The Revolution effected on a sudden and by a violent and convulsive effort, without any transition, without forethought, without mercy, that which would have happened little by little if left to itself. This was its work.

It is surprising that this view of the subject, which now seems so easy to discern, should have been so obscured and confused even to the clearest perceptions.

'Instead of redressing their grievances,' says Burke of the representatives of the French nation, 'and improving the fabric of their state, to which they were called by their monarch and sent by their country, they were made to take a very different course. They first destroyed all the balances and counterpoises which serve to fix the State and to give it a steady direction, and which furnish sure correctives to any violent spirit which may prevail in any of the orders. These balances existed in the oldest constitution and in the constitution of all the countries in Europe. These they rashly destroyed, and then they melted down the whole into one incongruous, ill-connected mass.' [1]

Burke did not perceive that he had before his eyes the very Revolution which was to abolish the ancient common law of Europe ; he could not discern that this and no other was the very question at issue.

[1] Burke's speech on the Army Estimates, 1790.

But why, we may ask, did this Revolution, which was imminent throughout Europe, break out in France rather than elsewhere, and why did it there display certain characteristics which have appeared nowhere else, or at least have appeared only in part? This second question is well worthy of consideration, and the inquiry will form the subject of the following book.

BOOK II.

CHAPTER I.

WHY FEUDAL RIGHTS HAD BECOME MORE ODIOUS TO THE PEOPLE
IN FRANCE THAN IN ANY OTHER COUNTRY.

IT must at first sight excite surprise that the Revolution, whose
peculiar object it was, as we have seen, everywhere to abolish the
remnant of the institutions of the Middle Ages, did not break out
in the countries in which these institutions, still in better preservation, caused the people most to feel their constraint and their
rigour, but, on the contrary, in the countries where their effects
were least felt; so that the burden seemed most intolerable where
it was in reality least heavy.

In no part of Germany, at the close of the eighteenth century,
was serfdom as yet completely abolished,[1] and in the greater part
of Germany the people were still literally *adscripti glebæ*, as in the
Middle Ages.   Almost all the soldiers who fought in the armies of
Frederic II. and of Maria Theresa were in reality serfs.[2]   In most
of the German States, as late as 1788, a peasant could not quit his
domain, and if he quitted it he might be pursued in all places
wherever he could be found, and brought back by force.   In that
domain he lived subject to the seignorial jurisdiction which controlled his domestic life and punished his intemperance or his sloth.
He could neither improve his condition, nor change his calling, nor
marry without the good pleasure of his master.   To the service of
that master a large portion of his time was due.   Labour rents
(*corvées*) existed to their full extent, and absorbed in some of these
countries three days in the week.   The peasant rebuilt and repaired
the mansion of the lord, carted his produce to market, drove his
carriage, and went on his errands.   Several years of the peasant's
early life were spent in the domestic service of the manor-house.
The serf might, however, become the owner of land, but his pro-

[1] See Note IV., Date of Abolition of Serfdom in Germany.
[2] See Note V.

perty always remained very incomplete. He was obliged to till his field in a certain manner under the eye of the master, and he could neither dispose of it nor mortgage it at will. In some cases he was compelled to sell its produce; in others he was restrained from selling it; his obligation to cultivate the ground was absolute. Even his inheritance did not descend without deduction to his offspring; a fine was commonly subtracted by the lord.

I am not seeking out these provisions in obsolete laws. They are to be met with even in the Code framed by Frederic the Great and promulgated by his successor at the very time of the outbreak of the French Revolution.[1]

Nothing of the kind had existed in France for a long period of time. The peasant came, and went, and bought, and sold, and dealt, and laboured, as he pleased. The last traces of serfdom could only be detected in one or two of the eastern provinces annexed to France by conquest; everywhere else the institution had disappeared; and indeed its abolition had occurred so long before that even the date of it was forgotten. The researches of archæologists of our own day have proved that as early as the thirteenth century serfdom was no longer to be met with in Normandy.

But in the condition of the people in France another and a still greater revolution had taken place. The French peasant had not only ceased to be a serf; he had become an Owner of Land. This fact is still at the present time so imperfectly established, and its consequences, as will presently be seen, have been so remarkable, that I must be permitted to pause for a moment to examine it.

It has long been believed that the subdivision of landed property in France dates from the Revolution of 1789, and was only the result of that Revolution. The contrary is demonstrable by every species of evidence.

Twenty years at least before that Revolution, Agricultural Societies were in existence which already deplored the excessive subdivision of the soil. ' The division of inheritances,' said M. de Turgot, about the same time, ' is such that what sufficed for a single family is shared among five or six children. These children and their families can therefore no longer subsist exclusively by the land.' Necker said a few years later that there was in France an *immensity* of small rural properties.

I have met the following expressions in a secret Report made to one of the provincial Intendants a few years before the Revo-

[1] See Note VI.

lution :—'Inheritances are divided in an equal and alarming manner, and as every one wishes to have something of everything, and everywhere, the plots of land are infinitely divided and perpetually subdivided.' Might not this sentence have been written in our days ?

I have myself taken the infinite pains to reconstruct, as it were, the survey of landed property as it existed in France before the Revolution, and I have in some cases effected my object. In pursuance of the law of 1790, which established the land-tax, each parish had to frame a return of the landed properties then existing within its boundaries. These returns have for the most part disappeared; nevertheless I have found them in a few villages, and by comparing them with the rolls of the present holders, I have found that, in these villages, the number of landed proprietors at that time amounted to one-half, frequently to two-thirds, of their present number: a fact which is the more remarkable if it be remembered that the total population of France has augmented by more than one-fourth since that period.

Already, as at the present time, the love of the peasant for property in land was intense, and all the passions which the possession of the soil has engendered in his nature were already inflamed. 'Land is always sold above its value,' said an excellent contemporary observer; 'which arises from the passion of all the inhabitants to become owners of the soil. All the savings of the lower orders which elsewhere are placed out at private interest, or in the public securities, are intended in France for the purchase of land.'

Amongst the novelties which Arthur Young observed in France, when he visited that country for the first time, none struck him more than the great division of the soil among the peasantry. He averred that half the soil of France belonged to them in fee. ' I had no idea,' he often says, ' of such a state of things;' and it is true that such a state of things existed at that time nowhere but in France, or in the immediate neighbourhood of France.

In England there had been peasant landowners, but the number of them had already considerably decreased. In Germany there had been at all times and in all parts of the country a certain number of peasant freeholders, who held portions of the soil in fee. The peculiar and often eccentric laws which regulated the property of these peasants are to be met with in the oldest of the Germanic customs; but this species of property was always of an exceptional character, and the number of these small proprietors was very limited.[1]

[1] See Note VII., Peasant Lands in Germany.

The districts of Germany in which, at the close of the eighteenth century, the peasants were possessed of land and lived almost as freely as in France, lay on the banks of the Rhine.[1] In those same districts the revolutionary passions of France spread with the utmost velocity, and have always been most intense. The tracts of Germany which remained, on the contrary, for the longest time inaccessible to these passions, are those where no such tenures of land had yet been introduced. The observation deserves to be made.

It is, then, a vulgar error to suppose that the subdivision of landed property in France dates from the Revolution. This state of things is far older. The Revolution, it is true, caused the lands of the Church and a great portion of the lands of the nobility to be sold; but if any one will take the trouble, as I have sometimes done, to refer to the actual returns and entries of these sales, it will be seen that most of these lands were purchased by persons who already held other lands; so that though the property changed hands, the number of proprietors increased far less than is supposed. There was already an *immensity* of these persons, to borrow the somewhat ambitious but, in this case, not inaccurate expression of M. Necker.

The effect of the Revolution was not to divide the soil, but to liberate it for a moment. All these small landowners were, in reality, ill at ease in the cultivation of their property, and had to bear many charges or easements on the land which they could not shake off.

These charges were no doubt onerous.[2] But the cause which made them appear insupportable was precisely that which might have seemed calculated to diminish the burden of them. The peasants of France had been released, more than in any other part of Europe, from the government of their lords, by a revolution not less momentous than that which had made them owners of the soil.

Although what is termed in France the Ancien Régime is still very near to us, since we live in daily intercourse with men born under its laws, that period seems already lost in the night of time. The radical revolution which separates us from it has produced the effect of ages : it has obliterated all that it has not destroyed. Few persons therefore can now give an accurate answer to the simple question—How were the rural districts of France administered before 1789 ? And indeed no answer can be

---

[1] See Note VIII., Nobility and Lands on the Rhine.
[2] See Note IX., Effect of Usury Laws on Land.

given to that question with precision and minuteness, without having studied, not books, but the administrative records of that period.

It is often said that the French nobility, which had long ceased to take part in the government of the State, preserved to the last the administration of the rural districts—the Seigneurs governed the peasantry. This again is very like a mistake.

In the eighteenth century all the affairs of the parish were managed by a certain number of parochial officers, who were no longer the agents of the manor or domain, and whom the Lord no longer selected. Some of these persons were nominated by the Intendant of the province, others were elected by the peasants themselves. The duty of these authorities was to assess the taxes, to repair the church, to build schools, to convoke and preside over the vestry or parochial meeting. They attended to the property of the parish and determined the application of it— they sued and were sued in its name. Not only the lord of the domain no longer conducted the administration of these small local affairs, but he did not even superintend it. All the parish officers were under the government or the control of the central power, as we shall show in a subsequent chapter. Nay, more, the Seigneur had almost ceased to act as the representative of the Crown in the parish, or as the channel of communication between the King and his subjects. He was no longer expected to apply in the parish the general laws of the realm, to call out the militia, to collect the taxes, to promulgate the mandates of the sovereign, or to distribute the bounty of the Crown. All these duties and all these rights belonged to others. The Seigneur was in fact no longer anything but an inhabitant of the parish, separated by his own immunities and privileges from all the other inhabitants. His rank was different, not his power. *The Seigneur is only the principal inhabitant* was the instruction constantly given by the Provincial Intendants to their Sub-delegates.

If we quit the parish, and examine the constitution of the larger rural districts, we shall find the same state of things. Nowhere did the nobles conduct public business either in their collective or their individual capacity. This was peculiar to France. Everywhere else the characteristic features of the old feudal society were partially preserved : the possession of the soil and the government of those who dwelt on the soil were still commingled.

England was administered as well as governed by the chief owners of the soil. Even in those parts of Germany, as in Prussia

and in Austria, in which the reigning princes had been most successful in shaking off the control of the nobles in the general
affairs of the state, they had left to that class, to a great degree,
the administration of rural affairs, and though the landed proprietor
was, in some places, controlled by the Government, his authority
had nowhere been superseded.

page:
(power
ed)

To say the truth, the French nobility had long since lost all
hold on the administration of public affairs, except on one single
point, that namely of justice. The principal nobles still retained
the right of having judges who decided certain suits in their name,
and occasionally established police regulations within the limits of
their domain; but the power of the Crown had gradually cut
down, limited, and subdued this seignorial jurisdiction to such a
degree that the nobles who still exercised it regarded it less as a
source of authority than as a source of income.

Such had been the fate of all the peculiar rights of the French
nobility. The political element had disappeared; the pecuniary
element alone remained, and in some instances had been largely
increased. —>Little political power.

I speak at this moment of that portion of the beneficial privileges of the aristocracy, which were especially called by the name
of feudal rights, since they were the privileges which peculiarly
touched the people.

It is not easy to ascertain in what these rights did precisely
still consist in 1789, for the number of them had been great, their
diversity amazing, and many of these rights had already vanished
or undergone a transformation; so that the meaning of the terms
by which they were designated was perplexing even to contemporaries, and is become obscure to us. Nevertheless by consulting
the works of the domanial jurists of the eighteenth century, and
from attentive researches into local customs, it will be found that
all the rights still in existence at that time may be reduced to a
small number of leading heads; all the others still subsisted, it is
true, but only in isolated cases.

The traces of seignorial labour-rents (*corvées*) may almost
everywhere be detected, but they were already half extinguished.
Most of the tolls on roads had been reduced or abolished; yet there
were few provinces in which some such tolls were not still to be
met with. Everywhere too Seigneurs levied dues on fairs and
markets. Throughout France they had the exclusive right of
sporting. Generally they alone could keep dovecotes and pigeons;
almost everywhere the peasant was compelled to grind at the
seignorial mill, and to crush his grapes in the seignorial wine-

press. A very universal and onerous seignorial right was that of the fine called *lods et ventes*, paid to the lord every time lands were bought or sold within the boundaries of his manor. All over the country the land was burdened with quit-rents, rent-charges, or dues in money or in kind, due to the lord from the copyholder, and not redeemable by the latter. Under all these differences one common feature may be traced. All these rights were more or less connected with the soil or with its produce; they all bore upon him who cultivates it.[1]

The spiritual lords of the soil enjoyed the same advantages; for the Church, which had a different origin, a different purpose, and a different nature from the feudal system, had nevertheless at last intimately mingled itself with that system; and though never completely incorporated with that foreign substance, it had struck so deeply into it as to be incrusted there.[2]

Bishops, canons, and incumbents held fiefs or charges on the land in virtue of their ecclesiastical functions. A convent had generally the lordship of the village in which it stood. The Church held serfs in the only part of France in which they still existed: it levied its labour-rents, its due on fairs and markets; it had the common oven, the common mill, the common wine-press, and the common bull. Moreover, the clergy still enjoyed in France, as in all the rest of Christendom, the right of tithe.[3]

But what I am here concerned to remark is, that throughout Europe at that time the same feudal rights—*identically the same* —existed, and that in most of the continental states they were far more onerous than in France. I may quote the single instance of the seignorial claim for labour: in France this right was unfrequent and mild; in Germany it was still universal and harsh.

Nay more, many of the rights of feudal origin which were held in the utmost abhorrence by the last generation of Frenchmen, and which they considered as contrary not only to justice but to civilisation—such as tithes, inalienable rent-charges or perpetual dues, fines or heriots, and what were termed, in the somewhat pompous language of the eighteenth century, *the servitude of the soil*, might all be met with at that time, to a certain extent, in England, and many of them exist in England to this day. Yet they do not prevent the husbandry of England from being the most perfect and the most productive in the world, and the English people is scarcely conscious of their existence.

---

[1] See Note X., Abuse of Feudal Rights.
[2] See Note XI., Ecclesiastical Feudal Rights.
[3] See Note XII., Rights of the Abbey of Cherbourg.

How comes it then that these same feudal rights excited in the hearts of the people of France so intense a hatred that this passion has survived its object, and seems therefore to be unextinguishable ? The cause of this phenomenon is, that, on the one hand, the French peasant had become an owner of the soil; and that, on the other, he had entirely escaped from the government of the great landlords. Many other causes might doubtless be indicated, but I believe these two to be the most important.

If the peasant had not been an owner of the soil, he would have been insensible to many of the burdens which the feudal system had cast upon landed property. What matters tithe to a tenant farmer? He deducts it from his rent. What matters a rent-charge to a man who is not the owner of the ground? What matter even the impediments to free cultivation to a man who cultivates for another?

On the other hand, if the French peasant had still lived under the administration of his landlord, these feudal rights would have appeared far less insupportable, because he would have regarded them as a natural consequence of the constitution of the country.

When an aristocracy possesses not only privileges but powers, when it governs and administers the country, its private rights may be at once more extensive and less perceptible. In the feudal times, the nobility were regarded pretty much as the government is regarded in our own; the burdens they imposed were endured in consideration of the security they afforded. The nobles had many irksome privileges; they possessed many onerous rights; but they maintained public order, they administered justice, they caused the law to be executed, they came to the relief of the weak, they conducted the business of the community. In proportion as the nobility ceased to do these things, the burden of their privileges appeared more oppressive, and their existence became an anomaly.

Picture to yourself a French peasant of the eighteenth century, or, I might rather say, the peasant now before your eyes, for the man is the same; his condition is altered, but not his character. Take him as he is described in the documents I have quoted—so passionately enamoured of the soil, that he will spend all his savings to purchase it, and to purchase it at any price. To complete this purchase he must first pay a tax, not to the government, but to other landowners of the neighbourhood, as unconnected as himself with the administration of public affairs, and hardly more influential than he is. He possesses it at last; his heart is buried in it with the seed he sows. This little nook of ground, which is

his own in this vast universe, fills him with pride and independence. But again these neighbours call him from his furrow, and
compel him to come to work for them without wages. He tries to
defend his young crops from their game ; again they prevent him.
As he crosses the river they wait for his passage to levy a toll.
He finds them at the market, where they sell him the right of
selling his own produce ; and when, on his return home, he wants
to use the remainder of his wheat for his own sustenance—of that
wheat which was planted by his hands, and has grown under his
eyes—he cannot touch it till he has ground it at the mill and
baked it at the bakehouse of these same men. A portion of the
income of his little property is paid away in quit-rents to them
also, and these dues can neither be extinguished nor redeemed.

Whatever he does, these troublesome neighbours are everywhere
on his path, to disturb his happiness, to interfere with his labour,
to consume his profits; and when these are dismissed, others in
the black garb of the Church present themselves to carry off the
clearest profit of his harvest. Picture to yourself the condition,
the wants, the character, the passions of this man, and compute, if
you are able, the stores of hatred and of envy which are accumulated in his heart.[1]

Feudalism still remained the greatest of all the civil institutions
of France, though it had ceased to be a political institution. Reduced to these proportions, the hatred it excited was greater than
ever ; and it may be said with truth that the destruction of a part
of the institutions of the Middle Ages rendered a hundred times
more odious that portion which still survived.[2]

[1] See Note XIII., Irritation caused
to the Peasantry by Feudal Rights, and
especially by the Feudal Rights of the
Clergy.

[2] See Note XIV., Effect of Feudalism on state of Real Property.

CHAPTER II.

SHOWING THAT ADMINISTRATIVE CENTRALISATION IS AN INSTITUTION
ANTERIOR IN FRANCE TO THE REVOLUTION OF 1789, AND NOT
THE PRODUCT OF THE REVOLUTION OR OF THE EMPIRE, AS IS
COMMONLY SAID.

AT a period when political assemblies still existed in France, I once
heard an orator, in speaking of administrative centralisation, call
it, 'that admirable achievement of the Revolution which Europe
envies us.' I will concede the fact that centralisation is an admirable achievement; I will admit that Europe envies us its possession,
but I maintain that it is not an achievement of the Revolution.
On the contrary, it is a product of the former institutions of France,
and, I may add, the only portion of the political constitution of the
monarchy which survived the Revolution, inasmuch as it was the
only one that could be made to adapt itself to the new social condition brought about by that Revolution. The reader who has the
patience to read the present chapter with attention will find that I
have proved to demonstration this proposition.

I must first beg to be allowed to put out of the question what
were called *les pays d'état*, that is to say, the provinces that
managed their own affairs, or rather had the appearance, in part,
of managing them. These provinces, placed at the extremities of
the kingdom, did not contain more than a quarter of the total
population of France; and there were only two among them in
which provincial liberty possessed any real vitality. I shall revert
to them hereafter, and show to what an extent the central power
had subjected these very states to the common mould.[1] But for
the present I desire to give my principal attention to what was
called in the administrative language of the day, *les pays d'élection*,
although, in truth, there were fewer elections in them than anywhere else. These districts encompassed Paris on every side, they
were contiguous, and formed the heart and the better part of the
territory of France.

---

[1] See the last chapter of this Book (xxi.) for a fuller account of the local
government of Languedoc.

To any one who may cast a glance over the ancient administration of the kingdom, the first impression conveyed is that of a diversity of regulations and authorities, and the entangled complication of the different powers. France was covered with administrative bodies and distinct officers, who had no connection with one another, but who took part in the government in virtue of a right which they had purchased, and which could not be taken from them; but their duties were frequently so intermingled and so nearly contiguous as to press and clash together within the range of the same transactions.

The courts of justice took an indirect part in the legislative power, and possessed the right of framing administrative regulations which became obligatory within the limits of their own jurisdiction. Sometimes they maintained an opposition to the administration, properly so called, loudly blamed its measures and proscribed its agents. Police ordinances were promulgated by simple justices in the towns and boroughs where they resided.

The towns had a great diversity of constitutions, and their magistrates bore different designations—sometimes as mayors, sometimes as consuls, or again as syndics, and derived their powers from different sources. Some were chosen by the king, others by the lord of the soil or by the prince holding the fief; some again were elected for a year by their fellow-citizens, whilst others purchased the right of governing them permanently.

These different powers were the last remains of the ancient system; but something comparatively new or greatly modified had by degrees established itself among them, and this I have yet to describe.

In the centre of the kingdom, and close to the throne, there had been gradually formed an administrative body of extraordinary authority, in the grasp of which every power was united after a new fashion: this was the King's Council. Its origin was ancient, but the greater part of its functions were of recent date. It was at once a supreme court of justice, inasmuch as it had the right to quash the judgments of all the ordinary courts, and a superior administrative tribunal, inasmuch as every special jurisdiction was dependent on it in the last resort. It possessed, moreover, as a Council of State, subject to the pleasure of the King, a legislative power, for it discussed and proposed the greater part of the laws, and fixed and assessed the taxes. As the superior administrative board, it had to frame the general regulations which were to direct the agents of the Government. Within its walls all important affairs were decided and all secondary powers controlled. Everything finally came home to it; from that centre was derived the movement which set everything in motion. Yet it possessed no inherent jurisdiction of its own. The King alone decided, even when the Council appeared to advise, and even when it seemed to administer justice, it consisted of no more than simple 'givers of advice'—an expression used by the Parliament in one of its remonstrances.

This Council was not composed of men of rank, but of personages of middling or even low extraction, former Intendants or other men of that class thoroughly versed in the management of business, all of whom were liable to dismissal by the Crown. It generally proceeded in its course quietly and discreetly, displaying less pretension than real power; and thus it had but little lustre of its own, or, rather, it was lost in the splendour of the throne to which it stood so near; at once so powerful that everything came within its scope, and so obscure that it has scarcely been remarked by history.

As the whole administration of the country was directed by a single body, so nearly the entire management of home affairs was entrusted to the care of one single agent—the Comptroller-General. On opening an almanack of France before the Revolution, it will be found that each province had its special minister; but on studying the administration itself in the legal records of the time, it will soon be seen that the minister of the province had but few occasions of any importance for exercising his authority. The common course of business was directed by the Comptroller-General, who gradually took upon himself all the affairs that had anything to do with money, that is to say, almost the whole public administration; and who thus performed successively the duties of minister of finance, minister of the interior, minister of public works, and minister of trade.

As, in truth, the central administration had but one agent in Paris, so it had likewise but a single agent in each province. Nobles were still to be found in the eighteenth century bearing the titles of governors of provinces; they were the ancient and often the hereditary representatives of feudal royalty. Honours were still bestowed upon them, but they no longer had any power. The Intendant was in possession of the whole reality of government.

This Intendant was a man of humble extraction, always a stranger to the province, and a young man who had his fortune to make. He never exercised his functions by any right of election, birth, or purchase of office; he was chosen by the government among the inferior members of the Council of State, and was always subject to dismissal. He represented the body from which he was thus severed, and, for that reason, was called, in the administrative language of the time, a Detached Commissioner. All the powers which the Council itself possessed were accumulated in his hands, and he exercised them all in the first instance. Like the Council, he was at once administrator and judge. He corresponded with all the ministers, and in the province was the sole agent of all the measures of the government.

In each canton was placed below him an officer nominated by himself, and removable at will, called the Sub-delegate. The Intendant was very commonly a newly-created noble; the Sub-delegate was always a plebeian. He nevertheless represented the entire Government in the small, circumscribed space assigned to him as much as the Intendant did in the whole; and he was amenable to the Intendant as the Intendant was to the minister.

The Marquis d'Argenson relates in his 'Memoirs,' that one day Law said to him, ' "I never could have believed what I saw, when I was Comptroller of Finance. Do you know that this kingdom of France is governed by thirty *Intendants*? You have neither parliament, nor estates, nor governors. It is upon thirty Masters of Requests, despatched into the provinces, that their evil or their good, their fertility or their sterility, entirely depends." '

These powerful officers of the Government were, however, completely eclipsed by the remnants of the ancient aristocracy, and lost in the brilliancy which that body still shed around it. So that, even in their own time, they were scarcely seen, although their finger was already on everything. In society the nobles had over such men the advantages of rank, wealth, and the consideration always attached to what is ancient. In the Government the nobility were immediately about the person of the Prince, and formed his Court, commanded the fleets, led the armies, and, in short, did all that most attracts the observation of contemporaries, and too often absorbs the attention of posterity. A man of high rank would have been insulted by the proposal to appoint him an Intendant. The poorest man of family would generally have disdained the offer. In his eyes the Intendants were the representatives of an upstart power, new men appointed to govern the middle classes and the peasantry, and, as for the rest, very sorry company. Yet, as Law said, and as we shall see, these were the men who governed France.

To commence with the right of taxation, which includes, as it were, all other rights. It is well known a part of the taxes were farmed. In these cases the King's Council negotiated with the financial companies, fixed the terms of the contract, and regulated the mode of collection. All the other taxes, such as the *taille*, the capitation-tax, and the *vingtièmes* were fixed and levied by the agents of the central administration or under their all-powerful control.

The Council, every year, by a secret decision, fixed the amount of the *taille* and its numerous accessories, and likewise its distribution among the provinces. The *taille* had thus increased from year to year, though public attention was never called to the fact, no noise being made about it.

As the *taille* was an ancient tax, its assessment and collection had been formerly confided to local agents, who were all, more or less, independent of the Government by right of birth or election, or by purchase of office; they were the lords of the soil, the parochial collectors, the treasurers of France, or officers termed the *élus*. These authorities still existed in the eighteenth century, but some had altogether ceased to busy themselves about the *taille*, whilst others only did so in a very secondary and entirely subordinate manner. Even here the entire power was in the hands of the Intendant and his agents; he alone, in truth, assessed the *taille* in the different parishes, directed and controlled the collectors, and granted delays of payments or exemptions.

As the other taxes, such as the capitation tax, were of recent date, the Government was no longer embarrassed in respect to them by the remnants of former powers, but dealt with them without any intervention of the parties governed. The Comptroller-General, the Intendant, and the Council fixed the amount of each quota.

Let us leave the question of money for that of men.

It is sometimes a matter of astonishment how the French can have so patiently borne the yoke of the military conscription at the time of the Revolution and ever since; but it must be borne in mind that they had been already broken in to bear it for a long period of time. The conscription had been preceded by the militia, which was a heavier burden, although the amount of men required was less. From time to time the young men in the country were made to draw lots, and from among them were taken a certain number of soldiers, who were formed into militia regiments, in which they served for six years.

As the militia was a comparatively modern institution, none of the ancient feudal powers meddled with it; the whole business was intrusted to the agents of the Central Government alone. The Council fixed the general amount of men and the share of each province. The Intendant regulated the number of men to be raised in each parish; his Sub-delegate superintended the drawing of the lots, decided all cases of exemption, designated those militia-men who were allowed to remain with their families and those who were to join the regiment, and finally delivered over the latter to the military authorities. There was no appeal except to the Intendant or the Council.

It may be said with equal accuracy that, except in the *pays d'état*, all the public works, even those that had a very special destination, were decided upon and managed by the agents of the central power alone.

There certainly existed local and independent authorities, who, like the seigneur, the boards of finance, and the *grands voyers* (surveyors of public roads), had the power of taking a part in such matters of public administration. But all these ancient authorities, as may be seen by the slightest examination of the administrative documents of the time, bestirred themselves but little, or bestirred themselves no longer. All the great roads, and even the cross-roads leading from one town to another, were made and kept up at the cost of the public revenue. The Council decided the plan and contracted for its execution. The Intendant directed the engineering works, and the Sub-delegate got together the com-pulsory labourers who were to execute them. The care of the by-roads was alone left to the old local authorities, and they became impassable.

As in our days, the body of the *Ponts et Chaussées* was the great agent of the Central Government in relation to public works, and, in spite of the difference of the times, a very remarkable resemblance is to be found in their constitution now and then. The administration of the *Ponts et Chaussées* had a council and a school, inspectors who annually travelled over the whole of France, and engineers who resided on the spot and who were appointed to direct the works under the orders of the Intendant. A far greater number of the institutions of the old monarchy than is commonly supposed have been handed down to the modern state of French society, but in their transmission they have generally lost their names, even though they still preserve the same forms. As a rare exception, the *Ponts et Chaussées* have preserved both one and the other.

The Central Government alone undertook, with the help of its agents, to maintain public order in the provinces. The *maréchaussée*, or mounted police, was dispersed in small detachments over the whole surface of the kingdom, and was everywhere placed under the control of the Intendants. It was by the help of these soldiers, and, if necessary, of regular troops, that the Intendant warded off any sudden danger, arrested vagabonds, repressed mendicity, and put down the riots, which were continually arising from the price of corn. It never happened, as had been formerly the case, that the subjects of the Crown were called upon to aid the Government in this task, except indeed in the towns, where there was generally a town-guard, the soldiers of which were chosen and the officers appointed by the Intendant.

The judicial bodies had preserved the right of making police regulations, and frequently exercised it ; but these regulations were only applicable to a part of the territory, and, more generally, to one spot only. The Council had the power of annulling them, and frequently did annul them in cases of subordinate jurisdiction. But the Council was perpetually making general regulations applicable to all parts of the kingdom, either relative to subjects different from those which the tribunals had already settled, or applicable to those which they had settled in another manner. The number of these regulations, or *arrêts du Conseil*, as they were then called, was immense ; and they seem to have constantly increased the nearer we approach the Revolution. There is scarcely a single matter of social economy or political organisation that was not reorganised by these *arrêts du Conseil* during the forty years preceding that event.

Under the ancient feudal state of society, the lord of the soil, if he possessed important rights, had, at the same time, very heavy obligations. It was his duty to succour the indigent in the interior of his domains. The last trace of this old European legislation is to be found in the Prussian Code of 1795, which says, 'The lord of the soil must see that the indigent peasants receive an education. It is his duty to provide means of subsistence to those of his vassals who possess no land, as far as he is able. If any of them fall into want, he must come to their assistance.'

But no law of the kind had existed in France for a long time. The lord, when deprived of his former power, considered himself liberated from his former obligations; and no local authority, no council, no provincial or parochial association, had taken his place. No single being was any longer compelled by law to take care of the poor in the rural districts, and the Central Government had boldly undertaken to provide for their wants by its own resources.

Every year the Council assigned to each province certain funds derived from the general produce of the taxes, which the Intendant distributed for the relief of the poor in the different parishes. It was to him that the indigent labourer had to apply, and, in times of scarcity, it was he who caused corn or rice to be distributed among the people. The Council annually issued ordinances for the establishment of charitable workshops (*ateliers de charité*) where the poorer among the peasantry were enabled to find work at low wages, and the Council took upon itself to determine the places where these were necessary. It may be easily supposed, that alms thus bestowed from a distance were indiscriminate, capricious, and always very inadequate.[1]

The Central Government, moreover, did not confine itself to relieving the peasantry in time of distress; it also undertook to teach them the art of enriching themselves, encouraged them in this task, and forced them to it, if necessary.[2] For this purpose, from time to time, it caused distributions of small pamphlets upon the science of agriculture to be made by its Intendants and their Sub-delegates, founded schools of agriculture, offered prizes, and kept up, at a great expense, nursery-grounds, of which it distributed the produce. It would seem to have been more wise to have lightened the weight and modified the inequality of the burdens which then oppressed the agriculture of the country, but such an idea never seems to have occurred.

Sometimes the Council insisted upon compelling individuals to prosper, whether they would or no. The ordinances constraining artisans to use certain methods and manufacture certain articles are innumerable; and as the Intendants had not time to superintend the application of all these regulations, there were inspectors-general of manufactures, who visited in the provinces to insist on their fulfilment. Some of the *arrêts du Conseil* even prohibited the cultivation of certain crops which the Council did not consider proper for the purpose; whilst others ordered the destruction of such vines as had been, according to its opinion, planted in an unfavourable soil. So completely had the Government already changed its duty as a sovereign into that of a guardian.

[1] See Note XV., Public Relief, and Note XVI.
[2] See Note XVII., Powers of the Intendant for the Regulation of Trade.

CHAPTER III.

SHOWING THAT WHAT IS NOW CALLED ADMINISTRATIVE TUTELAGE
WAS AN INSTITUTION IN FRANCE ANTERIOR TO THE REVOLUTION.

IN France municipal freedom outlived the feudal system. Long
after the landlords were no longer the rulers of the country districts, the towns still retained the right of self-government. Some
of the towns of France continued down to nearly the close of the
seventeenth century to form, as it were, small democratic common-
wealths, in which the magistrates were freely elected by the whole
people and were responsible to the people—in which municipal life
was still public and animated—in which the city was still proud of
her rights and jealous of her independence.

These elections were generally abolished for the first time in
1692. The municipal offices were then what was called put up to
sale (*mises en offices* was the technical expression), that is to say,
the King sold in each town to some of the inhabitants the right of
perpetually governing all their townsmen.

This measure cost the towns at once their freedom and their
well-being; for if the practice of the sale of commissions for a
public employment sometimes proved useful in its effects when
applied to the courts of justice—since the first condition of the
good administration of justice is the complete independence of the
judge—this system never failed to be extremely mischievous whenever it was applied to posts of administrative duty, which demand,
above all things, responsibility, subordination, and zeal. The
Government of the old French monarchy was perfectly aware of
the real effects of such a system. It took great care not to adopt
for itself the same mode of proceeding which it applied to the
towns, and scrupulously abstained from putting up to sale the
commissions of its own Intendants and Sub-delegates.

And it well deserves the whole scorn of history that this great
change was accomplished without any political motive. Louis XI.
had curtailed the municipal liberties of the towns, because he was
alarmed by their democratic character;[1] Louis XIV. destroyed them

[1] See Note XVIII., Spirit of the Government of Louis XI.

under no such fears.   The proof is that he restored these rights to all the towns which were rich enough to buy them back again.   In reality, his object was not to abolish them, but to traffic in them ; and if they were actually abolished, it was, without meaning it, by a mere fiscal expedient.   The same thing was carried on for more than eighty years.   Seven times within that period the Crown resold to the towns the right of electing their magistrates, and as soon as they had once more tasted this blessing, it was snatched away to be sold to them once more.   The motive of the measure was always the same, and frequently avowed.   'Our financial necessities,' says the preamble to an edict of 1722, 'compel us to have recourse to the most effectual means of relieving them.'   The mode was effectual, but it was ruinous to those who bore this strange impost.   'I am struck with the enormity of the sums which have been paid at all times to purchase back the municipal offices,' writes an Intendant to the Comptroller-General in 1764. 'The amount of these sums spent in useful improvements would have turned to the advantage of the town, which has, on the contrary, felt nothing but the weight of authority and the privileges of these offices.'   I have not detected a more shameful feature in the whole aspect of the government of France before the Revolution.

It seems difficult to say with precision at the present time how the towns of France were governed in the eighteenth century ; for, besides that the origin of the municipal authorities fluctuated incessantly, as has just been stated, each town still preserved some fragments of its former constitution and its peculiar customs.   There were not, perhaps, two towns in France in which everything was exactly similar ; but this apparent diversity is fallacious, and conceals a general resemblance.[1]

In 1764 the Government proposed to make a general law on the administration of the towns of France, and for this purpose it caused reports to be sent in by the Intendants of the Crown on the existing municipal government of the country.   I have discovered a portion of the results of this inquiry, and I have fully satisfied myself by the perusal of it that the municipal affairs of all these towns were conducted in much the same manner.   The distinctions are merely superficial and apparent—the groundwork is everywhere the same.

In most instances the government of the towns was vested in two assemblies.   All the great towns were thus governed, and some of the small ones.   The first of these assemblies was composed of

[1] See Note XIX., Administration of a French Town in the Eighteenth Century.

municipal officers, more or less numerous according to the place. These formed the executive body of the community, the corporation or *corps de la ville*, as it was then termed. The members of this body exercised a temporary power, and were elected when the King had restored the elective power, or when the town had been able to buy up its offices. They held their offices permanently upon a certain payment to the Crown, when the Crown had appropriated the patronage and succeeded in disposing of it by sale, which was not always the case; for this sort of commodity declined in value precisely in proportion to the increasing subordination of the municipal authority to the central power. These municipal officers never received any stipend, but they were remunerated by exemptions from taxation and by privileges. No regular gradation of authority seems to have been established among them—their administration was collective. The mayor was the president of the corporation, not the governor of the city.

The second assembly, which was termed the general assembly, or as we should say in England the *livery*, elected the corporation, wherever it was still subject to election, and always continued to take a part in the principal concerns of the town.

In the fifteenth century this general assembly frequently consisted of the whole population. 'This custom,' said one of the authors of these Reports, 'was consistent with the popular spirit of our forefathers.' At that time the whole people elected their own municipal officers; this body was sometimes consulted by the corporation, and to this body the corporation was responsible. At the end of the seventeenth century the same state of things might sometimes be met with.

In the eighteenth century the people acting as a body had ceased to meet in this general assembly; it had by that time become representative. But, it must be carefully remarked, that this body was no longer anywhere elected by the bulk of the community, or impressed with its spirit. It was invariably composed of *notables*, some of whom sate there in virtue of a personal right; others were deputed by guilds or companies, from which each of them received imperative instructions.

As this century rolled on, the number of these notables sitting in virtue of their own right augmented in the popular assembly; the delegates of the working guilds fell away or disappeared altogether. They were superseded by the delegates of the great companies, or, in other words, the assembly contained only burgesses and scarcely any artisans. Then the citizens, who are not so easily imposed on by the empty semblance of liberty as is sometimes supposed, ceased everywhere to take an interest in the affairs of the town, and lived like strangers within their own walls.   In vain the civic magistrates attempted from time to time to revive that civic patriotism which had done so many wonders in the Middle Ages. The people remained deaf.   The greatest interests of the town no longer appeared to affect the citizens.   They were asked to give their suffrages when the vain counterfeit of a free election had been retained; but they stood aloof.   Nothing is more frequent in history than such an occurrence.   Almost all the princes who have destroyed freedom have attempted at first to preserve the forms of freedom, from Augustus to our own times; they flattered themselves that they should thus combine the moral strength which public assent always gives, with the conveniences which absolute power can alone offer.   But almost all of them have failed in this endeavour, and have soon discovered that it is impossible to prolong these false appearances where the reality has ceased to exist.

In the eighteenth century the municipal government of the towns of France had thus everywhere degenerated into a contracted oligarchy.   A few families managed all the public business for their own private purposes, removed from the eye of the public, and with no public responsibility.   Such was the morbid condition of this administration throughout the whole of France.   All the Intendants pointed it out; but the only remedy they suggested was the increased subjection of the local authorities to the Central Government.

In this respect, however, it was difficult for success to be more complete.   Besides the Royal edicts, which from time to time modified the administration of all the towns in France, the local by-laws of each town were frequently overruled by Orders in Council, which were not registered—passed on the recommendation of the Intendants, without any previous inquiry, and sometimes without the citizens of the towns themselves knowing anything of the matter.[1]

'This measure,' said the inhabitants of a town which had been affected by a decree of this nature, ' has astonished all the orders of the city, who expected nothing of the kind.'

The towns of France at this period could neither establish an octroi on articles of consumption, nor levy a rate, nor mortgage, nor sell, nor sue, nor farm their property, nor administer that property, nor even employ their own surplus revenues, without the intervention of an Order in Council, made on the report of the Intendant.   All their public works were executed in conformity

[1] See Note XX.

to plans and estimates approved by the Council. These works were adjudged to contractors before the Intendant or his Sub-delegates, and were generally intrusted to the engineers or architects of the State.

These facts will doubtless excite the surprise of those who suppose that the whole present condition of France is a novelty.

But the Central Government interfered more directly in the municipal administration of the towns than even these rules would seem to indicate; its power was far more extended than its right to exercise it.

I meet with the following passage in a circular instruction, addressed about the middle of the last century by a Comptroller-General to all the Intendants of the Kingdom : ' You will pay particular attention to all that takes place in the municipal assemblies. You will take care to have a most exact report of everything done there and of all the resolutions taken, in order to transmit them to me forthwith, accompanied with your own opinion on the subject.'

In fact it may be seen, from the correspondence of the Intendant with his subordinate officers, that the Government had a finger in all the concerns of every town, the least as well as the greatest. The Government was always consulted—the Government had always a decided opinion on every point. It even regulated the public festivities, ordered public rejoicings, caused salutes to be fired, and houses to be illuminated. On one occasion I observe that a member of the burgher guard was fined twenty livres by the Intendant for having absented himself from a *Te Deum*.

The officers of these municipal corporations had therefore arrived at a becoming sense of their own insignificance. ' We most humbly supplicate you, Monseigneur' (such was the style in which they addressed the King's Intendant), ' to grant us your good-will and protection. We will endeavour not to show ourselves unworthy of them by the submission we are ready to show to all the commands of your Greatness.' ' We have never resisted your will, Monseigneur,' was the language of another body of these persons, who still assumed the pompous title of Peers of the City.

Such was the preparation of the middle classes for government, and of the people for liberty.

If at least this close dependence of the towns on the State had preserved their finances! but such was not the case. It is sometimes argued that without centralisation the towns would ruin themselves. I know not how that may be, but I know that in the eighteenth century centralisation did not prevent their ruin.   The whole administrative history of that time is replete with their embarrassments.

If we turn from the towns to the villages, we meet with different powers and different forms of government, but the same dependence.[1]

I find many indications of the fact, that in the Middle Ages the inhabitants of every village formed a community distinct from the Lord of the soil.   He, no doubt, employed the community, superintended it, governed it; but the village held in common certain property, which was absolutely its own ; it elected its own chiefs, and administered its affairs democratically.

This ancient constitution of the parish may be traced in all the nations in which the feudal system prevailed, and in all the countries to which these nations have carried the remnants of their laws.   These vestiges occur at every turn in England, and the system was in full vigour in Germany sixty years ago, as may be demonstrated by reading the code of Frederic the Great.   Even in France in the eighteenth century, some traces of it were still in existence.

I remember that, when I proceeded, for the first time, to ascertain from the archives of one of the old Intendancies of France, what was meant by a *parish* before the Revolution, I was surprised to find in this community, so poor and so enslaved, several of the characteristics which had struck me long ago in the rural townships of the United States, and which I had then erroneously conceived to be a peculiarity of society in the New World. Neither in the one nor in the other of these communities is there any permanent representation or any municipal body, in the strict sense of that term ; both the one and the other were administered by officers acting separately under the direction of the whole population.   In both, meetings were held from time to time, at which all the inhabitants, assembled in one body, elected their own magistrates and settled their principal affairs.   These two parishes, in short, are as much alike as that which is living can be like that which is dead.

Different as have been the destinies of these two corporate beings, their birth was in fact the same.

Transported at once to regions far removed from the feudal system, and invested with unlimited authority over itself, the rural parish of the Middle Ages in Europe is become the township of New England.   Severed from the lordship of the soil, but grasped

[1] See Note XXI., Administration of a Village in the Eighteenth Century.

in the powerful hand of the State, the rural parishes of France assumed the form I am about to describe.

In the eighteenth century the number and the name of the parochial officers varied in the different provinces of France. The ancient records show that these officers were more numerous when local life was more active, and that they diminished in number as that life declined. In most of the parishes they were, in the eighteenth century, reduced to two persons—the one named the 'Collector,' the other most commonly named the 'Syndic.' Generally, these parochial officers were either elected, or supposed to be so; but they had everywhere become the instruments of the State rather than the representatives of the community. The Collector levied the *taille*, under the direct orders of the Intendant. The Syndic, placed under the daily direction of the Sub-delegate of the Intendant, represented that personage in all matters relating to public order or affecting the Government. He became the principal agent of the Government in relation to military service, to the public works of the State, and to the execution of the general laws of the kingdom.

The Seigneur, as we have already seen, stood aloof from all these details of government; he had even ceased to superintend them, or to assist in them; nay more, these duties, which had served in earlier times to keep up his power, appeared unworthy of his attention in proportion to the progressive decay of that power. It would at last have been an offence to his pride to require him to attend to them. He had ceased to govern; but his presence in the parish and his privileges effectually prevented any good government from being established in the parish in place of his own. A private person differing so entirely from the other parishioners—so independent of them, and so favoured by the laws —weakened or destroyed the authority of all rules.

The unavoidable contact with such a person in the country had driven into the towns, as I shall subsequently have occasion to show, almost all those inhabitants who had either a competency or education, so that none remained about the Seigneur but a flock of ignorant and uncultivated peasants, incapable of managing the administration of their common interests. 'A parish,' as Turgot had justly observed, 'is an assemblage of cabins, and of inhabitants as passive as the cabins they dwell in.'

The administrative records of the eighteenth century are full of complaints of the incapacity, indolence, and ignorance of the parochial collectors and syndics. Ministers, Intendants, Sub-delegates, and even the country gentlemen, are for ever deploring these defects; but none of them had traced these defects to their cause.

Down to the Revolution the rural parishes of France had preserved in their government something of that democratic aspect which they had acquired in the Middle Ages. If the parochial officers were to be elected, or some matter of public interest to be discussed, the village bell summoned the peasants to the church-porch, where the poor as well as the rich were entitled to present themselves. In these meetings there was not indeed any regular debate or any decisive mode of voting, but every one was at liberty to speak his mind; and it was the duty of the notary, sent for on purpose, and operating in the open air, to collect these different opinions and enter them in a record of the proceedings.

When these empty semblances of freedom are compared with the total impotence which was connected with them, they afford an example, in miniature, of the combination of the most absolute government with some of the forms of extreme democracy; so that to oppression may be added the absurdity of affecting to disguise it. This democratic assembly of the parish could indeed express its desires, but it had no more power to execute its will than the corporate bodies in the towns. It could not speak until its mouth had been opened, for the meeting could not be held without the express permission of the Intendant, and, to use the expression of those times, which adapted their language to the fact, ' *under his good pleasure.*' Even if such a meeting were unanimous, it could neither levy a rate, nor sell, nor buy, nor let, nor sue, without the permission of the King's Council. It was necessary to obtain a minute of Council to repair the damage caused by the wind to the church steeple, or to rebuild the falling gables of the parsonage. The rural parishes most remote from Paris were just as much subject to this rule as those nearest to the capital. I have found records of parochial memorials to the Council for leave to spend twenty-five livres.

The inhabitants had indeed, commonly, retained the right of electing their parochial magistrates by universal suffrage; but it frequently happened that the Intendant designated to this small electoral body a candidate who never failed to be returned by a unanimity of suffrages. Sometimes, when the election had been made by the parishioners themselves, he set it aside, named the collector and syndic of his own authority, and adjourned indefinitely a fresh election. There are thousands of such examples.

It is difficult to conceive a more cruel fate than that of these parochial officers. The lowest agent of the Central Government, the Sub-delegate, bent them to every caprice. Often they were fined, sometimes imprisoned; for the securities which elsewhere defended the citizens against arbitrary proceedings had ceased to exist for them: ' I have thrown into prison,' said an Intendant in 1750, ' some of the chief persons in the villages who grumbled, and I have made these parishes pay the expense of the horsemen of the patrol. By these means they have been easily checkmated.' The consequence was, that these parochial functions were not considered as honours, but as burdens to be evaded by every species of subterfuge.

Yet these last remnants of the ancient parochial government were still dear to the peasantry of France; and even at the present day, of all public liberties the only one they thoroughly comprehend is parochial freedom. The only business of a public nature which really interests them is to be found there. Men, who readily leave the government of the whole nation in the hand of a master, revolt at the notion of not being able to speak their mind in the administration of their own village. So much weight is there yet in forms the most hollow.

What has been said of the towns and parishes of France may be extended to almost all the corporate bodies which had any separate existence and collective property.

Under the social condition of France anterior to the Revolution of 1789, as well as at the present day, there was no city, town, borough, village, or hamlet in the kingdom—there was neither hospital, church fabric, religious house, nor college, which could have an independent will in the management of its private affairs, or which could administer its own property according to its own choice. Then, as now, the executive administration therefore held the whole French people in tutelage; and if that insolent term had not yet been invented, the thing itself already existed.

CHAPTER IV.

ADMINISTRATIVE JURISDICTION AND THE IMMUNITY OF PUBLIC OFFI-
CERS ARE INSTITUTIONS OF FRANCE ANTERIOR TO THE REVOLU-
TION.[1]

IN no country in Europe were the ordinary courts of justice less
dependent on the Government than in France ; but in no country
were extraordinary courts of justice more extensively employed.
These two circumstances were more nearly connected than might
be imagined. As the King was almost entirely powerless in relation to the judges of the land—as he could neither dismiss them,
nor translate them, nor even, for the most part, promote them—as,
in short, he held them neither by ambition nor by fear, their
independence soon proved embarrassing to the Crown. The result
had been, in France, more than anywhere else, to withdraw from
their jurisdiction the suits in which the authority of the Crown
was directly interested, and to call into being, as it were beside
them, a species of tribunal more dependent on the sovereign,
which should present to the subjects of the Crown some semblance of justice without any real cause for the Crown to dread its
control.

In other countries, as, for instance, in some parts of Germany,
where the ordinary courts of justice had never been as independent
of the Government as those of France, no such precautions were
taken, and no administrative justice (as it was termed) existed.
The sovereign was so far master of the judges, that he needed no
special commissions.

[1] [*Que la justice administrative et
la garantie des fonctionnaires sont des
institutions de l'Ancien Régime.* The
difficulty of rendering these terms into
intelligible English arises from the fact
that at no time in the last two centuries of the history of England has
the executive administration assumed
a peculiar jurisdiction to itself or removed its officers from the jurisdiction
of the courts of common law in this
country. It will be seen in this chapter
that the ordinary jurisdictions of France
have always been liable to be superseded by extraordinary judicial authorities when the interests of the Government or the responsibility of its agents
were at stake. The arbitrary jurisdiction of all such irregular tribunals was,
in fact, abolished in England in 1641
by the Act under which fell the Court
of Star Chamber and the High Commission.]

The edicts and declarations of the Kings of France, published in the last century of the monarchy, and the Orders in Council promulgated within the same period, almost all provided on behalf of the Government, that the differences which any given measure might occasion and the litigation which might ensue, should be exclusively heard before the Intendants and before the Council. ' It is moreover ordered by his Majesty, that all the disputes which may arise upon the execution of this order, with all the circumstances and incidents thereunto belonging, shall be carried before the Intendant to be judged by him, saving an appeal to the Council, and all courts of justice and tribunals are forbidden to take cognisance of the same.' Such was the ordinary form of these decrees.

In matters which fell under laws or customs of an earlier date, when this precaution had not been taken, the Council continually intervened, by way of what was termed *evocation*, or the calling up to its own superior jurisdiction from the hands of the ordinary officers of justice suits in which the administration of the State had an interest. The registers of the Council are full of minutes of *evocation* of this nature. By degrees the exception became the rule, and a theory was invented to justify the fact.[1] It came to be regarded as a maxim of state, not in the laws of France, but in the minds of those by whom those laws were applied, that all suits in which a public interest was involved, or which arose out of the construction to be put on any act of the administration, were not within the competency of the ordinary judges, whose only business it was to decide between private interests. On this point we, in more recent times, have only added a mode of expression; the idea had preceded the Revolution of 1789.

Already at that time most of the disputed questions which arose out of the collection of the revenue were held to fall under the exclusive jurisdiction of the Intendant and the King's Council.[2] So, too, with reference to the regulation of public waggons and stage-coaches, drainage, the navigation of rivers, etc.; and in general all the suits in which the public authorities were interested came to be disposed of by administrative tribunals only. The Intendants took the greatest care that this exceptional jurisdiction should be continually extended. They urged on the Comptroller-General, and stimulated the Council. The reason one of these officers assigned to induce the Council to call up one of these suits deserves to be remembered. 'An ordinary judge,' said he, ' is subject to fixed rules, which compel him to punish any transgression of the law; but the Council can always set aside rules for a useful purpose.'

On this principle, it often happened that the Intendant or the Council called up to their own jurisdiction suits which had an almost imperceptible connection with any subject of administrative interest, or even which had no perceptible connection with such questions at all.   A country gentleman quarrels with his neighbour, and being dissatisfied with the apparent disposition of his judges, he asks the Council to *evoke* his cause.   The Intendant reports that, ' although this is a case solely affecting private rights, which fall under the cognisance of the courts of justice, yet that his Majesty can always, when he pleases, reserve to himself the decision of any suit whatever, without rendering any account at all of his motives.'

It was generally before the Intendant or before the Provost of the Maréchaussée that all the lower order of people were sent for trial, by this process of evocation, when they had been guilty of public disturbances.   Most of the riots so frequently caused by the high price of corn gave rise to transfers of jurisdiction of this nature.   The Intendant then summoned to his court a certain number of persons, who formed a sort of local council, chosen by himself, and with their assistance he proceeded to try criminals. I have found sentences delivered in this manner, by which men were condemned to the galleys, and even to death.   Criminal trials decided by the Intendant were still common at the close of the seventeenth century.

Modern jurists in discussing this subject of administrative jurisdictions assert, that great progress has been made since the Revolution.   ' Before that era,' they say, ' the judicial and administrative powers were confounded ; they have since been distinguished and assigned to their respective places.'   To appreciate correctly the progress here spoken of, it must never be forgotten, that if on the one hand the judicial power under the old monarchy was incessantly extending beyond the natural sphere of its authority, yet on the other hand that sphere was never entirely filled by it. To see one of these facts without the other is to form an incomplete and inaccurate idea of the subject.   Sometimes the courts of law were allowed to enact regulations on matters of public administration, which was manifestly beyond their jurisdiction ; sometimes they were restrained from judging regular suits, which was to exclude them from the exercise of their proper functions.   The modern law of France has undoubtedly removed the administration of justice from those political institutions into which it had very improperly been allowed to penetrate before the Revolution ; but at the same time, as has just been shown, the Government continually invaded the proper sphere of the judicial authorities, and this state of things is unchanged, as if the confusion of these powers were not equally dangerous on the one side as on the other, and even worse in the latter mode ; for the intervention of a judicial authority in administrative business is only injurious to the transaction of affairs ; but the intervention of administrative power in judicial proceedings depraves mankind, and tends to render men at once revolutionary and servile.

Amongst the nine or ten constitutions which have been established in perpetuity in France within the last sixty years, there is one in which it was expressly provided that no agent of the administration can be prosecuted before the ordinary courts of law without having previously obtained the assent of the Government to such a prosecution.[1] This clause appeared to be so well devised that when the constitution to which it belonged was destroyed, this provision was saved from the wreck, and it has ever since been carefully preserved from the injuries of revolutions. The administrative body still calls the privilege secured to them by this article one of the great conquests of 1789 ; but in this they are mistaken, for under the old monarchy the Government was not less solicitous than it is in our own times to spare its officers the unpleasantness of rendering an account in a court of law, like any other private citizens. The only essential difference between the two periods is this : before the Revolution the Government could only shelter its agents by having recourse to illegal and arbitrary measures ; since the Revolution it can legally allow them to violate the laws.

When the ordinary tribunals of the old monarchy allowed proceedings to be instituted against any officer representing the central authority of the Government, an Order in Council usually intervened to withdraw the accused person from the jurisdiction of his judges, and to arraign him before commissioners named by the Council ; for, as was said by a councillor of state of that time, a public officer thus attacked would have had to encounter an adverse prepossession in the minds of the ordinary judges, and the authority of the King would have been compromised. This sort of interference occurred not only at long intervals, but every day

---

[1] [The article referred to is the 75th article of the Constitution de l'An VIII., which provided that the agents of the executive government, other than the ministers, could only be prosecuted for their conduct in the discharge of their functions, in virtue of a decision of the Council of State.]

—not only with reference to the chief agents of the Government, but to the least. The slightest thread of a connection with the administration sufficed to relieve an officer from all other control. A mounted overseer of the Board of Public Works, whose business was to direct the forced labour of the peasantry, was prosecuted by a peasant whom he had ill-treated. The Council *evoked* the cause, and the chief engineer of the district, writing confidentially to the Intendant, said on this subject: ‘ It is quite true that the overseer is greatly to blame, but that is not a reason for allowing the case to follow the ordinary jurisdiction ; for it is of the utmost importance to the Board of Works that the courts of common law should not hear or decide on the complaints of the peasants engaged in forced labour against the overseers of these works. If this precedent were followed, those works would be disturbed by continual litigation, arising out of the animosity of the public against the officers of the Government.’

On another occasion the Intendant himself wrote to the Comptroller-General with reference to a Government contractor, who had taken his materials in a field which did not belong to him. ‘ I cannot sufficiently represent to you how injurious it would be to the interests of the Administration if the contractors were abandoned to the jurisdiction of the ordinary courts, whose principles can never be reconciled to those of the Government.’

These lines were written precisely a hundred years ago, but it appears as if the administrators who wrote them were our own contemporaries.

˙CHAPTER V.

SHOWING HOW CENTRALISATION HAD BEEN ABLE TO INTRODUCE
ITSELF AMONG THE ANCIENT INSTITUTIONS OF FRANCE, AND TO
SUPPLANT WITHOUT DESTROYING THEM.

LET us now briefly recapitulate what has been said in the three
preceding chapters. A single body or institution placed in the
centre of the kingdom regulated the public administration of the
whole country ; the same Minister directed almost all the internal
affairs of the kingdom ; in each province a single Government
agent managed all the details ; no secondary administrative bodies
existed, and none which could act until they had been set in
motion by the authority of the State ; courts of extraordinary
jurisdiction judged the causes in which the administration was
interested, and sheltered all its agents. What is this but the
centralisation with which we are so well acquainted ? Its forms
were less marked than they are at present; its course was less
regular, its existence more disturbed ; but it is the same being.
It has not been necessary to add or to withdraw any essential
condition ; the removal of all that once surrounded it at once
exposed it in the shape that now meets our eyes.

Most of the institutions which I have just described have been
imitated subsequently, and in a hundred different places ; [1] but
they were at that time peculiar to France ; and we shall shortly
see how great was the influence they had on the French Revolution and on its results.

But how came these institutions of modern date to be established in France amidst the ruins of feudal society ?

It was a work of patience, of address, and of time, rather than
of force or of absolute power. At the time when the Revolution
occurred, scarcely any part of the old administrative edifice of
France had been destroyed ; but another structure had been, as it
were, called into existence beneath it.

There is nothing to show that the Government of the old

[1] See Note XXIV., Traces in Canada of Centralisation of the old French
Monarchy.

French monarchy followed any deliberately concerted plan to effect this difficult operation. That Government merely obeyed the instinct which leads all governments to aim at the exclusive management of affairs—an instinct which ever remained the same in spite of the diversity of its agents. · The monarchy had left to the ancient powers of France their venerable names and their honours, but it had gradually subtracted from them their authority. They had not been expelled but enticed out of their domains. By the indolence of one man, by the egotism of another, the Government had found means to occupy their places. Availing itself of all their vices, never attempting to correct but only to supersede them, the Government at last found means to substitute for almost all of them its own sole agent, the Intendant, whose very name was unknown when those powers which he supplanted came into being.

The judicial institutions had alone impeded the Government in this great enterprise; but even there the State had seized the substance of power, leaving only the shadow of it to its adversaries. The Parliaments of France had not been excluded from the sphere of the administration, but the Government had extended itself gradually in that direction so as to appropriate almost the whole of it. In certain extraordinary and transient emergencies, in times of scarcity, for instance, when the passions of the people lent a support to the ambition of the magistrates, the Central Government allowed the Parliaments to administer for a brief interval, and to leave a trace upon the page of history; but the Government soon silently resumed its place, and gently extended its grasp over every class of men and of affairs.

In the struggles between the French Parliaments and the authority of the Crown, it will be seen on attentive observation that these encounters almost always took place on the field of politics, properly so called, rather than on that of administration. These quarrels generally arose from the introduction of a new tax; that is to say, it was not administrative power which these rival authorities disputed, but legislative power to which the one had as little rightful claim as the other.

This became more and more the case as the Revolution approached. As the passions of the people began to take fire, the Parliaments assumed a more active part in politics; and as at the same time the central power and its agents were becoming more expert and more adroit, the Parliaments took a less active part in the administration of the country. They acquired every day less of the administrator and more of the tribune.

The course of events, moreover, incessantly opens new fields of action to the executive Government, where judicial bodies have no aptitude to follow; for these are new transactions not governed by precedent, and alien to judicial routine. The great progress of society continually gives birth to new wants, and each of these wants is a fresh source of power to the Government, which is alone able to satisfy them. Whilst the sphere of the administration of justice by the courts of law remains unaltered, that of the executive Government is variable and constantly expands with civilisation itself.[1]

The Revolution which was approaching, and which had already begun to agitate the mind of the whole French people, suggested to them a multitude of new ideas, which the central power of the Government could alone realise. The Revolution developed that power before it overthrew it, and the agents of the Government underwent the same process of improvement as everything else. This fact becomes singularly apparent from the study of the old administrative archives. The Comptroller-General and the Intendant of 1780 no longer resemble the Comptroller-General and the Intendant of 1740; the administration was already transformed, the agents were the same, but they were impelled by a different spirit. In proportion as it became more minute and more comprehensive, it also became more regular and more scientific. It became more temperate as its ascendency became universal; it oppressed less, it directed more.

The first outbreak of the Revolution destroyed this grand institution of the monarchy; but it was restored in 1800. It was not, as has so often been said, the principles of 1789 which triumphed at that time and ever since in the public administration of France, but, on the contrary, the principles of the administration anterior to the Revolution, which then resumed their authority and have since retained it.

If I am asked how this fragment of the state of society anterior to the Revolution could thus be transplanted in its entirety, and incorporated into the new state of society which had sprung up, I answer that if the principle of centralisation did not perish in the Revolution, it was because that principle was itself the precursor and the commencement of the Revolution; and I add that when a people has destroyed Aristocracy in its social constitution, that people is sliding by its own weight into centralisation. Much less exertion is then required to drive it down that declivity than to hold it back. Amongst such a people all powers tend naturally

[1] See Note XXV., Example of the Intervention of the Council.

to unity, and it is only by great ingenuity that they can still be kept separate. The democratic Revolution which destroyed so many of the institutions of the French monarchy, served therefore to consolidate the centralised administration, and centralisation seemed so naturally to find its place in the society which the Revolution had formed that it might easily be taken for its offspring.

CHAPTER VI.

THE ADMINISTRATIVE HABITS OF FRANCE BEFORE THE REVOLUTION.

IT is impossible to read the letters addressed by an Intendant of one of the provinces of France, under the old monarchy, to his superiors and his subordinates, without admiring the similitude engendered by similar institutions between the administrators of those times and the administrators of our own. They seem to join hands across the abyss of the Revolution which lies between them. The same may be said of the people they govern. The power of legislation over the minds of men was never more distinctly visible.

The Ministers of the Crown had already conceived the design of taking actual cognisance of every detail of business and of regulating everything by their own authority from Paris. As time advanced and the administration became more perfect, this passion increased. Towards the end of the eighteenth century not a charitable workshop could be established in a distant province of France until the Comptroller-General himself had fixed the cost, drawn up the scheme, and chosen the site. If a poor-house was to be built the Minister must be informed of the names of the beggars who frequent it—when they arrive—when they depart. As early as the middle of the same century (in 1733) M. d'Argenson wrote—' The details of business thrown upon the Ministers are immense. Nothing is done without them, nothing except by them, and if their information is not as extensive as their powers, they are obliged to leave everything to be done by clerks, who become in reality the masters.'

The Comptroller-General not only called for reports on matters of business, but even for minute particulars relating to individuals. To procure these particulars the Intendant applied in his turn to his Sub-delegates, and of course repeated precisely what they told him, just as if he had himself been thoroughly acquainted with the subject.

In order to direct everything from Paris and to know everything there, it was necessary to invent a thousand checks and means of control. The mass of paper documents was already enormous, and such was the tedious slowness of these administrative proceedings, that I have remarked it always took at least a year before a parish could obtain leave to repair a steeple or to rebuild a parsonage : more frequently two or three years elapsed before the demand was granted.

The Council itself remarked in one of its minutes (March 29, 1773) that 'the administrative formalities lead to infinite delays, and too frequently excite very well-grounded complaints; these formalities are, however, all necessary,' added the Council.

I used to believe that the taste for statistics belonged exclusively to the administrators of the present day, but I was mistaken. At the time immediately preceding the Revolution of 1789 small printed tables were frequently sent to the Intendant, which he merely had to get filled up by his Sub-delegates and by the Syndics of parishes. The Comptroller-General required reports upon the nature of the soil, the methods of cultivation, the quality and quantity of the produce, the number of cattle, and the occupations and manners of the inhabitants. The information thus obtained was neither less circumstantial nor more accurate than that afforded under similar circumstances by Sub-prefects and Mayors at the present day. The opinions recorded on these occasions by the Sub-delegates, as to the character of those under their authority, were for the most part far from favourable. They continually repeated that 'the peasants are naturally lazy, and would not work unless forced to do so in order to live.' This economical doctrine seemed very prevalent amongst this class of administrators.

Even the official language of the two periods is strikingly alike. In both the style is equally colourless, flowing, vague, and feeble ; the peculiar characteristics of each individual writer are effaced and lost in a general mediocrity. It is much the same thing to read the effusions of a modern Prefect or of an ancient Intendant.

Towards the end of a century, however, when the peculiar language of Diderot and Rousseau had had time to spread and mingle with the vulgar tongue, the false sensibility, with which the works of those writers are filled, infected the administrators and reached even the financiers. The official style, usually so dry in its texture, was become more unctuous and even tender. A Sub-delegate laments to the Intendant of Paris 'that in the exercise of his functions he often feels grief most poignant to a feeling heart.'

Then, as at the present time, the Government distributed certain charitable donations among the various parishes, on condition that the inhabitants should on their part give certain alms. When the sum thus offered by them was sufficient, the Comptroller-General wrote on the margin of the list of contributions, ' Good ; express satisfaction ; ' but if the sum was considerable, he wrote, ' Good ; express satisfaction and sensibility.'

The administrative functionaries, nearly all belonging to the middle ranks, already formed a class imbued with a spirit peculiar to itself, and possessing traditions, virtues, an honour and a pride of its own. This was, in fact, the aristocracy of the new order of society, completely formed and ready to start into life ; it only waited until the Revolution had made room for it.

The administration of France was already characterised by the violent hatred which it entertained indiscriminately towards all those not within its own pale, whether belonging to the nobility or to the middle classes, who attempted to take any part in public affairs. The smallest independent body, which seemed likely to be formed without its intervention, caused alarm ; the smallest voluntary association, whatever was its object, was considered troublesome ; and none were suffered to exist but those which it composed in an arbitrary manner, and over which it presided. Even the great industrial companies found little favour in the eyes of the administration ; in a word, it did not choose that the citizens should take any concern whatever in the examination of their own affairs, and preferred sterility to competition. But, as it has always been necessary to allow the French people the indulgence of a little licence to console them for their servitude, the Government suffered them to discuss with great freedom all sorts of general and abstract theories of religion, philosophy, morals, and even politics. It was ready enough to allow the fundamental principles upon which society then rested to be attacked, and the existence of God himself to be discussed, provided no comments were made upon the very least of its own agents. Such speculations were supposed to be altogether irrelevant to the State.

Although the newspapers of the eighteenth century, or as they were then called the gazettes, contained more epigrams than polemics, the administration looked upon this small power with a very jealous eye. It was indulgent enough towards books, but already extremely harsh towards newspapers ; so, being unable altogether to suppress them, it endeavoured to turn them to its own purposes. Under the date of 1761 I find a circular addressed to all the Intendants throughout the kingdom, announcing that the King (Louis XV.) had directed that in future the ' Gazette de France ' should be drawn up under the inspection of the Government ; ' his Majesty being desirous,' says the circular, ' to render that journal interesting, and to ensure to it a superiority over all others.   In consequence whereof,' adds the Minister, ' you will take care to send me a bulletin of everything that happens in your district likely to engage the curiosity of the public, more especially whatever relates to physical science, natural history, or remarkable and interesting occurrences.'   This circular is accompanied by a prospectus setting forth that the new Gazette, though appearing oftener and containing more matter than the journal which it supersedes, will cost the subscribers much less.

Furnished with these documents, the Intendant wrote to his Sub-delegates and set them to work ; but at first they replied that they knew nothing.   This called forth a second letter from the Minister, complaining bitterly of the sterility of the province as to news.   'His Majesty commands me to tell you that it is his intention that you should pay very serious attention to this matter, and that you should give the most precise order to your agents.'   Hereupon the Sub-delegates undertake the task.   One of them reported that a smuggler of salt had. been hung, and had displayed great courage ; another that a woman in his district had been delivered of three girls at a birth ; a third that a dreadful storm had occurred, though without doing any mischief.   One of them declared that in spite of all his efforts he had been unable to discover anything worth recording, but that he would subscribe himself to so useful a journal, and would exhort all respectable persons to follow his example.   All these efforts seem, however, to have produced but little effect, for a fresh letter informs us that ' the King, who has the goodness,' as the Minister says, ' himself to enter into the whole detail of the measures for perfecting the Gazette, and who wishes to give to this journal the superiority and celebrity it deserves, has testified much dissatisfaction on seeing his views so ill carried out.'

History is a picture gallery, containing few originals and a great many copies.

It must be admitted, however, that in France the Central Government never imitated those Governments of the South of Europe which seem to have taken possession of everything only in order to render everything barren.   The French Government frequently showed great intelligence as to its functions, and always displayed prodigious activity.   But its activity was often unproductive and even mischievous, because at times it endeavoured to do that which was beyond its power, or that which no one could control.

It rarely attempted, or quickly abandoned, the most necessary reforms, which could only be carried out by persevering energy; but it constantly changed its by-laws and its regulations. Within the sphere of its presence nothing remained in repose for a moment. New regulations succeeded each other with such extraordinary rapidity that the agents of Government, amidst the multiplicity of commands they received, often found it difficult to discover how to obey them. Some municipal officers complained to the Comptroller-General himself of the extreme mobility of this subordinate legislation. 'The variation of the financial regulations alone,' said they, 'is such, that a municipal officer, even were his appointment permanent, has no time for anything but studying the new rules as fast as they come out, even to the extent of being forced to neglect his own business.'

Even when the law itself was not altered its application varied every day. Without seeing the working of the administration under the old French Government in the secret documents which are still in existence, it is impossible to imagine the contempt into which the law eventually falls, even in the eyes of those charged with the application of it, when there are no longer either political assemblies or public journals to check the capricious activity, or to set bounds to the arbitrary and changeable humour of the Ministers and their offices.

We hardly find a single Order in Council that does not recite some anterior laws, often of very recent date, which had been enacted but never executed. There was not an edict, a royal declaration, or any solemnly registered letters-patent, that did not encounter a thousand impediments in its application. The letters of the Comptrollers-General and the Intendants show that the Government constantly permitted things to be done, by exception, at variance with its own orders. It rarely broke the law, but the law was perpetually made to bend slightly in all directions to meet particular cases, and to facilitate the conduct of affairs.

An Intendant writes to the minister with reference to a duty of *octroi* from which a contractor of public works wanted to be exempted : ' It is certain that according to the strict letter of the edicts and decrees which I have just quoted, no person throughout the kingdom is exempted from these duties; but those who are versed in the knowledge of affairs are well aware that these imperative enactments stand on the same footing as to the penalties which they impose, and that although they are to be found in almost every edict, declaration, and decree for the imposition of taxes, they have never prevented exceptions from being made.'

The whole essence of the then state of France is contained

in this passage : rigid rules and lax practice were its characteristics.

Any one who should attempt to judge the Government of that period by the collection of its laws would fall into the most absurd mistakes.   Under the date 1757 I have found a royal declaration condemning to death any one who shall compose or print writings contrary to religion or established order.   The bookseller who sells and the pedlar who hawks them are to suffer the same punishment. Was this in the age of St. Dominic ?   It was under the supremacy of Voltaire.

It is a common subject of complaint against the French that they despise law ; but when, alas ! could they have learned to respect it ?   It may be truly said that amongst the men of the period I am describing, the place which should be filled in the human mind by the notion of *law* was empty.   Every petitioner entreated that the established order of things should be set aside in his favour with as much vehemence and authority as if he were demanding that it should be properly enforced ; and indeed its authority was never alleged against him but as a means of getting rid of his importunity   The submission of the people to the existing powers was still complete, but their obedience was the effect of custom rather than of will, and when by chance they were stirred up, the slightest excitement led at once to violence, which again was almost always repressed by counter-violence and arbitrary power, not by the law.

In the eighteenth century the central authority in France had not yet acquired that sound and vigorous constitution which it has since exhibited ; nevertheless, as it had already succeeded in destroying all intermediate authorities, and had left only a vast blank between itself and the individuals constituting the nation, it already appeared to each of them from a distance as the only spring of the social machine, the sole and indispensable agent of public life.

Nothing shows this more fully than the writings even of its detractors.   When the long period of uneasiness which preceded the Revolution began to be felt, all sorts of new systems of society and government were concocted.   The ends which these various reformers had in view were various, but the means they proposed were always the same.   They wanted to employ the power of the central authority in order to destroy all existing institutions, and to reconstruct them according to some new plan of their own device ; no other power appeared to them capable of accomplishing such a task.   The power of the State ought, they said, to be as unlimited as its rights; all that was required was to force it to make a proper use of both. The elder Mirabeau, a nobleman so imbued with the notion of the rights of his order that he openly called the Intendants 'intruders,' and declared that if the appointment of the magistrates was left altogether in the hands of the Government, the courts of justice would soon be mere 'bands of commissioners,'—Mirabeau himself looked only to the action of the central authority to realise his visionary schemes.

These ideas were not confined to books; they found entrance into men's minds, modified their customs, affected their habits, and penetrated throughout society, even into every-day life.

No one imagined that any important affair could be properly carried out without the intervention of the State. Even the agriculturists—a class usually refractory to precept—were disposed to think that if agriculture did not improve, it was the fault of the Government, which did not give them sufficient advice and assistance. One of them writes to an Intendant in a tone of irritation which foreshadows the coming Revolution. 'Why does not the Government appoint inspectors to go once a year into the provinces to examine the state of cultivation, to instruct the cultivators how to improve it—to tell them what to do with their cattle, how to fatten, rear, and sell them, and where to take them to market? These inspectors should be well paid; and the farmers who exhibited proofs of the best system of husbandry should receive some mark of honour.'

Agricultural inspectors and crosses of honour! Such means of encouraging agriculture never would have entered into the head of a Suffolk farmer.

In the eyes of the majority of the French the Government was alone able to ensure public order; the people were afraid of nothing but the patrols, and men of property had no confidence in anything else. Both classes regarded the gendarme on his rounds not merely as the chief defender of order, but as order itself. 'No one,' says the provincial assembly of Guyenne, 'can fail to observe that the sight of a patrol is well calculated to restrain those most hostile to all subordination.' Accordingly every one wanted to have a squadron of them at his own door. The archives of an intendancy are full of requests of this nature; no one seemed to suspect that under the guise of a protector a master might be concealed.[1]

Nothing struck the émigrés so much on their arrival in England as the absence of this military force. It filled them with surprise, and often even with contempt, for the English. One of

[1] See Note XXVI., Additional Patrols.

them, a man of ability, but whose education had not prepared him for what he was to see, wrote as follows :—'It is perfectly true that an Englishman congratulates himself on having been robbed, on the score that at any rate there is no patrol in his country. A man may lament anything that disturbs public tranquillity, but he will nevertheless comfort himself, when he sees the turbulént restored to society, with the reflection that the letter of the law is stronger than all other considerations. Such false notions, however,' he adds, 'are not absolutely universal ; there are some wise people who think otherwise, and wisdom must prevail in the end.'

But that these eccentricities of the English could have any connection with their liberties never entered into the mind of this observer. He chose rather to explain the phenomenon by more scientific reasons. ' In a country,' said he, ' where the moisture of the climate, and the want of elasticity in the air, give a sombre tinge to the temperament, the people are disposed to give them-selves up to serious objects. The English people are naturally inclined to occupy themselves with the affairs of government, to which the French are averse.'

The French Government having thus assumed the place of Providence, it was natural that every one should invoke its aid in his individual necessities. Accordingly we find an immense number of petitions which, while affecting to relate to the public interest, really concern only small individual interests.[1] The boxes containing them are perhaps the only place in which all the classes composing that society of France, which has long ceased to exist, are still mingled. It is a melancholy task to read them : we find peasants praying to be indemnified for the loss of their cattle or their horses; wealthy landowners asking for assistance in rendering their estates more productive; manufacturers soliciting from the Intendant privileges by which they may be protected from a troublesome competition, and very frequently confiding the embarrassed state of their affairs to him, and begging him to obtain for them relief or a loan from the Comptroller-General. It appears that some fund was set apart for this purpose.

Even the nobles were often very importunate solicitants; the only mark of their condition is the lofty tone in which they begged. The tax of twentieths was to many of them the principal link in the chain of their dependence.[2] Their quota of this tax was fixed every year by the Council upon the report of the Intendant, and

[1] See Note XXVII., Bureaux de Tabac.
[2] [It was a species of income-tax of five per cent. levied on a portion of the income.]

to him they addressed themselves in order to obtain delays and remissions. I have read a host of petitions of this nature made by nobles, nearly all men of title, and often of very high rank, in consideration, as they stated, of the insufficiency of their revenues, or the disordered state of their affairs. The nobles usually addressed the Intendant as 'Monsieur;' but I have observed that, under these circumstances, they invariably called him 'Monseigneur,' as was usually done by men of the middle class. Sometimes pride and poverty were drolly mixed in these petitions. One of the nobles wrote to the Intendant: 'Your feeling heart will never consent to see the father of a family of my rank strictly taxed by twentieths like a father of the lower classes.'

At the periods of scarcity, which were so frequent during the eighteenth century, the whole population of each district looked to the Intendant, and appeared to expect to be fed by him alone. It is true that every man already blamed the Government for all his sufferings. The most inevitable privations were ascribed to it, and even the inclemency of the seasons was made a subject of reproach to it.

We need not be astonished at the marvellous facility with which centralisation was re-established in France at the beginning of this century.[1] The men of 1789 had overthrown the edifice, but its foundations remained deep in the very minds of the destroyers, and on these foundations it was easy to build it up anew, and to make it more stable than it had ever been before.

[1] See Note XXVIII., Extinction of Loyal Activity.

CHAPTER VII.

OF ALL EUROPEAN NATIONS FRANCE WAS ALREADY THAT IN WHICH
THE METROPOLIS HAD ACQUIRED THE GREATEST PREPONDERANCE
OVER THE PROVINCES, AND HAD MOST COMPLETELY ABSORBED
THE WHOLE EMPIRE.

THE political preponderance of capital cities over the rest of the
empire is caused neither by their situation, their size, nor their
wealth, but by the nature of the government. London, which
contains the population of a kingdom, has never hitherto exercised
a sovereign influence over the destinies of Great Britain. No
citizen of the United States ever imagined that the inhabitants of
New York could decide the fate of the American Union. Nay
more, no one even in the State of New York conceives that the
will of that city alone could direct the affairs of the nation. Yet
New York at this moment numbers as many inhabitants as Paris
contained when the Revolution broke out.

At the time of the wars of religion in France Paris was thickly
peopled in proportion to the rest of the kingdom as in 1789.
Nevertheless, at that time it had no decisive power. At the time
of the Fronde Paris was still no more than the largest city in
France. In 1789 it was already France itself.

As early as 1740 Montesquieu wrote to one of his friends,
'Nothing is left in France but Paris and the distant provinces,
because Paris has not yet had time to devour them.' In 1750 the
Marquis de Mirabeau, a fanciful but sometimes deep thinker, said,
in speaking of Paris without naming it: ' Capital cities are necessary ; but if the head grows too large, the body becomes apoplectic
and the whole perishes. What then will be the result, if by giving
over the provinces to a sort of direct dependence, and considering
their inhabitants only as subjects of the Crown of an inferior order,
to whom no means of consideration are left and no career for
ambition is open, every man possessing any talent is drawn
towards the capital!' He called this a kind of silent revolution
which must deprive the provinces of all their men of rank, business,
and talent.

The reader who has followed the preceding chapters attentively already knows the causes of this phenomenon; it would be a needless tax on his patience to enumerate them afresh in this place.

This revolution did not altogether escape the attention of the Government, but chiefly by its physical effect on the growth of the city. The Government saw the daily extension of Paris and was afraid that it would become difficult to administer so large a city properly. A great number of ordinances issued by the Kings of France, chiefly during the seventeenth and eighteenth centuries, were destined to put a stop to the growth of the capital. These sovereigns were concentrating the whole public life of France more and more in Paris or at its gates, and yet they wanted Paris to remain a small city. The erection of new houses was forbidden, or else commands were issued that they should be built in the most costly manner and in unattractive situations which were fixed upon beforehand. Every one of these ordinances, it is true, declares, that in spite of all preceding edicts Paris had continued to spread. Six times during the course of his reign did Louis XIV., in the height of his power, in vain attempt to check the increase of Paris; the city grew continually in spite of all edicts. Its political and social preponderance increased even faster than its walls, not so much owing to what took place within them as to the events passing without.

During this period all local liberties gradually became extinct, the symptoms of independent vitality disappeared. The distinctive features of the various provinces became confused, and the last traces of the ancient public life were effaced. Not that the nation was falling into a state of languor; on the contrary, activity everywhere prevailed; but the motive principle was no longer anywhere but in Paris. I will cite but one example of this from amongst a thousand. In the reports made to the Minister on the condition of the bookselling trade, I find that in the sixteenth century and at the beginning of the seventeenth, many considerable printing offices existed in provincial towns which are now without printers, or where the printers are without work. Yet there can be no doubt that many more literary productions of all kinds were published at the end of the eighteenth century than during the sixteenth; but all mental activity now emanated from the centre alone; Paris had totally absorbed the provinces. At the time when the French Revolution broke out, this first revolution was fully accomplished.

The celebrated traveller Arthur Young left Paris soon after the meeting of the States-General, and a few days before the taking of the Bastille; the contrast between that which he had just seen in the city and that which he found beyond its walls filled him with surprise. In Paris all was noise and activity; every hour produced a fresh political pamphlet; as many as ninety-two were published in a week. 'Never,' said he, 'did I see such activity in publishing, even in London.' Out of Paris all seemed inert and silent; few pamphlets and no newspapers were printed. Nevertheless, the provinces were agitated and ready for action, but motionless; if the inhabitants assembled from time to time, it was in order to hear the news which they expected from Paris. In every town Young asked the inhabitants what they intended to do? 'The answer,' he says, 'was always the same: " Ours is but a provincial town; we must wait to see what will be done at Paris." These people,' he adds, ' do not even venture to have an opinion until they know what is thought at Paris.'

Nothing was more astonishing than the extraordinary ease with which the Constituent Assembly destroyed at a single stroke all the ancient French provinces, many of which were older than the monarchy, and then divided the kingdom methodically into eighty-three distinct portions, as though it had been the virgin soil of the New World. Europe was surprised and alarmed by a spectacle for which it was so little prepared. 'This is the first time,' said Burke, ' that we have seen men tear their native land in pieces in so barbarous a manner.' No doubt it appeared like tearing in pieces living bodies, but, in fact, the provinces that were thus dismembered were only corpses.

While Paris was thus finally establishing its supremacy externally, a change took place within its own walls equally deserving the notice of history. After having been a city merely of exchange, of business, of consumption, and of pleasure, Paris had now become a manufacturing town; a second fact, which gave to the first a new and more formidable character.

The origin of this change was very remote; it appears that even during the Middle Ages Paris was already the most industrious as well as the largest city of the kingdom. This becomes more manifest as we approach modern times. In the same degree that the business of administration was brought to Paris, industrial affairs found their way thither. As Paris became more and more the arbiter of taste, the sole centre of power and of the arts, and the chief focus of national activity, the industrial life of the nation withdrew and concentrated itself there in the same proportion.

Although the statistical documents anterior to the Revolution

F

are, for the most part, deserving of little confidence, I think it may safely be affirmed that, during the sixty years which preceded the French Revolution, the number of artisans in Paris was more than doubled; whereas during the same period the general population of the city scarcely increased one third.

Independently of the general causes which I have stated, there were other very peculiar causes which attracted working men to Paris from all parts of France, and agglomerated them by degrees in particular quarters of the town, which they ended by occupying almost exclusively. The restrictions imposed upon manufactures by the fiscal legislation of the time were lighter at Paris than anywhere else in France; it was nowhere so easy to escape from the tyranny of the guilds. Certain faubourgs, such as the Faubourg St. Antoine, and of the Temple specially, enjoyed great privileges of this nature. Louis XVI. considerably enlarged these immunities of the Faubourg St. Antoine, and did his best to gather together an immense working population in that spot, 'being desirous,' said that unfortunate monarch, in one of his edicts, 'to bestow upon the artisans of the Faubourg St. Antoine a further mark of our protection, and to relieve them from the restrictions which are injurious to their interests as well as to the freedom of trade.'

The number of workshops, manufactories, and foundries had increased so greatly in Paris, towards the approach of the Revolution, that the Government at length became alarmed at it. The sight of this progress inspired it with many imaginary terrors. Amongst other things, we find an Order in Council, in 1782, stating that 'the King, apprehending that the rapid increase of manufactures would cause a consumption of wood likely to become prejudicial to the supply of the city, prohibits for the future the creation of any establishment of this nature within a circuit of fifteen leagues round Paris.' The real danger likely to arise from such an agglomeration gave no uneasiness to any one.

Thus then Paris had become the mistress of France, and the popular army which was destined to make itself master of Paris was already assembling.

It is pretty generally admitted, I believe, now, that administrative centralisation and the omnipotence of Paris have had a great share in the overthrow of all the various governments which have succeeded one another during the last forty years. It will not be difficult to show that the same state of things contributed largely to the sudden and violent ruin of the old monarchy, and must be numbered among the principal causes of that first Revolution which has produced all the succeeding ones.

CHAPTER VIII.

FRANCE WAS THE COUNTRY IN WHICH MEN HAD BECOME THE MOST ALIKE.

IF we carefully examine the state of society in France before the Revolution we may see it under two very contrary aspects. It would seem that the men of that time, especially those belonging to the middle and upper ranks of society, who alone were at all conspicuous, were all exactly alike. Nevertheless we find that this monotonous crowd was divided into many different parts by a prodigious number of small barriers, and that each of these small divisions formed a distinct society, exclusively occupied with its own peculiar interests, and taking no share in the life of the community at large.

When we consider this almost infinitesimal division, we shall perceive that the citizens of no other nation were so ill prepared to act in common, or to afford each other a mutual support during a crisis; and that a society thus constituted might be utterly demolished in a moment by a great revolution. Imagine all those small barriers thrown down by an earthquake, and the result is at once a social body more compact and more homogeneous than any perhaps that the world had ever seen.

I have shown that throughout nearly the whole kingdom the independent life of the provinces had long been extinct; this had powerfully contributed to render all Frenchmen very much alike. Through the diversities which still subsisted the unity of the nation might already be discerned; uniformity of legislation brought it to light. As the eighteenth century advanced there was a great increase in the number of edicts, royal declarations, and Orders in Council, applying the same regulations in the same manner in every part of the empire. It was not the governing body alone but the mass of those governed, who conceived the idea of a legislation so general and so uniform, the same everywhere and for all: this idea was apparent in all the plans of reform which succeeded each other for thirty years before the outbreak of the Revolution. Two centuries earlier the very materials for such conceptions, if we may use such a phrase, would have been wanting.

Not only did the provinces become more and more alike, but in each province men of various classes, those at least who were placed above the common people, grew to resemble each other more and more, in spite of differences of rank. Nothing displays this more clearly than the perusal of the instructions to the several Orders of the States-General of 1789. The interests of those who drew them up were widely different, but in all else they were identical. In the proceedings of the earlier States-General the state of things was totally different; the middle classes and the nobility had then more common interests, more business in common; they displayed far less reciprocal animosity; yet they appeared to belong to two distinct races. Time, which had perpetuated, and, in many respects, aggravated the privileges interposed between two classes of men, had powerfully contributed to render them alike in all other respects. For several centuries the French nobility had grown gradually poorer and poorer. 'Spite of its privileges the nobility is ruined and wasted day by day, and the middle classes get possession of the large fortunes,' wrote a nobleman in a melancholy strain in 1755. Yet the laws by which the estates of the nobility were protected still remained the same, nothing appeared to be changed in their economical condition. Nevertheless, the more they lost their power the poorer they everywhere became, in exactly the same proportion.

It would seem as if, in all human institutions as in man himself, there exists, independently of the organs which manifestly fulfil the various functions of existence, some central and invisible force which is the very principle of life. In vain do the organs appear to act as before; when this vivifying flame is extinct the whole structure languishes and dies. The French nobility still had entails (indeed Burke remarked, that in his time entails were more frequent and more strict in France than in England), the right of primogeniture, territorial and perpetual dues, and whatever was called a beneficial interest in land. They had been relieved from the heavy obligation of carrying on war at their own charge, and at the same time had retained an increased exemption from taxation; that is to say, they kept the compensation and got rid of the burden. Moreover, they enjoyed several other pecuniary advantages which their forefathers had never possessed; nevertheless they gradually became impoverished in the same degree that they lost the exercise and the spirit of government. Indeed it is to this gradual impoverishment that the vast subdivision of landed property, which we have already remarked, must be partly attributed. The nobles had sold their lands piecemeal to the peasants, reserving to themselves only the seignorial rights which gave them the appearance rather than the reality of their former position. Several provinces of France, like the Limousin mentioned by Turgot, were filled with a small poor nobility, owning hardly any land, and living only on seignorial rights and rent-charges on their former estates.[1]

'In this district,' says an Intendant at the beginning of the century, 'the number of noble families still amounts to several thousands, but there are not fifteen amongst them who have twenty thousand livres a year.' I find in some minutes addressed by another Intendant (of Franche-Comté) to his successor, in 1750, 'the nobility of this part of the country is pretty good but extremely poor, and as proud as it is poor. It is greatly humbled compared to what it used to be. It is not bad policy to keep the nobles in this state of poverty in order to compel them to serve, and to stand in need of our assistance. They form,' he adds, 'a confraternity, into which those only are admitted who can prove four quarterings. This confraternity is not patented but only allowed; it meets only once a year, and in the presence of the Intendant. After dining and hearing mass together, these noblemen return, every man to his home, some on their rosinantes and the rest on foot. You will see what a comical assemblage it is.'

This gradual impoverishment of the nobility was more or less apparent, not only in France, but in all parts of the Continent, in which, as in France, the feudal system was finally dying out without being replaced by a new form of aristocracy. This decay was especially manifest and excited great attention amongst the German States on the banks of the Rhine. In England alone the contrary was the case. There the ancient noble families which still existed had not only kept, but greatly increased their fortunes; they were still first in riches as in power. The new families which had risen beside them had only copied but had not surpassed their wealth.

In France the non-noble classes alone seemed to inherit all the wealth which the nobility had lost; they fattened, as it were, upon its substance. Yet there were no laws to prevent the middle class from ruining themselves, or to assist them in acquiring riches; nevertheless they incessantly increased their wealth; in many instances they had become as rich as, and often richer than the nobles. Nay, more, their wealth was of the same kind, for, though dwelling

[1] See Note XXIX., Seignorial Dues in different Provinces of France.

in the town, they were often landowners in the country, and sometimes they even bought seignorial estates.

Education and habits of life had already created a thousand
other points of resemblance between these two classes of men. The
middle class man was as enlightened as the noble, and it deserves
to be remarked, his acquirements were derived from the very same
source. The same light shone upon both. Their education had
been equally theoretical and literary. Paris, which became more
and more the sole preceptor of France, had ended by giving to all
minds one common form and action.

At the end of the eighteenth century no doubt some difference
was still perceptible between the manners of the nobility and those
of the middle class, for nothing assimilates more slowly than that
surface of society which we call manners; at bottom, however, all
men above the rank of the common people were alike; they had the
same ideas, the same habits, the same tastes; they indulged in the
same pleasures, read the same books, and spoke the same language.
The only difference left between them was in their rights.

I much doubt whether this was the case in the same degree
anywhere else, even in England, where the different classes, though
firmly united by common interests, still differed in their habits and
feelings; for political liberty, which possesses the admirable power
of placing the citizens of a State in compulsory intercourse and
mutual dependence, does not on that account always make them
similar; it is the government of one man which, in the end, has
the inevitable effect of rendering all men alike, and all mutually
indifferent to their common fate.

CHAPTER IX.

SHOWING HOW MEN THUS SIMILAR WERE MORE DIVIDED THAN EVER
INTO SMALL GROUPS, ESTRANGED FROM AND INDIFFERENT TO
EACH OTHER.

LET us now look at the other side of the picture, and we shall see
that these same Frenchmen, who had so many points of resemblance amongst themselves, were, nevertheless, more completely
isolated from each other than perhaps the inhabitants of any other
country, or than had ever been the case in France.

It seems extremely probable that, at the time of the first establishment of the feudal system in Europe, the class which was
subsequently called the nobility did not at once form a *caste*, but
was originally composed of the chief men of the nation, and was
therefore, in the beginning, merely an aristocracy. This, however,
is a question which I have no intention of discussing here; it will
be sufficient to remark that, during the Middle Ages, the nobility
had become a caste, that is to say, that its distinctive mark was
birth.

It retained, indeed, one of the proper characteristics of an
aristocracy, that of being a governing body of citizens; but birth
alone decided who should be at the head of this body. Whoever
was not born noble was excluded from this close and particular
class, and could only fill a position more or less exalted but still
subordinate in the State.

Wherever on the continent of Europe the feudal system had
been established it ended in caste; in England alone it returned
to aristocracy.

It has always excited my surprise that a fact which distinguishes England from all other modern nations, and which alone
can throw light upon the peculiarities of its laws, its spirit, and its
history, has not attracted to a still greater degree the attention of
philosophers and statesmen, and that habit has rendered it, as it
were, imperceptible to the English themselves. It has frequently
been seen by glimpses, and imperfectly described, but no complete and distinct view has, I believe, ever been taken of it.

Montesquieu, it is true, on visiting Great Britain in 1739, wrote, ' I am now in a country which has little resemblance to the rest of Europe : ' but that is all.

It was indeed, not so much its parliament, its liberty, its publicity, or its jury, which at that time rendered England so unlike the rest of Europe ; it was something far more peculiar and far more powerful. England was the only country in which the system of caste had been not only modified, but effectually destroyed. The nobility and the middle classes in England followed the same business, embraced the same professions, and, what is far more significant, intermarried with each other. The daughter of the greatest nobleman could already without disgrace marry a man of yesterday.

In order to ascertain whether caste, with the ideas, habits, and barriers it creates amongst a nation, is definitely destroyed, look at its marriages. They alone give the decisive feature which we seek. At this very day, in France, after sixty years of democracy, we shall generally seek it in vain. The old and the new families, between which no distinction any longer appears to exist, avoid as much as possible to intermingle with each other by marriage.

It has often been remarked that the English nobility has been more prudent, more able, and less exclusive than any other. It would have been much nearer the truth to say, that in England, for a very long time past, no nobility, properly so called, has existed, if we take the word in the ancient and limited sense it has everywhere else retained.

This singular revolution is lost in the night of ages, but a living witness of it yet survives in the idiom of language. For several centuries the word *gentleman* has altogether changed its meaning in England, and the word *roturier* has ceased to exist. It would have been impossible to translate literally into English the well-known line from the 'Tartuffe,' even when Molière wrote it in 1664 :—

> Et tel qu'on le voit, il est bon gentilhomme.

If we make a further application of the science of languages to the science of history, and pursue the fate of the word *gentleman* through time and through space,—the offspring of the French word *gentilhomme*,—we shall find its application extending in England in the same proportion in which classes draw near one another and amalgamate. In each succeeding century it is applied to persons placed somewhat lower in the social scale. At length it travelled with the English to America, where it is used to desig-

nate every citizen indiscriminately. Its history is that of democracy itself.

In France the word *gentilhomme* has always been strictly
limited to its original meaning; since the Revolution it has been
almost disused, but its application has never changed. The word
which was used to designate the members of the caste was kept
intact, because the caste itself was maintained as separate from all
the rest as it had ever been.

I go even further, and assert that this caste had become far
more exclusive than it was when the word was first invented, and
that in France a change had taken place in the direction opposed
to that which had occurred in England.

Though the nobility and the middle class in France had become
far more alike, they were at the same time more isolated from each
other—two things which are so essentially distinct that the former,
instead of extenuating the latter, may frequently aggravate it.

During the Middle Ages, and whilst the feudal system was still
in force, all those who held land under a lord (and who were properly called vassals, in feudal law) were constantly associated with
the lord, though many of them were not noble, in the government
of the Seignory; indeed this was the principal condition of their
tenures. Not only were they bound to follow the lord to war, but
they were bound, in virtue of their holdings, to spend a certain
part of the year at his court, that is in helping him to administer
justice, and to govern the inhabitants. The lord's court was the
mainspring of the feudal system of government; it played a part
in all the ancient laws of Europe, and very distinct vestiges of it
may still be found in many parts of Germany. The learned feudal-
ist, Edmé de Fréminville, who, thirty years before the French
Revolution, thought fit to write a thick volume on feudal rights
and on the renovation of manor rolls, informs us that he had seen
in 'the titles of a number of manors, that the vassals were obliged
to appear every fortnight at the lord's court, and that being there
assembled they judged conjointly with the lord and his ordinary
judge, the assizes and differences which had arisen between the
inhabitants.' He adds, that he had found 'there were sometimes
eighty, one hundred and fifty, and even as many as two hundred
vassals in one lordship, a great number of whom were *roturiers*.'
I have quoted this, not as a proof, for a thousand others might be
adduced, but as an example of the manner in which at the beginning, and for long afterwards, the rural classes were united with
the nobility, and mingled with them daily in the conduct of affairs.
That which the lord's court did for the small rural proprietors, the

Provincial Estates, and subsequently the States-General, effected for the citizens of the towns.

It is impossible to study the records of the States-General of the fourteenth century, and above all of the Provincial Estates of the same period, without being astonished at the importance of the place which the *Tiers-Etat* filled in those assemblies, and at the power it wielded in them.

As a man the burgess of the fourteenth century was, doubtless, very inferior to the burgess of the eighteenth; but the middle class, as a body, filled a far higher and more secure place in political society. Its right to a share in the government was uncontested; the part which it played in political assemblies was always considerable and often preponderating. The other classes of the commmunity were forced to a constant reckoning with the people.

But what strikes us most is, that the nobility and the *Tiers-Etat* found it at that time so much easier to transact business together, or to offer a common resistance, than they have ever found it since. This is observable not only in the States-General of the fourteenth century, many of which had an irregular and revolutionary character impressed upon them by the disasters of the time, but in the Provincial Estates of the same period, where nothing seems to have interrupted the regular and habitual course of affairs. Thus, in Auvergne, we find that the three Orders took the most important measures in common, and that the execution of them was superintended by commissioners chosen equally from all three. The same thing occurred at the same time in Champagne. Every one knows the famous act by which, at the beginning of the same century, the nobles and burgesses of a large number of towns combined together to defend the franchises of the nation and the privileges of their provinces against the encroachments of the Crown. During that period of French history we find many such episodes, which appear as if borrowed from the history of England. In the following centuries events of this character altogether disappeared.[1]

The fact is, that as by degrees the government of the lordships became disorganised, and the States-General grew rarer or ceased altogether—that as the general liberties of the country were finally destroyed, involving the local liberties in their ruin—the burgess and the noble ceased to come into contact in public life. They no longer felt the necessity of standing by one another, or of a mutual compact; every day rendered them more independent of each other, but at the same time estranged them more and more. In the

[1] See Note XXX., Self-Government adverse to Spirit of Caste.

eighteenth century this revolution was fully accomplished; the two conditions of men never met but by accident in private life. Thenceforth the two classes were not merely rivals but enemies.[1]

One circumstance which seems very peculiar to France, was that at the very time when the order of nobility was thus losing its political powers, the nobles individually acquired several privileges which they had never possessed before, or increased those which they already enjoyed.. It was as if the members enriched themselves with the spoil of the body.   The nobility had less and less right to command, but the nobles had more and more the exclusive prerogative of being the first servants of the master.   It was more easy for a man of low birth to become an officer under Louis XIV. than under Louis XVI.; this frequently happened in Prussia at a time when there was no example of such a thing in France. Every one of these privileges once obtained adhered to the blood and was inseparable from it. The more the French nobility ceased to be an aristocracy, the more did it become a caste.

Let us take the most invidious of all these privileges, that of exemption from taxation.[2] It is easy to perceive that from the fifteenth century until the French Revolution, this privilege was continually increasing, and that it increased with the rapid progress of the public burdens. When, as under Charles VII., only 1,200,000 livres were raised by the *taille*, the privilege of being exempted from it was but small; but when, under Louis XVI., eighty millions were raised by the same tax, the privilege of exemption became very great. When the *taille* was the only tax levied on the non-noble classes, the exemption of the nobility was little felt; but when taxes of this description were multiplied a thousandfold under various names and shapes—when four other taxes had been assimilated with the *taille*—when burdens unknown in the Middle Ages, such as the application of forced labour by the Crown to all public works or services, the militia, &c.—had been added to the *taille* with its accessories, and were distributed with the same inequality, then indeed the exemption of birth appeared immense. The inequality, though great, was indeed still more apparent than real, for the noble was often reached through his farmer by the tax which he escaped in his own person; but in such matters as this the inequality which is seen does more harm than that which is felt.

Louis XIV., pressed by the financial difficulties which overwhelmed him towards the end of his reign, had established two common taxes—the capitation tax and the twentieths; but, as if the exemption from taxation had been in itself a privilege so venerable that it was necessary to respect it in the very act by which it was infringed, care was taken to render the mode of collection different even when the tax was common. For one class it remained harsh and degrading, for the other indulgent and honourable.[1]

Although inequality under taxation prevailed throughout the whole continent of Europe, there were very few countries in which it had become so palpable or was so constantly felt as in France. Throughout a great part of Germany most of the taxes were indirect; and even with respect to the direct taxes, the privilege of the nobility frequently consisted only in bearing a smaller share of the common burden.[2] There were, moreover, certain taxes which fell only upon the nobles, and which were intended to replace the gratuitous military service which was no longer exacted.

Now of all means of distinguishing one man from another and of marking the difference of classes, inequality of taxation is the most pernicious and the most calculated to add isolation to inequality, and in some sort to render both irremediable. Let us look at its effects. When the noble and the middle classes are not liable to the same tax, the assessment and collection of each year's revenue draws afresh with sharpness and precision the line of demarcation between them. Every year each member of the privileged order feels an immediate and pressing interest in not suffering himself to be confounded with the mass, and makes a fresh effort to place himself apart from it.[3]

As there is scarcely any matter of public business that does not either arise out of or result in a tax, it follows that as soon as the two classes are not equally liable to it, they can no longer have any reason for common deliberation, or any cause of common wants and desires; no effort is needed to keep them asunder; the occasion and the desire for common action have been removed.

In the highly-coloured description which Mr. Burke gave of the ancient constitution of France, he urged in favour of the constitution of the French nobility, the ease with which the middle classes could be ennobled by acquiring an office: he fancied that this bore some analogy to the open aristocracy of England. Louis XI. had, it is true, multiplied the grants of nobility; with him it was a means of lowering the aristocracy: his successors lavished

---

[1] See Note XXXIII., Indirect Privileges under Taxation.
[2] See Notes XXXIV. and XXXV.

[3] See Note XXXVI., Nobles favoured in Collection of Taxes.

them in order to obtain money. Necker informs us, that in his time the number of offices which conferred nobility amounted to four thousand. Nothing like this existed in any other part of Europe, but the analogy which Burke sought to establish between France and England on this score was all the more false.

If the middle classes of England, instead of making war upon the aristocracy, have remained so intimately connected with it, it is not specially because the aristocracy is open to all, but rather, as has been said, because its outline is indistinct and its limit unknown—not so much because any man could be admitted into it as because it was impossible to say with certainty when he took rank there—so that all who approached it might look upon themselves as belonging to it, might take part in its rule, and derive either lustre or profit from its influence.

Whereas the barrier which divided the nobility of France from the other classes, though easily enough passed, was always fixed and visible, and manifested itself to those who remained without, by striking and odious tokens. He who had once crossed it was separated from all those whose ranks he had just quitted by privileges which were burdensome and humiliating to them.

The system of creating new nobles, far from lessening the hatred of the *roturier* to the nobleman, increased it beyond measure ; it was envenomed by all the envy with which the new noble was looked upon by his former equals. For this reason the *Tiers-Etat*, in all their complaints, always displayed more irritation against the newly-ennobled than against the old nobility ; and far from demanding that the gate which led out of their own condition should be made wider, they continually required that it should be narrowed.

At no period of French history had it been so easy to acquire nobility as in 1789, and never were the middle classes and the nobility so completely separated. Not only did the nobles refuse to endure, in their electoral colleges, any one who had the slightest taint of middle-class blood, but the middle classes also as carefully excluded all those who might in any degree be looked upon as noble. In some provinces the newly-ennobled were rejected by one class because they were not noble enough, and by the other because they were too much so. This, it is said, was the case with the celebrated Lavoisier.

If, leaving the nobility out of the question, we turn our attention to the middle classes, we shall find the same state of things : the man of the middle classes living almost as far apart from the common people as the noble was from the middle class.

Almost the whole of the middle class before the Revolution dwelt in the towns. Two causes had principally led to this result— the privileges of the nobles and the *taille*. The Seigneur who lived on his estates usually treated his peasants with a certain good-natured familiarity, but his arrogance towards his neighbours of the middle class was unbounded. It had never ceased to augment as his political power had diminished, and for that very reason ; for on the one hand, as he had ceased to govern, he no longer had any interest in conciliating those who could assist him in that task ; whilst, on the other, as has frequently been observed, he tried to console himself for the loss of real power by an immoderate display of his apparent rights. Even his absence from his estates, instead of relieving his neighbours, only served to increase their annoyance. Absenteeism had not even that good effect, for privileges enforced by proxy were all the more insupportable.

I am not sure, however, that the *taille*, and all the taxes which had been assimilated to it, were not still more powerful causes.

I could show, I think, in very few words, why the *taille* and its accessories pressed much more heavily on the country than on the towns ; but the reader would probably think it superfluous. It will be sufficient to point out that the middle classes, gathered together in the towns, could find a thousand means of alleviating the weight of the *taille*, and often indeed of avoiding it altogether, which not one of them could have employed singly had he remained on the estate to which he belonged. Above all, he thereby escaped the obligation of collecting the *taille*, which he dreaded far more than that of paying it, and not without reason ; for there never was under the old French Government, or, I believe, under any Government, a worse condition than that of the parochial collector of the *taille*. I shall have occasion to show this hereafter. Yet no one in a village except the nobles could escape this office ; and rather than subject himself to it, the rich man of the middle class let his estates and withdrew to the neighbouring town. Turgot coincides with all the secret documents which I have had an opportunity of consulting, when he says, that ' the collecting of the *taille* converts all the non-noble landowners of the country into burgesses of the towns. Indeed this, to make a passing remark, was one of the chief causes why France was fuller of towns, and especially of small towns, than almost any other country in Europe.

Once ensconced within the walls of a town, a wealthy though low-born member of the middle class soon lost the tastes and ideas of rural life ; he became totally estranged from the labours and the affairs of those of his own class whom he had left behind. His whole life was now devoted to one single object: he aspired to become a public officer in his adopted town.

It is a great mistake to suppose that the passion for place, which fills almost all Frenchmen of our time, more especially those belonging to the middle ranks, has arisen since the Revolution; its birth dates from several centuries back, and it has constantly increased in strength, thanks to the variety of fresh food with which it has been continually supplied.

Places under the old Government did not always resemble those of our day, but I believe they were even more numerous; the number of petty places was almost infinite. It has been reckoned that between the years 1693 and 1790 alone, forty thousand such places were created, almost all within the reach of the lower middle class. I have counted that, in 1750, in a provincial town of moderate size, no less than one hundred and nine persons were engaged in the administration of justice, and one hundred and twenty-six in the execution of the judgments delivered by them—all inhabitants of the town. The eagerness with which the townspeople of the middle class sought to obtain these places was really unparalleled. No sooner had one of them become possessed of a small capital than, instead of investing it in business, he immediately laid it out in the purchase of a place. This wretched ambition has done more harm to the agriculture and the trade of France than the guilds or even the *taille*. When the supply of places failed, the imagination of place-hunters instantly fell to work to invent new ones. A certain Sieur Lemberville published a memorial to prove that it was quite in accordance with the interest of the public to create inspectors for a particular branch of manufactures, and he concluded by offering himself for the employment. Which of us has not known a Lemberville? A man endowed with some education and small means, thought it not decorous to die without having been a government officer. 'Every man according to his condition,' says a contemporary writer, 'wants to be something by command of the King.'

The principal difference in this respect between the time of which I have been speaking and the present is, that formerly the Government sold the places; whereas now it gives them away. A man no longer pays his money in order to purchase a place: he does more, he sells himself.

Separated from the peasantry by the difference of residence, and still more by the manner of life, the middle classes were also for the most part divided from them by interest. The privileges of the nobles with respect to taxation were justly complained of, but what then can be said of those enjoyed by the middle class? The offices which exempted them wholly or in part from public burdens were counted by thousands : one exempted them from the militia, another from the *corvée*, a third from the *taille*. 'Is there a parish,' says a writer of the time, 'that does not contain, independently of the nobles and ecclesiastics, a number of inhabitants who have purchased for themselves, by dint of places or commissions, some sort of exemption from taxation ?' One of the reasons why a certain number of offices destined for the middle classes were, from time to time, abolished is the diminution of the receipts caused by the exemption of so large a number of persons from the *taille*. I have no doubt that the number of those exempted among the middle class was as great as, and often greater than, among the nobility.

These miserable privileges filled those who were deprived of them with envy, and those who enjoyed them with the most selfish pride. Nothing is more striking throughout the eighteenth century than the hostility of the citizen of the towns towards the surrounding peasantry, and the jealousy felt by the peasants of the townspeople. 'Every single town,' says Turgot, 'absorbed by its own separate interests, is ready to sacrifice to them the country and the villages of its district.' 'You have often been obliged,' said he, elsewhere, in addressing his Sub-delegates, 'to repress the constant tendency to usurpation and encroachment which characterises the conduct of the towns towards the country people and the villages of their district.'

Even the common people who dwelt within the walls of the towns with the middle classes became estranged from and almost hostile to them. Most of the local burdens which they imposed were so contrived as to press most heavily on the lower classes. More than once I have had occasion to ascertain the truth of what Turgot also says in another part of his works, namely, that the middle classes of the towns had found means to regulate the *octrois* in such a manner that the burden did not fall on themselves.

What is most obvious in every act of the French middle classes, was their dread of being confounded with the common people, and their passionate desire to escape by every means in their power from popular control. 'If it were his Majesty's pleasure,' said the burgesses of a town, in a memorial addressed to the Comptroller-General, 'that the office of mayor should become elective, it would be proper to oblige the electors to choose

him only from the chief notables, and even from the corporation.'

We have seen that it was a part of the policy of the Kings of
France successively to withdraw from the population of the towns
the exercise of their political rights. From Louis XI. to Louis XV.
their whole legislation betrays this intention ; frequently the
burgesses themselves seconded that intention, sometimes they
suggested it.

At the time of the municipal reform of 1764, an Intendant
consulted the municipal officers of a small town on the point of
preserving to the artisans and working-classes—*autre menu peuple*
—the right of electing their magistrates. These officers replied
that it was true that ' the people had never abused this right, and
that it would doubtless be agreeable to preserve to them the
consolation of choosing their own masters; but that it would be
still better, in the interest of good order and the public tranquillity,
to make over this duty altogether to the Assembly of Notables.'
The Sub-delegate reported, on his side, that he had held a secret
meeting, at his own house, of the ' six best citizens of the town.'
These six best citizens were unanimously of opinion that the wisest
course would be to entrust the election, not even to the Assembly
of Notables, as the municipal officers had proposed, but to a
certain number of deputies chosen from the different bodies of
which that Assembly was composed. The Sub-delegate, more
favourable to the liberties of the people than these burgesses
themselves, reported their opinion, but added, as his own, that ' it
was nevertheless very hard upon the working-classes to pay,
without any means of controlling the expenditure of the money,
sums imposed on them by such of their fellow-citizens who were
probably, by reason of the privileged exemptions from taxation,
the least interested in the question.'

Let us complete this survey. Let us now consider the middle
classes as distinguished from the people, just as we have previously
considered the nobility as distinguished from the middle classes.[1]
We shall discover in this small portion of the French nation, thus
set apart from the rest, infinite subdivisions. It seems as if the
people of France was like those pretended simple substances in
which modern chemistry perpetually detects new elements by the

[1] [The use of the French term *bour-geois*, here and in some other passages
translated ' middle classes,' is a further
proof of the estimation of the power
once exercised by that class in the
community. In English the corre-
sponding term *burgess* has remained
inseparable from the exercise of municipal rights ; and we have no distinctive appellation, irrespective of political
rights, for the large class which separates the nobility from the populace.
That class is, in fact, in this country,
both socia'ly and politically, *the people.*]

force of its analysis. I have discovered not less than thirty-six distinct bodies among the notables of one small town. These distinct bodies, though already very diminutive, were constantly employed in reducing each other to still narrower dimensions. They were perpetually throwing off the heterogeneous particles they might still contain, so as to reduce themselves to the most simple elements. Some of them were reduced by this elaborate process to no more than three or four members, but their personality only became more intense and their tempers more contentious. All of them were separated from each other by some diminutive privileges, the least honourable of which was still a mark of honour. Between them raged incessant disputes for precedency. The Intendant, and even the Courts of Justice, were distracted by their quarrels. 'It has just been decided that holy-water is to be offered to the magistrates (*le présidial*) before it is offered to the corporation. The Parliament hesitated, but the King has called up the affair to his Council, and decided it himself. It was high time; this question had thrown the whole town into a ferment.' If one of these bodies obtained precedency over another in the general Assembly of Notables, the latter instantly withdrew, and preferred abandoning altogether the public business of the community rather than submit to an outrage on his dignity.—The body of periwig-makers of the town of La Flèche decided ' that it would express in this manner its well-founded grief occasioned by the precedency which had been granted to the bakers.' A portion of the notables of another town obstinately refused to perform their office, because, as the Intendant reported, ' some artisans have been introduced into the Assembly, with whom the principal burgesses cannot bear to associate.' ' If the place of sheriff,' said the Intendant of another province, ' be given to a notary, the other notables will be disgusted, as the notaries are here men of no birth, not being of the families of the notables, and all of them having been clerks.' The ' six best citizens,' whom I have already mentioned, and who so readily decided that the people ought to be deprived of their political rights, were singularly perplexed when they had to determine who the notables were to be, and what order of precedency was to be established amongst them. In such a strait they presume only to express their doubts, fearing, as they said, ' to cause to some of their fellow-citizens too sensible a mortification.'

The natural vanity of the French was strengthened and stimulated by the incessant collision of their pretensions in these small bodies, and the legitimate pride of the citizens was forgotten. Most of these small corporations, of which I have been speaking, already existed in the sixteenth century; but at that time their members, after having settled among themselves the business of their own fraternity, joined all the other citizens to transact in common the public business of the city.   In the eighteenth century these bodies were almost entirely wrapped up in themselves, for the concerns of their municipal life had become scarce, and they were all managed by delegates.   Each of these small communities, therefore, lived only for itself, was occupied only with itself, and had no affairs but its own interests.

Our forefathers had not yet acquired the term of *individuality*, - which we have coined for our own use, because in their times there was no such thing as an individual not belonging to some group of persons, and who could consider himself as absolutely alone; but each of the thousand little groups, of which French society was then composed, thought only of itself.   It was, if I may so express myself, a state of collective individuality, which prepared the French mind for that state of positive individuality which is the characteristic of our own time.

But what is most strange is that all these men, who stood so much aloof from one another, had become so extremely similar amongst themselves that if their positions had been changed no distinction could have been traced among them.   Nay more, if any one could have sounded their innermost convictions, he would have found that the slight barriers which still divided persons in all other respects so similar, appeared to themselves alike contrary to the public interest and to common sense, and that in theory they already worshipped the uniformity of society and the unity of power.   Each of them clung to his own particular condition, only because a particular condition was the distinguishing mark of others; but all were ready to confound their own condition in the same mass, provided no one retained any separate lot or rose above the common level.

CHAPTER X.

THE DESTRUCTION OF POLITICAL LIBERTY AND THE ESTRANGEMENT
OF CLASSES WERE THE CAUSES OF ALMOST ALL THE DISORDERS
WHICH LED TO THE DISSOLUTION OF THE OLD SOCIETY OF
FRANCE.

OF all the disorders which attacked the constitution of society in
France, as it existed before the Revolution, and led to the dissolution of that society, that which I have just described was the most
fatal. But I must pursue the inquiry to the source of so dangerous
and strange an evil, and show how many other evils took their
origin from the same cause.

If the English had, from the period of the Middle Ages, altogether lost, like the French, political freedom and all those local
franchises which cannot long exist without it, it is highly probable
that each of the different classes of which the English aristocracy
is composed would have seceded from the rest, as was the case in
France and more or less all over the continent, and that all those
classes together would have separated themselves from the people.
But freedom compelled them always to remain within reach of
each other, so as to combine their strength in time of need.

It is curious to observe how the British aristocracy, urged even
by its own ambition, has contrived, whenever it seemed necessary,
to mix familiarly with its inferiors, and to feign to consider them
as its equals. Arthur Young, whom I have already quoted, and
whose book is one of the most instructive works which exist on
the former state of society in France, relates that, happening to be
one day at the country-house of the Duc de la Rochefoucauld, at
La Roche Guyon, he expressed a wish to converse with some of
the best and most wealthy farmers of the neighbourhood. 'The
Duke had the kindness to order his steward to give me all the
information I wanted relative to the agriculture of the country,
and to speak to such persons as were necessary on points that he
was in doubt about. At an English nobleman's house there would
have been three or four farmers asked to meet me, who would have
dined with the family among ladies of the first rank. I do not

exaggerate when I say that I have had this at least an hundred times in the first houses of our islands. It is, however, a thing that in the present state of manners in France would not be met with from Calais to Bayonne, except by chance in the house of some great Lord, who had been much in England, and then not unless it were asked for. I once knew it at the Duke de Liancourt's.'[1]

Unquestionably the English aristocracy is of a haughtier nature than that of France, and less disposed to mingle familiarly with those who live in a humbler condition; but the obligations of its own rank have imposed that duty upon it. It submitted that it might command. For centuries no inequality of taxation has existed in England, except such exemptions as have been successively introduced for the relief of the indigent classes. Observe to what results different political principles may lead nations so nearly contiguous! In the eighteenth century, the poor man in England enjoyed the privilege of exemption from taxation; the rich in France. In one country the aristocracy has taken upon itself the heaviest public burdens, in order to retain the government of the State; in the other the aristocracy retained to the last exemption from taxation as a compensation for the loss of political power.

In the fourteenth century the maxim ' No tax without the consent of the taxed '—*n'impose qui ne veut*—appeared to be as firmly established in France as in England. It was frequently quoted; to contravene it always seemed an act of tyranny; to conform to it was to revert to the law. At that period, as I have already remarked, a multitude of analogies may be traced between the political institutions of France and those of England; but then the destinies of the two nations separated and constantly became more unlike, as time advanced. They resemble two lines starting from contiguous points at a slight angle, which diverge indefinitely as they are prolonged.

I venture to affirm that when the French nation, exhausted by the protracted disturbances which had accompanied the captivity of King John and the madness of Charles VI., suffered the Crown to levy a general tax without the consent of the people, and when the nobility had the baseness to allow the middle and lower classes to be so taxed on condition that its own exemption should be maintained, at that very time was sown the seed of almost all the vices and almost all the abuses which afflicted the ancient society of France during the remainder of its existence, and ended by causing. its violent dissolution; and I admire the rare sagacity of Philippe

[1] See Note XXXVII., Arthur Young's Tour.

de Comines when he says, 'Charles VII., who gained the point of laying on the *taille* at his pleasure, without the consent of the States of the Realm, laid a heavy burden on his soul and on that of his successors, and gave a wound to his kingdom which will not soon be closed.'

Observe how that wound widened with the course of years; follow step by step that fact to its consequences.

Forbonnais says with truth in his learned 'Researches on the Finances of France,' that in the Middle Ages the sovereigns generally lived on the revenues of their domains; and 'as the extraordinary wants of the State,' he adds, 'were provided for by extraordinary subsidies, they were levied equally on the clergy, the nobility, and the people.'

The greater part of the general subsidies voted by the three Orders in the course of the fourteenth century were, in point of fact, so levied. Almost all the taxes established at that time were *indirect*, that is, they were paid indiscriminately by all classes of consumers. Sometimes the tax was direct; but then it was assessed, not on property, but on income. The nobles, the priests, and the burgesses were bound to pay over to the King, for a year, a tenth, for instance, of all their incomes. This remark as to the charges voted by the Estates of the Realm applies equally to those which were imposed at the same period by the different Provincial Estates within their own territories. [1]

It is true that already, at that time, the direct tax known by the name of the *taille* was never levied on the noble classes. The obligation of gratuitous military service was the ground of their exemption; but the *taille* was at that time partially in force as a general impost, belonging rather to the seignorial jurisdictions than to the kingdom.

When the King first undertook to levy taxes by his own authority, he perceived that he must select a tax which did not appear to fall directly on the nobles; for that class, formidable and dangerous to the monarchy itself, would never have submitted to an innovation so prejudicial to their own interests. The tax selected by the Crown was, therefore, a tax from which the nobles were exempt, and that tax was the *taille*.

Thus to all the private inequalities of condition which already existed, another and more general inequality was added, which augmented and perpetuated all the rest. From that time this tax spread and ramified in proportion as the demands of the public Treasury increased with the functions of the central authority; it

[1] See Note XXXVIII.

was soon decupled, and all the new taxes assumed the character of the *taille*. Every year, therefore, inequality of taxation separated the classes of society and isolated the individuals of whom they consisted more deeply than before. Since the object of taxation was not to include those most able to pay taxes, but those least able to defend themselves from paying, the monstrous consequence was brought about that the rich were exempted and the poor burdened. It is related that Cardinal Mazarin, being in want of money, hit upon the expedient of levying a tax upon the principal houses in Paris, but that having encountered some opposition from the parties concerned, he contented himself with adding the five millions he required to the general brevet of the *taille*. He meant to tax the wealthiest of the King's subjects; he did tax the most indigent; but to the Treasury the result was the same.

The produce of taxes thus unjustly allotted had limits; but the demands of the Crown had none. Yet the Kings of France would neither convoke the States-General to obtain subsidies, nor would they provoke the nobility to demand that measure by imposing taxes on them without it.

Hence arose that prodigious and mischievous fecundity of financial expedients, which so peculiarly characterised the administration of the public resources during the last three centuries of the old French monarchy.

It is necessary to study the details of the administrative and financial history of that period, to form a conception of the violent and unwarrantable proceedings which the want of money may prescribe even to a mild Government, but without publicity and without control, when once time has sanctioned its power and delivered it from the dread of revolution—that last safeguard of nations.

Every page in these annals tells of possessions of the Crown first sold and then resumed as unsaleable; of contracts violated and of vested interests ignored; of sacrifices wrung at every crisis from the public creditor, and of incessant repudiations of public engagements.[1]

Privileges granted in perpetuity were perpetually resumed. If we could bestow our compassion on the disappointments of a foolish vanity, the fate of those luckless persons might deserve it who purchased letters of nobility, but who were exposed during the whole of the seventeenth and eighteenth centuries to buy over and over again the empty honours or the unjust privileges which they had already paid for several times. Thus Louis XIV.

[1] See Note XXXIX., Violation of Vested and Corporate Rights.

annulled all the titles of nobility acquired in the preceding ninety-two years, though most of them had been conferred by himself; but they could only be retained upon furnishing a fresh subsidy, *all these titles having been obtained by surprise*, said the edict. The same example was duly followed by Louis XV. eighty years later.

The militia-man was forbidden to procure a substitute, for fear, it was said, of raising the price of recruits to the State.

Towns, corporations, and hospitals were compelled to break their own engagements in order that they might be able to lend money to the Crown. Parishes were restrained from undertaking works of public improvement, lest by such a diversion of their resources they should pay their direct taxes with less punctuality.

It is related that M. Orry and M. Trudaine, of whom one was the Comptroller-General and the other the Director-General of Public Works, had formed a plan for substituting, for the forced labour of the peasantry on the roads, a rate to be levied on the inhabitants of each district for the repair of their thoroughfares. The reason which led these able administrators to forego that plan is instructive: they feared, it is said, that when a fund had been raised by such a rate it would be impossible to prevent the Treasury from appropriating the money to its own purposes, so that ere long the ratepayers would have had to support both the new money payment and the old charge of forced labour. I do not hesitate to say that no private person could have escaped the grasp of the criminal law who should have managed his own fortune as the Great Louis in all his glory managed the fortune of the nation.

If you stumble upon any old establishment of the Middle Ages which maintained itself with every aggravation of its original defects in direct opposition to the spirit of the age, or upon any mischievous innovation, search to the root of the evil—you will find it to be some financial expedient perpetuated in the form of an institution. To meet the pressure of the hour new powers were called into being which lasted for centuries.

A peculiar tax, which was called the due of *franc-fief*, had been levied from a distant period on the non-noble holders of noble lands. This tax established between lands the same distinction which existed between the classes of society, and the one constantly tended to increase the other. Perhaps this due of *franc-fief* contributed more than any other cause to separate the *roturier* and the noble, because it prevented them from mingling together in that which most speedily and most effectually assimilates men to each other—in the possession of land. A chasm was thus opened between the noble landowner on the one hand, and his neighbour, the non-noble landowner, on the other. Nothing, on the contrary, contributed to hasten the cohesion of these two classes in England more than the abolition, as early as the sixteenth century, of all outward distinctions between the fiefs held under the Crown and lands held in villenage.[1]

In the fourteenth century this feudal tax of *franc-fief* was light, and was only levied here and there; but in the eighteenth century, when the feudal system was well-nigh abolished, it was rigorously exacted in France every twenty years, and it amounted to one whole year's revenue. A son paid it on succeeding his father. 'This tax,' said the Agricultural Society of Tours in 1761, 'is extremely injurious to the improvement of the art of husbandry. Of all the imposts borne by the King's subjects there is indisputably none so vexatious and so onerous to the rural population.' 'This duty,' said another contemporary writer, 'which was at first levied but once in a lifetime, is become in course of time a very cruel burden.' The nobles themselves would have been glad that it should be abolished, for it prevented persons of inferior condition from purchasing their lands; but the fiscal demands of the State required that it should be maintained and increased.[2]

The Middle Ages are sometimes erroneously charged with all the evils arising from the trading or industrial corporations. But at their origin these guilds and companies served only as means to connect the members of a given calling with each other, and to establish in each trade a free government in miniature, whose business it was at once to assist and to control the working classes. Such, and no more, seems to have been the intention of St. Louis.

It was not till the commencement of the sixteenth century, in the midst of that period which is termed the Revival of Arts and Letters, that it was proposed for the first time to consider the right to labour in a particular vocation as a privilege to be sold by the Crown. Then it was that each Company became a small close aristocracy, and at last those monopolies were established which were so prejudicial to the progress of the arts and which so exasperated the last generation. From the reign of Henry III., who generalised the evil, if he did not give birth to it, down to Louis XVI., who extirpated it, it may be said that the abuse of the system of guilds never ceased to augment and to spread at the very time

[1] [This remark must be taken with some qualification as to the fact. These distinctions are not wholly eradicated at the present day in England, but they are mere questions of property, not of personal rank or political influence.]

[2] See Note XL.

when the progress of society rendered those institutions more insupportable, and when the common sense of the public was most
opposed to them.   Year after year more professions were deprived
of their freedom ; year after year the privileges of the incorporated
trades were increased.   Never was the evil carried to greater
lengths than during what are commonly called the prosperous
years of the reign of Louis XIV., because at no former period had
the want of money been more imperious, or the resolution not to
raise money with the assent of the nation more firmly taken.

Letrone said with truth in 1775—'The State has only established the trading companies to furnish pecuniary resources,
partly by the patents which it sells, partly by the creation of new
offices which the Companies are forced to buy up.   The Edict of
1673 carried the principles of Henry III. to their furthest consequences by compelling all the Companies to take out letters of con-
firmation upon payment for the same ; and all the workmen who
were not yet incorporated in some one of these bodies were compelled to enter them.   This wretched expedient brought in three
hundred thousand livres.'

We have already seen how the whole municipal constitution of
the towns was overthrown, not by any political design, but in the
hope of picking up a pittance for the Treasury.   This same want of
money, combined with the desire not to seek it from the States-
General of the kingdom, gave rise to the venality of public
offices, which became at last a thing so strange that its like had
never been seen in the world.   It was by this institution, engendered by the fiscal spirit of the Government, that the vanity of the
middle classes was kept on the stretch for three centuries and
exclusively directed to the acquisition of public employments, and
thus was the universal passion for places made to penetrate to the
bowels of the nation, where it became the common source of revolutions and of servitude.

As the financial embarrassments of the State increased, new
offices sprang up, all of which were remunerated by exemptions
from taxation and by privileges ; and as these offices were produced
by the wants of the Treasury, not of the administration, the result
was the creation of an almost incredible number of employments
which were altogether superfluous or mischievous.[1]   As early as
1664, upon an inquiry instituted by Colbert, it was found that the
capital invested in this wretched property amounted to nearly five
hundred millions of livres.   Richelieu had suppressed, it was said,
a hundred thousand offices : but they cropped out again under

[1] See Note XLI., Exemptions of Public Officers from Taxation.

other names.[1] For a little money the State renounced the right of
directing, of controlling, and of compelling its own agents. An
administrative engine was thus gradually built up so vast, so complicated, so clumsy, and so unproductive, that it came at last to be
left swinging on in space, whilst a more simple and handy instrument of government was framed beside it, which really performed the duties these innumerable public officers were supposed
to be doing.

It is clear that none of these pernicious institutions could have
subsisted for twenty years if they could have been brought under
discussion. None of them would have been established or aggravated if the Estates had been consulted, or if their remonstrances
had been listened to when by chance they were still called together.
Rarely as the States-General were convoked in the last ages of the
monarchy, they never ceased to protest against these abuses. On
several occasions these assemblies pointed out as the origin of all
these evils the power of arbitrarily levying taxes which had been
arrogated by the King, or, to borrow the identical terms employed
by the energetic language of the fifteenth century, ' the right of
enriching himself from the substance of the people without the
consent and deliberation of the Three Estates.' Nor did they confine themselves to their own rights alone ; they demanded with
energy, and frequently they obtained, greater deference to the
rights of the provinces and towns. In every session some voices
were raised in those bodies against the inequality of the public
burdens. They frequently demanded the abolition of the system or
close guilds ; they attacked with increasing vigour in each successive age the venality of public employments. ' He who sells office
sells justice, which is infamous,' was their language. When that
venality was established, they still complained of the abusive creation of offices. They denounced so many useless places and dangerous privileges, but always in vain. Three institutions had been
previously established against themselves ; they had originated in
the desire not to convoke these assemblies, and in the necessity of
disguising from the French nation the taxation which it was un-
safe to exhibit in its real aspect.

And it must be observed that the best kings were as prone to
have recourse to these practices as the worst. Louis XII. completed the introduction of the venality of public offices ; Henry IV.
extended the sale of them to reversions. The vices of the system
were stronger than the virtues of those who applied it.

The same desire of escaping from the control of the States-

[1] See Note XLII.

General caused the Parliaments to be entrusted with most of their political functions; the result was an intermixture of judicial and administrative offices, which proved extremely injurious to the good conduct of business. It was necessary to seem to afford some new guarantees in place of those which were taken away; for though the French support absolute power patiently enough, so long as it be not oppressive, they never like the sight of it; and it is always prudent to raise about it some appearance of barriers, which serve at least to conceal what they do not arrest.

Lastly, it was this desire of preventing the nation, when asked for its money, from asking back its freedom, which gave rise to an incessant watchfulness in separating the classes of society, so that they should never come together, or combine in a common resistance, and that the Government should never have on its hands at once more than a very small number of men separated from the rest of the nation. In the whole course of this long history, in which have figured so many princes remarkable for their ability, sometimes remarkable for their genius, almost always remarkable for their courage, not one of them ever made an effort to bring together the different classes of his people, or to unite them otherwise than by subjecting them to a common yoke. One exception there is, indeed, to this remark: one king of France there was who not only desired this end, but applied himself with his whole heart to attain it; that prince—for such are the inscrutable judgments of Providence—was Louis XVI.

The separation of classes was the crime of the old French monarchy, but it became its excuse; for when all those who constitute the rich and enlightened portion of a nation can no longer agree and co-operate in the work of government, a country can by no possibility administer itself, and a master *must* intervene.

'The nation,' said Turgot, with an air of melancholy, in a secret report addressed to the King, 'is a community, consisting of different orders ill compacted together, and of a people whose members have very few ties among themselves, so that every man is exclusively engrossed by his personal interest. Nowhere is any common interest discernible. The villages, the towns, have not any stronger mutual relations than the districts to which they belong. They cannot even agree among themselves to carry on the public works which they require. Amidst this perpetual conflict of pretensions and of undertakings your Majesty is compelled to decide everything in person or by your agents. Your special injunctions are expected before men will contribute to the public advantage, or respect the rights of others, or even sometimes before they will exercise their own.'

It is no slight enterprise to bring more closely together fellow-citizens who have thus been living for centuries as strangers or as enemies to each other, and to teach them how to carry on their affairs in common.

To divide them was a far easier task than it then becomes to reunite them. Such has been the memorable example given by France to the world. When the different classes which divided the ancient social system of France came once more into contact sixty years ago, after having been isolated so long, and by so many barriers, they encountered each other on those points on which they felt most poignantly, and they met in mutual hatred. Even in this our day their jealousies and their animosities have survived them.

CHAPTER XI.

OF THE SPECIES OF LIBERTY WHICH EXISTED UNDER THE OLD
MONARCHY, AND OF THE INFLUENCE OF THAT LIBERTY ON THE
REVOLUTION.

IF the reader were here to interrupt the perusal of this book, he
would have but a very imperfect impression of the government of
the old French monarchy, and he would not understand the state
of society produced by the Revolution.

Since the citizens of France were thus divided and thus contracted within themselves, since the power of the Crown was so
extensive and so great, it might be inferred that the spirit of independence had disappeared with public liberty, and that the whole
French people were equally bent in subjection. Such was not the
case; the Government had long conducted absolutely and alone all
the common affairs of the nation; but it was as yet by no means
master of every individual existence.

Amidst many institutions already prepared for absolute power
some liberty survived; but it was a sort of strange liberty, which
it is not easy at the present day to conceive aright, and which must
be very closely scrutinised to comprehend the good and the evil
resulting from it.

Whilst the Central Government superseded all local powers,
and filled more and more the whole sphere of public authority,
some institutions which the Government had allowed to subsist, or
which it had created, some old customs, some ancient manners,
some abuses even, served to check its action, to keep alive in the
hearts of a large number of persons a spirit of resistance, and to
preserve the consistency and the independent outline of many
characters.

Centralisation had already the same tendency, the same mode
of operation, the same aims as in our own time, but it had not yet
the same power. Government having, in its eagerness to turn
everything into money, put up to sale most of the public offices,
had thus deprived itself of the power of giving or withdrawing

those offices at pleasure. Thus one of its passions had considerably impaired the success of another: its rapacity had balanced its ambition. The State was therefore incessantly reduced to act through instruments which it had not forged, and which it could not break. The consequence was that its most absolute will was frequently paralysed in the execution of it. This strange and vicious constitution of the public offices thus stood in stead of a sort of political guarantee against the omnipotence of the central power. It was a sort of irregular and ill-constructed breakwater, which divided the action and checked the stroke of the supreme power.

Nor did the Government of that day dispose as yet of that countless multitude of favours, assistances, honours, and moneys which it has now to distribute; it was therefore far less able to seduce as well as to compel.

The Government moreover was imperfectly acquainted with the exact limits of its power.[1] None of its rights were regularly acknowledged or firmly established; its range of action was already immense, but that action was still hesitating and uncertain, as one who gropes along a dark and unknown track. This formidable obscurity, which at that time concealed the limits of every power and enshrouded every right, though it might be favourable to the designs of princes against the freedom of their subjects, was frequently not less favourable to the defence of it.

The administrative power, conscious of the novelty of its origin and of its low extraction, was ever timid in its action when any obstacle crossed its path. It is striking to observe, in reading the correspondence of the French Ministers and Intendants of the eighteenth century, how this Government, which was so absolute and so encroaching as long as its authority is not contested, stood aghast at the aspect of the least resistance; agitated by the slightest criticism, alarmed by the slightest noise, ready on all such occasions to stop, to hesitate, to parley, to treat, and often to fall considerably below the natural limits of its power. The nerveless egotism of Louis XV., and the mild benevolence of his successor, contributed to this state of things. It never occurred to these sovereigns that they could be dethroned. They had nothing of that harsh and restless temper which fear has since often imparted to those who govern. They trampled on none but those whom they did not see.

Several of the privileges, of the prejudices, of the false notions

[1] See Note XLIII.

most opposed to the establishment of a regular and salutary free government, kept alive amongst many persons a spirit of independence, and disposed them to hold their ground against the abuses of authority.

The Nobles despised the Administration, properly so called, though they sometimes had occasion to apply to it. Even after they had abandoned their former power, they retained something of that pride of their forefathers which was alike adverse to servitude and to law. They cared little for the general liberty of the community, and readily allowed the hand of authority to lie heavy on all about them; but they did not admit that it should lie heavy on themselves, and they were ready in case of need to run all risks to prevent it. At the commencement of the Revolution that nobility of France which was about to fall with the throne, still held towards the King, and still more towards the King's agents, an attitude far higher, and language far more free, than the middle class, which was so soon to overthrow the monarchy. Almost all the guarantees against the abuse of power which France possessed during the thirty-seven years of her representative government, were already loudly demanded by the nobles. In reading the instructions of that Order to the States-General, amidst its prejudices and its crotchets, the spirit and some of the great qualities of an aristocracy may still be felt.[1] It must ever be deplored that, instead of bending that nobility to the discipline of law, it was uprooted and struck to the earth. By that act the nation was deprived of a necessary portion of its substance, and a wound was given to freedom which will never be healed. A class which has marched for ages in the first rank has acquired, in this long and uncontested exercise of greatness, a certain loftiness of heart, a natural confidence in its strength, and a habit of being looked up to, which makes it the most resisting element in the frame of society. Not only is its own disposition manly, but its example serves to augment the manliness of every other class. By extirpating such an Order its very enemies are enervated. Nothing can ever completely replace it; it can be born no more; it may recover the titles and the estates, but not the soul of its progenitors.

The Clergy, who have since frequently shown themselves so servilely submissive to the temporal sovereign in civil matters, whosoever that temporal sovereign might be, and who become his most barefaced flatterers on the slightest indication of favour to the Church, formed at that time one of the most independent bodies in

[1] See Note XLIV., Instructions of the Order of Nobility at the States-General of 1789.

the nation, and the only body whose peculiar liberties would have enforced respect.[1]

The provinces had lost their franchises; the rights of the towns were reduced to a shadow. No ten noblemen could meet to deliberate together on any matter without the express permission of the King. But the Church of France retained to the last her periodical assemblies. Within her bosom even ecclesiastical power was circumscribed by limits which were respected.[2] The lower clergy enjoyed the protection of solid guarantees against the tyranny of their superiors, and was not prepared for passive obedience to the Sovereign by the uncontrolled despotism of the bishop. I do not attempt to pass any judgment on this ancient constitution of the Church; I merely assert that by this constitution the spirit of the priesthood was not fashioned to political servility.

Many of the ecclesiastics were moreover gentlemen of birth, and they brought with them into the Church the pride and indocility of their condition. All of them had, moreover, an exalted rank in the State, and certain privileges there. The exercise of those feudal rights, which had proved so fatal to the moral power of the Church, gave to its members, in their individual capacity, a spirit of independence towards the civil authority.

But that which especially contributed to give the clergy the opinions, the wants, the feelings, and often the passions of citizens, was the ownership of land. I have had the patience to read most of the reports and debates still remaining to us from the old Provincial Estates of France, and particularly those of Languedoc, a province in which the clergy participated even more than elsewhere in the details of the public administration; I have also examined the journals of the Provincial Assemblies which sat in 1779 and 1787. Bringing with me in this inquiry the impressions of our own times, I have been surprised to find bishops and priests, many of whom were equally eminent for their piety and for their learning, drawing up reports on the construction of a road or a canal, discussing with great science and skill the best methods to augment the produce of agriculture, to ensure the well-being of the inhabitants, and to encourage industry, these churchmen being always equal, and often superior, to all the laymen engaged with them in the transaction of the same affairs.

I maintain, in opposition to an opinion which is very generally

---

[1] See Note XLV., Religious Administration of an Ecclesiastical Province in the Eighteenth Century.

[2] See Note XLVI., Spirit of the Clergy.

and very firmly established, that the nations which deprive the Roman Catholic clergy of all participation in landed property, and convert their incomes into salaries, do in fact only promote the interests of the Papacy, and those of the temporal Ruler, whilst they renounce an important element of freedom amongst themselves.

A man who, as far as the best portion of his nature is concerned, is the subject of a foreign authority, and who in the country where he dwells can have no family, will only be linked to the soil by one durable tie—namely, landed property. Break that bond, and he belongs to no place in particular. In the place where the accident of birth may have cast him, he lives like an alien in the midst of a civil community, scarcely any of whose civil interests can directly affect him. His conscience binds him to the Pope; his maintenance to the Sovereign. His only country is the Church. In every political event he perceives little more than the advantage or the loss of his own profession. Let but the Church be free and prosperous, what matters all the rest? His most natural political state is that of indifference—an excellent member of the Christian commonwealth, but elsewhere a worthless citizen. Such sentiments and such opinions as these in a body of men who are the directors of childhood, and the guardians of morality, cannot fail to enervate the soul of the entire nation in relation to public life.

A correct impression of the revolution which may be effected in the human mind by a change wrought in social conditions, may be obtained from a perusal of the Instructions given to the Delegates of the Clergy at the States-General of 1789.[1]

The clergy in those documents frequently showed their intolerance, and sometimes a tenacious attachment to several of their former privileges; but, in other respects, not less hostile to despotism, not less favourable to civil liberty, not less enamoured of political liberty, than the middle classes or the nobility, this Order proclaimed that personal liberty must be secured, not by promises alone, but by a form of procedure analogous to the Habeas Corpus Act. They demanded the destruction of the State prisons, the abolition of extraordinary jurisdictions and of the practice of calling up causes to the Council of State, publicity of procedure, the permanence of judicial officers, the admissibility of all ranks to public employments, which should be open to merit alone; a system of military recruiting less oppressive and humiliating to the people, and from which none should be exempted; the extinction by purchase of seignorial rights, which sprung from the feudal system were, they said, contrary to freedom; unrestricted freedom of

[1] See Note XLVII.

labour; the suppression of internal custom-houses; the multiplication of private schools, insomuch that one gratuitous school should exist in every parish; lay charitable institutions in all the rural districts, such as workhouses and workshops of charity; and every kind of encouragement to agriculture.

In the sphere of politics, properly so called, the clergy proclaimed, louder than any other class, that the nation had an indefeasible and inalienable right to assemble to enact laws and to vote taxes. No Frenchman, said the priests of that day, can be forced to pay a tax which he has not voted in person or by his representative. The clergy further demanded that States-General freely elected should annually assemble; that they should in presence of the nation discuss all its chief affairs; that they should make general laws paramount to all usages or particular privileges; that the deputies should be inviolable and the ministers of the Crown constantly responsible. The clergy also desired that assemblies of States should be created in all the provinces, and municipal corporations in all the towns. Of divine right not a word.

Upon the whole, and notwithstanding the notorious vices of some of its members, I question if there ever existed in the world a clergy more remarkable than the Catholic clergy of France at the moment when it was overtaken by the Revolution—a clergy more enlightened, more national, less circumscribed within the bounds of private duty and more alive to public obligations, and at the same time more zealous for the faith:—persecution proved it. I entered on the study of these forgotten institutions full of prejudices against the clergy of that day : I conclude that study full of respect for them. They had in truth no defects but those inherent in all corporate bodies, whether political or religious, when they are strongly constituted and knit together; such as a tendency to aggression, a certain intolerance of disposition, and an instinctive —sometimes a blind—attachment to the particular rights of their Order.

The Middle Classes of the time preceding the Revolution were also much better prepared than those of the present day to show a spirit of independence. Many even of the defects of their social constitution contributed to this result. We have already seen that the public employments occupied by these classes were even more numerous than at present, and that the passion for obtaining these situations was equally intense. But mark the difference of the age. Most of those places being neither given nor taken away by the Government, increased the importance of those who filled them without placing them at the mercy of the ruler; hence, the very cause which now completes the subjection of so many persons was precisely that which most powerfully enabled them at that time to maintain their independence.

The immunities of all kinds which so unhappily separated the middle from the lower classes, converted the former into a spurious aristocracy, which often displayed the pride and the spirit of resistance of the real aristocracy. In each of those small particular associations which divided the middle classes into so many sections, the general advantage was readily overlooked, but the interests and the rights of each body were always kept in view. The common dignity, the common privileges were to be defended.[1] No man could ever lose himself in the crowd, or find a hiding-place for base subserviency. Every man stood, as it were, on a stage, extremely contracted it is true, but in a glare of light, and there he found himself in presence of the same audience, ever ready to applaud or to condemn him.

The art of stifling every murmur of resistance was at that time far less perfected than it is at present. France had not yet become that dumb region in which we dwell : every sound on the contrary had an echo, though political liberty was still unknown, and every voice that was raised might be heard afar.

That which more especially in those times ensured to the oppressed the means of being heard was the constitution of the Courts of Justice. France had become a land of absolute government by her political and administrative institutions, but her people were still free by her institutions of justice. The judicial administration of the old monarchy was complicated, troublesome, tedious, and expensive : these were no doubt great faults, but servility towards the Government was not to be met with there—that servility which is but another form of venality, and the worst form. That capital vice, which not only corrupts the judge, but soon infects the whole body of the people, was altogether unknown to the elder magistracy. The judges could not be removed, and they sought no promotion—two things alike necessary to their independence ; for what matters it that a judge cannot be coerced if there are a thousand means of seduction ?

It is true that the power of the Crown had succeeded in depriving the Courts of ordinary jurisdiction of the cognisance of almost all the suits in which the public authorities were interested ; but though they had been stripped, they still were feared. Though they might be prevented from recording their judgments, the Government did not always dare to prevent them from receiv-

[1] See Note XLVIII.

ing complaints or from recording their opinions; and as the language of the Courts still preserved the tone of that old language of France which loved to call things by their right names, the magistrates not unfrequently stigmatised the acts of the Government as arbitrary and despotic.[1] The irregular intervention of the Courts in the affairs of government, which often disturbed the conduct of them, thus served occasionally to protect the liberties of the subject. The evil was great, but it served to curb a greater evil.

In these judicial bodies and all around them the vigour of the ancient manners of the nation was preserved in the midst of modern opinions. The Parliaments of France doubtless thought more of themselves than of the commonwealth; but it must be acknowledged that, in defence of their own independence and honour, they always bore themselves with intrepidity, and that they imparted their spirit to all that came near them.

When in 1770 the Parliament of Paris was broken, the magistrates who belonged to it submitted to the loss of their profession and their power without a single instance of any individual yielding to the will of the sovereign. Nay, more, some Courts of a different kind, such as the Court of Aids, which were neither affected nor menaced, voluntarily exposed themselves to the same harsh treatment, when that treatment had become certain. Nor is this all: the leading advocates who practised before the Parliament resolved of their own accord to share its fortune; they renounced all that made their glory and their wealth, and condemned themselves to silence rather than appear before dishonoured judges. I know of nothing in the history of free nations grander than what occurred on this occasion, and yet this happened in the eighteenth century, hard by the court of Louis XV.

The habits of the French Courts of justice had become in many respects the habits of the nation. The Courts of justice had given birth to the notion that every question was open to discussion and every decision subject to appeal, and likewise to the use of publicity, and to a taste for forms of proceeding—things adverse to servitude: this was the only part of the education of a free people which the institutions of the old monarchy had given to France. The administration itself had borrowed largely from the language and the practice of the Courts. The King considered himself obliged to assign motives for his edicts, and to state his reasons before he drew the conclusion; the Council of State caused its orders to be preceded by long preambles; the Intendants promul-

[1] See Note XLIX., Example of the Language of the Courts of Justice.

gated their ordinances in the forms of judicial procedure. In all the administrative bodies of any antiquity, such, for example, as the body of the Treasurers of France or that of the *élus* (who assessed the *taille*), the cases were publicly debated and decided after argument at the bar. All these usages, all these formalities, were so many barriers to the arbitrary power of the sovereign.

The people alone, applying that term to the lower orders of society, and especially the people of the rural districts, were almost always unable to offer any resistance to oppression except by violence.

Most of the means of defence which I have here passed in review were, in fact, beyond their reach; to employ those means, a place in society where they could be seen, or a voice loud enough to make itself heard, was requisite. But above the ranks of the lower orders there was not a man in France who, if he had the courage, might not contest his obedience and resist in giving way.

The King spoke as the chief of the nation rather than as its master. 'We glory,' said Louis XVI., at his accession, in the preamble of a decree, 'we glory to command a free and generous nation.' One of his ancestors had already expressed the same idea in older language, when, thanking the States-General for the boldness of their remonstrances, he said, 'We like better to speak to freemen than to serfs.'

The men of the eighteenth century knew little of that sort of passion for comfort which is the mother of servitude—a relaxing passion, though it be tenacious and unalterable, which mingles and intertwines itself with many private virtues, such as domestic affections, regularity of life, respect for religion, and even with the lukewarm, though assiduous, practice of public worship, which favours propriety but proscribes heroism, and excels in making decent livers but base citizens. The men of the eighteenth century were better and they were worse.

The French of that age were addicted to joy and passionately fond of amusement; they were perhaps more lax in their habits, and more vehement in their passions and opinions than those of the present day, but they were strangers to the temperate and decorous sensualism that we see about us. In the upper classes men thought more of adorning life than of rendering it comfortable; they sought to be illustrious rather than to be rich. Even in the middle ranks the pursuit of comfort never absorbed every faculty of the mind; that pursuit was often abandoned for higher and more refined enjoyments; every man placed some object beyond the love of money before his eyes. 'I know my countrymen,' said a contemporary writer, in language which, though eccentric, is spirited, 'apt to melt and dissipate the metals, they are not prone to pay them habitual reverence, and they will not be slow to turn again to their former idols, to valour, to glory, and, I will add, to magnanimity.'

The baseness of mankind is, moreover, not to be estimated by the degree of their subserviency to a sovereign power; that standard would be an incorrect one.   However submissive the French may have been before the Revolution to the will of the King, one sort of obedience was altogether unknown to them: they knew not what it was to bow before an illegitimate and contested power —a power but little honoured, frequently despised, but which is willingly endured because it may be serviceable or because it may hurt.   To this degrading form of servitude they were ever strangers. The King inspired them with feelings which none of the most absolute princes who have since appeared in the world have been able to call forth, and which are become incomprehensible to the present generation, so entirely has the Revolution extirpated them from the hearts of the nation.   They loved him with the affection due to a father; they revered him with the respect due to God. In submitting to the most arbitrary of his commands they yielded less to compulsion than to loyalty, and thus they frequently preserved great freedom of mind even in the most complete depend- ence.   To them the greatest evil of obedience was compulsion; to us it is the least: the worst is in that servile sentiment which leads men to obey.   We have no right to despise our forefathers. Would to God that we could recover, with their prejudices and their faults, something of their greatness!

It would then be a mistake to think that the state of society in France before the Revolution was one of servility and dependence.[1] Much more liberty existed in that society than in our own time; but it was a species of irregular and intermittent liberty, always contracted within the bounds of certain classes, linked to the notion of exemption and of privilege, which rendered it almost as easy to defy the law as to defy arbitrary power, and scarcely ever went far enough to furnish to all classes of the community the most natural and necessary securities.[2]   Thus reduced, and thus deformed, liberty was still not unfruitful.   It was this liberty which, at the very time when centralisation was tending more and more to equalise, to emasculate, and to dim the character of the nation, still preserved

[1] See Note L.
[2] See Note LI., Of the Reasons which frequently put a restraint on Absolute Government under the Mon- archy.

amongst a large class of private persons their native vigour, their colour, and their outline, fostered self-respect in the heart, and often caused the love of glory to predominate over every other taste. By this liberty were formed those vigorous characters, those proud and daring spirits which were about to appear, and were to make the French Revolution at once the object of the admiration and the terror of succeeding generations. It would have been so strange that virtues so masculine should have grown on a soil where freedom was no more.

But if this sort of ill-regulated and morbid liberty prepared the French to overflow despotism, perhaps it likewise rendered them less fit than any other people to establish in lieu of that despotism the free and peaceful empire of constitutional law.

CHAPTER XII.

IN the eighteenth century the French peasantry could no longer be preyed upon by petty feudal despots; they were seldom the object of violence on the part of the Government; they enjoyed civil liberty, and were owners of a portion of the soil; but all the other classes of society stood aloof from this class, and perhaps in no other part of the world had the peasantry ever lived so entirely alone. The effects of this novel and singular kind of oppression deserve a very attentive separate consideration.

As early as the beginning of the seventeenth century, Henry IV. complained, as we learn from Pérófix, that the nobles were quitting the rural districts. In the middle of the eighteenth century this desertion had become almost general; all the records of the time indicate and deplore the fact, economists in their writings, the Intendants in their reports, agricultural societies in their proceedings. A more authentic proof of the same fact is to be found in the registers of the capitation tax. The capitation tax was levied at the actual place of residence, and it was paid by the whole of the great nobility and by a portion of the landed gentry at Paris.

In the rural districts none remained but such of the gentry as their limited means compelled to stay there. These persons must have found themselves placed in a position with reference to the peasants, his neighbours, such as no rich proprietor can be conceived to have occupied before.[1] Being no longer in the position of a chief, they had not the same interest as of old to attend to, or assist, or direct the village population; and, on the other hand, not being subject to the same burdens, they could neither feel much sympathy with poverty which they did not share, nor with grievances to which they were not exposed. The peasantry were

[1] See Notes LII. and LIII.

no longer the subjects of the gentry; the gentry were not yet the fellow-citizens of the peasantry—a state of things unparalleled in history.

This gave rise to a sort of absenteeism of feeling, if I may so express myself, even more frequent and more effectual than absenteeism properly so called. Hence it arose that a gentleman residing on his estate frequently displayed the views and sentiments which his steward would have entertained in his absence; like his steward, he learned to look upon his tenants as his debtors, and he rigorously exacted from them all that he could claim by law or by custom, which sometimes rendered the application of the last remnant of feudal rights more harsh than it had been in the feudal times.

Often embarrassed, and always needy, the small gentry lived shabbily in their country-houses, caring only to amass money enough to spend in town during the winter. The people, who often find an expression which hits the truth, had given to these small squires the name of the least of the birds of prey, a *hobereau*, a sort of Squire Kite.

No doubt individual exceptions might be presented to these observations: I speak of classes, which ought alone to detain the attention of history. That there were in those times many rich landowners who, without any necessary occasion and without a common interest, attended to the welfare of the peasantry, who will deny? But these were persons who struggled successfully against the law of their new condition, which, in spite of themselves, was driving them into indifference, as it was driving their former vassals into hatred.

This abandonment of a country life by the nobility has often been attributed to the peculiar influence of certain ministers and certain kings—by some to Richelieu, by others to Louis XIV. It was, no doubt, an idea almost always pursued by the Kings of France, during the three last centuries of the monarchy, to separate the gentry from the people, and to attract the former to Court and to public employments. This was especially the case in the seventeenth century, when the nobility were still an object of fear to royalty. Amongst the questions addressed to the Intendants, they were sometimes asked—'Do the gentry of your province like to stay at home, or to go abroad?'

A letter from an Intendant has been found giving his answer on this subject: he laments that the gentry of his province like to remain with their peasants, instead of fulfilling their duties about the King. And let it here be well remarked, that the province of which this Intendant was speaking was Anjou—that province which was afterwards La Vendée. These country gentlemen who refused, as he said, to fulfil their duties about the King, were the only country gentlemen who defended with arms in their hands the monarchy in France, and died there fighting for the Crown ; they owed this glorious distinction simply to the fact that they had found means to retain their hold over the peasantry—that peasantry with whom they were blamed for wishing to live.

Nevertheless the abandonment of the country by the class which then formed the head of the French nation must not be mainly attributed to the direct influence of some of the French kings. The principal and permanent cause of this fact lay not so much in the will of certain men as in the slow and incessant influence of institutions; and the proof is, that when, in the eighteenth century, the Government endeavoured to combat this evil, it could not even check the progress of it. In proportion as the nobility completely lost its political rights without acquiring others, and as local freedom disappeared, this emigration of the nobles increased. It became unnecessary to entice them from their homes; they cared not to remain there. Rural life had become distasteful to them.

What I here say of the nobles applies in all countries to rich landowners. In all centralised countries the rural districts lose their wealthy and enlightened inhabitants. I might add that in all centralised countries the art of cultivation remains imperfect and unimproved—a commentary on the profound remark of Montesquieu, which determines his meaning, when he says that ' land produces less by reason of its own fertility than of the freedom of its inhabitants.' But I will not transgress the limits of my subject.

We have seen elsewhere that the middle classes, equally ready to quit the rural districts, sought refuge from all sides in the towns. On no point are all the records of French society anterior to the Revolution more agreed. They show that a second genera-tion of rich peasants was a thing almost unknown. No sooner had a farmer made a little money by his industry than he took his son from the plough, sent him to the town, and bought him a small appointment. From that period may be dated the sort of strange aversion which the French husbandman often displays, even in our own times, for the calling which has enriched him. The effect has survived the cause.

To say the truth, the only man of education—or, as he would be called in England, the only *gentleman*—who permanently resided amongst the peasantry and in constant intercourse with them, was the parish priest. · The result was that the priest would have become the master of the rural populations, in spite of Voltaire, if ho had not been himself so nearly and ostensibly linked to the political order of things; the possession of several political privileges exposed him in some degree to the hatred inspired by those political institutions.[1]

The peasant was thus almost entirely separated from the upper classes; he was removed from those of his fellow-creatures who might have assisted and directed him. In proportion as they attained to enlightenment or competency, they turned their backs on him; he stood, as it were, tabooed and set apart in the midst of the nation.

This state of things did not exist in an equal degree amongst any of the other civilised nations of Europe, and even in France it was comparatively recent. The peasantry of the fourteenth century were at once more oppressed and more relieved. The aristocracy sometimes tyrannised over them, but never forsook them.

In the eighteenth century, a French village was a community of persons, all of whom were poor, ignorant, and coarse; its magistrates were as rude and as contemned as the people; its syndic could not read; its collector could not record in his own handwriting the accounts on which the income of his neighbours and his own depended. Not only had the former lord of the manor lost the right of governing this community, but he had brought himself to consider it a sort of degradation to take any part in the government of it. To assess the *taille*, to call out the militia, to regulate the forced labour, were servile offices, devolving on the syndic. The central power of the State alone took any care of the matter, and as that power was very remote, and had as yet nothing to fear from the inhabitants of the villages, the only care it took of them was to extract revenue.

Let me show you what a forsaken class of society becomes which no one desires to oppress, but which no one attempts to enlighten or to serve.

The heaviest burdens which the feudal system had imposed on the rural population had without doubt been withdrawn and mitigated; but it is not sufficiently known that for these burdens others had been substituted, perhaps more onerous. The peasant had not to endure all the evils endured by his forefathers, but he supported many hardships which his forefathers had never known.

[1] See Note LIV., Example of the Mischievous Effects of the Pecuniary Rights of the Clergy.

The *taille* had been decupled, almost exclusively at the cost of the peasantry, in the preceding two centuries. And here a word must be said of the manner in which this tax was levied, to show what barbarous laws may be founded and maintained in civilised ages, when the most enlightened men in the nation have no personal interest in changing them.

I find in a confidential letter, written by the Comptroller-General himself, in 1772, to the Intendants, a description of this tax, which is a model of brevity and accuracy. 'The *taille*,' said that minister, 'arbitrarily assessed, collectively levied as a personal, not a real, tax in the great part of France, is subject to continual variations from all the changes which happen every year in the fortunes of the taxpayers.' The whole is in these three phrases. It is impossible to depict more ably the evil by which the writer profited.

The whole sum to be paid by each parish was fixed every three years. It perpetually varied, as the minister says, so that no farmer could foresee a year beforehand what he would have to pay in the year following. In the internal economy of each parish any one of the peasants named by the collector was entrusted with the apportionment of the tax on the rest.

I have said I would explain what was the condition of this collector. Let us take this explanation in the language of the Assembly of the Province of Berri in 1779, a body not liable to suspicion, for it was entirely composed of privileged persons, who paid no *taille*, and were chosen by the King. ' As every one seeks to evade this office of collector,' said this Assembly, ' each person must fill it in turn. The levy of the *taille* is therefore entrusted every year to a fresh collector, without regard to his ability or his integrity ; the preparation of each roll of assessment bears marks, therefore, of the personal character of the officer who makes it. The collector stamps on it his own fears, or foibles, or vices. How, indeed, could he do better ? He is acting in darkness, for who can tell with precision the wealth of his neighbour or the proportion of his wealth to that of another ? Nevertheless the opinion of the collector alone is to decide these points, and he is responsible with all his property and even his person for the receipts. He is commonly obliged for two whole years to lose half his days in running after the taxpayers. Those who cannot read are obliged to find a neighbour to perform the office for them.'

Turgot had already said of another province, a short time before, 'This office of collector drives to despair, and generally to ruin, those on whom it is imposed; by this means all the wealthier families of a village are successively reduced to poverty.'

This unhappy officer was, however, armed with the most arbitrary powers;[1] he was almost as much a tyrant as a martyr. Whilst he was discharging functions by which he ruined himself, he had it in his power to ruin everybody else. 'Preference for his relations,' to recur to the language of the Provincial Assembly, 'or for his friends and neighbours, hatred and revenge against his enemies, the want of a patron, the fear of affronting a man of property who had work to give, were at issue with every feeling of justice.' Personal fear often hardened the heart of the collector; there were parishes in which he never went out but escorted by constables and bailiffs. 'When he comes without the constable,' said an Intendant to a Minister, in 1764, 'the persons liable to the tax will not pay.' 'In the district of Villefranche alone,' says the Provincial Assembly of Guienne, 'there were one hundred and six officers constantly out to serve writs and levy distraints.'

To evade this violent and arbitrary taxation the French peasantry, in the midst of the eighteenth century, acted like the Jews in the Middle Ages. They were ostensibly paupers, even when by chance they were not so in reality. They were afraid to be well off; and not without reason, as may be seen from a document which I select, not from Guienne, but a hundred leagues off. The Agricultural Society of Maine announced in its Report of 1761, that it proposed to distribute cattle by way of prizes and encouragements. 'This plan was stopped,' it adds, 'on account of the dangerous consequences to be apprehended by a low jealousy of the winners of these prizes, which, by means of the arbitrary assessment of the public taxes, would occasion them annoyance in the following year.'

Under this system of taxation each tax-payer had, in fact, a direct and permanent interest to act as a spy on his neighbours, and to denounce to the collector the progress of their fortunes. The whole population was thus trained to delation and to hatred. Were not such things rather to be expected in the domains of a rajah of Hindostan?

There were, however, at the same time in France certain districts in which the taxes were raised with regularity and moderation; these were called the *pays d'état*.[2] It is true that to these districts the right of levying their own taxes had been left. In Languedoc, for example, the *taille* was assessed on real property,

---

[1] See Note LV.
[2] See Note LVI., Superiority of Method adopted in the *Pays d'État*.

and did not vary according to the means of the holder.   Its fixed
and known basis was a survey which had been carefully made, and
was renewed every thirty years, and in which the lands were
divided, according to their fertility, into three classes.   Every tax-
payer knew beforehand exactly what his proportion of the charge
amounted to.   If he failed to pay, he alone, or rather his land
alone, was liable.   If he thought the assessment unjust, he might
always require that his share should be compared with that of any
other inhabitant of the parish, on the principle of what is now
termed in France an appeal to proportionate equality.

The'se regulations are precisely those which are now followed in
France ; they have not been improved since that time, but they
have been generalised : for it deserves observation, that although
the form of the public administration in France has been taken
from the Government anterior to the Revolution, nothing else has
been copied from that Government.   The best of the administrative forms of proceeding in modern France have been borrowed
from the old Provincial Assemblies, and not from the Government.
The machine was adopted, but its produce rejected.

The habitual poverty of the rural population had given birth
to maxims little calculated to put an end to it.   'If nations were
well off,' said Richelieu, in his Political Testament, 'hardly would
they keep within the rules.'   In the eighteenth century this maxim
was modified, but it was still believed that the peasantry would
not work without the constant stimulus of necessity, and that want
was the only security against idleness.   That is precisely the
theory which is sometimes professed with reference to the negro
population of the colonies.   It was an opinion so generally diffused
amongst those who governed that almost all the economists thought
themselves obliged to combat it at length.

The primary object of the *taille* was to enable the King to
purchase recruits so as to dispense the nobles and their vassals
from military service; but in the seventeenth century the obligation of military service was again imposed, as we have seen, under
the name of the militia, and henceforth it weighed upon the common people only, and almost exclusively on the peasantry.

The infinite number of police reports from the constables,
which are still to be found amongst the records of any intendancy,
all relating to the pursuit of refractory militia-men or deserters,
suffice to prove that this force was not raised without obstacles.
It seems, indeed, that no public burden was more insupportable to
the peasantry than this : to evade it they frequently fled into the
woods, where they were pursued by the armed authorities.   This

is the more singular, when we see the facility with which the conscription works in France in the present times.

This extreme repugnance of the peasantry of France before the Revolution to the militia was attributable less to the principle of the law than to the manner in which the law was executed; more especially from the long period of uncertainty, during which it threatened those liable to be drawn (they could be taken until forty years of age, unless they were married)—from the arbitrary power of revision, which rendered the advantage of a lucky number almost useless—from the prohibition to hire a substitute—from disgust at a hard and perilous profession, in which all hope of advancement was forbidden; but, above all, from the feeling that this oppressive burden rested on themselves alone, and on the most wretched amongst themselves, the ignominy of this condition rendering its hardships more intolerable.

I have had means of referring to many of the returns of the draft for the militia, as it was made in 1769 in a large number of parishes. In all these returns there are some exemptions: this man is a gentleman's servant; that, the gamekeeper of an abbey; a third is only the valet of a man of inferior birth, but who, at least, 'lives like a nobleman.' Wealth alone afforded an exemption; when a farmer annually figured amongst those who paid the largest sum in taxes, his sons were dispensed from the militia; that was called encouragement of agriculture. Even the economists, who, in all other points, were great partisans of social equality, were not shocked by this privilege; they only suggested that it should be extended, or, in other words, that the burden of the poorest and most friendless of the peasants should become more severe. 'The low pay of the soldier,' said one of these writers, 'the manner in which he is lodged, dressed, and fed, and his entire state of dependence, would render it too cruel to take any but a man of the lowest orders.'

Down to the close of the reign of Louis XIV. the high roads were not repaired, or were repaired at the cost of those who used them, namely, the State and the adjacent landowners. But about that time the roads began to be repaired by forced labour only, that is to say, exclusively at the expense of the peasantry.[1] This expedient for making roads without paying for them was thought so ingenious, that in 1737 a circular of the Comptroller-General Orry established it throughout France. The Intendants were armed with the right of imprisoning the refractory at pleasure, or of sending constables after them.[2]

[1] See Note LVII., Repair of Roads, how regarded.
[2] See Note LVIII., Commitments for Non-performance of Compulsory Labour.

From that time, whenever trade augmented, so that more roads were wanted or desired, the *corvée* or forced labour extended to new lines, and had more work to do. It appears from the Report made in 1779 to the Provincial Assembly of Berri, that the works executed by forced labour in that poor province were estimated in one year at 700,000 livres. In 1787 they were computed at about the same sum in Lower Normandy. Nothing can better demonstrate the melancholy fate of the rural population; the progress of society, which enriched all the other classes, drove them to despair, and civilisation itself turned against that class alone.

I find about the same time, in the correspondence of the Intendants, that leave was to be refused to the peasants to do their forced labour on the private roads of their own villages, since this labour was to be reserved to the great high roads only, or, as they were then called, 'the King's highway.' The strange notion that the cost of the roads was to be defrayed by the poorest persons, and by those who were the least likely to travel by them, though of recent date, took such root in the minds of those who were to profit by it, that they soon imagined that the thing could not be done differently.[1] In 1766 an attempt was made to commute this forced labour into a local rate, but the same inequality survived, and affected this new species of tax.

Though originally a seignorial right, the system of forced labour, by becoming a royal right, was gradually extended to almost all public works. In 1719 I find it was employed to build barracks. 'Parishes are to send their best workmen,' said the Ordinance, 'and all other works are to give way to this.' The same forced service was used to escort convicts to the galleys and beggars to the workhouse;[2] it had to cart the baggage of troops as often as they changed their quarters, a burden which was very onerous at a time when each regiment carried heavy baggage after it. Many carts and oxen had to be collected for the purpose.[3] This sort of obligation, which signified little at its origin, became one of the most burdensome when standing armies grew more numerous. Sometimes the Government contractors loudly demanded the assistance of forced labour to convey timber from the forests to the naval arsenals. These peasants commonly received certain wages, but they were arbitrarily fixed and low.[4] The burden of an impost so ill-assessed sometimes became so heavy as to excite the uneasiness of the receivers of the *taille*. 'The outlay

---

[1] See Note LIX.
[2] See Note LX., Escort of Galley-slaves.
[3] See Note LXI.
[4] See Note LXII.

required of the peasants on the roads,' said one of these officers in 1751, ' is such, that they will soon be quite unable to pay the *taille*.'

Could all these new oppressions have been established if there had been in the vicinity of these peasants any men of wealth and education, disposed and able, if not to defend them, at least to intercede for them, with that common master who already held in his grasp the fortunes of the poor and of the rich ?

I have read a letter of a great landowner, writing in 1774 to the Intendant of his province, to induce him to open a road. This road, he said, would cause the prosperity of the village, and for several reasons ; he then went on to recommend the establishment of a fair, which would double, he thought, the price of produce. With excellent motives, he added that with the assistance of a small contribution a school might be established, which would furnish the King with more industrious subjects. It was the first time that these necessary ameliorations had occurred to him ; he had only thought of them in the preceding two years, which he had been compelled by a *lettre de cachet* to spend in his own house. ' My exile for the last two years in my estates,' he candidly observed, ' has convinced me of the extreme utility of these things.'

It was more especially in times of scarcity that the relaxation or total interruption of the ties of patronage and dependence, which formerly connected the great rural proprietors and the peasantry, was manifest. At such critical times the Central Government, alarmed by its own isolation and weakness, sought to revive for the nonce the personal influences or the political associations which the Government itself had destroyed ; they were summoned to its aid, but they were summoned in vain, and the State was astonished to find that those persons were defunct whom it had itself deprived of life.

In this extremity some of the Intendants—Turgot, for instance —in the poorest provinces, issued illegal ordinances to compel the rich landowners to feed their tenants till the next harvest. I have found, under the date of 1770, letters from several parish priests, who propose to the Intendants to tax the great landowners, both clerical and lay, ' who possess vast estates which they do not inhabit, and from which they draw large revenues to be spent elsewhere.'

At all times the villages were infested with beggars; for, as Letronne observes, the poor were relieved in the towns, but in the country, during the winter, mendicity was their only resource.

Occasionally these poor wretches were treated with great violence. In 1767 the Duc de Choiseul, then Minister, resolved suddenly to suppress mendicity in France. The correspondence of the Intendants still shows with what rigour his measures were taken. The patrol was ordered at once to take up all the beggars found in the kingdom; it is said that more than 50,000 of them were seized. Able-bodied vagabonds were to be sent to the galleys; as for the rest, more than forty workhouses were opened to receive them. It would have been more to the purpose to have opened the hearts of the rich.

This Government of the ancient French monarchy, which was, as I have said, so mild, and sometimes so timid, so full of formalities, of delays, and of scruples, when it had to ᶜdo with those who were placed above the common people, was always harsh and always prompt in proceeding against the lower orders, especially against the peasantry. Amongst the records which I have examined, I have not seen one relating to the arrest of a man of the middle class by order of the Intendant; but the peasants were arrested continually, some for forced labour, some for begging, some for the militia, some by the police or for a hundred other causes. The former class enjoyed independent courts of justice, long trials, and a public procedure; the latter fell under the control of the provost-marshal, summarily and without appeal.[1]

'The immense distance which exists between the common people and all the other classes of society,' Necker wrote in 1785, 'contributes to avert our observation from the manner in which authority may be handled in relation to all those persons lost in a crowd. Without the gentleness and humanity which characterise the French and the spirit of this age, this would be a continual subject of sorrow to those who can feel for others under burdens from which they are themselves exempt.'

But this oppression was less apparent in the positive evil done to those unhappy classes than in the impediments which prevented them from improving their own condition. They were free and they were owners of land, yet they remained almost as ignorant, and often more indigent, than the serfs, their forefathers. They were still without industrial employment, amidst all the wonderful creations of the modern arts; they were still uncivilised in a world glittering with civilisation. If they retained the peculiar intelligence and perspicacity of their race, they had not been taught to use these qualities; they could not even succeed in the cultivation of the soil, the only thing they had to do. 'The husbandry I see before me is that of the tenth century,' was the remark of a

[1] See Note LXIII.

celebrated English agriculturist in France. They excelled in no profession but in that of arms; there at least they came naturally and necessarily into contact with the other classes.

In this depth of isolation and indigence the French peasantry lived; they lived enclosed and inaccessible within it. I have been surprised and almost shocked to perceive that less than twenty years before the Catholic worship was abolished without resistance in France and the churches desecrated, the means taken to ascertain the population of a district were these: the parish priests reported the number of persons who had attended at Easter at the Lord's table—an estimate was added for the probable number of children and of the sick; the result gave the whole body of the population. Nevertheless the spirit of the age had begun to penetrate by many ways into these untutored minds; it penetrated by irregular and hidden channels, and assumed the strangest shapes in their narrow and obscure capacities. Yet nothing seemed as yet externally changed; the manners, the habits, the faith of the peasant seemed to be the same; he was submissive, and was even merry.

There is something fallacious in the merriment which the French often exhibit in the midst of the greatest calamities. It only proves that, believing their ill fortune to be inevitable, they seek to throw it off by not thinking of it, but not that they do not feel it. Open to them a door of escape from the evil they seem to bear so lightly, and they will rush towards it with such violence as to pass over your body without so much as seeing you, if you are on their path.

These things are clear to us, from our point of observation; but they were invisible to contemporary eyes. It is always with great difficulty that men belonging to the upper classes succeed in discerning with precision what is passing in the mind of the common people, and especially of the peasantry. The education and the manner of life of the peasantry give them certain views of their own, which remain shut to all other classes. But when the poor and the rich have scarcely any common interests, common grievances, or common business, the darkness which conceals the mind of the one from the mind of the other becomes impenetrable, and the two classes might live for ever side by side without the slightest interpenetration. It is curious to observe in what strange security all those who inhabited the upper or the middle storeys of the social edifice were living at the very time when the Revolution was beginning, and to mark how ingeniously they discoursed on the virtues of the common people, on their gentleness, on their attachment to themselves, on their innocent diversions; the absurd and terrible contrast of '93 was already beneath their feet.

Let us here pause for a moment as we proceed to consider, amidst all these minute particulars which I have been describing, one of the greatest laws of Providence in the government of human societies.

The French nobility persisted in standing aloof from the other classes; the landed gentry ended by obtaining exemptions from most of the public burdens which rested upon them; they imagined that they should preserve their rank whilst they evaded its duties, and for a time this seemed to be so. But soon an internal and invisible malady appeared to have infected their condition; it dwindled away though no one touched it, and whilst their immunities increased their substance declined. The middle classes, with which they had been so reluctant to mingle, grew in wealth and in intelligence beside them, without them, and against them; they had rejected the middle classes as associates and as fellow-citizens; but they were about to find in those classes their rivals, soon their enemies, at length their masters. A superior power had relieved them from the care of directing, of protecting, of assisting their vassals; but as that power had left them in the full enjoyment of their pecuniary rights and their honorary privileges, they conceived that nothing was lost to them. As they still marched first, they still thought they were leading; and indeed they had still about them men whom, in the language of the law, they named their *subjects*—others were called their vassals, their tenants, their farmers. But, in reality, none followed them; they were alone, and when those very classes rose against them, flight was their only resource.

Although the destinies of the nobility and the middle classes have differed materially from each other, they have had one point of resemblance: the men of the middle classes had ended by living as much apart from the common people as those of the upper classes. Far from drawing nearer to the peasantry, they had withdrawn from all contact with their hardships; instead of uniting themselves closely to the lower orders, to struggle in common against a common inequality, they only sought to establish fresh preferences in their own favour; and they were as eager to obtain exemptions for themselves as the nobles were to maintain their privileges. These peasants, from whom the middle classes had sprung, were not only become strangers to their descendants, but were literally unknown by them; and it was not until arms had been placed by the middle classes in their hands that those classes perceived what unknown passions they had kindled—passions which they could neither guide nor control, and which ended by turning the instigators of those passions into their victims.

In all future ages the ruins of that great House of France, which had seemed destined to extend over the whole of Europe, will be the wonder of mankind; but those who read its history with attention will understand without difficulty its fall. Almost all the vices, almost all the errors, almost all the fatal prejudices I have had occasion to describe, owed either their origin, or their duration, or their extent to the arts practised by most of the kings of France to divide their subjects in order to govern them more absolutely.

But when the middle classes were thus thoroughly severed from the nobility, and the peasantry from the nobility, as well as from the middle classes—when, by the progress of the same influences within each class, each of them was internally subdivided into minute bodies, almost as isolated from each other as the classes to which they belonged, the result was one homogeneous mass, the parts of which no longer cohered. Nothing was any longer so organised as to thwart the Government—nothing so as to assist it; insomuch that the whole fabric of the grandeur of the monarchy might fall to pieces at once and in a moment as soon as the society on which it rested was disturbed.

And the people, which alone seem to have learnt something from the misconduct and the mistakes of all its masters, if indeed it escaped their empire, failed to shake off the false notions, the vicious habits, the evil tendencies which those masters had imparted to it, or allowed it to assume. Sometimes that people has carried the predilections of a slave into the enjoyment of its liberty, alike incapable of self-government and hostile to those who would have directed it.

I now resume my track; and, losing sight of the old and general facts which have prepared the great Revolution I design to paint, I proceed to the more particular and more recent incidents which finally determined its occurrence, its origin, and its character.

CHAPTER XIII.

SHOWING THAT TOWARDS THE MIDDLE OF THE EIGHTEENTH CENTURY
MEN OF LETTERS BECAME THE LEADING POLITICAL MEN OF FRANCE,
AND OF THE EFFECTS OF THIS OCCURRENCE.

FRANCE had long been the most literary of all the nations of Europe ;
although her literary men had never exhibited such intellectual
powers as they displayed about the middle of the eighteenth
century, or occupied such a position as that which they then
assumed.   Nothing of the kind had ever been seen in France, or
perhaps in any other country.   They were not constantly mixed
up with public affairs as in England : at no period, on the contrary,
had they lived more apart from them.   They were invested with
no authority whatever, and filled no public offices in a society
crowded with public officers; yet they did not, like the greater
part of their brethren in Germany, keep entirely aloof from the
arena of politics and retire into the regions of pure philosophy and
polite literature.   They busied themselves incessantly with matters
appertaining to government, and this was, in truth, their special
occupation.   Thus they were continually holding forth on the
origin and primitive forms of society, the primary rights of the
citizen and of government, the natural and artificial relations of
men, the wrong or right of customary laws, and the principles of
legislation.   While they thus penetrated to the fundamental basis
of the constitution of their time, they examined its structure with
minute care and criticised its general plan.   All, it is true, did
not make a profound and special study of these great problems :
the greater part only touched upon them cursorily, and as it were
in sport : but they all dealt with them more or less.   This species
of abstract and literary politics was scattered in unequal proportions
through all the works of the period ; from the ponderous treatise
to the popular song, not one of them but contained some grains
of it.

As for the political systems of these writers, they varied so
greatly one from the other that any attempt to reconcile them, or
to form any one theory of government out of them, would be an

impracticable task.   Nevertheless, by discarding matters of detail,
so as to get at the first leading ideas, it may be easily discovered
that the authors of these different systems agreed at least in one
very general notion, which all of them seem to have alike conceived,
and which appears to have pre-existed in their minds before all the
notions peculiar to themselves and to have been their common
fountain-head.   However widely they may have diverged in the
rest of their course, they all started from this point.   They all
agreed that it was expedient to substitute simple and elementary
rules, deduced from reason and natural law, for the complicated
traditional customs which governed the society of their time.
Upon a strict scrutiny it may be seen that what might be called
the political philosophy of the eighteenth century consisted, properly speaking, in this one notion.

These opinions were by no means novel; for three thousand
years they had unceasingly traversed the imaginations of mankind,
though without being able to stamp themselves there.   How came
they at last to take possession of the minds of all the writers of this
period ?   Why, instead of progressing no farther than the heads of a
few philosophers, as had frequently been the case, had they at last
reached the masses, and assumed the strength and the fervour of a
political passion to such a degree, that general and abstract theories
upon the nature of society became daily topics of conversation,
and even inflamed the imaginations of women, and of the peasantry ?
How was it that literary men, possessing neither rank, nor honours,
nor fortune, nor responsibility, nor power, became, in fact, the
principal political men of the day, and even the only political men,
inasmuch as whilst others held the reins of government, they alone
grasped its authority ?

A few words may suffice to show what an extraordinary and
terrible influence these circumstances, which apparently belong
only to the history of French literature, exercised upon the
Revolution, and even upon the present condition of France.

It was not by chance that the philosophers of the eighteenth
century thus coincided in entertaining notions so opposed to those
which still served as bases to the society of their time : these ideas
had been naturally suggested to them by the aspect of the society
which they had all before their eyes.   The sight of so many unjust
or absurd privileges, the burden of which was more and more felt
whilst their cause was less and less understood, urged, or rather
precipitated, the minds of one and all towards the idea of the
natural equality of man's condition.   Whilst they looked upon so
many strange and irregular institutions, born of other times, which

no one had attempted either to bring into harmony with each other or to adapt to modern wants, and which appeared likely to perpetuate their existence though they had lost their worth, they learned to abhor what was ancient and traditional, and naturally became desirous of re-constructing the social edifice of their day upon an entirely new plan—a plan which each one traced solely by the light of his reason.[1]

These writers were predisposed, by their own position, to relish general and abstract theories upon the subject of government, and to place in them the blindest confidence. The almost immeasurable distance in which they lived from practical duties afforded them no experience to moderate the ardour of their character; nothing warned them of the obstacles which the actual state of things might oppose to reforms, however desirable. They had no idea of the perils which always accompany the most needful revolutions; they had not even a presentiment of them, for the complete absence of all political liberty had the effect of rendering the transaction of public affairs not only unknown to them, but even invisible. They were neither employed in those affairs themselves, nor could they see what those employed in them were doing. They were consequently destitute of that superficial instruction which the sight of a free community, and the tumult of its discussions, bestow even upon those who are least mixed up with government. Thus they became far more bold in innovation, more fond of generalising and of systems, more disdainful of the wisdom of antiquity, and still more confident in their individual reason, than is commonly to be seen in authors who write speculative books on politics.

The same state of ignorance opened to them the ears and hearts of the people. It may be confidently affirmed that if the French had still taken part, as they formerly had done, in the States-General, or if even they had found a daily occupation in the administration of the affairs of the country in the assemblies of their several provinces, they would not have allowed themselves to be inflamed as they were by the ideas of the writers of the day, since they would have retained certain habits of public business which would have preserved them from the evils of pure theory.

Had they been able, like the English, gradually to modify the spirit of their ancient institutions by practical experience without destroying them, they would perhaps have been less inclined to invent new ones. But there was not a man who did not daily feel himself injured in his fortune, in his person, in his comfort, or his pride by some old law, some ancient political custom, or some

[1] See Note LXIV.

other remnant of former authority, without perceiving at hand any remedy that he could himself apply to his own particular hardship. It appeared that the whole constitution of the country must either be endured or destroyed.

The French, however, had still preserved one liberty amidst the ruin of every other: they were still free to philosophise almost without restraint upon the origin of society, the essential nature of governments, and the primordial rights of mankind.

All those who felt themselves aggrieved by the daily application of existing laws were soon enamoured of these literary politics. The same taste soon reached even those who by nature or by their condition of life seemed the farthest removed from abstract speculations. Every tax-payer wronged by the unequal distribution of the *taille* was fired by the idea that all men ought to be equal; every little landowner devoured by the rabbits of his noble neighbour was delighted to be told that all privileges were, without distinction, contrary to reason. Every public passion thus assumed the disguise of philosophy; all political action was violently driven back into the domain of literature; and the writers of the day, undertaking the guidance of public opinion, found themselves at one time in that position which the heads of parties commonly hold in free countries. No one in fact was any longer in a condition to contend with them for the part they had assumed.

An aristocracy in all its vigour not only carries on the affairs of a country, but directs public opinion, gives a tone to literature, and the stamp of authority to ideas; but the French nobility of the eighteenth century had entirely lost this portion of its supremacy; its influence had followed the fortunes of its power; and the position it had occupied in the direction of the public mind had been entirely abandoned to the writers of the day, to occupy as they pleased. Nay more, this very aristocracy whose place they thus assumed, favoured their undertaking. So completely had it forgotten the fact that general theories, once admitted, inevitably transform themselves in time into political passions and deeds, that doctrines the most adverse to the peculiar rights, and even to the existence, of the nobility were looked upon as ingenious exercises of the mind; the nobles even shared äs a pleasant pastime in these discussions, and quietly enjoyed their immunities and privileges whilst they serenely discussed the absurdity of all established customs.

Astonishment has frequently been expressed at the singular blindness with which the higher classes under the old monarchy of France thus contributed to their own ruin. But whence could they have become more enlightened? Free institutions are not less necessary to show the greater citizens their perils than to secure to the lesser their rights. For more than a century since the last traces of public life had disappeared in France, no shock, no rumour had ever warned those most directly interested in the maintenance of the ancient constitution that the old building was tottering to its fall. As nothing had changed in its external aspect, they imagined that everything had remained the same. Their minds were thus bounded by the same horizon at which that of their fathers had stopped. In the public documents of the year 1789 the nobility appears to have been as much preoccupied with the idea of the encroachments of the royal power as it could possibly have been in those of the fifteenth century. On the other hand, the unfortunate Louis XVI. just before his own destruction by the incursion of democracy, still continued (as has been justly remarked by Burke) to look upon the aristocracy as the chief rival of the royal power, and mistrusted it as much as if he was still living in the days of the *Fronde*. The middle and lower classes on the contrary were in his eyes, as in those of his forefathers, the surest support of the throne.

But that which must appear still more strange to men of the present day—men who have the shattered fragments of so many revolutions before their eyes—is the fact, that not the barest notion of a violent revolution ever entered into the minds of the generation which witnessed it. Such a notion was never discussed, for it was never conceived. Those minor shocks which the exercise of political liberty is continually imparting to the best constituted societies, serve daily to call to mind the possibility of an earthquake, and to keep public vigilance on the alert; but in the state of society of France in the eighteenth century, on the brink of this abyss, nothing had yet indicated that the fabric leaned.

On examining with attention the Instructions drawn up by the three Orders before their convocation in 1789—by all the three, the nobility and clergy, as well as the *Tiers-État*—noting *seriatim* all the demands made for the changes of laws or customs, it will be seen with a sort of terror, on terminating this immense labour, and casting up the sum total of all these particular requirements, that what was required is no less than the simultaneous and systematic abolition of every law and every usage current throughout the country; and that what was impending must be one of the most extensive and dangerous revolutions that ever appeared in the world. Yet the very men who were so shortly to become its victims knew nothing of it. They fancied that the total and sudden transformation of so ancient and complicated a state of society was to be effected, without any concussion, by the aid and efficacy of reason alone; and they fatally forgot that maxim which their forefathers, four hundred years before, had expressed in the simple and energetic language of their time : ' *Par requierre de trop grande franchise et libertés chet-on en trop grande servaige.*' (By requiring too great liberty and franchise, men fall into too great servitude.)

It was not surprising that the nobility and middle classes, so long excluded from all public action, should have displayed this strange inexperience ; but what astonishes far more is, that the very men who had the conduct of public affairs, the ministers, the magistrates, and the Intendants, should not have evinced more foresight. Many of them, nevertheless, were very clever men in their profession, and were thoroughly possessed of all the details of the public administration of their time ; but in that great science of government, which teaches the comprehension of the general movement of society, the appreciation of what is passing in the minds of the masses, and the foreknowledge of the probable results—they were just as much novices as the people itself. In truth, it is only the exercise of free institutions that can teach the statesman this principal portion of his art.

This may easily be seen in the Memoir addressed by Turgot to the King in 1775, in which, among other matters, he advised his Majesty to summon a representative assembly, freely elected by the whole nation, to meet every year, for six weeks, about his own person, but to grant it no effective power. His proposal was, that this assembly should take cognisance of administrative business, but never of the government—should offer suggestions rather than express a will—and, in fact, should be commissioned to discuss laws, but not to make them. ' In this wise,' said the Memoir, ' the royal power would be enlightened, but not thwarted, and public opinion contented without danger: for these assemblies would have no authority to oppose any indispensable operation ; and if, which is most improbable, they should not lend themselves to this duty, his Majesty would still be the master to do as he pleases.'

It was impossible to show greater ignorance of the true bearing of such a measure; and of the spirit of the times. It has frequently happened, it is true, that towards the end of a revolutionary period, such a proposal as that made by Turgot has been carried into effect with impunity, and that a shadow of liberty has been granted without the reality. Augustus made the experiment with

success.   A nation fatigued by a prolonged struggle may willingly
consent to be duped in order to obtain repose; and history shows
that enough may then be done to satisfy it, by collecting from all
parts of the country a certain number of obscure or dependent individuals, and making them play before it the part of a political
assembly for the wages they receive.   There have been several
examples of the kind.   But at the commencement of a revolution such experiments always fail; they inflame, without satisfying
the people.   This truth, known to the humblest citizen of a
free country, was not known to Turgot, great administrator as he
was.

If now it be taken into consideration that this same French
nation, so ignorant of its own public affairs, so utterly devoid of
experience, so hampered by its institutions, and so powerless to
amend them, was also in those days the most lettered and witty
nation of the earth, it may readily be understood how the writers
of the time became a great political power, and ended by being the
first power in the country.

In England those who wrote on the subject of government were
connected with those who governed; the latter applied new ideas
to practice—the former corrected or controlled their theories by
practical observation.   But in France the political world remained
divided into two separate provinces, with no mutual intercourse.
One portion governed; the other established abstract principles on
which all government ought to be founded.   Here measures were
taken in obedience to routine; there general laws were propounded,
without even a thought as to the means of their application.   These
kept the direction of affairs; those guided the intelligence of the
nation.

Above the actual state of society—the constitution of which was
still traditional, confused, and irregular, and in which the laws
remained conflicting and contradictory, ranks sharply sundered, the
conditions of the different classes fixed whilst their burdens were
unequal—an imaginary state of society was thus springing up, in
which everything appeared simple and co-ordinate, uniform, equit-
able, and agreeable to reason.   The imagination of the people
gradually deserted the former state of things in order to seek
refuge in the latter.   Interest was lost in what was, to foster dreams
of what might be; and men thus dwelt in fancy in this ideal city,
which was the work of literary invention.

The French Revolution has been frequently attributed to that
of America.   The American Revolution had certainly considerable
influence upon the French; but the latter owed less to what was

actually done in the United States than to what was thought at the same time in France. Whilst to the rest of Europe the Revolution of America still only appeared a novel and strange occurrence, in France it only rendered more palpable and more striking that which was already supposed to be known. Other countries it astonished; to France it brought more complete conviction. The Americans seemed to have done no more than execute what the literary genius of France had already conceived; they gave the substance of reality to that which the French had excogitated. It was as if Fénelon had suddenly found himself in Salentum.

This circumstance, so novel in history, of the whole political education of a great people being formed by its literary men, contributed more than anything perhaps to bestow upon the French Revolution its peculiar stamp, and to cause those results which are still perceptible.

The writers of the time not only imparted their ideas to the people who effected the Revolution, but they gave them also their peculiar temperament and disposition. The whole nation ended, after being so long schooled by them, in the absence of all other leaders and in profound ignorance of practical affairs, by catching up the instincts, the turn of mind, the tastes, and even the humours of those who wrote; so that, when the time for action came, it transported into the arena of politics all the habits of literature.

A study of the history of the French Revolution will show that it was carried on precisely in that same spirit which has caused so many abstract books to be written on government. There was the same attraction towards general theories, complete systems of legislation, and exact symmetry in the laws—the same contempt of existing facts—the same reliance upon theory—the same love of the original, the ingenious, and the novel in institutions—the same desire to reconstruct, all at once, the entire constitution by the rules of logic, and upon a single plan, rather than seek to amend it in its parts. The spectacle was an alarming one; for that which is a merit in a writer is often a fault in a statesman : and the same things which have often caused great books to be written, may lead to great revolutions.

Even the political language of the time caught something of the tone in which the authors spoke : it was full of general expressions, abstract terms, pompous words, and literary turns. This style, aided by the political passions which it expressed, penetrated through all classes, and descended with singular facility even to the lowest. Considerably before the Revolution, the edicts of Louis

XVI. frequently spoke of the law of nature and the rights of man; and I have found instances of peasants who, in their memorials called their neighbours 'fellow-citizens,' their *Intendant* 'a respectable magistrate,' their parish-priest ' the minister of the altar,' and God ' the Supreme Being,' and who wanted nothing but spelling to become very indifferent authors.

These new qualities became so completely incorporated with the old stock of the French character, that habits resulting only from this singular education have frequently been attributed to the natural disposition of the French. It has been asserted that the taste, or rather the passion, which the French have displayed during the last sixty years for general ideas and big words in political discussion, arose from some characteristic peculiar to the French race, which has been somewhat pedantically called ' the genius of France,' as if this pretended characteristic could suddenly have displayed itself at the end of the last century, after having remained concealed during the whole history of the country.

It is singular that the French have preserved the habits which they had derived from literature, whilst they have almost entirely lost their ancient love of literature itself. I have been frequently astonished in the course of my own public life, to see that men who had never read the works of the eighteenth century, or of any other, and who had a great contempt for authors, nevertheless so faithfully retain some of the principal defects which were displayed before their birth by the literary spirit of that day.

CHAPTER XIV.

SHOWING HOW IRRELIGION HAD BECOME A GENERAL AND DOMINANT
PASSION AMONGST THE FRENCH OF THE EIGHTEENTH CENTURY,
AND WHAT INFLUENCE THIS FACT HAD ON THE CHARACTER OF
THE REVOLUTION.

FROM the time of the great Revolution of the sixteenth century,
when the spirit of free inquiry undertook to decide which were
false and which were true among the different traditions of
Christianity, it had never ceased to engender certain minds of a
more curious or a bolder stamp, who contested or rejected them
all. The same spirit that, in the days of Luther, had at once
driven several millions of Catholics out of the pale of Catholicism,
continued .to drive in individual cases some few .Christians out of
the pale of Christianity itself. Heresy was followed by unbelief.

It may be said generally that in the eighteenth century
Christianity had lost over the whole of the continent of Europe
a great part of its power; but in most countries it was rather
neglected than violently contested, and even those who forsook it
did so with regret. Irreligion was disseminated among the Courts
and wits of the age; but it had not yet penetrated into the hearts
of the middle and lower classes. It was still the caprice of some
leading intellects, not the opinion of the vulgar. 'It is a prejudice commonly diffused throughout Germany,' said Mirabeau, in
1787, 'that the Prussian provinces are full of atheists; when, in
truth, although some freethinkers are to be met with there, the
people of those parts are as much attached to religion as in the
most superstitious countries, and even a great number of fanatics
are to be found there.' To this he added, that it was much to be
regretted that Frederick II. had not sanctioned the marriage of
the Catholic clergy, and, above all, had refused to leave those
priests who married in possession of the income of their ecclesiastical preferment; 'a measure,' he continued, 'which we should
have ventured to consider worthy of the great man.' Nowhere
but in France had irreligion become a general passion, fervid,
intolerant, and oppressive.

There the state of things was such as had never occurred before.   In other times, established religions had been attacked with violence ; but the ardour evinced against them had always taken rise in the zeal inspired by a new faith.   Even the false and detestable religions of antiquity had not had either numerous or passionate adversaries until Christianity arose to supplant them ; till then they were quietly and noiselessly dying out in doubt and indifference—dying, in fact, the death of religions, by old age. But in France the Christian religion was attacked with a sort of rage, without any attempt to substitute any other belief.   Continuous and vehement efforts having been made to expel from the soul of man the faith that had filled it, the soul was left empty. A mighty multitude wrought with ardour at this thankless task. That absolute incredulity in matters of religion which is so contrary to the natural instincts of man, and places his soul in so painful a condition, appeared attractive to the masses.   That which until then had only produced the effect of a sickly languor, began to generate fanaticism and a spirit of propagandism.

The occurrence of several great writers, all disposed to deny the truths of the Christian religion, can hardly be accepted as a sufficient explanation of so extraordinary an event.   For how, it may be asked, came all these writers, every one of them, to turn their talents in this direction rather than any other ?   Why, among them all, cannot one be found who took it into his head to support the other side ? and, finally, how was it that they found the ears of the masses far more open to listen to them than any of their predecessors had done, and men's minds so inclined to believe them ? The efforts of all these writers, and above all their success, can only be explained by causes altogether peculiar to their time and their country.   The spirit of Voltaire had already been long in the world : but Voltaire himself, in truth, could never have attained his supremacy, except in the eighteenth century and in France.

It must first be acknowledged that the Church was not more open to attack in France than elsewhere.   The corruptions and abuses which had been allowed to creep into it were less, on the contrary, there than in most other Catholic countries.   The Church of France was infinitely more tolerant than it had ever been previously and than the Church still was in other nations.   Consequently, the peculiar causes of this phenomenon must be looked for less in the condition of religion itself than in that of society.

For the thorough comprehension of this fact, what was said in the preceding chapter must not be lost sight of—namely, that the whole spirit of political opposition excited by the corruption of the

K

Government, not being able to find a vent in public affairs, had taken refuge in literature, and that the writers of the day had become the real leaders of the great party which tended to overthrow the social and political institutions of the country.

This being well understood, the question is altered. We no longer ask in what the Church of that day erred as a religious institution, but how far it stood opposed to the political revolution which was at hand, and how it was more especially irksome to the writers who were the principal promoters of this revolution.

The Church, by the first principles of her ecclesiastical government, was adverse to the principles which they were desirous of establishing in civil government. The Church rested principally upon tradition; they professed great contempt for all institutions based upon respect for the past. The Church recognised an authority superior to individual reason; they appealed to nothing but that reason. The Church was founded upon a hierarchy: they aimed at an entire subversion of ranks. To have come to a common understanding it would have been necessary for both sides to have recognised the fact, that political society and religious society, being by nature essentially different, cannot be regulated by analogous laws. But at that time they were far enough from any such conclusion; and it was fancied that, in order to attack the institutions of the State, those of the Church must be destroyed which served as their foundation and their model.

Moreover, the Church was itself the first of the political powers of the time; and, although not the most oppressive, the most hated; for she had contrived to mix herself up with those powers, without having any claim to that position either by her nature or her vocation; she often sanctioned in them the very defects she blamed elsewhere; she covered them with her own sacred inviolability, and seemed desirous of rendering them as immortal as herself. An attack upon the Church was sure at once to chime in with the strong feeling of the public.

But, besides these general reasons, the literary men of France had more special, and, so to say, personal reasons for attacking the Church in the first instance. The Church represented precisely that portion of the Government which stood nearest and most directly opposed to themselves. The other powers of the State were only felt by them from time to time; but the ecclesiastical authority being specially employed in keeping watch over the progress of thought, and the censorship of books, was a daily annoyance to them. By defending the common liberties of the human mind against the Church, they were combating in their own cause, and they began by bursting the shackles which pressed most closely upon themselves.

Moreover, the Church appeared to them to be, and was, in fact, the most open and the worst defended side of all the vast edifice which they were assailing. Her strength had declined at the same time that the temporal power of the Crown had increased. After having been first the superior of the temporal powers, then their equal, she had come down to be their client; and a sort of reciprocity had been established between them. The temporal powers lent the Church their material force, whilst the Church lent them her moral authority; they caused the Church to be obeyed, the Church caused them to be respected—a dangerous interchange of obligations in times of approaching revolution, and always disadvantageous to a power founded not upon constraint but upon faith.

Although the Kings of France still called themselves the eldest sons of the Church, they fulfilled their obligations towards her most negligently: they evinced far less ardour in her protection than in the defence of their own government. They did not, it is true, permit any direct attack upon her, but they suffered her to be transfixed from a distance by a thousand shafts.

The sort of semi-constraint which was at that time imposed upon the enemies of the Church, instead of diminishing their power, augmented it. There are times when the restraint imposed on literature succeeds in arresting the progress of opinions; there are others when it accelerates their course: but a species of control similar to that then exercised over the press, has invariably augmented its power a hundredfold.

Authors were persecuted enough to excite compassion—not enough to inspire them with terror. They suffered from that kind of annoyance which irritates to opposition, not from the heavy yoke which crushes. The prosecutions directed against them, which were almost always dilatory, noisy, and vain, appeared less calculated to prevent their writing than to excite them to the task. A complete liberty of the press would have been less prejudicial to the Church.

'You consider our intolerance more favourable to the progress of the mind than your unlimited liberty,' wrote Diderot to David Hume in 1768. 'D'Holbach, Helvetius, Morelet, and Suard, are not of your opinion.' Yet it was the Scotchman who was right; he possessed the experience of the free country in which he lived. Diderot looked upon the matter as a literary man—Hume, as a politician.

If the first American who might be met by chance, either in his own country or abroad, were to be stopped and asked whether he considered religion useful to the stability of the laws and the good order of society, he would answer, without hesitation, that no civilised society, but more especially none in a state of freedom, can exist without religion. Respect for religion is, in his eyes, the greatest guarantee of the stability of the State and of the safety of the community. Those who are ignorant of the science of government know that fact at least. Yet there is not a country in the world where the boldest doctrines of the philosophers of the eighteenth century, on political subjects, have been more adopted than in America : their anti-religious doctrines alone have never been able to make way there, even with the advantage of an un-limited liberty of the press.

As much may be said of the English.[1] French irreligious philosophy had been preached to them even before the greater part of the French philosophers were born. It was Bolingbroke who set up Voltaire. Throughout the eighteenth century infidelity had celebrated champions in England. Able writers and profound thinkers espoused that cause, but they were never able to render it triumphant as in France ; inasmuch as all those who had any-thing to fear from revolutions eagerly came to the rescue of the established faith. Even those who were the most mixed up with the French society of the day, and who did not look upon the doctrines of French philosophy as false, rejected them as dangerous. Great political parties, as is always the case in free countries, were interested in attaching their cause to that of the Church ; and Bolingbroke himself became the ally of the bishops. The clergy, animated by these examples, and never finding itself deserted, combated manfully in its own cause. The Church of England, in spite of the defects of its constitution, and the abuses of every kind that swarmed within it, supported the shock victoriously. Authors and orators rose within it, and applied themselves with ardour to the defence of Christianity. The theories hostile to that religion, after having been discussed and refuted, were finally rejected by the action of society itself, and without any interference on the part of the Government.

It is not necessary, however, to seek examples beyond France itself. What Frenchman would ever think in our times of writing such books as those of Diderot or Helvetius ? Who would read them now ? and, it may almost be said, who even knows their titles ? The imperfect experience of public life which France has

[1] See Note LXV., Infidelity in England.

acquired during the last sixty years has been sufficient to disgust the French with this dangerous literature. It is only necessary to see how much the respect for religion has gradually resumed its sway among the different classes of the nation, according as each of them acquired that experience in the rude school of Revolution. The old nobility, which was the most irreligious class before 1789, became the most fervent after 1793 : it was the first infected, and the first cured. When the *bourgeoisie* felt itself struck down in its triumph, it began also, in its turn, gradually to revert to religious faith. Little by little, respect for religion penetrated to all the classes in which men had anything to lose by popular disturbances; and infidelity disappeared, or at least hid its head more and more, as the fear of revolutions arose.

But this was by no means the case at the time immediately preceding the Revolution of 1789. The French had so completely lost all practical experience in the great affairs of mankind, and were so thoroughly ignorant of the part held by religion in the government of empires, that infidelity first established itself in the minds of the very men who had the greatest and most pressing personal interest in keeping the State in order and the people in obedience. Not only did they themselves embrace it, but in their blindness they disseminated it below them. They made impiety the pastime of their vacant existence.

The Church of France, so prolific down to that period in great orators, when she found herself deserted by all those who ought to have rallied by a common interest to her cause, became mute. It seemed at one time that, provided she retained her wealth and her rank, she was ready to renounce her faith.

As those who denied the truths of Christianity spoke aloud, and those who still believed held their peace, a state of things was the result which has since frequently occurred again in France, not only on the question of religion, but in very different matters. Those who still preserved their ancient belief, fearing to be the only men who still remained faithful to it, and more afraid of isolation than of error, followed the crowd without partaking its opinions. Thus, that which was still only the feeling of a portion of the nation, appeared to be the opinion of all, and, from that very fact, seemed irresistible even to those who had themselves given it this false appearance.

The universal discredit into which every form of religious belief had fallen, at the end of the last century, exercised without any doubt the greatest influence upon the whole of the French Revolution: it stamped its character. Nothing contributed more to give its features that terrible expression which they wore.

In seeking to distinguish between the different effects which irreligion at that time produced in France, it may be seen that it was rather by disturbing men's minds than by degrading their hearts, or even corrupting their morals, that it disposed the men of that day to go to such strange excesses.

When religion thus deserted the souls of men, it did not leave them, as is frequently the case, empty and debilitated. They were filled for the time with sentiments and ideas that occupied its place, and did not, at first, allow them to be utterly prostrate.

If the French who effected the Revolution were more incredulous than those of the present day in matters of religion, at least they had one admirable faith which the present generation has not. They had faith in themselves. They never doubted of the perfectibility and power of man: they were burning with enthusiasm for his glory: they believed in his worth. They placed that proud confidence in their own strength which so often leads to error, but without which a people is only capable of servitude: they never doubted of their call to transform the face of society and regenerate the human race. These sentiments and passions became like a sort of new religion to them, which, as it produced some of those great effects which religions produce, kept them from individual selfishness, urged them on even to self-sacrifice and heroism, and frequently rendered them insensible to all those petty objects which possess the men of the present day.

After a profound study of history we may still venture to affirm that there never was a revolution, in which, at the commencement, more sincere patriotism, more disinterestedness, more true greatness, were displayed by so great a number of men. The nation then exhibited the principal defect, but, at the same time, the principal ornament, which youth possesses, or rather did possess, namely, inexperience and generosity.

Yet irreligion had produced an enormous public evil. In most of the great political revolutions, which, up to that period, had appeared in the world, those who had attacked the established laws had respected the creeds of the country; and, in the greater part of the religious revolutions, those who attacked religion made no attempt to change, at one blow, the nature and order of all the established authorities, and to raze to the ground the ancient constitution of the government. In the greatest convulsions of society one point, at least, had remained unshaken.

But in the French Revolution, the religious laws having been abolished at the same time that the civil laws were overthrown, the minds of men were entirely upset: they no longer knew either to what to cling, or where to stop; and thus arose a hitherto unknown species of revolutionists, who carried their boldness to a pitch of madness, who were surprised by no novelty and arrested by no scruple, and who never hesitated to put any design whatever into execution.   Nor must it be supposed that these new beings have been the isolated and ephemeral creation of a moment, and destined to pass away as that moment passed.   They have since formed a race of beings which has perpetuated itself, and spread into all the civilised parts of the world, everywhere preserving the same physiognomy, the same passions, the same character.   The present generation found it in the world at its birth : it still remains before our eyes.

CHAPTER XV.

THAT THE FRENCH AIMED AT REFORM BEFORE LIBERTY.

IT is worthy of observation that amongst all the ideas and all the feelings which led to the French Revolution, the idea and the taste for political liberty, properly so called, were the last to manifest themselves and the first to disappear.

For some time past the ancient fabric of the Government had begun to be shaken; it tottered already, but liberty was not yet thought of. Even Voltaire had scarcely thought about it; three years' residence in England had shown him what that liberty is, but without attaching him to it. The sceptical philosophy which was then in vogue in England enchanted him; the political laws of England hardly attracted his attention; he was more struck by their defects than by their merits. In his letters on England, which are one of his best pieces, Parliament is hardly mentioned; the fact was that he envied the English their literary freedom without caring for their political freedom, as if the former could ever long exist without the latter.

Towards the middle of the eighteenth century, a certain number of writers began to appear who devoted themselves especially to questions of public administration, and who were designated, in consequence of several principles which they held in common, by the general name of political economists or *physiocrates*. These economists have left less conspicuous traces in history than the French philosophers; perhaps they contributed less to the approach of the Revolution; yet I think that the true character of the Revolution may best be studied in their works. The French philosophers confined themselves for the most part to very general and very abstract opinions on government; the economists, without abandoning theory, clung more closely to facts. The former said what might be thought; the latter sometimes pointed out what might be done. All the institutions which the Revolution was about to annihilate for ever were the peculiar objects of their attacks; none found favour in their sight. All the institutions, on the contrary, which may be regarded as the product of the Revolution, were announced beforehand by these economical writers, and ardently recommended; there is hardly one of these institutions of which the germ may not be discovered in some of their writings; and those writings may be said to contain all that is most substantial in the Revolution itself.

Nay, more, their books already bore the stamp of that revolutionary and democratic temper which we know so well : they breathe not only the hatred of certain privileges, but even diversity was odious to them ; they would adore equality, even in servitude. All that thwarts their designs is to be crushed. They care little for plighted faith, nothing for private rights—or rather, to speak accurately, private rights have already ceased in their eyes to exist —public utility is everything. Yet these were men, for the most part, of gentle and peaceful lives, worthy persons, upright magistrates, able administrators; but the peculiar spirit of their task bore them onwards.

The past was to these economists a subject of endless contempt. 'This nation has been governed for centuries on false principles,' said Letronne, 'everything seems to have been done by haphazard.' Starting from this notion, they set to work; no institution was so ancient or so well-established in the history of France that they hesitated to demand its suppression from the moment that it incommoded them or deranged the symmetry of their plans. One of these writers proposed to obliterate at once all the ancient territorial divisions of the kingdom, and to change all the names of the provinces, forty years before the Constituent Assembly executed this scheme.

They had already conceived the idea of all the social and administrative reforms which the Revolution has accomplished before the idea of free institutions had begun to cross their minds. They were, indeed, extremely favourable to the free exchange of produce, and to the doctrine of *laissez faire et laissez passer*, the basis of free trade and free labour; but as for political liberties, properly so called, these did not occur to their minds, or, if perchance they did occur to their imaginations, such ideas were at once rejected. Most of them began to display considerable hostility to deliberative assemblies, to local or secondary powers, and, in general, to all the checks which have been established, at different times, in all free nations, to balance the central power of the Government. 'The system of checks,' said Quesnay, 'is a fatal idea in government.' 'The speculations on which a system of checks has been devised are chimerical,' said a friend of the same writer.

The sole guarantee invented by them against the abuse of power was public education; for, as Quesnay elsewhere observes, 'despotism is impossible when the nation is enlightened.' 'Struck by the evils arising from abuses of authority,' said another of his disciples, 'men have invented a thousand totally useless means of resistance, whilst they have neglected the only means which are truly efficacious, namely, public, general, and continual instruction in the principles of essential justice and natural order.' This literary nonsense was, according to these thinkers, to supply the place of all political securities.

Letronne, who so bitterly deplored the forlorn condition in which the Government had left the rural districts, who described them as without roads, without employment, and without information, never conceived that their concerns might be more successfully carried on if the inhabitants themselves were entrusted with the management of them.

Turgot himself, who deserves to rank far above all the rest for the elevation of his character and the singular merits of his genius, had not much more taste than the other economists for political liberty, or, at least, that taste came to him later, and when it was forced upon him by public opinion. To him, as well as to all the others, the chief political security seemed to be a certain kind of public instruction, given by the State, on a particular system and with a particular tendency. His confidence in this sort of intellectual drug, or, as one of his contemporaries expressed it, 'in the mechanism of an education regulated by principles,' was boundless. 'I venture to assure your Majesty,' said he, in a report to the King, proposing a plan of this nature, 'that in ten years your people will have changed out of knowledge; and that by their attainments, by their morality, and by their enlightened zeal for your service and for that of the country, France will be raised far above all other nations. Children who are now ten years of age will then have grown up as men prepared for the public service, attached to their country, submissive, not through fear but through reason, to authority, humane to their fellow-citizens, accustomed to recognise and to respect the administration of justice.'

Political freedom had been so long destroyed in France that men had almost entirely forgotten what are its conditions and its effects. Nay, more, the shapeless ruins of freedom which still remained, and the institutions which seem to have been formed to supply its place, rendered it an object of suspicion and of prejudice. Most of the Provincial Assemblies which were still in existence retained the spirit of the Middle Ages as well as their obsolete formalities, and they checked rather than advanced the progress of society. The Parliaments, which alone stood in lieu of political bodies, had no power to prevent the evil which the Government did, and frequently prevented the good which the Government attempted to do.

To accomplish the revolution which they contemplated by means of all these antiquated instruments appeared impracticable to the school of economists. To confide the execution of their plans to the nation, mistress of herself, was not more agreeable to them; for how was it possible to cause a whole people to adopt and follow a system of reform so extensive and so closely connected in all .its parts? It seemed to them more easy and more proper to make the administrative power of the Crown itself the instrument of their designs.

That new administrative power had not sprung from the institutions of the Middle Ages, nor did it bear the mark of that period; in spite of its errors they discovered in it some beneficial tendencies. Like themselves it was naturally favourable to equality of conditions and to uniformity of rules; as much as themselves it cordially detested all the ancient powers which were born of feudalism or tended to aristocracy. In all Europe no machine of government existed so well organised, so vast, or so strong. To find such a government ready to their hands seemed to them a most fortunate circumstance; they would have called it providential, if it had been the fashion then, as it now is, to cause Providence to intervene on all occasions. 'The state of France,' said Letronne, ' is infinitely better than that of England, for here reforms can be accomplished which will change the whole condition of the country in a moment; whilst among the English such reforms may always be thwarted by political parties.'

The point was, then, not to destroy this absolute power, but to convert it. 'The State must govern according to the rules of essential order,' said Mercier de la Rivière, ' and when this is the case it ought to be all powerful.' ' Let the State thoroughly understand its duty, and then let it be altogether free.' From Quesnay to the Abbé Bodeau they were all of the same mind. They not only relied on the royal administration to reform the social condition of their own age, but they partially borrowed from it the idea of the future government they hoped to found. The latter was framed in the image of the former.

These economists held that it is the business of the State not only to command the nation, but to fashion it in a certain manner, to form the character of the population upon a certain preconceived model, to inspire the mind with such opinions and the heart with such sentiments as it may deem necessary. In fact, they set no limits to the rights of the State, nor to what it could effect. The State was not only to reform men, but to transform them—perhaps if it chose, to make others! 'The State can make men what it pleases,' said Bodeau. That proposition includes all their theories.

This unlimited social power which the French economists had conceived was not only greater than any power they ever beheld, but it differed from every other power by its origin and its nature. It did not flow directly from the Deity, it did not rest on tradition; it was an impersonal power; it was not called the King, but the State; it was not the inheritance of a family, but the product and the representative of all. It entitled them to bend the right of every man to the will of the rest.

That peculiar form of tyranny which is called Democratic Despotism, and which was utterly unknown to the Middle Ages, was already familiar to these writers. No gradations in society, no distinctions of classes, no fixed ranks—a people composed of individuals nearly alike and entirely equal—this confused mass being recognised as the only legitimate sovereign, but carefully deprived of all the faculties which could enable it either to direct or even to superintend its own government. Above this mass a single officer, charged to do everything in its name without consulting it. To control this officer, public opinion, deprived of its organs; to arrest him, revolutions, but no laws. In principle, a subordinate agent; in fact, a master.

As nothing was as yet to be found about them which came up to this ideal, they sought it in the depths of Asia. I affirm, without exaggeration, that there is not one of these writers who has not, in some of his productions, passed an emphatic eulogy on China. That, at least, is always to be found in their books; and, as China was still very imperfectly known, there is no trash they have not written about that empire. That stupid and barbarous government, which a handful of Europeans can overpower when they please, appeared to them the most perfect model to be copied by all the nations of the earth. China was to them what England, and subsequently the United States, became for all Frenchmen. They expressed their emotion and enchantment at the aspect of a country, whose sovereign, absolute but unprejudiced, drives a furrow once a year with his own hands in honour of the useful arts; where all public employments are obtained by competitive examination, and which has a system of philosophy for its religion, and men of letters for its aristocracy.

It is supposed that the destructive theories which are designated in our times by the name of *socialism* are of recent origin : this, again, is a mistake ; these theories are contemporary with the first French school of economists. Whilst they were intent on employing the all-powerful government they had conceived in order to change the form of society, other writers grasped in imagination the same power to subvert its foundations.

In the *Code de la Nature,* by Morelly, will be found, side by side with the doctrines of the economists on the omnipotence and unlimited rights of the State, several of the political theories which have most alarmed the French nation in these later times, and which are supposed to have been born before our eyes—community of goods, the right to labour, absolute equality of conditions, uniformity in all things, a mechanical regularity in all the movements of individuals, a tyranny to regulate every action of daily life, and the complete absorption of the personality of each member of the community into the whole social body.

'Nothing in society shall belong in singular property to any one,' says the first article of this code. 'Property is detestable, and whosoever shall attempt to re-establish it, shall be shut up for life, as a maniac or an enemy of mankind. Every citizen is to be supported, maintained, and employed at the public expense,' says Article II. 'All productions are to be stored in public magazines, to be distributed to the citizens and to supply their daily wants. Towns will be erected on the same plan ; all private dwellings or buildings will be alike ; at five years of age all children will be taken from their parents and brought up in common at the cost of the State and in a uniform manner.'

Such a book might have been written yesterday : it is a hundred years old. It appeared in 1755, at the very time when Quesnay founded his school. So true it is that centralisation and socialism· are products of the same soil ; they are to each other what the grafted tree is to the wild stock.

Of all the men of their time, these economists are those who would appear most at home in our own ; their passion for equality is so strong, and their taste for freedom is so questionable, that one might fancy they are our contemporaries. In reading the speeches and the books of the men who figured in the Revolution of 1789, we are suddenly transported into a place and a state of society quite unknown to us ; but in perusing the books of this school of economists one may fancy we have been living with these people, and have just been talking with them.

About the year 1750 the whole French nation would not have

been disposed to exact a larger amount of political freedom than the economists themselves. The taste and even the notion of freedom had perished with the use of it. The nation desired reform rather than rights; and if there had been at that time on the throne of France a sovereign of the energy and the character of Frederick the Great, I doubt not that he would have accomplished in society and in government many of the great changes which have been brought about by the Revolution, and this not only without the loss of his crown, but with a considerable augmentation of his power. It is said that one of the ablest ministers of Louis XV., M. de Machault, had a glimpse of this idea, and imparted it to his master; but such undertakings are not the result of advice : to be able to perform them a man must have been able to conceive them.

Twenty years later the state of things was changed. A vision of political freedom had visited the mind of France, and was every day becoming more attractive, as may be inferred from a variety of symptoms. The provinces began to conceive the desire to manage once more their own affairs. The notion that the whole people has a right to take part in the government diffused itself and took possession of the public. Recollections of the old States-General were revived. The nation, which detested its own history, recalled no other part of it with pleasure but this. This fresh current of opinion bore away the economists themselves, and compelled them to encumber their unitarian system with some free institutions.

When, in 1771, the Parliaments were destroyed, the same public, which had so often suffered from their prejudices, was deeply affected by their fall. It seemed as if with them fell the last barrier which could still restrain the arbitrary power of the Crown.

This opposition astonished and irritated Voltaire. ' Almost all the kingdom is in a state of effervescence and consternation,' he wrote to one of his friends; ' the ferment is as great in the provinces as at Paris itself. Yet this edict seems to be full of useful reforms. To abolish the sale of public offices, to render the administration of justice gratuitous, to prevent suitors from coming from all corners of the kingdom to Paris to ruin themselves there, to charge the Crown with the payment of the expenses of the seignorial jurisdictions—are not these great services rendered to the nation ? These Parliaments, moreover, have they not been often barbarous and persecutors ? I am really amazed at the out-of-the-way people who take the part of these insolent and indocile citizens. For my own part I think the King right ; and since we must serve, I think it better to serve under a lion born of a good family, and who is by birth much stronger than I am, than under two hundred rats of my own condition.' And he adds, by way of excuse, ' Remember that I am bound to appreciate highly the favour the King has conferred on all the lords of manors, by undertaking to pay the expenses of their jurisdictions.'

Voltaire, who had long been absent from Paris, imagined that public opinion still remained at the point where he had left it. But he was mistaken. The French people no longer confined themselves to the desire that their affairs should be better conducted; they began to wish to conduct their affairs themselves, and it was manifest that the great Revolution, to which everything was contributing, would be brought about not only with the assent of the people, but by their hands.

From that moment, I believe that this radical Revolution, which was to confound in common ruin all that was worst and all that was best in the institutions and condition of France, became inevitable. A people so ill-prepared to act for themselves could not undertake a universal and simultaneous reform without a universal destruction. An absolute sovereign would have been a less dangerous innovator. For myself, when I reflect that this same Revolution, which destroyed so many institutions, opinions, and habits adverse to freedom, also destroyed so many of those things without which freedom can hardly exist, I incline to the belief that had it been wrought by a despot it would perhaps have left the French nation less unfit one day to become a free people, than wrought as it was by the sovereignty of the people and by the people themselves.

What has here been said must never be lost sight of by those who would understand the history of the French Revolution.

When the love of the French for political freedom was awakened, they had already conceived a certain number of notions on matters of government, which not only did not readily ally themselves with the existence of free institutions, but which were almost contrary to them.

They had accepted as the ideal of society a people having no aristocracy but that of its public officers, a single and all-powerful administration, directing the affairs of State, protecting those of private persons. Meaning to be free, they by no means meant to deviate from this first conception : only they attempted to reconcile it with that of freedom.

They, therefore, undertook to combine an unlimited administrative centralisation with a preponderating legislative body—the administration of a bureaucracy with the government of electors. The nation as a whole had all the rights of sovereignty ; each citizen taken singly was thrust into the strictest dependence; the former was expected to display the experience and the virtues of a free people—the latter the qualities of a faithful servant.

This desire of introducing political freedom in the midst of institutions and opinions essentially alien or adverse to it, but which were already established in the habits or sanctioned by the taste of the French themselves, is the main cause of the abortive attempts at free government which have succeeded each other in France for more than sixty years ; and which have been followed by such disastrous revolutions, that, wearied by so many efforts, disgusted by so laborious and so sterile a work, abandoning their second intentions for their original aim, many Frenchmen have arrived at the conclusion that to live as equals under a master is after all not without some charm.   Thus it is that the French of the present day are infinitely more similar to the Economists of 1750 than to their fathers in 1789.

I have often asked myself what is the source of that passion for political freedom which in all ages has been the fruitful mother of the greatest things which mankind have achieved—and in what feelings that passion strikes root and finds its nourishment.

It is evident that when nations are ill directed they soon conceive the wish to govern themselves ; but this love of independence, which only springs up under the influence of certain transient evils produced by despotism, is never lasting : it passes away with the accident that gave rise to it ; and what seemed to be the love of freedom was no more than the hatred of a master. That which nations made to be free really hate is the curse of dependence.

Nor do I believe that the true love of freedom is ever born of the mere aspect of its material advantages ; for this aspect may frequently happen to be overcast.   It is very true that in the long run freedom ever brings, to those who know how to keep it, ease, comfort, and often wealth ; but there are times at which it disturbs for a season the possession of these blessings ; there are other times when despotism alone can confer the ephemeral enjoyment of them.   The men who prize freedom only for such things as these are not men who ever long preserved it.

That which at all times has so strongly attached the affection of certain men is the attraction of freedom itself, its native charms independent of its gifts—the pleasure of speaking, acting, and breathing without restraint, under no master but God and the law. He who seeks in freedom aught but herself is fit only to serve.

There are nations which have indefatigably pursued her through every sort of peril and hardship. They loved her not for her material gifts; they regard herself as a gift so precious and so necessary that no other could console them for the loss of that which consoles them for the loss of everything else. Others grow weary of freedom in the midst of their prosperities; they allow her to be snatched without resistance from their hands, lest they should sacrifice by an effort that well-being which she had bestowed upon them. For them to remain free, nothing was wanting but a taste for freedom. I attempt no analysis of that lofty sentiment to those who feel it not. It enters of its own accord into the large hearts God has prepared to receive it; it fills them, it enraptures them; but to the meaner minds which have never felt it, it is past finding out.

CHAPTER XVI.

SHOWING THAT THE REIGN OF LOUIS XVI. WAS THE MOST PRO-
SPEROUS EPOCH OF THE OLD FRENCH MONARCHY, AND HOW THIS
VERY PROSPERITY ACCELERATED THE REVOLUTION.

IT cannot be doubted that the exhaustion of the kingdom under
Louis XIV. began long before the reverses of that monarch.   The
first indication of it is to be perceived in the most glorious years
of his reign.   France was ruined long before she had ceased to
conquer.   Vauban left behind him an alarming essay on the
administrative statistics of his time.   The Intendants of the
provinces, in the reports addressed by them to the Duke of
Burgundy at the close of the seventeenth century, and before the
disastrous War of the Spanish Succession had begun, all alluded to
the gradual decline of the nation, and they speak of it not as a
very recent occurrence: ' The population has considerably decreased in this district,' says one of them.   ' This town, formerly
so rich and flourishing, is now without employment,' says another.
Or again : ' There have been manufactures in this province, but
they are now abandoned ;' or, ' The farmers formerly raised much
more from the soil than they do at present; agriculture was in a
far better condition twenty years ago.'   ' Population and production have diminished by about one-fifth in the last thirty
years,' said an Intendant of Orleans at the same period.   The
perusal of these reports might be recommended to those persons
who are favourable to absolute government, and to those princes
who are fond of war.

As these hardships had their chief source in the evils of the
constitution, the death of Louis XIV., and even the restoration of
peace, did not restore the prosperity of the nation.   It was the
general opinion of all those who wrote on the art of government or
on social economy in the first half of the eighteenth century, that
the provinces were not recovering themselves; many even thought
that their ruin was progressive.   Paris alone, they said, grows in
wealth and in extent.   Intendants, ex-ministers, and men of
business were of the same opinion on this point as men of letters.

For myself, I confess that I do not believe in this continuous decline of France throughout the first half of the eighteenth century; but an opinion so generally entertained amongst persons so well informed, proves at least that the country was making at that time no visible progress. All the administrative records connected with this period of the history of France which have fallen under my observation denote, indeed, a sort of lethargy in the community. The government continued to revolve in the orbit of routine without inventing any new thing; the towns made scarcely an effort to render the condition of their inhabitants more comfortable or more wholesome; even in private life no considerable enterprise was set on foot.

About thirty or forty years before the Revolution broke out the scene began to change. It seemed as if a sort of inward perturbation, not remarked before, thrilled through the social frame. At first none but a most attentive eye could discern it; but gradually this movement became more characterised and more distinct. Year by year it gained in rapidity and in extent; the nation stirs, and seems about to rise once more. But, beware! It is not the old life of France which re-animates her. The breath of a new life pervades the mighty body, but pervades it only to complete its dissolution. Restless and agitated in their own condition, all classes are straining for something else; to better that condition is the universal desire, but this desire is so feverish and wayward that it leads men to curse the past, and to conceive a state of society altogether the reverse of that which lies before them.

Nor was it long before the same spirit penetrated to the heart of the Government. The Government was thus internally transformed without any external alteration; the laws of the kingdom were unchanged, but they were differently applied.

I have elsewhere remarked that the Comptrollers-General and the Intendants of 1760 had no resemblance to the same officers in 1780. The correspondence of the public offices demonstrates this fact in detail. Yet the Intendant of 1780 had the same powers, the same agents, the same arbitrary authority as his predecessor, but not the same purposes; the only care of the former was to keep his province in a state of obedience, to raise the militia, above all to collect the taxes; the latter has very different views, his head is full of a thousand schemes for the augmentation of the wealth of the nation. Roads, canals, manufactures, commerce, are the chief objects of his thoughts; agriculture more particularly attracts his notice.   Sully came into fashion amongst the administrators of that age.

Then it was that they began to form the agricultural societies, which I have already mentioned ; they established exhibitions, they distributed prizes.   Some of the circulars of the Comptrollers-General were more like treatises on husbandry than official correspondence.

In the collection of all the taxes the change which had come over the mind of the governing body was especially perceptible. The existing law was still unfair, arbitrary and harsh, as it had long been, but all its defects were mitigated in the application of it.

'When I began to study our fiscal laws,' says M. Mollien,[1] in his Memoirs, 'I was terrified by what I found there : fines, imprisonment, corporal punishment, were placed at the disposal of exceptional courts for mere oversights; the clerks of the revenue farms had almost all property and persons in their power, subject to the discretion of their oaths.   Fortunately I did not confine myself to the mere perusal of this code, and I soon had occasion to find out that between the text of the law and its application there was the same difference as between the manners of the old and the new race of financiers.'

' The collection of taxes may undoubtedly give rise to infinite abuses and annoyances,' said the Provincial Assembly of Lower Normandy in 1787 ; 'we must, however, do justice to the gentleness and consideration with which these powers have been exercised for some years past.'

The examination of public records fully bears out this assertion. They frequently show a genuine respect for the life and liberty of man, and more especially a sincere commiseration for the sufferings of the poor, which before would have been sought for in vain. Acts of violence committed by the fiscal officers on paupers had become rare ; remissions of taxation were more frequent, relief more abundant.   The King augmented all the funds intended to establish workshops of charity in the rural districts, or to assist the indigent, and he often founded new ones.   Thus more than

---

[1] [Count Mollien was educated in the fiscal service of the old monarchy, and after having escaped the perils of the Revolution he became Minister of the Treasury to the Emperor Napoleon, and under the Restoration a Peer of France.   He left Memoirs of his Administration, which have been printed for private circulation by his widow, the estimable Countess Mollien, in four volumes octavo, but not yet published. These Memoirs are a model of personal integrity and financial judgment, the more remarkable as it was the fate of M. Mollien to live in times when these qualities were equally rare.   The work was reviewed in the 'Quarterly Review,' 1849-1850, and this article was republished in 1872, in Mr. Reeve's ' Royal and Republican France.']

80,000 livres were distributed by the State in this manner in the district of Upper Guienne alone in 1779; 40,000 in 1784 in that of Tours; 48,000 in that of Normandy in 1787. Louis XVI. did not leave this portion of the duties of government to his Ministers only; he sometimes took it upon himself. When in 1776, an edict of the Crown fixed the compensation due to the peasantry whose fields were devastated by the King's game in the neighbourhood of the Royal seats, and established a simple and certain method of enforcing the payment of it, the King himself drew the preamble of the decree. Turgot relates that this virtuous and unfortunate Prince handed the paper to him with these words : ' You see that I too have been at work.' If we were to pourtray the Government of the old French monarchy such as it was in the last years of its existence, the image would be too highly flattered and too unlike the reality.

As these changes were brought about in the minds of the governing class and of the governed, the prosperity of the nation expanded with a rapidity heretofore unknown. It was announced by numerous symptoms : the population largely augmented ; the wealth of the country augmented more largely still. The American War did not arrest this movement; the State was embarrassed by it, but the community continued to enrich itself by becoming more industrious, more enterprising, more inventive.

' Since 1774,' says one of the members of the administration of that time, ' different kinds of industry have by their extension enlarged the area of taxation on all commodities.' If we compare the terms of arrangement agreed upon at different periods of the reign of Louis XVI. between the State and the financial companies which farmed the public revenue, the rate of payment will be found to have risen at each renewal with increasing rapidity. The farm of 1786 produced fourteen millions more than that of 1780. ' It may be reckoned that the produce of duties on consumption is increasing at the rate of two millions per annum,' said Necker, in his Report of 1781.

Arthur Young declared that, in 1788, Bordeaux carried on a larger trade than Liverpool. He adds : ' Latterly the progress of maritime commerce has been more rapid in France than in England ; trade has doubled there in the last twenty years.'

With due regard to the difference of the times we are speaking of, it may be established that in no one of the periods which have followed the Revolution of 1789 has the national prosperity of France augmented more rapidly than it did in the twenty years preceding that event.[1] The period of thirty-seven years of the constitutional monarchy of France, which were times of peace and progress, can alone be compared in this respect to the reign of Louis XVI.

The aspect of this prosperity, already so great and so rapidly increasing, may well be matter of surprise, if we think of all the defects which the Government of France still included, and all the restrictions against which the industry of the nation had still to contend. Perhaps there may be politicians who, unable to explain the fact, deny it, being of the opinion of Molière's physician that a patient cannot recover against the rules of art. How are we to believe that France prospered and grew rich with unequal taxation, with a diversity of customary law, with internal custom-houses, with feudal rights, with guilds, with purchased offices, &c. ? In spite of all this, France was beginning to grow rich and expand on every side, because within all this clumsy and ill-regulated machinery, which seemed calculated to check rather than to impel the social engine, two simple and powerful springs were concealed, which, already, sufficed to keep the fabric together, and to drive it along in the direction of public prosperity—a Government which was still powerful enough to maintain order throughout the kingdom, though it had ceased to be despotic ; a nation which, in its upper classes, was already the most enlightened and the most free on the continent of Europe, and in which every man could enrich himself after his own fashion and preserve the fortune he had once acquired.

The King still spoke the language of an arbitrary ruler, but in reality he himself obeyed that public opinion which inspired or influenced him day by day, and which he constantly consulted, flattered, feared ; absolute by the letter of the laws, limited by their application. As early as 1784, Necker said in a public document as a thing not disputed : 'Most foreigners are unable to form an idea of the authority now exercised in France by public opinion ; they can hardly understand what is that invisible power which makes itself obeyed even in the King's palace ; yet such is the fact.'

Nothing is more superficial than to attribute the greatness and the power of a people exclusively to the mechanism of its laws ; for, in this respect, the result is obtained not so much by the perfection of the engine as by the amount of the propelling power. Look at England, whose administrative laws still at the present day appear so much more complicated, more anomalous, more

[1] See Note LXVI., Progress of France.

irregular, than those of France![1] Yet is there a country in
Europe where the national wealth is greater, where private property is more extended, varied, and secure, or where society is
more stable and more rich ? This is not caused by the excellence
of any laws in particular, but by the spirit which pervades the
whole legislation of England. The imperfection of certain organs
matters nothing, because the whole is instinct with life.

As the prosperity, which I have just described, began to
extend in France, the community nevertheless became more unsettled and uneasy ; public discontent grew fierce ; hatred against
all established institutions increased. The nation was visibly
advancing towards a revolution.

Nay, more, those parts of France which were about to become
the chief centres of this revolution were precisely the parts of the
territory where the work of improvement was most perceptible.
An examination of what remains of the archives of the ancient
circumscription of the Ile de France readily shows that the abuses
of the monarchy had been soonest and most effectually reformed
in the immediate vicinity of Paris.[2] There, the liberty and property of the peasants were already better secured than in any
other of what were termed the *pays d'élection.* Personal forced
service had disappeared long before 1789. The *taille* was levied
with greater regularity, moderation, and fairness than in any
other part of France. The ordinance made in 1772 for the amelioration of this tax in this district is a striking proof of what an
Intendant could do for the advantage or for the misery of a whole
province. As seen through this document, the aspect of the tax
was already changed. Government commissioners were to proceed
every year to each parish ; the community was to assemble before
them ; the value of the taxable property was to be publicly established, and the resources of every tax-payer to be ascertained in his
presence ; in short, the *taille* was assessed with the assent of all
those who had to pay it. The arbitrary powers of the village
syndic, the unprofitable violence of the fiscal officers, were at an
end. The *taille* no doubt retained its inherent defects under any
system of collection : it lighted upon but one class of taxpayers,
and lay as heavy on industry as upon property ; but in all other
respects it widely differed from that which still bore the same
name in the neighbouring divisions of the territory.

Nowhere, on the contrary, were the institutions of the whole
monarchy less changed than on the banks of the Loire, near the

---

[1] See Note LXVII., Judicial Institutions of England.
[2] See Note LXVIII., Privileges of the District of Paris.

mouths of that river, in the marshes of Poitou and the heaths of
Brittany. Yet there it was that the fire of civil war was kindled
and kept alive, and that the fiercest and longest resistance was
opposed to the Revolution; so that it might be said that the
French found their position the more intolerable the better it
became. Surprising as this fact is, history is full of such contra-
dictions.

It is not always by going from bad to worse that a country
falls into a revolution. It happens most frequently that a people,
which had supported the most crushing laws without complaint,
and apparently as if they were unfelt, throws them off with violence as soon as the burden begins to be diminished. The state
of things destroyed by a revolution is almost always somewhat
better than that which immediately preceded it; and experience
has shown that the most dangerous moment for a bad government
is usually that when it enters upon the work of reform. Nothing
short of great political genius can save a sovereign who undertakes
to relieve his subjects after a long period of oppression. The evils
which were endured with patience so long as they were inevitable
seem intolerable as soon as a hope can be entertained of escaping
from them. The abuses which are removed seem to lay bare those
which remain, and to render the sense of them more acute; the
evil has decreased, it is true, but the perception of the evil is more
keen. Feudalism in all its strength had not inspired as much
aversion to the French as it did on the eve of its disappearance.
The slightest arbitrary proceedings of Louis XVI. seemed more
hard to bear than all the despotism of Louis XIV.[1] The brief
detention of Beaumarchais produced more excitement in Paris
than the Dragonnades.

No one any longer contended in 1780 that France was in a
state of decline; there seemed, on the contrary, to be just then
no bounds to her progress. Then it was that the theory of the
continual and indefinite perfectibility of man took its origin.
Twenty years before nothing was to be hoped of the future: then
nothing was to be feared. The imagination, grasping at this near
and unheard-of felicity, caused men to overlook the advantages
they already possessed, and hurried them forward to something
new.

Independently of these general reasons, there were other causes
of this phenomenon which were more peculiar and not less powerful. Although the financial administration had improved with
everything else, it still retained the vices which are inherent in

[1] See Note LXIX.

absolute government. As the financial department was secret and uncontrolled, many of the worst practices which had prevailed under Louis XIV. and Louis XV. were still followed. The very efforts which the Government made to augment the public prosperity—the relief and the rewards it distributed—the public works it caused to be executed—continually increased the expenditure without adding to the revenue in the same proportion; hence the King was continually thrown into embarrassments greater than those of his predecessors. Like them, he left his creditors unpaid; like them, he borrowed in all directions, but without publicity and without competition, and the creditors of the Crown were never sure of receiving their interest; even their capital was always at the mercy of the sovereign.

A witness worthy of credit, for he had seen these things with his own eyes and was better qualified than any other person to see them well, remarks on this subject:—' The French were exposed to nothing but risks in their relations with their own Government. If they placed their capital in the State stocks, they could never reckon with certainty on the payment of interest to a given day; if they built ships, repaired the roads, clothed the army, they had nothing to cover their advance and no certainty of repayment, so that they were reduced to calculate the chances of a Government contract as if it were a loan on terms of the utmost risk.' And the same person adds, very judiciously: ' At this time, when the rapid growth of industry had developed amongst a larger number of men the love of property and the taste and the desire of comfort, those who had entrusted a portion of their property to the State were the more impatient of a breach of contract on the part of that creditor who was especially bound to fulfil his obligations.'

The abuses which are here imputed to the French administration were not at all new; what was new was the impression they produced. The vices of the financial system had even been far more crying in former times; but changes had taken place in Government and in society which rendered them infinitely more perceptible than they were of old.

The Government, having become more active in the last twenty years, and having embarked in every species of undertaking which it had never thought of before, was at last become the greatest consumer of the produce of industry and the greatest contractor of public works in the kingdom. The number of persons who had pecuniary transactions with the State, who were interested in Government loans, lived by Government wages, or speculated in Government contracts, had prodigiously increased. Never before had the fortune of the nation and the fortunes of private persons been so much intermingled. The mismanagement of the public finances, which had long been no more than a public evil, thus became to a multitude of families a private calamity. In 1789 the State was indebted nearly 600 millions of francs to creditors who were almost all in debt themselves, and who inoculated with their own dissatisfaction against the Government all those whom the irregularity of the public Treasury caused to participate in their embarrassments. And it must be observed, that as malcontents of this class became more numerous, they also became more exasperated; for the love of speculation, the thirst for wealth, the taste for comfort, having grown and extended in proportion to the business transacted, the same evils which they might have endured thirty years before without complaint now appeared altogether insupportable.

Hence it arose that the fundholders, the traders, the manufacturers, and other persons engaged in business or in monetary affairs, who generally form the class most hostile to political innovation, the most friendly to existing governments, whatever they may be, and the most submissive to the laws even when they despise and detest them, were on this occasion the class most eager and resolute for reform. They loudly demanded a complete revolution in the whole system of finance, without reflecting that to touch this part of the Government was to cause every other part to fall.

How could such a catastrophe be averted? On the one hand, a nation in which the desire of making fortunes extended every day—on the other, a Government which incessantly excited this passion, which agitated, inflamed, and beggared the nation, driving by either path on its own destruction.

CHAPTER XVII.

SHOWING THAT THE FRENCH PEOPLE WERE EXCITED TO REVOLT BY THE MEANS TAKEN TO RELIEVE THEM.

As the common people of France had not appeared for one single moment on the theatre of public affairs for upwards of one hundred and forty years, no one any longer imagined that they could ever again resume their position. They appeared unconscious, and were therefore believed to be deaf; accordingly, those who began to take an interest in their condition talked about them in their presence just as if they had not been there. It seemed as if these remarks could only be heard by those who were placed above the common people, and that the only danger to be apprehended was that they might not be fully understood by the upper classes.

The very men who had most to fear from the fury of the people declaimed loudly in their presence on the cruel injustice under which the people had always suffered. They pointed out to each other the monstrous vices of those institutions which had weighed most heavily upon the lower orders: they employed all their powers of rhetoric in depicting the miseries of the common people and their ill-paid labour; and thus they infuriated while they endeavoured to relieve them. I do not speak of the writers, but of the Government, of its chief agents, and of those belonging to the privileged class itself.

When the King, thirteen years before the Revolution, tried to abolish the use of compulsory labour, he said, in the preamble to this decree, 'With the exception of a small number of provinces (the *pays d'état*), almost all the roads throughout the kingdom have been made by the gratuitous labour of the poorest part of our subjects. Thus the whole burden has fallen on those who possess nothing but their hands, and who are interested only in a secondary degree in the existence of roads; those really interested are the landowners, nearly all privileged persons, whose estates are increased in value by the construction of roads. By forcing the poor to keep them up unaided, and by compelling them to give their time and labour without remuneration, they are deprived of their sole resource against want and hunger, because they are made to labour for the profit of the rich.'

When, at the same period, an attempt was made to abolish the restrictions which the system of trading companies or guilds imposed on artisans, it was proclaimed, in the King's name, 'that the right to work is the most sacred of all possessions; that every law by which it is infringed violates the natural rights of man, and is null and void in itself; that the existing corporations are moreover grotesque and tyrannical institutions, the result of selfishness, avarice, and violence.' Such words as these were dangerous, no doubt, but, what was infinitely more so, was that they were spoken in vain. A few months later the corporations and the system of compulsory labour were again established.

It is said that Turgot was the Minister who put this language into the King's mouth, but most of Turgot's successors made him hold no other. When, in 1780, the King announced to his subjects that the increase of the *taille* would, for the future, be subject to public registration, he took care to add, by way of commentary, 'Those persons who are subject to the *taille*, besides being harassed by the vexations incident to its collection, have likewise hitherto been exposed to unexpected augmentations of the tax, insomuch that the contributions paid by the poorest part of our subjects have increased in a much greater proportion than those paid by all the rest.' When the King, not yet venturing to place all the public burdens on an equal footing, attempted at least to establish equality of taxation in those which were already imposed on the middle class, he said, 'His Majesty hopes that rich persons will not consider themselves aggrieved by being placed on the common level, and made to bear their part of a burden which they ought long since to have shared more equally.'

But it was, above all, at periods of scarcity that nothing was left untried to inflame the passions of the people far more than to provide for their wants. In order to stimulate the charity of the rich, one Intendant talked of 'the injustice and insensibility of those landowners who owe all they possess to the labours of the poor, and who let them die of hunger at the very moment they are toiling to augment the returns of landed property.' The King, too, thus expressed himself on a similar occasion: 'His Majesty is determined to defend the people against manœuvres which expose them to the want of the most needful food, by forcing them to give their labour at any price that the rich choose to bestow. The King will not suffer one part of his subjects to be sacrificed to the avidity of the other.'

Until the very end of the monarchy the strife which subsisted among the different administrative powers gave occasion for all sorts of demonstrations of this kind; the contending parties readily imputed to each other the miseries of the people. A strong instance of this appeared in the quarrel which arose, in 1772, between the Parliament of Toulouse and the King, with reference to the transport of grain. 'The Government, by its bad measures, places the poor in danger of dying of hunger,' said the Parliament. 'The ambition of the Parliament and the avidity of the rich are the cause of the general distress,' retorted the King. Thus both the parties were endeavouring to impress the minds of the common people with the belief that their superiors are always to blame for their sufferings.

These things are not contained in the secret correspondence of the time, but in public documents which the Government and the Parliaments themselves took care to have printed and published by thousands. The King took occasion incidentally to tell very harsh truths both to his predecessors and to himself. 'The treasure of the State,' said he on one occasion, 'has been burdened by the lavish expenditure of several successive reigns. Many of our inalienable domains have been granted on leases at nominal rents.' On another occasion he was made to say, with more truth than prudence, 'The privileged trading companies mainly owed their origin to the fiscal avidity of the Crown.' Farther on, he remarked that 'if useless expenses have often been incurred, and if the *taille* has increased beyond all bounds, it has been because the Board of Finance found an increase of the *taille* the easiest resource inasmuch as it was clandestine, and was therefore employed, although many other expedients would have been less burdensome to our people.'[1]

All this was addressed to the enlightened part of the nation, in order to convince it of the utility of certain measures which private interests rendered unpopular. As for the common people, it was assumed that if they listened they did not understand.

It must be admitted that at the bottom of all these charitable feelings there remained a strong bias of contempt for these wretched beings whose miseries the higher classes so sincerely wished to relieve: and that we are somewhat reminded, by this display of compassion, of the notion of Madame Duchâtelet, who, as Voltaire's secretary tells us, did not scruple to undress herself before her attendants, not thinking it by any means proved that lackeys are men. And let it not be supposed that Louis XVI.

---

[1] See Note LXX., Arbitrary Augmentation of Taxes.

or his ministers were the only persons who held the dangerous
language which I have just cited; the privileged persons, who
were about to become the first objects of the popular fury, expressed
themselves in exactly the same manner before their inferiors. It
must be admitted that in France the higher classes of society had
begun to pay attention to the condition of the poor before they
had any reason to fear them; they interested themselves in their
fate at a time when they had not begun to believe that the sufferings of the poor were the precursors of their own perdition. This
was peculiarly visible in the ten years which preceded 1789; the
peasants were the constant objects of compassion, their condition
was continually discussed, the means of affording them relief were
examined, the chief abuses from which they suffered were exposed,
and the fiscal laws which pressed most heavily upon them were
condemned; but the manner in which this new-born sympathy
was expressed was as imprudent as the long-continued insensibility
which had preceded it.

If we read the reports of the Provincial Assemblies which met
in some parts of France in 1779, and subsequently throughout the
kingdom, and if we study the other public records left by them,
we shall be touched by the generous sentiments expressed in
them, and astonished at the wonderful imprudence of the language
in which they are expressed.

The Provincial Assembly of Lower Normandy said, in 1787,
'We have too frequently seen the money destined by the King for
roads serve only to increase the prosperity of the rich without any
benefit to the people. It has often been employed to embellish
the approach to a country mansion instead of making a more convenient entrance to a town or village.' In the same assembly the
Orders of nobility and clergy, after describing the abuses of compulsory labour, spontaneously offered to contribute out of their
own funds 50,000 livres towards the improvement of the roads, in
order, as they said, that the roads of the province might be made
practicable without any further cost to the people. It would probably have cost these privileged classes less to abolish the compulsory system, and to substitute for it a general tax of which they
should pay their quota; but though willing to give up the profit
derived from inequality of taxation, they liked to maintain the
appearance of the privilege. While they gave up that part of their
rights which was profitable, they carefully retained that which was
odious.

Other assemblies, composed entirely of landowners exempt
from the *taille*, and who fully intended to continue so, nevertheless

depicted in the darkest colours the hardships which the *taille* inflicted on the poor. They drew a frightful picture of all its abuses, which they circulated in all directions. But the most singular part of the affair is that to these strong marks of the interest they felt in the common people, they from time to time added public expressions of contempt for them. The people had already become the object of their sympathy without having ceased to be the object of their disdain.

The Provincial Assembly of Upper Guienne, speaking of the peasants whose cause they so warmly pleaded, called them *coarse and ignorant creatures, turbulent spirits, and rough and intractable characters.* Turgot, who did so much for the people, seldom spoke of them otherwise.[1]

These harsh expressions were used in acts intended for the greatest publicity, and meant to meet the eyes of the peasants themselves. It seemed as though the framers of them imagined that they were living in a country like Galicia, where the higher classes speak a different language from the lower, and cannot be understood by them. The feudalists of the eighteenth century, who frequently displayed towards the ratepayers and others who owed them feudal services, a disposition to indulgence, moderation, and justice, unknown to their predecessors, still spoke occasionally of ‘vile peasants.’ These insults seem to have been ‘in proper form,’ as the lawyers say.

The nearer we approach towards 1789, the more lively and imprudent does this sympathy with the hardships of the common people become. I have held in my hands the circulars addressed by several Provincial Assemblies in the very beginning of 1788 to the inhabitants of the different parishes, calling upon them to state in detail all the grievances of which they might have to complain.

One of these circulars is signed by an abbé, a great lord, three nobles, and a man of the middle class, all members of the Assembly, and acting in its name. This committee directed the Syndic of each parish to convoke all the peasants, and to inquire of them what they had to say against the manner in which the various taxes which they paid were assessed and collected. ‘We are generally aware,’ they say, ‘that most of the taxes, especially the *gabelle* and the *taille*, have disastrous consequences for the cultivators, but we are anxious to be acquainted with every single abuse.’ The curiosity of the Provincial Assembly did not stop there; it investigated the number of persons in the parish enjoying any privileges

[1] See Note LXXI., Manner in which Turgot spoke of the Country People.

with respect to taxes, whether nobles, ecclesiastics, or *roturiers*, and the precise nature of these privileges; the value of the property of those thus exempted; whether or not they resided on their estates; whether there was much Church property, or, as the phrase then was, land in mortmain, which was out of the market, and its value. All this even was not enough to satisfy them; they wanted to be told the share of duties, *taille*, additional dues, poll-tax, and forced labour-rate which the privileged class would have to pay, supposing equality of taxation existed.

This was to inflame every man individually by the catalogue of his own grievances; it pointed out to him the authors of his wrongs, emboldened him by showing him how few they were in number, and fired his heart with cupidity, envy, and hatred. It seemed as if the Jacquerie, the Maillotins, and the Sixteen were totally forgotten, and that no one was aware that the French people, which is the quietest and most kindly disposed in the world, so long as it remains in its natural frame of mind, becomes the most barbarous as soon as it is roused by violent passions.

Unfortunately I have not been able to procure all the returns sent in by the peasants in reply to these fatal questions; but I have found enough to show the general spirit which pervaded them.

In these reports the name of every privileged person, whether of the nobility or the middle class, is carefully mentioned; his mode of life is frequently described, and always in an unfavourable manner. The value of his property is curiously examined; the number and extent of his privileges are insisted on at length, and especially the injury they do to all the other inhabitants of the village. The bushels of corn which have to be paid to him as dues are reckoned up; his income is calculated in an envious tone—an income by which no one profits, they say. The casual dues of the parish priest—his stipend, as it was already called—are pronounced to be excessive; it is remarked with bitterness that everything at church must be paid for, and that a poor man cannot even get buried gratis. As to the taxes, they are all unfairly assessed and oppressive; not one of them finds favour, and they are all spoken of in a tone of violence which betrays exasperation.

'The indirect taxes are detestable,' they say; 'there is not a household in which the clerk of the excise does not come and search, nothing is sacred from his eyes and hands. The registration dues are crushing. The collector of the *taille* is a tyrant, whose rapacity leads him to avail himself of every means of harassing the poor. The bailiffs are no better; no honest farmer

can be secure from their ferocity. The collectors are forced to
ruin their neighbours in order to avoid exposing themselves to the
voracity of these despots.'

The Revolution not only announces its approach in this inquiry ;
it is already there, speaking its own proper language and showing
its face without disguise.

Amid all the differences which exist between the religious
Revolution of the sixteenth century and the French Revolution of
the eighteenth, one contrast is peculiarly striking : in the sixteenth
century most of the great nobles changed their religion from
motives of ambition or cupidity ; the people, on the contrary, from
conviction and without any hope of profit. In the eighteenth
century the reverse was the case; disinterested convictions and
generous sympathies then agitated the enlightened classes and
incited them to revolution, while a bitter feeling of their wrongs
and an ardent desire to alter their position excited the common
people. The enthusiasm of the former put the last stroke to
inflaming and arming the rage and the desires of the latter.

CHAPTER XVIII.

CONCERNING SOME PRACTICES BY WHICH THE GOVERNMENT COM-
PLETED THE REVOLUTIONARY EDUCATION OF THE PEOPLE OF
FRANCE.

THE Government itself had long been at work to instil into and
rivet upon the mind of the common people many of the ideas which
have been called revolutionary—ideas hostile to individual liberty,
opposed to private rights, and favourable to violence.

The King was the first to show with how much contempt it
was possible to treat the most ancient, and apparently the best
established, institutions. Louis XV. shook the monarchy and
hastened the Revolution quite as much by his innovations as by his
vices, by his energy as by his indolence. When the people beheld
the fall and disappearance of a Parliament almost contemporary
with the monarchy itself, and which had until then seemed as
immovable as the throne, they vaguely perceived that they were
drawing near a time of violence and of chance when everything
may become possible, when nothing, however ancient, is respected,
and nothing, however new, may not be tried.

During the whole course of his reign Louis XVI. did nothing
but talk of reforms to be accomplished. There are few institutions
of which he did not foreshadow the approaching ruin, before the
Revolution came to effect it. After removing from the statute-book
some of the worst of these institutions he very soon replaced them ;
it seemed as if he wanted only to loosen their roots, leaving to
others the task of striking them down. By some of the reforms
which he effected himself, ancient and venerable customs were suddenly changed without sufficient preparation, and established rights
were occasionally violated. These reforms prepared the way for the
Revolution, not so much by overthrowing the obstacles in its way,
as by showing the people how to set about making it. The evil
was increased by the very purity and disinterestedness of the intentions which actuated the King and his ministers; for no example
is more dangerous than that of violence exerted for a good purpose
by honest and well-meaning men.

At a much earlier period Louis XIV. had publicly broached in his edicts the theory that all the land throughout the kingdom had originally been granted conditionally by the State, which was thus declared to be the only true landowner, and that all others were possessors whose titles might be contested, and whose rights were imperfect. This doctrine had arisen out of the feudal system of legislation; but it was not proclaimed in France until feudalism was dying out, and was never adopted by the Courts of justice. It is, in fact, the germ of modern socialism, and it is curious enough to see it first springing up under royal despotism.

During the reigns which followed that of Louis XIV., the administration day by day instilled into the people in a manner still more practical and comprehensible the contempt in which private property was to be held. When during the latter half of the eighteenth century the taste for public works, especially for roads, began to prevail, the Government did not scruple to seize all the land needed for its undertakings, and to pull down the houses which stood in the way. The French Board of Works was already just as enamoured of the geometrical beauty of straight lines as it has been ever since; it carefully avoided following the existing roads if they were at all crooked, and rather than make the slightest deviation it cut through innumerable estates. The ground thus damaged or destroyed was never paid for but at an arbitrary rate and after long delay, or frequently not at all.[1]

When the Provincial Assembly of Lower Normandy took the administration out of the hands of the Intendant, it was discovered that the price of all the land seized by authority in the preceding twenty years for making roads was still unpaid. The debt thus contracted by the State, and not discharged, in this small corner of France, amounted to 250,000 livres. The number of large pro-prietors thus injured was limited; but the small ones who suffered were very numerous, for even then the land was much subdivided.[2] Every one of these persons had learnt by his own experience how little respect the rights of an individual can claim when the interest of the public requires that they should be invaded—a doc-trine which he was not likely to forget when the time came for applying it to others for his own advantage.

In a great number of parishes charitable endowments had formerly existed, destined by their founders to relieve the inhabit-ants in certain cases, and in conformity to testamentary bequest. Most of these endowments were destroyed during the later days of

[1] See Note LXXII., Growth of Revolutionary Opinions under the Old Monarchy.
[2] See Note LXXIII.

the monarchy, or diverted from their original objects by mere
Orders in Council, that is to say, by the arbitrary act of Government.   In most instances the funds thus left to particular villages
were taken from them for the benefit of neighbouring hospitals. At
the same time the property of these hospitals was in its turn
diverted to purposes which the founder had never had in view, and
would undoubtedly not have approved.   An edict of 1780 authorised all these establishments to sell the lands which had been
devised to them at various times to be held by them for ever, and
permitted them to hand over the purchase-money to the State,
which was to pay the interest upon it. This, they said, was making
a better use of the charity of their forefathers than they had done
themselves.   They forgot that the surest way of teaching mankind
to violate the rights of the living is to pay no regard to the will of
the dead.   The contempt displayed by the Administration of the
old French monarchy for testamentary dispositions has never been
surpassed by any succeeding power. Nothing could be more unlike
the scrupulous anxiety which leads the English to invest every
individual citizen with the force of the whole social body in order
to assist him in maintaining the effect of his last dispositions, and
which induces them to pay even more respect to his memory than
to himself.

Compulsory requisitions, the forced sale of provisions, and the
maximum, are measures not without their precedents under the old
monarchy.   I have discovered instances in which the officers of
Government, during periods of scarcity, fixed beforehand the price
of the provisions which the peasants brought to market; and
when the latter stayed away from fear of this constraint, ordinances were promulgated to compel them to come under penalty
of a fine.

But nothing taught a more pernicious lesson than some of the
forms adopted by criminal justice when the common people were
in question.   The poor were even then far better protected than
has generally been supposed against the aggressions of any citizen
richer or more powerful than themselves; but when they had to do
with the State, they found only, as I have already described,
exceptional tribunals, prejudiced judges, a hasty and illusory procedure, and a sentence executed summarily and without appeal.
'The Provost of the Constables and his lieutenant are to take
cognisance of the disturbances and gatherings which may be
occasioned by the scarcity of corn; the prosecution is to take place
in due form, and judgment to be passed by the Provost, and without appeal.   His Majesty inhibits the jurisdiction of all courts of

justice in these cases.' We learn by the Reports of the Constables, that on these occasions suspected villages were surrounded during the night, that houses were entered before daybreak, and peasants who had been denounced were arrested without further warrant. A man thus arrested frequently remained for a long time in prison before he could speak to his judge, although the edicts directed that every accused person should be examined within four-and-twenty hours. This regulation was as precise and as little respected then as it is now.

By these means a mild and stable government daily taught the people the code of criminal procedure most appropriate to a period of revolution, and best adapted to arbitrary power. These lessons were constantly before their eyes ; and to the very last the old monarchy gave the lower classes this dangerous education. Even Turgot himself, in this respect, faithfully imitated his predecessors. When, in 1775, his change in the corn-laws occasioned resistance in the Parliament and disturbances in the rural districts, he obtained a Royal ordonnance transferring the mutineers from the jurisdiction of the tribunals to that of the Provost-Marshal, 'which is chiefly destined,' so the phrase runs, ' to repress popular tumults when it. is desirable that examples should be quickly made.' Nay, worse than this, every peasant leaving his parish without being provided with a certificate signed by the parish priest and by the Syndic, was to be prosecuted, arrested, and tried before the Provost-Marshal as a vagabond.

It is true that under this monarchy of the eighteenth century, though the forms of procedure were terrific, the punishment was almost always light. The object was to inspire fear rather than to inflict pain; or rather, perhaps, those in power were violent and arbitrary from habit or from indifference, and mild by temperament. But this only increased the taste for this summary kind of justice. The lighter the penalty the more readily was the manner forgotten in which it had been pronounced. The mildness of the sentence served to veil the horror of the mode of procedure.

I may venture to affirm, from the facts I have in my possession, that a great number of the proceedings adopted by the Revolutionary Government had precedents and examples in the measures taken with regard to the common people during the last two centuries of the monarchy. The monarchy gave to the Revolution many of its forms ; the latter only added to them the atrocity of its own spirit.

CHAPTER XIX.

NOTHING had yet been changed in the form of the French Government, but already the greater part of the secondary laws which regulated the condition of persons and the administration of affairs had been abolished or modified.

The destruction of the Guilds, followed by their partial and incomplete restoration, had totally changed all the old relations between workmen and their employers. These relations had become not only different, but uncertain and difficult. The police of the masters was at an end; the authority of the State over the trades was imperfectly established; and the artisan, placed in a constrained and undecided position between the Government and his employer, did not know to whom he was to look for protection, or from whom he was to submit to restraint. This state of discontent and anarchy, into which the whole lower class of the towns had been plunged at one blow, produced very great consequences as soon as the people began to reappear on the political stage.

One year before the Revolution a Royal edict had disturbed the order of the administration of justice in all its parts; several new jurisdictions had been created, a multitude of others abolished, and all the rules of judicial competence changed. Now in France, as I have already shown, the number of persons engaged in administering justice and in executing the sentences of the law was enormous. In fact, it may be said that the whole of the middle class was more or less connected with the tribunals. The effect of this law, therefore, was to unsettle the station and property of thousands of families, and to place them in a new and precarious position. The edict was little less inconvenient to litigants, who found it difficult, in the midst of this judicial revolution, to discover what laws were applicable to their cases, and by what tribunals they were to be decided.

But it was the radical reform which the Administration, properly so called, underwent in 1787, which more than all the rest first threw public affairs into disorder, and shook the private existence of every individual citizen.

I have already mentioned that in what were termed the *pays d'élection*, that is to say, in about three-quarters of France, the whole administration of each district was abandoned to one man, the Intendant, who acted not only without control, but without advice.

In 1787, in addition to the Intendant, a Provincial Assembly was created, which assumed the real administration of the country. In each village an elective municipal body likewise took the place of the ancient parochial assemblies, and in most cases of the Syndic.

A state of the law so opposed to that which had preceded it, and which so completely changed not only the whole course of affairs, but the relative position of persons, was applied in all places at the same moment and almost in the same manner, without the slightest regard to previous usages or to the peculiar situation of each province, so fully had the passion for unity which characterised the Revolution taken possession of the ancient Government, which the Revolution was about to destroy.

These changes served to display the force of habit in the action of political institutions, and to show how much easier it is to deal with obscure and complicated laws, which have long been in use, than with a totally new system of legislation, however simple.

Under the old French monarchy there existed all sorts of authorities, which varied almost infinitely, according to the provinces; but as none of these authorities had any fixed or definite limits, the field of action of each of them was always common to several others besides. Nevertheless, affairs had come to be transacted with a certain regularity and convenience; whereas the newly established authorities, which were fewer in number, carefully circumscribed, and exactly similar, instantly conflicted and became entangled in hopeless confusion, frequently reducing each other mutually to impotence.

Moreover the new law had one great vice which in itself would have sufficed, especially at first, to render it difficult of execution: all the powers it created were collective [1] or corporate.

Under the old monarchy there had been only two methods of administration. Where the administration was entrusted to one man, he acted without the assistance of any assembly; wherever

[1] See Note LXXIV.

assemblies existed, as in the *pays d'état* or in the towns, the executive power was not vested in any particular person; the Assembly not only governed and superintended the administration, but administered itself, or by means of temporary commissions which it appointed.

As these were the only two modes of operation which were then understood, when one was given up the other was adopted. It is strange that in the midst of a community so enlightened, and where the administration of the Government had long played so prominent a part, no one ever thought of uniting the two systems and of drawing a distinction, without making a separation, between the power which has to execute and that which superintends and directs. This idea, which appears so simple, never occurred to any one; it was not discovered until the present century, and may be said to be the only great invention in the field of public administration which we can claim. We shall see hereafter the results of the contrary practice when these administrative habits were transferred to political life, and when, in obedience to the traditions of the old institutions of the monarchy, hated as they were, the system which had been followed by the provincial estates and the small municipalities of the towns was applied in the National Convention; and the causes which had formerly occasioned a certain embarrassment in the transaction of business suddenly engendered the Reign of Terror.

The Provincial Assemblies of 1787 were invested with the right of governing themselves in most of the cases in which, until then, the Intendant had acted alone; they were charged, under the authority of the Central Government, with the assessment of the *taille* and with the superintendence of its collection—with the power of deciding what public works were to be undertaken, and with their execution. All the persons employed in public works, from the inspector down to the driver of the road-gang, were under their control. They were to order what they thought proper, to render an account of the services performed to the Minister, and to suggest to him the fitting remuneration. The parochial trusts were almost entirely placed under the direction of these assemblies; they were to decide, in the first instance, most of the litigated matters which had until then been tried before the Intendant. Many of these functions were unsuitable for a collective and irresponsible body, and moreover they were to be performed by men who were now, for the first time, to take a part in the administration.

The confusion was made complete by depriving the Intendant

of all power, though his office was not suppressed. After taking from him the absolute right of doing everything, he was charged with the task of assisting and superintending all that was to be done by the Assembly ; as if it were possible for a degraded public officer to enter into the spirit of the law by which he has been dispossessed and to assist its operation.

That which had been done to the Intendant was now extended to his Sub-delegate. By his side, and in the place which he had formerly occupied, was placed a District Assembly, which was to act under the direction of the Provincial Assembly, and upon analogous principles.

All that we know of the acts of the Provincial Assemblies of 1787,[1] and even their own reports, show that as soon as they were created they engaged in covert hostilities and often in open war with the Intendants, who made use of their superior experience only to embarrass the movements of their successors. Here an Assembly complained that it was only with difficulty that it could extract the most necessary documents from the hands of the Intendant. There an Intendant accused the members of the Assembly of endeavouring to usurp functions, which, as he said, the edicts had still left to himself. He appealed to the Minister, who often returned no answer, or merely expressed doubts, for the subject was as new and as obscure to him as to every one else. Sometimes the Assembly resolved that the Intendant had administered badly, that the roads which he had caused to be made were ill planned or ill kept up, and that the corporate bodies under his trust have gone to ruin. Frequently these assemblies hesitated in the obscurity of laws so imperfectly known ; they sent great distances to consult one another, and constantly sent each other advice. The Intendant of Auch asserted that he had the right to oppose the will of the Provincial Assembly which had authorised a parish to tax itself; the Assembly maintained that this was a subject on which the Intendant could not longer give orders, but only advice, and it asks the Assembly of the Ile de France for its opinion.

Amidst all these recriminations and consultations the course of administration was impeded and often altogether stopped; the vital functions of the country seemed almost suspended. ' The stagnation of affairs is complete,' says the Provincial Assembly of Lorraine, which in this was only the echo of several others, ' and all good citizens are grieved at it.'

On other occasions these new governing bodies erred on the

---

[1] See Note LXXV., Contests in the Provincial Assemblies of 1787.

side of over-activity and excessive self-confidence; they were
filled with a restless and uneasy zeal, which led them to seek to
change all the old methods suddenly, and hastily to reform all the
most ancient abuses. Under the pretext that henceforth they
were to be the guardians of the towns, they assumed the control
of municipal affairs; in a word, they put the finishing stroke to
the general confusion by aiming at universal improvement.

Now, when we consider what an immense space the administrative powers of the State had so long filled in France, the numerous
interests which were daily affected by them, and all that depended
upon them or stood in need of their co-operation; when we reflect
that it was to the Government rather than to themselves that
private persons looked for the success of their own affairs, for the
encouragement of their manufactures, to ensure their means of
subsistence, to lay out and keep up their roads, to maintain their
tranquillity, and to preserve their wealth, we shall have some idea
of the infinite number of people who were personally injured by the
evils from which the administration of the kingdom was suffering.

But it was in the villages that the defects of the new organisation were most strongly felt; in them it not only disturbed the
course of authority, it likewise suddenly changed the relative
position of society, and brought every class into collision.

When, in 1775, Turgot proposed to the King to reform the
administration of the rural districts, the greatest difficulty he
encountered, as he himself informs us, arose from the unequal
incidence of taxation: for how was it possible to make men who
were not all liable to contribute in the same manner, and some of
whom were altogether exempt from taxation, act and deliberate
together on parochial affairs relating chiefly to the assessment and
the collection of those very taxes and the purposes to which they
were to be applied? Every parish contained nobles and the clergy
who did not pay the *taille*, peasants who were partially or wholly
exempt, and others who paid it all. It was as three distinct
parishes, each of which would have demanded a separate administration. The difficulty was insoluble.

Nowhere, indeed, was the inequality of taxation more apparent
than in the rural districts; nowhere was the population more
effectually divided into different groups frequently hostile to one
another. In order to make it possible to give to the villages a
collective administration and a free government on a small scale,
it would have been necessary to begin by subjecting all the
inhabitants to an equal taxation and lessening the distance by
which the classes were divided.

This was not, however, the course taken when the reform was begun in 1787. Within each parish the ancient distinction of classes was maintained, together with the inequality of taxation, which was its principal token, but, nevertheless, the whole administration was placed in the hands of elective bodies. This instantly led to very singular results.

When the electoral assembly met in order to choose municipal officers, the Curé and the Seigneur were not to appear; they belonged, it was alleged, to the orders of the nobility and the clergy, and this was an occasion on which the commonalty had principally to choose its representatives.

When, however, the municipal body was once elected, the Curé and the Seigneur were members of it by right; for it would not have been decent altogether to exclude two such considerable inhabitants from the government of the parish. The Seigneur even presided over the parochial representatives in whose election he had taken no part, but in most of their proceedings he had no voice. For instance, when the assessment and division of the *taille* were discussed, the Curé and the Seigneur were not allowed to vote, for were they not both exempt from this tax? On the other hand, the municipal council had nothing to do with their capitation-tax, which continued to be regulated by the Intendant according to peculiar forms.

For fear that this President, isolated as he was from the body which he was supposed to direct, should still exert an indirect influence prejudicial to the interests of the Order to which he did not belong, it was demanded that the votes of his own tenants should not count; and the Provincial Assemblies, being consulted on this point, gave it as their opinion that this omission was proper, and entirely conformable to principle. Other persons of noble birth, who might be inhabitants of the parish, could not sit in the same plebeian corporation unless they were elected by the peasants and then, as the by-laws carefully pointed out, they were only entitled to represent the lower classes.

The Seigneur, therefore, only figured in this Assembly in a position of absolute subjection to his former vassals, who were all at once become his masters; he was their prisoner rather than their chief. In gathering men together by such means as these, it seemed as if the object was not so much to connect them more closely with each other as to render more palpable the differences of their condition and the incompatibility of their interests.

Was or was not the village Syndic still that discredited officer whose duties no one would accept but upon compulsion, or was the condition of the Syndic raised with that of the community to which he belonged as its chief agent?[1] Even this question was not easily answered. I have found the letter of a village bailiff, written in 1788, in which he expresses his indignation at having been elected to the office of Syndic, 'which was,' he said, 'contrary to all the privileges of his other post.' To this the Comptroller-General replies that this individual must be set right : that he must be made to understand that he ought to be proud of the choice of his fellow-citizens; and that moreover the new Syndics were not to resemble the local officers who had formerly borne the same appellation, and that they would be treated with more consideration by the Government.

On the other hand some of the chief inhabitants of parishes, and even men of rank, began at once to draw nearer to the peasantry, as soon as the peasantry had become a power in the State. A landed proprietor exercising a heritable jurisdiction over a village near Paris complained that the King's Edict debarred him from taking part, even as a mere inhabitant, in the proceedings of the Parochial Assembly. Others consented, from mere public spirit, as they said, to accept even the office of Syndic.

It was too late: but as the members of the higher classes of society in France thus began to approach the rural population and sought to combine with the people, the people drew back into the isolation to which it had been condemned and maintained that position. Some parochial assemblies refused to allow the Seigneur of the place to take his seat among them; others practised every kind of trick to evade the reception of persons as low-born as themselves, but who were rich. 'We are informed,' said the Provincial Assembly of Lower Normandy, 'that several municipal bodies have refused to receive among their members landowners not being noble and not domiciled in the parish, though these persons have an undoubted right to sit in such meetings. Some other bodies have even refused to admit farmers not having any property in land in the parish.'

Thus then the whole reform of these secondary enactments was already novel, obscure, and conflicting before the principal laws affecting the government of the State had yet been touched at all. But all that was still untouched was already shaken, and it could barely be said that any law was in existence which had not already been threatened with abolition or a speedy change by the Central Government itself.

This sudden and comprehensive renovation of all the laws and

[1] See Note LXXVI.

all the administrative habits of France, which preceded the political Revolution of 1789, is a thing scarcely thought of at the present time, yet it was one of the severest perturbations which ever occurred in the history of a great people. This first revolution exercised a prodigious influence on the Revolution which was about to succeed it, and caused the latter to be an event different from all the events of the same kind which had ever till then happened in the world and from those which have happened since.[1]

The first English Revolution, which overthrew the whole political constitution of the country and abolished the monarchy itself, touched but superficially the secondary laws of the land and changed scarcely any of the customs and usages of the nation. . The administration of justice and the conduct of public business retained their old forms and followed even their past aberrations. In the heat of the Civil Wars the twelve judges of England are said to have continued to go the circuit twice a year. Everything was not, therefore, abandoned to agitation at the same time. The Revolution was circumscribed in its effects, and English society, though shaken at its apex, remained firm upon its base.

France herself has since 1789 witnessed several revolutions which have fundamentally changed the whole structure of her government. Most of them have been very sudden and brought about by force, in open violation of the existing laws. Yet the disorder they have caused has never been either long or general; scarcely have they been felt by the bulk of the nation, sometimes they have been unperceived.

The reason is that since 1789 the administrative constitution of France has ever remained standing amidst the ruins of her political constitutions. The person of the sovereign or the form of the government was changed, but the daily course of affairs was neither interrupted nor disturbed: every man still remained submissive, in the small concerns which interested himself, to the rules and usages with which he was already familiar; he was dependent on the secondary powers to which it had always been his custom to defer; and in most cases he had still to do with the very same agents; for, if at each revolution the administration was decapitated, its trunk still remained unmutilated and alive; the same public duties were discharged by the same public officers, who carried with them through all the vicissitudes of political legislation the same temper and the same practice. They judged and they administered in the name of the King, after-

---

[1] See Note LXXVII., Definition of Feudal Rights.

wards in the name of the Republic, at last in the name of the Emperor. And when Fortune had again given the same turn to her wheel, they began once more to judge and to administer for the King, for the Republic, and for the Emperor, the same persons doing the same thing, for what is there in the name of a master? Their business was not so much to be good citizens as to be good administrators and good judicial officers. As soon as the first shock was over, it seemed, therefore, as if nothing had stirred in the country.

But when the Revolution of 1789 broke out, that part of the Government which, though subordinate, makes itself daily felt by every member of the commonwealth, and which affects his well-being more constantly and decisively than anything else, had just been totally subverted : the administrative offices of France had just changed all their agents and revised all their principles. The State had not at first appeared to receive a violent shock from this immense reform ; but there was not a man in the country who had not felt it in his own particular sphere. Every one had been shaken in his condition, disturbed in his habits, or put to inconvenience in his calling. A certain order still prevailed in the more important and general affairs of the nation ; but already no one knew whom to obey, whom to apply to, nor how to proceed in those lesser and private affairs which form the staple of social life. The nation having lost its balance in all these details, one more blow sufficed to upset it altogether, and to produce the widest catastrophe and the most frightful confusion that the world had ever beheld.

CHAPTER XX.

SHOWING THAT THE REVOLUTION PROCEEDED NATURALLY FROM THE EXISTING STATE OF FRANCE.

I PROPOSE ere I conclude to gather up some of the characteristics which I have already separately described, and to trace the Revolution, proceeding as it were of itself from the state of society in France which I have already pourtrayed.

If it be remembered that in France the Feudal system, though it still kept unchanged all that could irritate or could injure, had most effectually lost all that could protect or could be of use, it will appear less surprising that the Revolution, which was about virtually to abolish this ancient constitution of Europe, broke forth in France rather than elsewhere.

If it be observed that the French nobility, after having lost its ancient political rights, and ceased more than in any other country of feudal Europe to govern and guide the nation, had, nevertheless, not only preserved, but considerably enlarged its pecuniary immunities, and the advantages which the members of this body personally possessed; that whilst it had become a subordinate class it still remained a privileged and close body, less and less an aristocracy, as I have said elsewhere, but more and more a caste; it will be no cause of surprise that the privileges of such a nobility had become so inexplicable and so abhorrent to the French people, as to inflame the envy of the democracy to so fierce a pitch that it is still burning in their hearts.

If, lastly, it be borne in mind that the French nobility, severed from the middle classes whom they had repelled, and from the people whose affections they had lost, was thus alone in the midst of the nation—apparently the head of an army, but in reality a body of officers without soldiers—it will be understood how that which had stood erect for a thousand years came to perish in a night.

I have shown how the King's Government, having abolished the franchises of the provinces, and having usurped all local powers in three-quarters of the territory of France, had thus drawn all public affairs into its own hands, the least as well as the greatest. I have shown, on the other hand, how, by a necessary consequence, Paris had made itself the master of the kingdom of which till then it had been the capital, or rather had itself become the entire country. These two facts, which were peculiar to France, would alone suffice, if necessary, to explain why a riot could fundamentally destroy a monarchy which had for ages endured so many violent convulsions; and which, on the eve of its dissolution, still seemed unassailable even to those who were about to overthrow it.

France being one of the states of Europe in which all political life had been for the longest time and most effectually extinguished, in which private persons had most lost the usage of business, the habit of reading the course of events, the experience of popular movements and almost the notion of the people, it may readily be imagined how all Frenchmen came at once to fall into a frightful Revolution without foreseeing it; those who were most threatened by that catastrophe leading the way, and undertaking to open and widen the path which led to it.

As there were no longer any free institutions, or consequently any political classes, no living political bodies, no organised or disciplined parties, and as, in the absence of all these regular forces, the direction of public opinion, when public opinion came again into being, devolved exclusively on the French philosophers, it might be expected that the Revolution would be directed less with a view to a particular state of facts, than with reference to abstract principles and very general theories: it might be anticipated that instead of endeavouring separately to amend the laws which were bad, all laws would be attacked, and that an attempt would be made to substitute for the ancient constitution of France an entirely novel system of government, conceived by these writers.

The Church being naturally connected with all the old institutions which were doomed to perish, it could not be doubted that the Revolution would shake the religion of the country when it overthrew the civil government; wherefore it was impossible to foretell to what pitch of extravagance these innovators might rush, delivered at once from all the restraints which religion, custom, and law impose on the imagination of mankind.

He who should thus have studied the state of France would easily have foreseen that no stretch of audacity was too extreme to be attempted there, and no act of violence too great to be endured. 'What,' said Burke, in one of his eloquent pamphlets, 'is there not a man who can answer for the smallest district—nay, more, not one man who can answer for another? Every one is arrested in his own home without resistance, whether he be accused of royalism, of *moderantism*, or of anything else.' But Mr. Burke knew but little of the condition in which that monarchy which he regretted had abandoned France to her new masters. The administration which had preceded the Revolution had deprived the French both of the means and of the desire of mutual assistance. When the Revolution arrived, it would have been vain to seek in the greater part of France for any ten men accustomed to act systematically and in concert, or to provide for their own defence; the Central Power had alone assumed that duty, so that when this Central Power had passed from the hands of the Crown into those of an irresponsible and sovereign Assembly, and had become as terrible as it had before been good-natured, nothing stood before it to stop or even to check it for a moment. The same cause which led the monarchy to fall so easily rendered everything possible after its fall had occurred.

Never had toleration in religion, never had mildness in authority, never had humanity and goodwill to mankind been more professed, and, it seemed, more generally admitted than in the eighteenth century. Even the rights of war, which is the last refuge of violence, had become circumscribed and softened. Yet from this relaxed state of manners a Revolution of unexampled inhumanity was about to spring, though this softening of the manners of France was not a mere pretence, for no sooner had the Revolution spent its fury than the same gentleness immediately pervaded all the laws of the country, and penetrated into the habits of political society.

This contrast between the benignity of its theories and the violence of its actions, which was one of the strangest characteristics of the French Revolution, will surprise no one who has remarked that this Revolution had been prepared by the most civilised classes of the nation, and that it was accomplished by the most barbarous and the most rude. The members of those civilised classes having no pre-existing bond of union, no habit of acting in concert, no hold upon the people, the people almost instantly became supreme when the old authorities of the State were annihilated. Where the people did not actually assume the government it gave its spirit to those who governed; and if, on the other hand, it be recollected what the manner of life of that people had been under the old monarchy, it may readily be surmised what it would soon become.

Even the peculiarities of its condition had imparted to the French people several virtues of no common occurrence. Emancipated early, and long possessed of a part of the soil, isolated rather than dependent, the French showed themselves at once temperate and proud; sons of labour, indifferent to the delicacies of life, resigned to its greatest evils, firm in danger—a simple and manly race who were about to fill those mighty armies before which Europe was to bow. But the same cause made them dangerous masters. As they had borne almost alone for centuries all the burden of public wrongs—as they had lived apart feeding in silence on their prejudices, their jealousies, and their hatreds, they had become hardened by the rigour of their destiny, and capable both of enduring and of inflicting every evil.

Such was the state of the French people when, laying hands on the government, it undertook to complete the work of the Revolution. Books had supplied the theory; the people undertook the practical application, and adapted the conceptions of those writers to the impulse of their own passions.

Those who have attentively considered, in these pages, the state of France in the eighteenth century must have remembered the birth and development of two leading passions, which, however, were not contemporaneous, and which did not always tend to the same end.

The first, more deeply seated and proceeding from a more remote source, was the violent and inextinguishable hatred of inequality. This passion, born and nurtured in presence of the inequality it abhorred, had long impelled the French with a continuous and irresistible force to raze to their foundations all that remained of the institutions of the Middle Ages, and upon the ground thus cleared to construct a society in which men should be as much alike and their conditions as equal as human nature admits of.

The second, of a more recent date and a less tenacious root, led them to desire to live, not only equal but free.

At the period immediately preceding the Revolution of 1789, these two passions were equally sincere and appeared to be equally intense. At the outbreak of the Revolution they met and combined; for a moment they were intimately mingled, they inflamed each other by mutual contact, and kindled at once the whole heart of France. Such was 1789, a time of inexperience no doubt, but a time of generosity, of enthusiasm, of virility, and of greatness—a time of immortal memory, towards which the eyes of mankind will turn with admiration and respect long after those who witnessed it and we ourselves shall have disappeared. Then, indeed, the French were sufficiently proud of their cause and of them-

selves to believe that they might be equal in freedom. Amidst
their democratic institutions they therefore everywhere placed free
institutions. Not only did they crush to the dust all that effete
legislation which divided men into castes, corporations, and classes,
and which rendered their rights even more unequal than their conditions, but they shattered by a single blow those other laws, more
recently imposed by the authority of the Crown, which had deprived
the French nation of the free enjoyment of its own powers, and
had placed by the side of every Frenchman the Government, as
his preceptor, his guardian, and, if need be, his oppressor. Centralisation fell with absolute government.

But when that vigorous generation, which had commenced the
Revolution was destroyed or enervated, as commonly happens to
any generation which engages in such enterprises—when, following the natural course of events of this nature, the love of freedom
had been damped and discouraged by anarchy and popular tyranny,
and the bewildered nation began to grope after a master—absolute
government found prodigious facilities for recovering and consoli-
dating its authority, and these were easily discovered by the
genius of the man who was to continue the Revolution and to
destroy it.

France under the old Monarchy had, in fact, contained a whole
system of institutions of modern date, which, not being adverse to
social equality, could easily have found a place in the new state of
society, but which offered remarkable opportunities to despotism.
These were sought for amidst the ruins of all other institutions,
and they were found there. These institutions had formerly
given birth to habits, to passions, and to opinions, which tended
to retain men in a state of division and obedience : and such
were the institutions which were restored and set to work. Centralisation was disentangled from the ruins and re-established ;
and as, whilst this system rose once more, everything by which it
had before been limited was destroyed, from the bowels of that
nation which had just overthrown monarchy a power suddenly
came forth more extended, more comprehensive, more absolute
than that which had ever been exercised by any of the French
kings. This enterprise appeared strangely audacious, and its success
unparalleled, because men were thinking of what they saw, and had
forgotten what they had seen. The Dominator fell, but all that
was most substantial in his work remained standing ; his government had perished, but the administration survived ; and every time
that an attempt has since been made to strike down absolute power,
all that has been done is to place a head of Liberty on a servile body.

Several times, from the commencement of the Revolution to the present day, the passion of liberty has been seen in France to expire, to revive—and then to expire again, again to revive. Thus will it long be with a passion so inexperienced and ill-directed, so easily discouraged, alarmed, and vanquished; a passion so superficial and so transient. During the whole of this period, the passion for equality has never ceased to occupy that deep-seated place in the hearts of the French people which it was the first to seize : it clings to the feelings they cherish most fondly. Whilst the love of freedom frequently changes its aspect, wanes and waxes, grows or declines with the course of events, that other passion is still the same, ever attracted to the same object with the same obstinate and indiscriminating ardour, ready to make any sacrifice to those who allow it to sate its desires, and ready to furnish every government which will favour and flatter it with the habits, the opinions, and the laws which Despotism requires to enable it to reign.

The French Revolution will ever be wrapped in clouds and darkness to those who direct their attention to itself alone. The only light that can illuminate its course must be sought in the times which preceded it. Without a clear perception of the former society of France, of its laws, of its defects, of its prejudices, of its littleness, of its greatness, it is impossible to comprehend what the French have been doing in the sixty years which have followed its dissolution; but even this perception will not suffice without penetrating to the very quick into the character of this nation.

When I consider this people in itself it strikes me as more extraordinary than any event in its own annals. Was there ever any nation on the face of the earth so full of contrasts and so extreme in all its actions; more swayed by sensations, less by principles; led therefore always to do either worse or better than was expected of it, sometimes below the common level of humanity, sometimes greatly above it ;—a people so unalterable in its leading instincts, that its likeness may still be recognised in descriptions written two or three thousand years ago, but at the same time so mutable in its daily thoughts and in its tastes as to become a spectacle and an amazement to itself, and to be as much surprised as the rest of the world at the sight of what it has done ;—a people beyond all others the child of home and the slave of habit, when left to itself, but when once torn against its will from the native hearth and from its daily pursuits, ready to go to the end of the world and to dare all things ; indocile by temperament, yet accepting the arbitrary and even the violent rule of a sovereign more readily than the free and regular government of the chief citizen ;

to-day the declared enemy of all obedience, to-morrow serving with a sort of passion which the nations best adapted for servitude cannot attain; guided by a thread as long as no one resists, ungovernable when the example of resistance has once been given; always deceiving its masters, who fear it either too little or too much; never so free that it is hopeless to enslave it, or so enslaved that it may not break the yoke again; apt for all things but excelling only in war; adoring chance, force, success, splendour and noise, more than true glory; more capable of heroism than of virtue, of genius than of good sense, ready to conceive immense designs rather than to accomplish great undertakings; the most brilliant and the most dangerous of the nations of Europe and that best fitted to become by turns an object of admiration, of hatred, of pity, of terror, but never of indifference!

Such a nation could alone give birth to a Revolution so sudden, so radical, so impetuous in its course, and yet so full of reactions, of contradictory incidents and of contrary examples. Without the reasons I have related the French would never have made the Revolution; but it must be confessed that all these reasons united would not have sufficed to account for such a Revolution anywhere else but in France.

I am arrived then at the threshold of this great event. My intention is not to go beyond it now, though perhaps I may do so hereafter. I shall then proceed to consider it not only in its causes but in itself, and I shall venture finally to pass a judgment on the state of society which it has produced.

SUPPLEMENTARY CHAPTER.

ON THE PAYS D'ÉTATS, AND ESPECIALLY ON THE CONSTITUTIONS OF LANGUEDOC.

IT is not my intention minutely to investigate in this place how public business was carried on in each of the provinces called Pays d'États, which were still in existence at the outbreak of the Revolution. I wish only to indicate the number of them ; to point out those in which local life was still most active ; to show what were the relations of these provinces with the administration of the Crown ; how far they formed an exception to the general rules I have previously established ; how far they fell within those rules ; and lastly, to show by the example of one of these provinces what they might all have easily become.

Estates had existed in most of the provinces of France—that is, each of them had been administered under the King's government by the *gens des trois états*, as they were then called, which meant the representatives of the Clergy, the Nobility, and the Commons. This provincial constitution, like most of the other political institutions of the Middle Ages, occurred, with the same features, in almost all the civilised parts of Europe—in all those parts, at least, into which Germanic manners and ideas had penetrated. In many of the provinces of Germany these States subsisted down to the French Revolution ; in those provinces in which they had been previously destroyed they had only disappeared in the course of the seventeenth and eighteenth centuries. Everywhere, for two hundred years, the sovereigns had carried on a clandestine or an open warfare against them. Nowhere had they attempted to improve this institution with the progress of time, but only to destroy and deform it whenever an opportunity presented itself and when they could not do worse.

In France, in 1789, these States only existed in five provinces of a certain extent and in some insignificant districts. Provincial liberty could, in truth, only be said to exist in two provinces—in Brittany and in Languedoc : everywhere else the institution had entirely lost its virility, and was reduced to a mere shadow.

I shall take the case of Languedoc separately, and devote to it in this place a closer examination.

Languedoc was the most extensive and the most populous of all the *pays d'états*. It contained more than two thousand parishes, or, as they were then called, ' communities,' and nearly two millions of inhabitants. It was, besides, the best ordered and the most prosperous of all these provinces as well as the largest. Languedoc is, therefore, the fairest specimen of what provincial liberty might be under the old French monarchy, and to what an extent, even in the districts where it appeared strongest, it had been subjected to the power of the Crown.

In Languedoc the Estates could only assemble upon the express order of the King, and under a writ of summons addressed by the King individually every year to the members of whom they were composed, which caused one of the malcontents of the time to say, ' Of the three bodies composing our Estates, one—that of the clergy —sits at the nomination of the King, since he names to the bishoprics and benefices ; and the two others may be supposed to be so, since an order of the Court may prevent any member it pleases from attending the Assembly, and this without exiling or prosecuting him, by merely not summoning him.'

The Estates were not only to meet, but to be prorogued on certain days appointed by the King. The customary duration of their session had been fixed at forty days by an Order in Council. The King was represented in the Assembly by commissioners, who had always free access when they required it, and whose business it was to explain the will of the Government. The Assembly was, moreover, strictly held in restraint. They could take no resolution of any importance, they could determine on no financial measure at all, until their deliberations had been approved by an Order in Council ; for a tax, a loan, or a suit at law they require the express permission of the King. All their standing orders, down to that which related to the order of their meetings, had to be authorised before they became operative. The aggregate of their receipts and expenditure—their budget, as it would now be called—was subjected every year to the same control.

The Central Power, moreover, exercised in Languedoc the same political rights which were everywhere else acknowledged to belong to it. The laws which the Crown was pleased to promulgate, the general ordinances it was continually passing, the general measures of its policy, were applicable there as well as in the rest of the kingdom. The Crown exercised there all the natural functions of government ; it had there the same police and the same agents ;

there, as well as everywhere else, it created numerous new public officers, whose places the province was compelled to buy up at a large price.

Languedoc was governed, like the other provinces of France, by an Intendant. This Intendant had, in each district, his Sub-delegates, who corresponded with the heads of the parishes and directed them. The Intendant exercised the tutélage of the administration as completely as in the *pays d'élection*. The humblest village in the gorges of the Cevennes was precluded from making the smallest outlay until it had been authorised by an Order of the King's Council from Paris. That part of the judicial administration which is now denominated in France the *contentieux administratif*, or the litigated questions referred to the Council of State, was not only not less, but more comprehensive than in the remainder of France. The Intendant decided, in the first instance, all questions relating to the public ways; he judged all suits relating to roads; and, in general, he pronounced on all the matters in which the Government was, or conceived itself to be, interested. The Government extended the same protection as elsewhere to all its agents against the rash prosecutions of the citizens whom they might have oppressed.

What then did Languedoc possess which distinguished it from the other provinces of the kingdom, and which caused them to envy its institutions? Three things sufficed to render it entirely different from the rest of France.

I. An Assembly, composed of men of station, looked up to by the population, respected by the Crown, to which no officer of the Central Power, or, to use the phraseology then in use, 'no officer of the King,' could belong, and in which, every year, the special interests of the province were freely and gravely discussed. The mere fact that the royal administration was placed near this source of light caused its privileges to be very differently exercised; and though its agents and its instincts were the same, its results in no degree resembled what they were elsewhere.

II. In Languedoc many public works were executed at the expense of the King and his agents. There were other public works, for which the Central Government provided the funds and partly directed the execution, but the greater part of them were executed at the expense of the province alone. When the King had approved the plan and authorised the estimates for these last-mentioned works, they were executed by officers chosen by the Estates, and under the inspection of commissioners taken from this Assembly.

III. Lastly, the province had the right of levying itself, and in the manner it preferred, a part of the royal taxes and all the rates which were imposed by its own authority for its own wants.

Let us see the results which Languedoc continued to extract from these privileges: they deserve a minute attention.

Nothing is more striking in the other parts of France—the *pays d'élection*—than the almost complete absence of local charges. The general imposts were frequently oppressive, but a province spent nothing on itself. In Languedoc, on the contrary, the annual expenditure of the province on public works was enormous; in 1780 it exceeded two millions of livres.

The Central Government was sometimes alarmed at witnessing so vast an outlay. It feared that the province, exhausted by such an effort, would be unable to acquit the share of the taxes due to the State; it blamed the Estates for not moderating this expenditure. I have read a document, framed by the Assembly, in answer to these animadversions: the passages I am about to transcribe from it will depict, better than all I could say, the spirit which animated this small Government.

It is admitted in this statement that the province has commenced and is still carrying on immense public works; but, far from offering any apology for this proceeding, it is added that, saving the opposition of the Crown, these works will be still further extended and persevered in. The province had already improved or rectified the channel of the principal rivers within its territory, and it was then engaged in adding to the Canal of Burgundy, dug under Louis XIV., but already insufficient, a prolongation which, passing through Lower Languedoc, should proceed by Cette and Agen to the Rhone. The port of Cette had been opened to trade, and was maintained at great cost. All these expenses had, as was observed, a national rather than a provincial character; yet the province, as the party chiefly interested, had taken them on itself. It was also engaged in draining and restoring to agriculture the marshes of Aigues-Mortes. · Roads had been the object of its peculiar care: all those which connect the province with the rest of the kingdom had been opened or put in good order; even the cross-roads between the towns and villages of Languedoc had been repaired. All these different roads were excellent even in winter, and formed the greatest contrast with the hard, uneven, and ill-constructed roads which were to be found in most of the adjacent provinces, such as Dauphiny, Quercy, and the government of Bordeaux—all *pays d'élection*, it was remarked. On this point the Report appeals to the opinion of travellers and traders; and this

appeal was just, for Arthur Young, when he visited the country
ten years afterwards, put on his notes, ' Languedoc, *pays d'états* :
good roads, made without compulsory labour.'

' If the King would allow it,' this Report continued, ' the States
will do more : they will undertake the improvement of the cross-
roads in the villages, which are not less interesting than the others.
For if produce cannot be removed from the barns of the grower to
market, what use is it that it can be sent to a distance ?' ' The
doctrine of the States on questions of public works has always
been,' they say, ' that it is not the grandeur of these undertakings
but their utility that must be looked to.' Rivers, canals, roads
which give value to all the produce of the soil and of manufactures,
by enabling them to be conveyed at all times and at little cost
wherever they are wanted, and by means of which commerce can
penetrate to every part of the province—these are things which
enrich a country, whatever they may cost it. Besides, works of this
nature, undertaken in moderation at the same time, in various parts
of the country, and somewhat equally distributed, keep up the rate
of wages, and stand in lieu of relief to the poor. ' The King
has not needed to establish charitable workhouses at his cost in
Languedoc, as has been done in other parts of France,' said the
province, with honest pride ; ' we do not ask for that favour ; the
useful works we ourselves carry on every year supersede such
establishments, and give to all our people productive labour.'

The more I have studied the general regulations established by
the States of Languedoc, with the permission of the King (though
generally not originating with the Crown), in that portion of the
public administration which was left in their hands, the more I
have been struck with the wisdom, the equity, and the moderation
they display ; the more superior do the proceedings of the local
government appear in comparison with all I have found in the
districts administered by the King alone.

The province was divided into ' communities ' (towns or villages) ; into administrative districts, called *dioceses* ; and, lastly,
into three great departments called *stewardries*. Each of these
parts had a distinct representation, and a little separate government of its own, which acted under the guidance either of the
Estates or of the Crown. If it be a question of public works
which interest one of these small political bodies, they are only to
be undertaken at the request of the interested parties. If the improvements of a community are of advantage to the diocese, the
diocese contributed to the expense in a certain proportion. If the
stewardry was interested, the stewardry contributed likewise. So

again these several divisions were all to assist the townships, even for the completion of undertakings of local interest, if they were necessary and above its strength, for, said the States frequently, 'the fundamental principle of our constitution is that all parts of Languedoc are reciprocally bound together, and ought successively to help each other.'

The works executed by the province were to be carefully prepared beforehand, and first submitted to the examination of the lesser bodies which were to contribute to them. They were all paid for: forced labour was unknown. I have observed that in the other parts of France—the *pays d'élection*—the land taken from its owners for public works was always ill and tardily paid for, and often not paid for at all. This was one of the great grievances complained of by the Provincial Assemblies when they were convoked in 1787. In some cases the possibility of liquidating debts of this nature had been taken away, for the object taken had been altered or destroyed before the valuation. In Languedoc every inch of ground taken from its owner was to be carefully valued before the works were begun, and paid for in the first year of the execution.

The regulations of these Estates relating to different public works, from which these details are copied, seemed so well conceived that even the Central Government admired, though without imitating them. The King's Council, after having sanctioned the application of them, caused them to be printed at the Royal press, and to be transmitted to all the Intendants of France as a document to be consulted.

What I have said of public works is à fortiori applicable to that other not less important portion of the provincial administration which related to the levy of taxes. In this respect, more particularly, the contrast was so great between the kingdom and the provinces that it is difficult to believe they formed part of the same empire.

I have had occasion to say elsewhere that the methods of proceeding used in Languedoc for the assessment and collection of the *taille* were in part the same as are now employed in France in the levy of the public taxes. Nor shall I here revert to this subject, merely adding that the province was so attached to its own superior methods of proceeding, that when new taxes were imposed by the Crown, the States of Languedoc never hesitated to purchase at a very high price the right of levying them in their own manner and by their own agents exclusively.

In spite of all the expenses which I have successively

enumerated, the finances of Languedoc were nevertheless in such good order, and its credit so well established, that the Central Government often had recourse to it, and borrowed, in the name of the province, sums of money which would not have been lent on such favourable terms to the Government itself. Thus Languedoc borrowed, on its own security, but for the King's service, in the later years of the monarchy, 73,200,000 livres, or nearly three millions sterling.

The Government and the Ministers of the Crown looked, however, with an unfavourable eye on these provincial liberties. Richelieu had first mutilated and afterwards abolished them. The spiritless and indolent Louis XIII., who loved nothing, detested them; the horror he felt for all provincial privileges was such, said Boulainvilliers, that his anger was excited by the mere name of them. It is hard to sound the hatred of feeble souls for whatever compels them to exert themselves. All that they retain of manhood is turned in that direction, and they exhibit strength in their animosity, however weak they may be in everything else. Fortunately the ancient constitution of Languedoc was restored under the minority of Louis XIV., who consequently respected it as his own work. Louis XV. suspended it for a couple of years, but afterwards allowed it to go on.

The creation of municipal offices for sale exposed the constitution of the province to dangers less direct, but not less formidable. That pernicious institution not only destroyed the constitution of the towns; it tended to vitiate that of the provinces. I know not whether the deputies of the commons in the Provincial Assemblies had ever been elected *ad hoc*, but at any rate they had long ceased to be so; the municipal officers of the towns were *ex officio* the sole representatives of the burgesses and the people in those bodies.

This absence of a direct constituency acting with reference to the affairs of the day was but little remarked as long as the towns freely elected their own magistrates by universal suffrage, and generally for a very limited period. Thus the mayor, the council, or the syndic represented the wishes of the population in the Hall of the Estates as faithfully as if they had been elected by their fellow-citizens for that purpose. But very different was the case with a civic officer who had purchased for money the right of governing. Such an officer represented no one but himself, or, at best, the petty interests or the petty passions of his own coterie. Yet this magistrate by contract retained the powers which had been exercised by his elected predecessors. The character of the

institution was, therefore, immediately changed. The nobles and
the clergy, instead of having the representatives of the people
sitting with them or opposite to them in the Provincial Assembly,
met there none but a few isolated, timid, and powerless burgesses,
and thus the commons occupied a more subordinate place in the
government at the very time when they were every day becoming
richer and stronger in society. This was not the case in Languedoc,
the province having always taken care to buy up these offices as
fast as they were established by the Crown. The loan contracted
by the States for this purpose, in the year 1773 only, amounted to
more than four millions of livres.

Other causes of still greater power had contributed to infuse a
new spirit into these ancient institutions, and to give to the States
of Languedoc an incontestable superiority over those of all the
other provinces.

In this province, as in a great portion of the south of France,
the *taille* was real and not personal—that is to say, it was regulated by the value of property, and not by the personal condition
of the proprietor. Some lands had, no doubt, the privilege of not
paying this tax: these lands had, in former times, belonged to the
nobility, but, by the progress of time and of capital, it had happened that a portion of this property had fallen into the hands of
non-noble holders. On the other hand, the nobles had become
the holders of many lands which were liable to the *taille*. The
privilege of exemption, being thus removed from persons to things,
was doubtless more abused; but it was less felt, because, though
still irksome, it was no longer humiliating. Not being indis-
solubly connected with the idea of a class, not investing any class
with interests altogether alien and opposed to those of the other
classes, such a privilege no longer opposed a barrier to the co-
operation of all in public affairs. In Languedoc especially, more
than in any other part of France, all classes did so co-operate, and
this on a footing of complete equality.

In Brittany the landed gentry of the province had the right of
all appearing in their own persons at the States, which made these
Assemblies in some sort resemble the Polish Diets. In Languedoc
the nobles only figured at the States of the province by their
representatives: twenty-three of them sat for the whole body.
The clergy also sat in the person of the twenty-three bishops of
the province, and it deserves especial observation that the towns
had as many votes as the two upper orders.

As the Assembly sat in one house and the orders did not vote
separately, but conjointly, the commons naturally acquired much

importance, and their spirit gradually infused itself into the whole body. Nay, more, the three magistrates, who, under the name of Syndics-General, were charged, in the name of the States, with the ordinary management of the business, were almost always lawyers,—that is to say, commoners. The nobility was strong enough to maintain its rank, but no longer strong enough to reign alone. The clergy, though consisting to a great extent of men of gentle birth, lived on excellent terms with the commons; they eagerly adopted most of the plans of that Order, and laboured in conjunction with it to increase the material prosperity of the whole community, by encouraging trade and manufactures, thus placing their own great knowledge of mankind and their singular dexterity in the conduct of affairs at the service of the people. A priest was almost always chosen to proceed to Versailles to discuss with the Ministers of the Crown the questions which sometimes set at variance the royal authority and that of the States. It might be said that throughout the last century Languedoc was administered by the Commons, who were controlled by the Nobles and assisted by the Bishops.

Thanks to this peculiar constitution of Languedoc, the spirit of the age was enabled peacefully to pervade this ancient institution, and to modify it altogether without at all destroying it.

It might have been so everywhere else in France. A small portion of the perseverance and the exertions which the sovereigns of France employed for the abolition or the dislocation of the Provincial Estates would have sufficed to perfect them in this manner, and to adapt them to all the wants of modern civilisation, if those sovereigns had ever had any other aim than to become and to remain the masters of France.

[THE chapters which follow were not included in the work first published by M. de Tocqueville in 1855. They are the continuation of it, left unfinished at the time of his death in 1859, and published in 1865 by M. de Beaumont amongst the posthumous works of his friend. They are now translated for the first time. Although they must be regarded as incomplete, since they never received the final revision of the author, and the latter portions of them are fragmentary, yet they are not, I think, unworthy to form part of the work to which they were intended to belong, and a melancholy interest attaches to them as the last meditations of a great and original thinker. In the French text an attempt has been made to distinguish, by a different type, the passages which are more carefully finished from those which consisted merely of notes for further elaboration. But as this arrangement breaks the uniformity of the text more than is necessary, I have not adopted it.—H. R.]

BOOK III.

CHAPTER I.

OF THE VIOLENT AND UNDEFINED AGITATION OF THE HUMAN MIND
AT THE MOMENT WHEN THE FRENCH REVOLUTION BROKE OUT.

WHAT I have previously said of France is applicable to the whole
Continent. In the ten or fifteen years preceding the French
Revolution, the human mind was abandoned, throughout Europe,
to strange, incoherent, and irregular impulses, symptoms of a new
and extraordinary disease, which would have singularly alarmed
the world if the world had understood them.

A conception of the greatness of man in general, and of the
omnipotence of his reason and the boundless range of his intelligence, had penetrated and pervaded the spirit of the age; yet this
lofty conception of mankind in general was commingled with a
boundless contempt for the age in which men were living and the
society to which they belonged. Never was so much humility
united to so much pride—the pride of humanity was inflated to
madness; the estimate each man formed of his age and country
was singularly low.

All over the Continent that instinctive attachment and in-
voluntary respect which the men of all ages and all countries are
wont in general to feel for their own peculiar institutions, for their
traditional customs, and for the wisdom or the virtues of their
forefathers, had almost ceased to exist among the educated classes.
Nothing was spoken of but the decrepitude and incoherence of
existing institutions, the vices and corruption of existing society.

Traces of this state of mind may be discovered throughout the
literature of Germany. The philosophy, the history, the poetry,
even the novels of the time, are full of it. Every product of the
intellect was so stamped by it, that the books of that epoch bear a
mark that distinguishes them from the works of every other age.
All the memoirs of that day, which gave birth to a profusion of

memoirs—all the correspondence of the time which has been published—attest a state of mind so different from the present, that nothing short of this concurrence of certain and abundant evidence could convince us of the fact.

Every page of Schlosser's 'History of the Eighteenth Century' reveals this general presentiment, that a great change was about to take place in the condition of mankind.

George Forster, one of the companions of Captain Cook, to whose expedition he had been attached with his father as a naturalist, writes to Jacobi in 1779: 'Things cannot remain as they are: this is announced by every symptom in the world of science, in the world of theology, and in that of politics. Much as my heart has hitherto desired peace, not less do I desire to see the arrival of this crisis on which such mighty hopes are founded.'[1] 'Europe,' he writes again in 1782, 'seems to me on the brink of a horrible revolution; in truth the mass is so corrupt that bleeding may well be necessary.'[2] 'The present state of society,' said Jacobi, 'presents to me nothing but the aspect of a dead and stagnant sea: that is why I could desire an inundation, be it what it may, even of barbarians, to sweep away this reeking marsh and lay bare a fresh soil.'[3] 'We are living in the midst of shattered institutions and forms—a monstrous chaos which everywhere reflects an image of dismay[4] and of death.' These things were written in a pretty country house, by wealthy people, surrounded by their literary friends, who passed their time in endless philosophical discussions which affected, excited, and inflamed them till they shed torrents of daily tears—in imagination.

It was not the princes, the ministers, the rulers, or those, in short, who, in different capacities, were directing the march of affairs, who perceived that some great change was at hand. The idea that government could become quite different from what government then was,—that all which had lasted so long might be destroyed and superseded by that which as yet only existed in the brain of a few men of letters—the thought that the existing

---

[1] 'Correspondence of George Forster,' i. 257.

[2] *Idem*, ii. 286.

[3] See 'Waldemar': a philosophical novel, by Jacobi, written in 1779. Notwithstanding its defects, which are immense, this book made a great impression, because these defects were those of the age.

[4] The word in the French text is *confiance*—'l'image de la *confiance* et de la mort.' But this expression appears to me unintelligible, and the word has probably been wrongly printed or wrongly transcribed. M. de Tocqueville's handwriting was singularly illegible, and these detached notes were written in characters which he was himself not always able to read. The passage here cited is from Vandelbourg's French translation of Jacobi's 'Waldemar,' where it might be verified (Tom. i. p. 154.)—H. R.

order of things might be overthrown to establish a new order in the midst of disorder and ruin, would have appeared to them an absurd illusion and a fantastic dream. The gradual improvement of society seemed to them the limit of the possible.

It is a common error of the people who are called wise and practical in ordinary times, to judge by certain rules the men whose very object is to change or to destroy those rules. When a time is come at which passion takes the guidance of affairs, the beliefs of men of experience are less worthy of consideration than the schemes which engage the imagination of dreamers.

It is curious to see in the official correspondence of that epoch, civil officers of ability and foresight laying their plans, framing their measures, and calculating scientifically the use they will make of their powers, at a time when the Government they are serving, the laws they are applying, the society they are living in, and they themselves shall be no more.

'What scenes are passing in France!' writes Johann Müller on the 6th of August, 1789.[1] 'Blessed be the impression they produce on the nations and on their masters! I know there are excesses, but the cost of a free constitution is not too great. Is not a storm which purifies the air better than an atmosphere tainted as with the plague, even though here and there it should strike a few heads?' 'What an event,' exclaimed Fox, 'how much the greatest it is that ever happened in the world! and how much the best!'[2]

Can we be surprised that this conception of the Revolution as a general uprising of humanity, a conception which enlarged and invigorated so many small and feeble souls, should have taken possession at once of the mind of France, when even other countries partook of it? Nor is it astonishing that the first excesses of the Revolution should have affected the best patriots of France so little, when even foreigners who were not excited by the struggle or embittered by personal grievances could extend so much indulgence to them.

Let it not be supposed that this sort of abhorrence of themselves and of their age, which had thus strangely fallen upon almost all the inhabitants of the continent of Europe, was a superficial or a transient sentiment.

Ten years later, when the French Revolution had inflicted on Germany all sorts of violent transformations accompanied by death

[1] Letter of Johann Müller to Baron de Salis, August 6th, 1789.
[2] Fox to Mr. Fitzpatrick, July 30th, 1789. ('Memorials and Correspondence of Fox,' ii. 361.)

and destruction, even then, one of those Germans, in whom enthusiasm for France had turned to bitter hatred, exclaims, mindful of the past, in a confidential effusion, ' What was is no more. What new edifice will be raised on the ruins, I know not. But this I know, that it would be the direst calamity if this tremendous era were again to give birth to the apathy and the worn-out forms of the past.' ' Yes,' replied the person to whom these words were addressed, ' the old social body must perish.' [1]

The years which preceded the French Revolution were, in almost every part of Europe, years of great national prosperity. The useful arts were everywhere more cultivated. The taste for enjoyments, which follow in the train of affluence, was more diffused. Industry and commerce, which supply these wants, were improving and spreading. It seemed as if the life of man becoming thus more busy and more sensual, the human mind would lose sight of those abstract studies which embrace society, and would centre more and more on the petty cares of daily life. But the contrary took place. Throughout Europe, almost as much as in France, all the educated classes were plunged in philosophical discussions and dogmatical theories. Even in places ordinarily the most remote from speculations of this nature, the same train of argument was eagerly pursued. In the most trading cities of Germany, in Hamburg, Lubeck, and Dantzig, the merchants, traders, and manufacturers would meet after the labours of the day to discuss amongst themselves the great questions which affect the existence, the condition, the happiness of man. Even the women, amidst their petty household cares, were sometimes distracted by these enigmas of life. ' We thought,' says Perthes, ' that by becoming highly enlightened, one might become perfect.'

' Der König sey der beste Mann, sonst sey der bessere König,'

said the poet Claudius.

This period too gave birth to a new passion, embodied in a new word—*cosmopolitism*—which was to swallow up patriotism. It seemed as if all classes were bent on escaping whenever they could from the care of their private affairs, to give themselves up to the grand interests of humanity.

As in France the love of letters filled a large space even in the busiest times, the publication of a new book was an event of interest in the smallest towns as well as in the chief cities. Everything was a subject of inquiry; everything was a source of

---

[1] Life of Perthes, p. 177; and of Stolberg, p. 179—in same book.

emotion. Treasures of passion seemed accumulated in every breast, which sought but an occasion to break forth.

Thus, a traveller who had been round the globe was an object of general attention. When Forster went to Germany in 1774, he was received with enthusiasm. Not a town but gave him an ovation. Crowds flocked about him to hear his adventures from his own lips, but still. more to hear him describe the unknown countries he had visited, and the strange customs of the men among whom he had been living. Was not their savage simplicity worthy more than all our riches and our arts : were not their instincts above our virtues ? [1]

A certain unfrocked Lutheran priest, one Basidow, ignorant, quarrelsome, and a drunkard, a caricature of Luther, excogitated a new system of schools which was, he said, to change the ideas and manners of his countrymen. He put forth his scheme in coarse and intemperate language. The object, as he took care to announce, was not only to regenerate Germany, but the human race. Forthwith, all Germany is in movement. Princes, nobles, commons, towns, cities, abet the great innovator. Lords and ladies of high estate write to Basidow to ask his advice. Mothers of families place his books in the hands of their children. The old schools founded by Melanchthon are forsaken. A college, designed to educate these reformers of mankind, is founded under the name of the ' Philanthropian,' blazes for a moment, and disappears. The enthusiasm drops, leaving behind it confusion and doubt.

The real spirit of the age was to reject every form of mysticism, and to cling in all things to the evidence most palpable to the understanding. Nevertheless, in this violent perturbation of mind, men, not knowing as yet which way to look, cast themselves suddenly on the supernatural. On the eve of the French Revolution, Europe was covered with strange fraternities and secret societies, which only revived under new names delusions that had long been forgotten. Such were the doctrines of Swedenborg, of the Martinists, of the Freemasons, the Illuminati, the Rosicrucians, the disciples of Strict Abstinence, the Mesmerists, and many other varieties of similar sects. Many of these sects originally contemplated no more than the private advantage of their members.

[1] Not a man of education, of whatever rank, would pass through the town where Forster lived without coming to converse with him. Princes invited him, nobles courted him, the commonalty thronged about him, the learned were intensely interested by his conversation. To Michaelis, Heyne, Herder, and others who were endeavouring to solve the mystery of the antiquity and history of mankind, Forster seemed to open the sources of the primæval world by describing those populations of another hemisphere which had not come in contact with any form of civilisation.

But all of them now aspired to embrace the destinies of mankind. Most of them had been, at the time of their birth, wholly philosophical or religious: all now turned at once to politics, and were absorbed in them. By different means they all proposed to bring about the regeneration of society and the reform of governments. It is especially worthy of remark that this sense of unrest, this perturbation of the human mind which I am describing, did not manifest itself in the lower classes, which bore nevertheless the burden of existing abuses. Those classes were still motionless and inert. Not the poor man, but the rich man was tossing in this feverish condition : the movement sunk not lower than the upper rank of the middle classes. Nowadays secret societies are filled by poor workmen, obscure artisans, or ignorant peasants. At the time I am speaking of they consisted entirely of princes, great nobles, capitalists, merchants, and men of letters.

When in 1786 the secret papers of the Illuminati were seized in the hands of their principal chiefs, many anarchical documents were found among them, in which personal property was denounced as the source of all evil, and absolute equality of conditions was vaunted. In the archives of the same sect a list of adepts was found. It consisted entirely of the most distinguished names in Germany, princes, great nobles, and ministers : the founder of the sect was himself a professor of canon law. The King of Poland and Prince Frederick of Prussia were Rosicrucians. The new King of Prussia, who had just succeeded Frederick the Great on the throne, immediately sent for the leading Rosicrucians, and intrusted to them important missions.[1] ' It is asserted,' says Mounier [2] in his books on these sects, ' that several great personages of France and Germany, some of whom were Protestants, took the tonsure in order to be admitted into the sect of Strict Observance.'

Another thing well worthy of notice : it was a time when the sciences had discredited the marvellous, as they became more positive and more certain—when the inexplicable was easily taken for the false, and when in all things reason claimed to supersede authority, reality the imaginary, and free inquiry faith : nevertheless there was not one of the sects I have just mentioned but had some point of contact with the supernatural; all of them ended in some fantastic conclusion. Some of them were imbued with mystical conceptions : others fancied they had found out the secret to change some of the laws of nature. At that moment

[1] See for these details Schlosser's 'History of the Eighteenth Century,' and Forster's Correspondence.

[2] Mounier's book, published at Tü- bingen in 1801, is entitled ' Influence attribué aux Philosophes, aux Francs-maçons et aux Illuminés sur la Révolution.'

every species of enthusiasm might pass for science, every dreamer could find listeners, every impostor could find believers: nothing is more characteristic of the perplexed and agitated condition of men's minds, running to and fro, like a benighted traveller who has lost his way, and who, instead of getting onward, doubles back upon his own footsteps. And it was not the common herd of the people who were at the head of these extravagances; men of letters, men of learning believed in alchemy, in the visible action of the demon, in the transmutation of metals, in the apparition of ghosts. Strange instance of belief in every form of absurdity, growing amidst the decay of religious convictions—of men putting faith in every invisible and supernatural influence, except in that of God !

These mountebanks were the especial delight of sovereigns. Forster writes to his father from Cassel in 1782 : 'An old French adventuress is here who shows spirits to the Landgrave, and receives 150 louis d'or. He is vain enough to think that the devil may take the trouble to tempt him in person. She has with her another Frenchman who casts out bad spirits from the afflicted,' etc. etc. Great monarchs had at their courts charlatans of the first water—Cagliostro, the Count de St. Germain or Mesmer: the little princes were fain to put up, for want of better, with ridiculous little tricksters.

The aspect of this society was nevertheless one of the most imposing which has ever been presented to the world, in spite of the errors and follies of the age. Never had humanity been prouder of itself than at that moment, for at no other moment, from the birth of all the ages, had man believed in his own omnipotence. The whole of Europe resembled a camp, awakening at break of day, bustling at first in different directions, until the rising sun points out the destined track and illuminates the road of march. Alas! how little do those who come at the close of a great revolution resemble those who begin it,—full of lofty hopes, of generous designs, of stores of energy they are ready to pour forth, of noble delusions, of unselfish disinterestedness. Many contemporary writers, unable to discern the general causes which had produced the strange subversion of society they were witnessing, attributed it to a conspiracy of secret societies.[1] As if any private conspiracy could ever explain a movement of such depth and so destructive of human institutions. The secret societies were certainly not the cause of the Revolution : but they

[1] This was the view taken by the Abbé Barruel in his book on Jacobinism. In 4 vols.

must be considered as one of the most conspicuous signs of its approach.

They were not the only signs.

It would be a mistake to suppose that the American Revolution was hailed with ardent sympathy in France alone : the noise of it went forth to the ends of Europe : everywhere it was regarded as a beacon. Steffens, who fifty years later took so active a part in rousing Germany against France, relates in his Memoirs, that in early childhood the first thing that excited him was the cause of American independence.

'I still remember vividly,' says he, ' what happened at Elsinore and in the roadstead, on the day when that peace was signed which secured the triumph of freedom. The day was fine ; the roadstead was full of people of all nations. We awaited with eager impatience the very dawn. All the ships were dressed—the masts ornamented with pennons, everything covered with flags ; the weather was calm, with just wind enough to cause the gay bunting to flutter in the breeze ; the boom of cannon, the cheers of the crews on deck, completed the festal character of the day. My father had invited some friends to his table ; they drank to the victory of the Americans and the triumph of the popular cause, whilst a dim presentiment that great events would result from this triumph mingled with their rejoicings. It was the bright and cheering dawn of a bloody day. My father sought to imbue us with the love of political freedom. Contrary to the habit of the house, he had us brought to table ; where he impressed on us the importance of the event we were witnessing, and bade us drink with him and his guests to the welfare of the new commonwealth.' [1]

Of the men who, in every corner of old Europe, felt themselves thus moved by the deeds of a small community in the New World, not one thoroughly understood the deep and secret cause of his own emotion, yet all heard a signal in that distant sound. What it announced was still unknown. It was the voice of John crying in the wilderness that new times were at hand.

Seek not to assign to these facts which I have been relating any peculiar cause : all of them were different symptoms of the same social disease. On all hands the old institutions and the old powers no longer fitted accurately the new condition and the new wants of man. Hence that strange unrest which led even the great and the worldly to regard their own state of life as intolerable. Hence that universal thirst for change, which came unbidden

[1] 'Memoirs of Henry Steffens.' Breslau : 1840. Steffens was born in 1775, at Stavagner, in Norway.

to every mind, though no one knew as yet how that change could be brought about. An internal and spontaneous impulse seemed to shake at once the whole fabric of society, and disturbed to their foundations the ideas and habits of every man. To hold back was felt to be impossible : yet none knew on which side they would incline; and the whole of Europe was in the condition of a huge mass which oscillates before it falls.

CHAPTER II.

HOW THIS VAGUE PERTURBATION OF THE HUMAN MIND SUDDENLY
BECAME IN FRANCE A POSITIVE PASSION, AND WHAT FORM THIS
PASSION AT FIRST ASSUMED.

IN the year 1787 this vague perturbation of the human mind, which
I have just described, and which had for some time past been
agitating the whole of Europe without any precise direction,
suddenly became in France an active passion directed to a positive
object.   But, strange to say, this object was not that which the
French Revolution was to attain : and the men who were first and
most keenly affected by this new passion were precisely those whom
the Revolution was to devour.

At first, indeed, it was not so much the equality of rights as
political freedom which was looked for ; and the Frenchmen who
were first moved themselves, and who set society in motion, belonged
not to the lower but to the highest order.   Before it sunk down
to the people, this new-born detestation of absolute and arbitrary
power burst forth amongst the nobles, the clergy, the magistracy,
the most privileged of the middle classes,—those in short who,
coming nearest in the State to the master, had more than others
the means of resisting him and the hope of sharing his power.

But why was the hatred of despotism the first symptom ?   Was
it not because in this state of general dissatisfaction, the common
ground on which it was most easy to agree was that of war against
a political power, which either oppressed every one alike or supported that by which every one was oppressed ; and because the
noble and the rich found in liberty the only mode of expressing this
dissatisfaction, which they felt more than any other class ?

I shall not relate how Louis XVI. was led by financial considerations to convoke about him, in an assembly, the members of
the nobility, the clergy, and the upper rank of the commons, and
to submit to this body of ' Notables ' the state of affairs.   I am discussing history, not narrating it.   It is well known that this
assembly, which met at Versailles on the 22nd February, 1787,
consisted of nine peers of France, twenty noblemen, eight privy

councillors, four masters of requests, ten marshals of France, thirteen archbishops or bishops, eighteen chief judges, twenty-two municipal officers of different cities, twelve deputies of the provinces which had retained their local estates, and some other magistrates—in all from 125 to 130 members.[1]   Henry IV. had once before used the same means to postpone the meeting of the States-General and to obtain without them a sort of public sanction to his measures : but the times were changed.   In 1596 France was at the close of a long revolution, wearied by her efforts, and distrustful of her powers, seeking nothing but rest, and asking of her rulers no more than an external deference.   The Notables caused her without difficulty to forget the States-General.   But in 1787 they only revived the recollection of them in her memory.   In the reign of Henry IV., these princes, these nobles, these bishops, these wealthy commoners who were summoned to advise the King, were still the masters of society.   They could therefore control the movement they had set on foot.   Under Louis XVI. in 1787 these same classes retained only the externals of power.   We have seen that the substance of it was lost to them for ever.   They were, so to speak, hollow bodies, resonant but easily crushed : still capable of exciting the people, incapable of directing it.

This great change had come about insensibly and imperceptibly.   By none was it clearly perceived.   Those most affected by it knew not that it had taken place.   Even their opponents doubted it.   The whole nation had lived so long apart from its own concerns, that it took but a hazy view of its condition.   All the evils from which it suffered seemed to have merged in a spirit of opposition and a dislike for the existing Government.   No sooner were the Notables assembled than, forgetting that they were the nominees of the sovereign, chosen by him to give their advice and not their injunctions, they proceeded to act as the representatives of the country.   They demanded the public accounts, they censured the acts of the Government, they attacked most of the measures, the execution of which they were merely asked to facilitate.   Their assistance was sought : they proffered their opposition.

Public opinion instantly rose in their favour, and threw its whole weight on their side.   Then was witnessed the strange spectacle of a Government proposing measures favourable to the people without ceasing to be unpopular, and of an Assembly resisting these measures with the support of public favour.

Thus the Government proposed to reform the salt tax (*la gabelle*), which pressed so heavily and often so cruelly on the

---

[1] Buchez and Roux, 'Parliamentary History of the Revolution,' p. 480.

people.   It would have abolished forced labour, reformed the *taille*, and suppressed the *twentieths*, a species of tax from which the upper classes had continued to make themselves exempt.   In place of these taxes, which were to be abolished or reformed, a land-tax was to be imposed, on the very same basis which has since become the basis of the land-tax of France, and the custom-houses, which placed grievous restrictions on trade and industry, were to be removed to the frontier of the kingdom.   Beside, and almost in the place of, the Intendants who administered each province, an elective body was to be constituted, with the power not only of watching the conduct of public business, but, in most cases, of directing it. All these measures were conformable to the spirit of the times. They were resisted or postponed by the Notables.   Nevertheless, the Government remained unpopular, and the Notables had the public cry in their favour.

Fearing that he had not been understood, the Minister, Calonne, explained in a public document that the effect of the new laws would be to relieve the people from a portion of the taxes, and to throw that portion on the rich.   That was true, but the Minister was still unpopular.   'The clergy,' said he elsewhere, 'are, before all things, citizens and subjects.   They must pay taxes like all the rest.   If the clergy have debts, a part of their property must be sold to discharge them.'   That again was to aim at one of the tenderest points of public opinion : the point was touched, but the public were unmoved.

On the question of the reform of the *taille*, the Notables opposed it on the ground that it could not relieve those who paid it without imposing an excessive burden on the other tax-payers, especially on the nobility and clergy, *whose privileges on the score of taxation had already been reduced to almost nothing.*   The abolition of internal custom-houses was objected to peremptorily on behalf of the privileges of certain provinces, which were to be treated with great forbearance.

They highly approved in principle the creation of provincial assemblies.   But they desired that, instead of uniting together the three Orders in these small local bodies, they should be separated, and always be presided over by a nobleman or a prelate, for, said some of the Committees of Notables, 'these assemblies would tend to democracy if they were not guided by the superior lights of the first Order.'

Nevertheless, the popularity of the Notables remained unshaken to the end : nay, it was continually on the increase.   They were applauded, incited, encouraged : and when they resisted the

Government, they were loudly cheered on to the attack. The King, hastening to dismiss them, thought himself obliged to offer them his public thanks.

Not a few of these persons are said to have been amazed at this degree of public favour and sudden power. They would have been far more astonished at it if they could have foreseen what was about to follow: if they had known that these same laws, which they had resisted with so much popular applause, were founded on the very principles which were to triumph in the Revolution; that the traditional institutions which they opposed to the innovations of the Government were precisely the institutions which the Revolution was about to destroy.

That which caused the popularity of these Notables was not the form of their opposition, but the opposition itself. They criticised the abuses of the Government; they condemned its prodigality; they demanded an account of its expenditure; they spoke of the constitutional laws of the country, of the fundamental principles which limit the unlimited power of the Crown, and, without precisely demanding the interposition of the nation in the government by the States-General, they perpetually suggested that idea. This was enough.

The Government had already long been suffering from a malady which is the endemic and incurable disease of powers that have undertaken to order, to foresee, to do everything. It had assumed a universal responsibility. However men might differ in the grounds of their complaints, they agreed in blaming the common source of them; what had hitherto been no more than a general inclination of mind, then became a universal and impetuous passion. All the secret sores caused by daily contact with dilapidated institutions, which chafed both manners and opinion in a thousand places—all the smothered animosities kept alive by divided classes, by contested positions, by absurd or oppressive distinctions, rose against the supreme power. Long had they sought a pathway to the light of day: that path once opened they rushed blindly along it. It was not their natural path, but it was the first they found open. Hatred of arbitrary power became then their sole passion, and the Government their common enemy.

CHAPTER III.

HOW THE PARLIAMENTS OF FRANCE, FOLLOWING PRECEDENT, OVERTHREW THE MONARCHY.

THE feudal Government, whose ruins still sheltered the nation, had been a government in which arbitrary power, violence, and great freedom were commingled. Under its laws, if actions had often been restricted, speech was habitually independent and bold. The legislative power was exercised by kings, but never without control. When the great political assemblies of France ceased to be, the Parliaments took, in some sort, the place of them ; and before they enregistered in the code that regulated their judicial proceedings a new law decreed by the King, they stated to the sovereign their objections, and made known to him their opinions.

Much inquiry has been made as to the first origin of this usurpation of legislative power by judicial authority. It is vain to seek that origin elsewhere than in the general manners of the time, which could not tolerate, or even conceive, a power so absolute and secret, as not, at least, to admit of discussion on the terms of obedience. The institution was in nowise premeditated. It sprang spontaneously from the very root of the ideas then prevalent and from the usages alike of subjects and of kings.

An edict, before it was put in force, was sent down to the Parliament. The agents of the Crown explained its principles and its merits ; the magistrates discussed it. All this was done in public, in open debate, with that virility which characterised all the institutions of the Middle Ages. It frequently happened that the Parliament sent deputies to the King, several times over, to supplicate him to modify or withdraw an edict. If the King came down in person, he allowed his own law to be debated with vivacity, sometimes with violence, in his presence. But when at last his will was made known, all was silence and obedience : for the magistracy acknowledged that they were no more than the first officers and representatives of the sovereign ; their duty was to advise but not to coerce him.

In 1787, the ancient precedents of the monarchy were faithfully and strictly followed. The old machine of Royal government was again set in motion : but it became apparent that the machine was propelled by some new motive power of an unknown kind, which, instead of causing it to move onwards, was about to break it in pieces.

The King then, according to custom, caused the new edicts to be brought down to the Parliament : and the Parliament, equally according to custom, laid its humble remonstrance at the steps of the throne.[1]

The King replied; and Parliaments insisted. For centuries things had gone on thus, and the nation heard from time to time this sort of political dialogue carried on above its head between the sovereign and his magistrates. The practice had only been interrupted during the reign of Louis XIV. and for a time. But the novelty lay in the subject of the debate and the nature of the arguments.

This time the Parliament, before it proceeded to register the edicts, called for all the accounts of the finance department, which we should now call the budget of the State, in support of the measures; and as the King naturally declined to hand over the entire government to a body which was irresponsible and non-elected, and so to share the legislative power with a Court of Justice, the Parliament then declared that the nation alone had the right to raise fresh taxes,[2] and thereupon demanded that the nation should be convoked. The Parliament grasped the very heart of the people, but held it only for a moment.

---

[1] The Edicts of the 17th June, 1787, were :
1. For the free transport of grain.
2. To establish provincial assemblies.
3. For the commutation of forced labour.
4. A land subsidy.
5. A Stamp Act.

The Parliament accepted the three first, and resisted the two last. When the importance of the Edict on Provincial Assemblies is considered, which created new local powers, and comprised an immense revolution in government and society, one cannot but be amazed at the concurrence which existed, on this occasion, between the two most ancient powers of the monarchy, the one to present, the other to accept it. Nothing can show more forcibly to what a degree, amongst this people, who were all perpetually engaged, even to the women, in debating on government,

the true science of human affairs was unknown, and how the Government, which had plunged the nation in this ignorance, had ended by sinking into the same darkness. This Edict completed the destruction of the whole ancient political system of Europe, overthrew at once whatever remained of feudal monarchy, substituted democracy for aristocracy, the commonwealth for the Crown. I do not pronounce on the value of this change. I merely affirm that it amounted to an immediate and radical overthrow of all the old institutions of the realm, and that if the Parliament and the King plunged together thus resolutely on this course, it was because neither of them saw whither they were going. Hand in hand they leapt into the dark.

[2] 16th July, 1787. The nation assembled in the States-General has alone the right to grant subsidies to the King.

The arguments put forward by the Magistracy in support of their demands were not less novel than the demands themselves. The King, they said, was only the administrator and not the owner of the public fortune : the representative and chief officer of the nation, not its master. Sovereignty resided in the nation itself. The nation alone could decide great questions : its rights were not dependent on the will of the sovereign ; they took their being from the nature of man ; they were as inalienable and indestructible as human nature itself. 'The institution of the States-General,' they declared, ' is a principle founded on the rights of man and confirmed by reason.'[1] 'Common interest has combined men in society, and given rise to governments : that alone can maintain them.'[2] 'No prescription of the States-General can run against the nature of things or against the imperishable rights of the nation.'[3] 'Public opinion is rarely mistaken : it is rare that men receive impressions contrary to truth.'[4]

The King having exiled the Parliament from Paris, that body protested that liberty of speech and action was an inalienable right of man, and could not be wrested from him without tyranny, save by the regular forms of judicial procedure.

It must not be supposed that the Parliaments alleged these principles as novelties :[5] they were, on the contrary, very industriously traced up to the cradle of the monarchy. The judgments or decrees of the Parliament of Paris were crammed with historical quotations, frequently borrowed from the Middle Ages, in barbarous Latin. They are full of provincial capitulations, royal ordinances, beds of justice, rules, privileges, and precedents, which lost themselves in the shadows of the past.

Strangely enough, at the same moment that the Parliament of Franche-Comté proclaimed the indestructible rights of the nation, it protested against any infraction of the peculiar privileges of the province as they existed at the period of annexation under Louis XIV. So again the Parliament of Normandy invoked the States-General of the kingdom 'to inaugurate a new order of things,' but not the

---

[1] Remonstrance of the Parliament of Paris, 24th July, 1787. Notes taken from the official documents.

[2] Parliament of Grenoble, 5th January, 1678. ' Despotic measures,' said the Parliament of Besançon (1787), 'are not more binding on a nation than a military constitution, and cannot run against the inalienable rights of the nation.'

[3] Remonstrance of the Parliament of Grenoble, 20th December, 1787.

[4] Remonstrance of the Parliament of Paris, 24th July, 1787.

[5] In the speech of M. de Simonville, of the 16th July, 1787, delivered in the Parliament of Paris, he went back to 1301 to prove the utility, necessity, and safety of the States-General. He spoke at the same time of the Constitution, of patriotism, rights of the nation, ministers of the altars, &c. (Official Documents.)

less did it demand, in the name of its own feudal traditions, the restoration of the States of Normandy, as the peculiar privilege of that province : so curiously were ideas, just born into the world, enclosed and swathed in these remains of antiquity.

It was a tradition of the old monarchy that the Parliament should use in its remonstrances animated and almost violent language : a certain exaggeration of words was conceded to it. The most absolute sovereigns had tolerated this licence of speech, by reason, indeed, of the powerlessness of those who uttered it : as they were certain in the end to be reduced to obedience and compressed within narrow limits, the indulgence of a free utterance was readily left to them. The Parliament, moreover, was wont to make a great deal of noise for a small result : what it said went beyond what it meant: this franchise had become a sort of right of the magistracy.

On this occasion the Parliament carried their ancient freedom to a degree of licence never heard before; for a new-born fire was burning in their hearts and unconsciously inflamed their language. Certainly, among the governments of our own time, which are almost all, nevertheless, governments maintained by the sword, not one could allow its ministers and its measures to be attacked in such terms by the representatives of its own authority.

' Despotism, Sire,' said the Parliament of Paris, ' is substituted for the laws of the realm, and the magistracy is no more than the instrument of arbitrary power. . . . Would that Your Majesty could interrogate the victims of that power, confined forgotten in impenetrable prisons, the abode of silence and injustice; those whom intrigue, cupidity, the jealousy of power, the thirst of vengeance, the fear or the hatred of justice, private pique or personal convenience, have caused to be put there.' Then drawing a parallel between two citizens, one rich and the other poor, the latter being oppressed by the former, the Parliament added—' Is indigence then a crime ? Have flesh and blood no claims? Does a man without credit, or a poor man, cease to be a citizen ? '

It was especially on the subject of taxation and against the collectors of the revenue that, even in the calmest times, the judicial bodies were accustomed to inveigh with extreme violence. No sooner was the new tax announced than the Parliament of Paris declared it to be disastrous ; consternation followed the proposal ; its adoption would give rise to a general mourning.[1] The population, harassed by fiscal exactions, were at their wits' end.[2]

---

[1] Histoire du Gouvernement Français du 22 Février, 1787, au 31 Décembre.
[2] Parlement de Normandie, 1787.

To arrogate to one's self the power of levying tribute without the States-General was to declare aloud that the sovereign seeks not to be a king of France, but a king of serfs.[1] The substance of the people was become the prey of the cupidity of courtiers and the rapacity of contractors.[2]

Great as was the excitement of that time, it would still be very difficult to account for the language of these magistrates without recalling what had been said so many times before on the same subject. As under the old monarchy most of the taxes were levied on account of private persons, who held them on farm, or by their agents ; for centuries past men had accustomed themselves to look upon taxation as it bore on the private emolument of certain individuals, and not as the common income of the nation. Taxes were commonly denounced as *odious exactions*. The salt duty was styled the *infernal machine of the gabelle* : those who collected the taxes were spoken of as public robbers, enriched by the poverty of everybody else. So said the tax-payers ; the courts of justice held the same language ; and even the Government, which had leased to these very farmers the rights they exercised, scarcely spoke differently of them. It seemed as if their business was not its own, and that it sought a way of escape amidst the clamour which pursued its own agents.

When, therefore, the Parliament of Paris spoke in this manner on the subject of taxes, it merely followed an old and general practice. The play was the same, but the audience was changed ; and the clamour, instead of dying away as it had commonly done within the limit of the classes whom their privileges caused to be but little affected by taxation, was now so loud and so reiterated that it penetrated to those classes which bore the heaviest burden, and ere long filled them with indignation.

If the Parliament employed new arguments to vindicate its own rights, the Government employed arguments not less new in defence of its ancient prerogatives. For example, in a pamphlet attributed to the Court, which appeared about that time, the following passage occurs :— 'It is a question of *privilege* which excites the Parliament. They want to retain their exemption from taxation ; this is nothing but a formidable combination between the nobility of sword and gown to continue under colour of liberty to humble and enslave the commons, whom the King alone defends, and means to raise.'[3]

[1] Parlement de Toulouse, 27 Août, 1787.

[2] Parlement de Besançon, 1787.

[3] A pamphlet entitled, 'Réclamation du Tiers-État au Roi.'

' My object has been,' said Calonne, ' to slay the hydra of privileges, exemptions, and abuses.' [1]

Whilst, however, these discussions were going on upon the principle of government, the daily work of administration threatened to stop: there was no money. The Parliament had rejected the measures relating to taxation. It refused to sanction a loan. In this perplexity the King, seeing that he could not gain over the Assembly, attempted to coerce it. He went down to the Chamber, and before he proceeded to command their submission, less eager to exercise his rights than to confirm them, he caused the Edicts to be again debated in his presence. He began by laying down that his authority was absolute. The legislative power resided in its integrity in his hands. He required no extraordinary powers to carry on the government. The States-General, when he chose to consult them, could only tender advice; he was still the supreme arbiter of their representations and their grievances. This sitting took place on November 19th, 1787. Having said thus much, every one was allowed to speak in his presence. The most opposite and often violent propositions were asserted to his face during a discussion of eight hours; after which he withdrew, declaring, as his last word, that he refused to convoke the States-General at present, though he promised them for the year 1791.

Yet, after having thus suffered his most acknowledged and least formidable rights to be contested in his own presence, the King resolved to resume the exercise of those which were most disputed and most unpopular. His own act had opened the mouths of the speakers, but he sought to punish them for having spoken. In one of its remonstrances the Parliament of Paris had said, ' Sire, the French monarchy would be reduced to a state of despotism if, under the King's authority, Ministers could dispose of personal freedom by *lettres de cachet*, and of the rights of property by *lits de justice*, of civil and criminal affairs by *scire facias*,[2] and of the judicature itself by partial exile or by the arbitrary translation of judges.'

To which the King replied : ' If the greater number of votes in my Courts can constrain my will, the monarchy would become a mere aristocracy of magistrates.' ' Sire,' rejoined the Parliament, ' no aristocracy in France, but no despotism.' [3]

[1] Mémoire Apologétique,' 1787.

[2] The word in the original is *évocation*. I have adopted the English law term which most nearly approaches it.—*Trans.*

[3] Remonstrances of the 4th January, 1788, and 4th May, 1788. A pamphlet of the time, written in defence of the King, is a mere diatribe against aristocracy. It was attributed to Lecesne des Maisons.

Two men, in the course of this struggle, had especially distinguished themselves by the boldness of their speeches and by their revolutionary attitude : these were M. Goislard and M. d'Eprémenil. It was resolved to arrest them. Then occurred a scene, the prelude, so to speak, of the great tragedy that was to follow, well calculated to exhibit an easy-going Government under the aspect of tyranny.

Informed of the resolution taken against them, these two magistrates left their homes, and took refuge in the Parliament itself, in the full dress of their Order, where they were lost amidst the crowd of judges forming that great body. The Palace of Justice was surrounded by troops, and the doors guarded. Viscount d'Agoult, who commanded them, appeared alone in the great Chamber. The whole Parliament was assembled, and sitting in the most solemn form. The number of the judges, the venerable antiquity of the Court, the dignity of their dress, the simplicity of their demeanour, the extent of their power, the majesty of the very hall, filled with all the memorials of our history, all contributed to make the Parliament the greatest and most honoured thing in France, after the Throne.

In presence of such an Assembly the officer stood at first at gaze. He was asked who sent him there. He answered in rough but embarrassed accents, and demanded that the two members whom he was ordered to arrest should be pointed out to him. The Parliament sat motionless and silent. The officer withdrew— re-entered—then withdrew again ; the Parliament, still motionless and silent, neither resisting nor yielding. The time of year was that when the days are shortest. Night came on. The troops lit fires round the approaches to the Palace, as round a besieged fort. The populace, astonished by so unwonted a sight, surrounded them in crowds, but stood aloof : the populace was touched but not yet excited, and therefore stood aloof to contemplate, by the light of those bivouac fires, a scene so new and unwonted under the monarchy. For there it might see how the oldest Government in Europe applied itself to teach the people to outrage the majesty of the oldest institutions, and to violate in their sanctuary the most august of ancient powers.

This lasted till midnight, when D'Eprémenil at last rose. He thanked the Parliament for the effort it had made to save him. He declined to trespass longer on the generous sympathy of his colleagues. He commended the commonwealth and his children to their care, and, descending the steps of the court, surrendered himself to the officer. It seemed as if he was leaving that assembly to mount the scaffold. The scaffold, indeed, he was one day to mount, but that was in other times and under other powers. The only living witness of this strange scene, Duke Pasquier, has told me that at these words of D'Eprémenil the whole Assembly burst into tears, as if it had been Regulus marching out of Rome to return to the horrid death which awaited him in Carthage. The Marshal de Noailles sobbed aloud. Alas! how many tears were ere long to be shed on loftier woes than these. Such grief was no doubt exaggerated, but not unreal. At the commencement of a revolution the vivacity of emotions greatly exceeds the importance of events, as at the close of revolutions it falls short of them.

Having thus struck a blow at the whole body of the Parliaments, represented by their chief, it only remained to annihilate their power. Six edicts were simultaneously published.[1] These edicts, which roused all France, were designed to effect several of the most important and useful reforms which the Revolution has since accomplished : the separation of the legislative and judicial powers, the abolition of exceptional courts of justice, and the establishment of all the principles which, to this day, govern the judicial organisation of France, both civil and criminal. All these reforms were conceived in the true spirit of the age, and met the real and lasting wants of society. But, as they were aimed at the privileged jurisdiction of the Parliaments, they struck down the idol of the hour, and they emanated from a power which was detested. That was enough. In the eyes of the nation these new edicts were a triumph of absolute government. The time had not yet come when everything may be pardoned by democracy to despotism in exchange for order and equality. In a moment the nation rose. Each Parliament became at once a focus of resistance round which the Orders of the province grouped themselves, so as

---

[1] The object of the Edicts, which were sent down to the Parliament on the 8th May, 1788, is well known. The first and second of these established a new order of judicature. Exceptional courts of justice were abolished. Small courts were scattered over the country, which have since become the French Courts of First Instance. Higher courts were established to hear appeals, to sit on criminal cases, and on civil cases under 20,000 livres in value : these were the germ of the appeal courts of France ; lastly, the Parliaments were to hear causes in appeal of more than 20,000 livres value—but this was a needless provision, and it has disappeared Such was the reform comprised in the two first edicts. The third contained reforms of equal importance, in criminal and penal law. No capital executions were henceforth to take place, without such a respite as would afford time for the exercise of the prerogative of mercy : no coercive interrogatory was to be used : the felon's bench was abolished : no criminal sentence to be given without reasons : compensation was to be awarded to those who should be unjustly indicted. The fourth and fifth edicts related exclusively to the Parliaments, and were designed to modify or rather to destroy them. (See the 'History of the Revolution,' by Buchez and Roux.)

to present a firm front to the action of the central power of government.

France was at that time divided, as is well known, into thirteen judicial provinces, each of which was attached to a Parliament. All these Parliaments were absolutely independent of one another, all of them had equal prerogatives, all of them were invested with the same right of discussing the mandates of the legislator before submitting to them. This organisation will be seen to have been natural, on looking back to the time when most of these courts of justice were founded. The different parts of France were so dissimilar in their interests, their disposition, their customs, and their manners, that the same legislation could not be applied to all of them at once. As a distinct law was usually enacted for each province, it was natural that in each province there should be a Parliament whose duty it was to test this law. In more recent times, the French having become more similar, one law sufficed for all : but the right of testing the law remained divided.

An edict of the King applying equally to the whole of France, after it had been accepted and executed in a certain manner in one part of the territory, might still be modified or contested in the twelve other parts. That was the right, but that was not the custom. For a long period of time the separate Parliaments had ceased to contest anything, save the administrative rules, which might be peculiar to their own province. They did not debate the general laws of the kingdom, unless the peculiar interests of their own province seemed to be affected by some one of their provisions. As for the principle of such laws, their opportunity or efficiency, these were considerations they did not commonly entertain. On these points they were wont to rely on the Parliament of Paris, which, by a sort of tacit agreement, was looked up to by all the other Parliaments as their political guide.

On this occasion each Parliament chose to examine these edicts, as if they concerned its own province alone, and as if it had been the sole representative of France ; each province chose, too, to distinguish itself by a separate resistance in the midst of the general resistance they encountered. All of these discussed the principle of each edict, as well as its special application. A clause which had been accepted without difficulty by one of these bodies was obstinately opposed elsewhere : one of them barely notices what called forth the indignation of another. Assailed by thirteen adversaries at once, each of which attacked with different weapons and struck in different places, the Government, amidst all these bodies, could not lay its hand upon a single head.

But, what was even more remarkable than the diversity of these attacks, was the uniform intention which animated them. Each of the thirteen courts struggled after its own fashion and upon its own soil, but the sentiment which excited them was identically the same. The remonstrances made at that time by the different Parliaments, and published by them, would fill many volumes; but open the book where you will, you seem to be reading the same page : always the same thoughts expressed for the most part in the same words. All of them demanded the States-General in the name of the imprescriptible rights of the nation : all of them approved the conduct of the Parliament of Paris, protested against the acts of violence directed against it, encouraged it to resist, and imitated, as well as it could, not only its measures, but the philosophical language of its opposition. 'Subjects,' said the Parliament of Grenoble, 'have rights as well as the sovereign —rights which are essential to all who are not slaves.' 'The just man,' said the Parliament of Normandy, 'does not change his principles when he changes his abode.' 'The King,' said the Parliament of Besançon, 'cannot wish to have for his subjects humiliated slaves.'[1] The tumult raised at the same time by all these magistrates scattered over the surface of the country sounds like the confused noise of a multitude : listen attentively to what they are saying : it is as the voice of one man.

What is it then that the country was saying thus simultaneously? Everywhere you find the same ideas and the same expressions, so that beneath the unity of the judicature you discover the unity of the nation : and through this multiplicity of old institutions, of local customs, of provincial privileges, of different usages, which seemed to sever France into so many different peoples, each living a separate life, you discern one of the nations of the earth in which the greatest degree of similarity subsists between man and man. This movement of the Parliaments, at once multiple and uniform, attacking like a crowd, striking like a single arm,—this judicial insurrection was more dangerous to the Government than all other insurrections, even military revolt; because it turned against the Government that regular, civil, and moral power which is the habitual instrument of authority. The strength of an army may coerce for a day, but the constant defence of Governments lies in courts of justice. Another striking point in this resistance of the judicial bodies, was not so much the mischief they themselves did to the Government, as that which they allowed to be done to it by others. They established, for

_____
[1] These citations are from official documents.

instance, the worst form of liberty of the press : that, namely, which springs not from a right, but from the non-execution of the laws.   They introduced, too, the right of holding promiscuous meetings, so that the different members of each Order and the Orders themselves could remove for a time the barrier which divided them, and concert a common course of action.

Thus it was that all the Orders in each province engaged gradually in the struggle, but not all at the same time or in the same manner.   The nobility were the first and boldest champions in that contest against the absolute powers of the King.[1]   It was in the place of the aristocracy that absolute government had taken root : they were the first to be humbled and annoyed by some obscure agent of the central power, who, under the name of an Intendant, was sent perpetually to regulate and transact behind their backs the smallest local affairs : they had produced not a few of the writers who had protested with the greatest energy against despotism ; free institutions and the new opinions had almost everywhere found in the nobles their chief supporters.   Independently of their own grievances, they were carried away by the common passion which had become universal, as is demonstrated by the nature of their attacks.   Their complaint was not that their peculiar privileges had been violated, but that the common law of the realm had been trampled under foot, the provincial Estates abolished, the States-General interrupted, the nation treated like a minor, and the country deprived of the management of its own affairs.

At this first period of the Revolution, when hostilities had not yet broken out amongst the ranks of society, the language of the aristocracy was exactly the same as that of the other classes, distinguished only by going greater lengths and taking a higher tone.   Their opposition had something republican about it : it was the same feeling animating prouder men and souls more accustomed to live in contact with the world's greatness.

A man who had till then been a violent enemy of the privileged orders, having been present at one of the meetings where the opposition was organised and where the nobles had made a sacrifice of all their rights amidst the applause of the commons, relates this scene in a letter to a friend and exclaims with enthusiasm, ' Our nobility (how truly a nobility !) has come down to point out our

[1] ' Will posterity believe,' said a pamphlet of the time, ' that the seditious views of the Parliaments are shared by princes of the blood, by dukes, counts, marquises, and by spiritual as well as temporal peers ? ' (' Lettres flamandes à un Ami.')

rights, to defend them with us: I have heard it with my own ears; free elections, equality of numbers, equality of taxation—every heart was touched by their disinterestedness and kindled by their patriotism.' [1]

When public rejoicings took place at Grenoble upon the news of the dismissal of the Archbishop of Sens, August 29th, 1788, the city was instantly illuminated and covered with transparencies, on one of which the following lines were read :—

> ' Nobles, vous méritez le sort qui vous décore,
> De l'État chancelant vous êtes les soutiens.
> La nation, par vous, va briser ses liens ;
> Déjà du plus beau jour on voit briller l'aurore.'

In Brittany the nobles were ready to arm the peasants, in order to resist the Royal authorities; and at Paris when the first riot broke out (August 24th, 1788) which was feebly and indecisively repressed by the army, several of the officers, who belonged, as is well known, to the nobility, resigned their commissions rather than shed the blood of the people. The Parliament complimented them on their conduct, and called them ' those noble and generous soldiers whom the purity and delicacy of their sentiments had compelled to resign their commissions.' [2]

The opposition of the clergy was not less decided though more discreet. It naturally assumed the forms appropriate to the clerical body. When the Parliament of Paris was exiled to Troyes and received the homage of all the public bodies of that city, the Chapter of the Cathedral, as the organ of the clergy, complimented the Parliament in the following terms :—' The vigour restored to the constitutional maxims of the monarchy has succeeded in defeating the territorial subsidy, and you have taught the Treasury to respect the sacred rights of property.' ' The general mourning of the nation and your own removal from your duties and from the bosom of your families were to us a poignant spectacle, and whilst these august walls echoed the sounds of public grief, we carried into the Sanctuary our private sorrow and our prayers.'—(Official Papers, 1787.)

[1] Letter of Charles R—— to the Commons of Brittany, 1788.

[2] Decree of September 25th, 1788. (Official documents). On the occasion of the partial riot caused at Grenoble by the triumphant return of the Parliament (October 12th, 1788), the army, instead of repressing it, was incited by its own officers to take part in the movement. 'The officers of the regiment' (said an eye-witness) 'did not show less ardour; they waited in a body on the First President to express the joy they felt on his return. On this occasion we cannot refuse ourselves the pleasure of paying them a tribute of praise. Their prudence, their humanity, their patriotism have earned for them the esteem of the city.' I think Bernadotte was serving in this regiment.

Wherever the three Orders combined in opposition, the clergy made their appearance.   Usually the Bishop spoke little, but he took the chair which was offered him.   The famous meeting at Romans, that which protested with the greatest violence against the Edicts of May, was alternately presided over by the Archbishop of Narbonne and the Archbishop of Vienne.[1]

Generally speaking, parish priests were seen at all the meetings of the Orders, where they took a lively and direct part in the debates.

At the outset of the struggle the middle classes had shown themselves timid and irresolute.   Yet it was on those classes especially that the Government had relied for consolation in its distress, and for aid without abandoning its ancient prerogatives : the propositions of the Government had been framed with peculiar regard to the interests of the middle classes and to their passions.   Long habituated to obedience, they did not engage without apprehension in a course of resistance.   Their opposition was tempered with caution.   They still flattered the power to which they were opposed, and acknowledged its rights while they contested the use of them. They seemed partly seduced by its favours, and ready to yield to the Government, provided some share of government were bestowed on themselves.   Even when they appeared to direct, the middle classes never ventured to walk alone ; impelled by an internal heat which they did not care to show, they sought rather to turn the passions of the upper classes to their own advantage than to increase the violence of them.   But as the struggle was prolonged the *bourgeoisie* became more excited, more animated, more bold, until it outstripped the other classes, assumed the leading part and kept it, until the People appeared upon the stage.

At this period of the contest not a trace is to be seen of a war of classes.   'All the Orders,' said the Parliament of Toulouse, 'breathe nothing but concord, and their only ambition is to promote the common happiness.'

A man, then unknown, but who afterwards became celebrated for his talents and for his misfortunes, Barnave, in a paper written in defence of the *Tiers-État* pointed out this agreement of the three Orders, and exclaimed, with the enthusiasm of the time, 'Ministers of religion ! you obtained from the reverence of our forefathers the right to form among yourselves the first Order of the State ; you are an integral part of the French Constitution,

---

[1] September 14th, 1788. The Archbishop, as chairman, alone signed the letter written in the name of the three Orders which appears by its style to have been drafted by Mounier, November 8th, 1788.

and you ought to maintain it. And you, illustrious families! the monarchy has never ceased to flourish under your protection; you created it at the cost of your blood, you have many times saved it from the foreigner; save it now from internal enemies. Secure to your children the splendid benefits your fathers have handed down to you; the name of hero is not honoured under a servile sky.'[1]

These sentiments might be sincere; one sole passion paramount to other passions pervaded all classes, namely, a spirit of resistance to the Government as the common enemy, a spirit of opposition throughout, in small as well as in great affairs, which struck at everything, and assumed all shapes, even those which disfigured it. Some, in order to resist the Government, laid stress on what remained of old local franchises. Here a man stood up for some old privilege of his class, some secular right of his calling or his corporation; there, another man, forgetting his grievances and animosity against the privileged classes, denounced an edict which, he said, would reduce to nothing the seignorial jurisdictions, and would thus *strip the nobles of all the dignity of their fiefs.*

In this violent struggle every man grasped, as if by chance, the weapon nearest at hand, even when it was the least suited to him. If one took note of all the privileges, all the exclusive rights, all the old municipal and provincial franchises which were at this epoch claimed, asserted, and loudly demanded, the picture would be at once very exact and very deceptive; it would appear as if the object of the impending Revolution was not to destroy, but to restore, the old order of society. So difficult is it for the individuals who are carried along by one of the great movements of human society to distinguish the true motive power amongst the causes by which they are themselves impelled. Who would have imagined that the impulse which caused so many traditional rights to be asserted was the very passion which was leading irresistibly to their entire abolition?[2]

---

[1] Published between May 8th, 1788, and the Restoration of the Parliaments.

[2] A single instance will suffice to show how the hatred of despotism, and public or corporate interests, caused the very principles of this Revolution to be repudiated by those who were to be its champions. After the Edicts of May, 1788, the whole bar of the Parliament of Aix signed a protest, in which the following sentences occur: 'Is uniformity in legislation so absolute a benefit? In a vast monarchy, composed of several distinct populations, may not the difference of manners and customs bring about some difference in the laws? The customs and franchises of each province are the patrimony of all the subjects of the Crown. It is proposed to degrade and destroy the seignorial jurisdictions, which are the sacred heritage of the nobility. What confusion! What disorder!' This document was the production of the great lawyer Portalis (afterwards one of the chief authors of the Code Civil): it was signed by him, by Simeon, and by eighty members of the Bar.

Now let us close our ears for a moment to these tumultuous sounds, proceeding from the middle and upper classes of the nation, to catch, if we may, some whisper beginning to make itself heard from the midst of the People. No sign that I can discover from this distance of time announced that the rural population was at all agitated. The peasant plodded onwards in his wonted track. That vast section of the nation was still neutral, and, as it were, unseen.[1]

Even in the towns the people remained a stranger to the excitement of the upper classes, and indifferent to the stir which was going on above its head. They listen; they watch, with some surprise, but with more curiosity than anger. But no sooner did the agitation make itself felt among them than it was found to have assumed a new character. When the magistrates re-entered Paris in triumph, the people, which had done nothing to defend these members of Parliament, arrested in their places, gathered together tumultuously to hail their return.

I have said in another part of this book that nothing was more frequent under the old *régime* than riots. The Government was so strong that it willingly allowed these transient ebullitions to have free scope. But on this occasion there were numerous indications that a very different state of things had begun. It was a time when everything old assumed new features—riots like everything else. Corn-riots had perpetually occurred in France; but they were made by mobs without order, object, or consistence. Now, on the contrary, broke out insurrection, as we have since so often witnessed it, with its tocsin, its nocturnal cries, its sanguinary placards; a fierce and cruel apparition; a mob infuriated, yet organised and directed to some end, which rushes at once into civil war, and shatters every obstacle.

Upon the intelligence that the Parliament had prevailed, and that the Archbishop of Sens retired from the Ministry, the populace of Paris broke out in disorderly manifestations, burnt the minister in effigy, and insulted the watch. These disturbances were, as usual, put down by force; but the mob ran to arms, burnt the guard-houses, disarmed the troops, attempted to set fire to the Hôtel Lamoignon, and was only driven back by the King's house-

---

[1] Yet in a paper, published a short time before the convocation of the States-General, the following lines occur: 'In some provinces the inhabitants of the country are persuaded that they are to pay no more taxes, and that they will share among themselves the property of the landowners. They already hold meetings to ascertain what these estates are, and to adjust the distribution of them. The States-General are expected only to give a shape to these aggressions.' ('Tableau Moral du Clergé en France sur la fin du 18ème Siècle, 1789.')

hold troops.   Such was the early but terrible germ of the insurrections of the Revolution.[1]

The Reign of Terror was already visible in disguise.   Paris,
which nowadays a hundred thousand men scarcely keep in order,
was then protected by an indifferent sort of police called the watch.
Paris had in it neither barracks nor troops.   The household
troops and the Swiss Guards were quartered in the environs.
This time the watch was powerless.

In presence of so general and so novel an opposition, the
Government showed signs at first of surprise and of annoyance
rather than of defeat.   It employed all its old weapons—proclamations, *lettres de cachet*, exile—but it employed them in vain.
Force was resorted to, enough to irritate, not enough to terrify ;
moreover, a whole people cannot be terrified.   An attempt was
made to excite the passions of the multitude against the rich, the
citizens against the aristocracy, the lower magistrates against the
courts of justice.   It was the old game ; but this too was played
in vain.   New judges were appointed, but most of the new magistrates refused to sit.   Favours, money were proffered ; venality
itself had given way to passion.   An effort was made to divert the
public attention ; but it remained concentrated.   Unable to stop
or even to check the liberty of writing, the Government sought to
use it by opposing one press to another press.   A number of little
pamphlets were published on its side, at no small cost.[2]   Nobody
read the defence, but the myriad pamphlets that attacked it were
devoured.   All these pamphlets were evolved from the abstract
principles of Rousseau's *Contrat Social*.   The Sovereign was to be
a citizen king ; every infraction of the law was treason *against
the nation*.   Nothing in the whole fabric of society was sound ;
the Court was a hateful den in which famished courtiers devoured the spoils of the people.

At length an incident occurred which hurried on the crisis.
The Parliament of Dauphiny had resisted like all the other
Parliaments, and had been smitten like them all.   But nowhere
did the cause which it defended find a more general sympathy or

---

[1] 24th August, 1788. All the pamphlets of the time laid down a theory
of insurrection. 'It is the business of
the people to break the fetters laid
upon it. Every citizen is a soldier, &c.'
See 'Remarks on the Cabinet Order
for suppressing discussions in opposition to the Edicts of the 8th of May.'
(' Bibliothèque,' No. 595.)

[2] Some of the authors of these papers
favourable to Government we e said to
be Beaumarchais, the Abbé Maury,
Linguet, the Abbé Mosellet, &c. The
Abbé Maury alone was said to be receiving a pension of 22,000 francs.
(' Lettres d'un Français rétiré à Lon-
dres,' July 1788.)

more resolute champions. Mutual class grievances were there perhaps more intense than in any other place ; but the prevailing excitement lulled for a time all private passions ; and, whereas in most of the other provinces each class carried on its warfare against the Government separately and without combination, in Dauphiny they regularly constituted themselves into a political body and prepared for resistance. Dauphiny had enjoyed for ages its own States, which had been suspended in 1618, but not abolished. A few nobles, a few priests, and a few citizens having met of their own accord in Grenoble, dared to call upon the nobility, the clergy, and the commons to meet as provincial Estates in a country-house near Grenoble, named Vizille. This building was an old feudal castle, formerly the residence of the Dukes of Lesdiguières, but recently purchased by a new family, that of Périer, to whom it belongs to this day. No sooner had they met in this place, than the three Orders constituted themselves, and an air of regularity was thrown over their irregular proceedings. Forty-nine members of the clergy were present, two hundred and thirty-three members of the nobility, three hundred and ninety-one of the commons. The members of the whole meeting were counted ; but not to divide the Orders, it was decided, without discussion, that the president should be chosen from one of the two higher Orders, and the secretary from the commons : the Count de Morges was called to the chair, M. Mounier was named secretary. The Assembly then proceeded to deliberate, and protested in a body against the Édicts of May and the suppression of the Parliament. They demanded the restoration of the old Estates of the province which had been arbitrarily and illegally suspended ; they demanded that in these Estates a double number of representatives should be given to the commons ; they called for the prompt convocation of the States-General, and decided that on the spot a letter should be addressed to the King stating their grievances and their demands. This letter, couched in violent language and in a tone of civil war, was in fact immediately signed by all the members. Similar protests had already been made, similar demands had been expressed with equal violence ; but nowhere as yet had there been so signal an example of the union of all classes. ' The members of the nobility and the clergy,' says the Journal of the House, ' were complimented by a member of the commons on the loyalty with which, laying aside former pretensions, they had hastened to do justice to the commons, and on their zeal to support the union of the three Orders.' The President replied that the peers would always be ready to act with their fellow-citizens for the salvation of the country.[1]

The Assembly of Vizille produced an amazing effect throughout France. It was the last time that an event, happening elsewhere than in Paris, has exercised a great influence on the general destinies of the country. The Government feared that what Dauphiny had dared to do might be imitated everywhere. Despairing at last of conquering the resistance opposed to it, it declared itself beaten. Louis XVI. dismissed his ministers, abolished or suspended his edicts, recalled the Parliaments, and granted the States-General. This was not, it must be well remarked, a concession made by the King on a point of detail, it was a renunciation of absolute power; it was a participation in the Government that he admitted and secured to the country by at length conceding in earnest the States-General. One is astonished in reading the writings of that time to find them speaking of a great revolution already accomplished before 1789. It was in truth a great revolution, but one destined to be swallowed up and lost in the immensity of the Revolution about to follow.

Numerous indeed and prodigious in extent were the faults that had to be committed to bring affairs to the state they then were in. But the Government of Louis XVI., having allowed itself to be driven to such a point, cannot be condemned for giving way. No means of resistance were at its disposal. Material force it could not use, as the army lent a reluctant, a nerveless support to its policy. The law it could not use, for the courts of justice were in opposition. In the old kingdom of France, moreover, the absolute power of the Crown had never had a force of its own nor possessed instruments depending solely on itself. It had never assumed the aspect of military tyranny; it was not born in camps and never had recourse to arms. It was essentially a civil power, a work not of violence but of art. This Government was so organised as

---

[1] In the meetings which followed that of Vizille, and which took place either at Grenoble or at St. Rambert or at Romans, the same union was maintained and drawn closer. The nobility and the clergy steadily demanded that the representatives of the commons should be doubled, taxation made equal, and the votes taken individually. The commons continued to express their gratitude. 'I am instructed by my Order,' said the Speaker of the Commons at one of these meetings (held at Romans, September 15th, 1788), 'to repeat our thanks; we shall never forget your anxiety to do us justice.' Similar compliments were renewed at an Assembly, also held at Romans on November 2nd, 1788. In a letter addressed to the Municipalities of Brittany, an inhabitant of Dauphiny writes: 'I have seen the clergy and the nobility renounce with a fairness worthy of all respect their old pretensions in the States, and unanimously acknowledge the rights of the Commons. I could no longer doubt the salvation of the country.' ('Letters of Charles R—— to the Municipality of Brittany.')

easily to overpower individual resistance, but its constitution, its precedents, its habits, and those of the nation forbade it to govern against a majority in opposition. The power of the Crown had only been established by dividing classes, by hedging them round with the prejudices, the jealousies, the hatreds, peculiar to each of them, so as never to have to do with more than one class at once, and to bring the weight of all the others to bear against it. No sooner had these different classes, sinking for a moment the barriers by which they had been divided, met and agreed upon a common resistance, though but for a single day, than the absolute power of the Government was conquered. The Assembly of Vizille was the outward and visible sign of this new union and of what it might bring to pass. And although this occurrence took place in the depths of a small province and in a corner of the Alps, it thus became the principal event of the time. It exhibited to every eye that which had been as yet visible but to few, and in a moment it decided the victory.

CHAPTER IV.

THE PARLIAMENTS DISCOVER THAT THEY HAVE LOST ALL AUTHORITY, JUST WHEN THEY THOUGHT THEMSELVES MASTERS OF THE KINGDOM.

WHEN the Royal authority had been conquered, the Parliaments at first conceived that the triumph was their own. They returned to the bench, less as reprieved delinquents than as conquerors, and thought that they had only to enjoy the sweets of victory.

The King, when he withdrew the edicts which had raised to the bench new judges, ordered that at least the judgments and decrees of those judges should be maintained. The Parliaments declared that whatever had been adjudged without themselves was not adjudged at all. They summoned before them the insolent magistrates who had presumed to aspire to their seats, and, borrowing an old expression of mediæval law to meet this novel incident, they *noted them infamous*. All France saw that the King's friends were punished for their fidelity to the Crown, and learnt that henceforth safety was not to be found on the side of obedience.

The intoxication of these magistrates may easily be understood. Louis XIV. in all his glory had never been the object of more universal adulation, if that word can be applied to immoderate praise prompted by genuine and disinterested passions.

The Parliament of Paris, exiled to Troyes, was received in that city by all the public bodies, which hastened to pay it the homage due to the sovereign, and to utter to its face the most extravagant compliments. 'August senators!' they said, 'generous citizens! strict and compassionate magistrates! you all deserve in every French heart the title of fathers of your country. You are the consolation of the nation's ills. Your actions are sublime examples of energy and patriotism. The French nation looks upon you with tenderness and veneration.' The Chapter of the Cathedral of Troyes, complimenting them in the name of the Church, said: 'Our country and our religion solicit some durable monument of what you have done.' Even the University came forth, in gowns

and square caps, to drawl out its homage in bad Latin, 'Illus-
trissimi Senatûs princeps, præsides insulati, Senatores integerrimi!
We share the general emotion, and we are here to express our
lively admiration of your patriotic heroism.   Hitherto the highest
courage was that military valour which calls legions of heroes from
their homes; we now see the heroes of peace in the sanctuary of
justice; like those generous citizens who were the pride of Rome
in their day of triumph, you have earned a triumph which secures
to you immortal fame.'   The First President replied to all these
addresses curtly, like a sovereign, and assured the speakers of the
good will of his Court.

In several provinces the arrest or exile of the judges had
provoked riots.   In all, their return gave rise to almost insane
explosions of popular rejoicing.   At Grenoble, when the courier
arrived, who brought the news of the restoration of the Parliaments, he was carried in triumph through the town, and overpowered with caresses and acclamations; women, unable to reach
his person, kissed his horse.   In the evening the whole town was
spontaneously illuminated.   All the public bodies and guilds
defiled before the Parliament, declaiming bombastic compliments.

At Bordeaux on the same day there was a similar ovation.
The people took the horses from the carriage of the First President, and drew him to his chambers.   The judges who had obeyed
the King's orders were hooted.   The First President reprimanded
them in public.   In the midst of this scene the oldest member of
the Parliament exclaimed, 'My children, tell this to your descendants, that the remembrance of this day may keep alive the fire of
patriotism.'   He who said this was an aged man, born ninety
years before, whose youth had been spent under the reign of
Louis XIV.   What changes may not take place in the opinions
and the language of a people within the lifetime of a man!   They
ended by burning a cardinal in effigy on the market-place; which
did not prevent the clergy from singing a *Te Deum*.   These
events took place at the end of October, 1788.

Suddenly the acclamations which surrounded the Parliaments
ceased; the enthusiasm dropped; silence and solitude gathered
about them.   Not only were they the objects of public indifference,
but all sorts of charges were brought against them, the same which
the Government had vainly attempted to urge.   The country was
inundated with vituperative pamphlets against them.   'These
judges,' it was said in these pamphlets, 'know nothing of politics;
in reality they have only been aiming at power.   They are at one
with the nobles and the priests, and as hostile as these are to the

commons, who constitute almost the entire nation. They fancied that their attack on despotism would cause all this to be forgotten; but, in asserting the rights of the nation, they have allowed them to be questioned: those rights are derived from the Social Contract; to discuss them, is to clothe them in the false colours of voluntary concession. Indeed, the demands they made from the King were in some respects excessive. They are an aristocracy of lawyers who want to be masters of the King himself.'[1] Another pamphlet, attributed to Volney, apostrophised them in these terms: 'August body of Magistrates! we are under sacred obligations to you which we do not disown, but we cannot forget that during all these years that you have represented the people, you have allowed it to be oppressed: you, the teachers of the people, have allowed almost all the books calculated to enlighten it to be burnt; and when you resisted despotism it was because it was about to crush yourselves.'

Especially for the Parliament of Paris was the fall sudden and terrible. How shall I describe the mighty void, the death-like silence which encompassed that great Court, and its own sense of impotence and despair, or the scornful vengeance of the Crown, when, in reply to fresh remonstrances, Louis XVI. said, 'I have no answer to make to my Parliament or to its supplications: with the assembled nation I am about to concert measures to consolidate for ever public order and the prosperity of the kingdom'?

The same measure which recalled the Parliament to its hall of justice restored d'Eprémenil to liberty. The reader will remember the dramatic scene of his arrest, his address in the style of Regulus, the emotion of the audience, and the immense popularity of the martyr. He was confined in the Ile Ste. Marguérite, off Cannes: the warrant for his discharge arrives, and he starts. On the road he is at first treated as a great man, but as he proceeds the radiance that surrounded him fades away: once at Paris, nobody cares about him, unless it be to cut a joke. To descend thus from the sublime to the ridiculous, he had only to post across the territory some two hundred leagues.

The Parliament, wretched at the discovery of its unpopularity, endeavoured to regain the favour of the public. Recourse was had to stirring means: the same language which had so often served to excite the people in its favour was again employed. The cry for

---

[1] See a pamphlet attributed to Servan (1789), and entitled 'Glose sur l'arrêté du Parlement'; and one entitled 'Despotisme des Parlements,' published on the 25th September, 1788, after the decree which suddenly made the Parliaments unpopular.

periodical sessions of the States-General, for the responsibility of Ministers, for personal freedom, for the liberty of the press: all was in vain. The amazement of the judges was extreme: they were totally unable to comprehend what was happening before their eyes. They continued to speak of the *constitution* to be defended, not seeing that this word was popular enough when the constitution was opposed to the King, but hateful to public opinion when it was opposed to equality. They condemned a publication which attacked the old institutions of the kingdom to be burnt by the common hangman, not perceiving that the ruin of these institutions was precisely what was desired. They asked of one another what could possibly have brought about such a change in the public mind. They fancied they had a strength of their own, not being aware that they had only been the blind auxiliaries of another power: everything, as long as that power made them its instruments; nothing, as soon as, being able to act on its own behalf, it ceased to need their assistance. They did not see that the same wave which had driven them along, and raised them so high, carried them back with it as it retired.

Originally the Parliament consisted of jurists and advocates chosen by the King from the ablest members of their profession. A path to honours and to the highest offices of State was thus opened by merit to men born in the humblest conditions of fortune. The Parliament was then, with the Church, one of those powerful democratic institutions, which were born and had implanted themselves on the aristocratic soil of the Middle Ages.

At a later period the Crown, to make money, put up to sale the right of administering justice. The Parliament was then filled by a certain number of wealthy families, who considered the national judicature as a privilege of their own, to be guarded from the intrusion of others with increasing jealousy; they obeyed in this the strange impulse which seemed to impel each particular body to dwindle more and more into a small close aristocracy, at the very time when the opinions and general habits of the nation caused society to incline more and more to democracy.

Nothing certainly could be more opposed to the ideas of the time than a judicial caste, exercising by purchase the whole jurisdiction of the country. No practice, indeed, had been more often and more bitterly censured, for a century past, than the sale of these offices. This magistracy, vicious as it was in principle, had nevertheless a merit which the better constituted tribunals of our own time do not always possess. The judges were independent. They administered justice in the name of the sovereign, but not in compliance with his will.   They obeyed no passions but their own.

When all the intermediate powers which might counter-balance or attenuate the unlimited power of the King had been struck down, the Parliament alone still remained firm. The Parliament could still speak when all the world was silent, and maintain itself erect, for a time, when all the world had long been forced to bow.   The consequence was that it became popular as soon as the Government was out of favour with the nation.   And when, for a moment, hatred of despotism had become a fervent passion and a sentiment common to all Frenchmen, the Parliaments appeared to be the sole remaining barrier against absolute power. The defects which had been most blamed in them acted as a sort of guarantee of their political honesty.   Even their vices were a pro-tection, and their love of power, their presumption, and their prejudices were arms which the nation used.   But no sooner had absolute power been definitely conquered, and the nation felt assured that it could defend its own rights, than the Parliament again at once became what it was before—an old, decrepit, and discredited institution ; a legacy of the Middle Ages, again exposed to the full tide of public aversion.   To effect its destruction, the King had only to endure its triumph.

CHAPTER V.

ABSOLUTE POWER BEING SUBDUED, THE TRUE SPIRIT OF THE REVOLUTION FORTHWITH BECAME MANIFEST.

THE bond of a common passion had for an instant linked all classes together. No sooner was that bond relaxed than they flew asunder, and the veritable spirit of the Revolution, disguised before, was suddenly unveiled. After the triumph which had been obtained over the King, the next thing was to ascertain who should win the fruits of the victory ; the States-General having been conceded, who should predominate in that assembly. The King could no longer refuse to convoke them ; but he had still the power to determine the form they were to assume. One hundred and seventy-five years had elapsed since their last meeting. They had become a mere indistinct tradition. None knew precisely what should be the number of the deputies, the mutual relations of the three Orders, the mode of election, the forms of deliberation. The King alone could have settled these questions : he did not settle them. After having allowed the disputed powers, which he sought to retain, to be snatched away from him, he failed to use those which were not disputed.

M. de Brienne, the First Minister, had strange notions on this subject, and caused his master to adopt a resolution unparalleled in history. He regarded the questions, whether the electoral franchise was to be universal or limited, whether the assembly was to be numerous or restricted, whether the Orders were to be separated or united, whether they were to be equal or unequal in their rights, as a matter of erudition. Consequently an Order in Council commanded all the constituted bodies of the realm to make researches as to the structure of the old States-General and the forms used by them ; and added that ' His Majesty invited all the learned persons of the kingdom, more especially those who belonged to the Academy of Belles-lettres and Antiquities, to address to the Keeper of the Seals papers and information on this subject.'

Thus was the constitution of the country treated like an academical essay, put up to competition. The call was heard.

All the local powers deliberated on the answer to be given to the King. All the corporate bodies put in their claims. All classes endeavoured to rake up from the ruins of the old States-General the forms which seemed best adapted to secure their own peculiar interests. Every one had something to say; and as France was the most literary country in Europe, there was a deluge of publications. The conflict of classes was inevitable; but that conflict, which should naturally have been reserved for the States-General themselves, where it might have been kept within bounds when it arose on given questions, finding a boundless field before it, and being fed by general controversy, speedily assumed a degree of strange boldness and excessive violence, to be accounted for by the secret excitement of the public mind, but which no external symptom had as yet prepared men for. Between the time when the King renounced his absolute authority and the commencement of the elections about five months elapsed. In this interval little was changed in the actual state of things, but the movement which was driving the French nation to a total subversion of society dashed onwards with increasing velocity.

At first nothing was talked of but the constitution of the States-General; big books were hastily filled with crude erudition, in which an attempt was made to reconcile the traditions of the Middle Ages with the demands of the present time: then the question of the old States-General was dropped. This heap of mouldy precedents was flung aside, and it was asked what, on general and abstract principles, the legislative power ought to be. At each step the horizon extended: beyond the constitution of the legislature the discussion embraced the whole framework of government: beyond the frame of government the whole fabric of society was to be shaken to its foundations. At first men spoke of a better ponderation of powers, a better adjustment of the rights of classes, but soon they advanced, they hurried, they rushed to pure democracy. At first Montesquieu was cited and discussed, at last Rousseau was the only authority; he, and he alone, became and was to remain the Teacher of the first age of the Revolution. The old *régime* was still in complete existence, and already the institutions of England were deemed superannuated and inadequate. The root of every incident that followed was implanted in men's minds. Scarcely an opinion was professed in the whole course of the Revolution which might not already be traced in its germ: there was not an idea realised by the Revolution, that some theory had not at once reached and even surpassed.

'In all things the majority of numbers is to give the law':

such was the keynote of the whole controversy. Nobody dreamed
that the concession of political rights could be determined by any
other element than that of number. 'What can be more absurd,'
exclaims a writer who was one of the most moderate of the time,
' than that a body which has twenty millions of heads should be
represented in the same manner as one which has an hundred
thousand?'[1] After having shown that there were in France eighty
thousand ecclesiastics and about a hundred and twenty thousand
nobles, Siéyès merely adds, 'Compare this number of these two
hundred thousand privileged persons to that of twenty-six million
souls, and judge the question.'[2]

The most timid among the innovators of the Revolution, those
who wished that the reasonable prerogatives of the different Orders
should be respected, talked, nevertheless, as if there were neither
class nor Order, and still took the numerical majority[3] as the sole
basis of their calculations. Everybody framed his own statistics,
but all was statistical. 'The relation of privileged persons to those
not privileged,' said Lafon-Ladebat, ' is as one to twenty-two.'[4]
According to the city of Bourg,[5] the commons formed nineteen-
twentieths of the population; according to the city of Nîmes,[6]
twenty-nine thirtieths. It was, as you see, a mere question of
figures. From this political arithmetic, Volney deduced, as a
natural consequence, universal suffrage;[7] Roederer, universal
eligibility;[8] Péthion, the unity of the assembly.[9]

Many of these writers, in drawing out their figures, knew
nothing of the quotient : and the calculation frequently led them
beyond their hopes, and even beyond their wishes.

The most striking thing, at this passionate epoch, was not so
much the passions which broke forth, as the power of the opinions
that prevailed; and the opinion that prevailed above all others
was, that not only there were no privileges, but even that there
were no private rights. Even those who professed the largest
consideration for privileges and private rights considered such
privileges and rights as wholly indefensible—not only those exercised in their own time, but those existing at any time and in any

[1] 'Le Tiers-État au Roi,' by M.
Louchet, December 20th, 1788.
    [2] 'Qu'est-ce-que le Tiers ?' p. 53.
    [3] Lacretelle, 'Convocation des États-
Généraux'; Bertrand de Molleville,
'Observations adressées à l'Assemblée
des Notables.'
    [4] 'Observations lues aux représen-
tants du Tiers-État à Bordeaux,' December, 1788.
    [5] 'Requête du Tiers-État de la ville

de Bourg,' December, 1788.
    [6] 'Délibérations de la ville de Nîmes
en Conseil général.'
    [7] 'Des conditions nécessaires à la
légalité des États-Généraux.'
    [8] 'De la députation aux États-Géné-
raux.'
    [9] 'Avis aux Français,' 1788. A pam-
phlet written in 1788, but full of the
true revolutionary spirit of 1792.

country.   The conception of a temperate and ponderated Government, that is to say, of a Government in which the different classes of society, and the different interests which divide them, balance each other—in which men are weighed not only as individuals, but by reason of their property, their patronage, and their influence in the scale of the common weal,—these conceptions were wanting in the mind of the multitude ; they were replaced by the notion of a crowd, consisting of similar elements, and they were superseded by votes, not as the representatives of interests or of persons, but of numerical force.[1]

Another thing well worthy of remark in this singular movement of the mind, was its *pace*, at first so easy and regulated, at last so headlong and impetuous.   A few months' interval marked this difference.   Read what was written in the first weeks of 1788 by the keenest opponents of the old *régime*, you will be struck by the forbearance of their language : then take the publications of the most moderate reformers in the last five months of the same year, you will find them revolutionary.

The Government had challenged discussion on itself : no bounds therefore would be set to the theme.   The same impulse which had been given to opinions soon drove the passions of the nation with furious rapidity in the same direction.   At first the commons complained that the nobility carried their rights too far.   Later on, the existence of any such rights was denied.   At first it was proposed to share power with the upper classes : soon all power was refused to them.   The aristocracy was to become a sort of extraneous substance in the uniform texture of the nation.   Some said the privileged classes were a hundred thousand, some that they were five hundred thousand.   All agreed in thinking that they formed a mere handful, foreign to the rest of the nation, only to be tolerated in the interest of public tranquillity.   'Take away in your imagination,' said Rabaut Saint-Etienne, 'the whole of the clergy—take away even the whole nobility, there still remains the nation.'   The commons were a complete social body : all the rest was vain superfluity : not only the nobles had no right to be masters of the rest, they had scarcely the right to be their fellow-citizens.

[1] Mounier himself was just as little able as the most violent revolutionists, who were soon to appear, to conceive the idea of rights derived from the past ; of political usages and customs which are in reality laws, though unwritten, and only to be touched with caution, of interests to be respected and very gradually modified without causing a rupture between that which has been and that which is to be—the idea, in short, which is the first principle of practical and regular political liberty. See Mounier's 'Nouvelles Observations sur les États-Généraux.'

For the first time perhaps in the history of the world, the upper classes had separated and isolated themselves to such a degree from all other classes, that their members could be counted one by one and set apart like sheep draughted from a flock: whilst the middle classes were bent on *not* mixing with the class above them, but, on the contrary, stood carefully aloof from all contact. These two symptoms, had they been understood, would have revealed the immensity of the Revolution which was about to take place, or rather which was already made.

Now follow the movement of passion in the track of opinion. At first hatred was expressed against privileges, none against persons. But by degrees the tone becomes more bitter, emulation becomes jealousy, enmity becomes detestation, a thousand conflicting associations are piled together to form the mighty mass which a thousand arms are at once to lift, and drop upon the head of the aristocracy so as to crush it.

The privileged ranks were attacked in countless publications. They were defended in so few, that it is somewhat difficult to ascertain what was said in their favour. It may seem surprising that the assailed classes, holding most of the great offices of State and owning a large portion of the land of the country, should have found so few defenders, though so many eloquent voices have pleaded their cause since they have been conquered, decimated, ruined. But this is explained by the extreme confusion into which the aristocracy was thrown, when the rest of the nation, having proceeded for a time in the track marked out by itself, suddenly turned against it. With astonishment, it perceived that the opinions used to attack it were its own opinions. The notions which compassed its annihilation were familiar to its own mind. What had been the amusement of aristocratic leisure became a terrible weapon against aristocratic society. In common with their adversaries, these nobles were ready enough to believe that the most perfect form of society would be that most nearly akin to the natural equality of man ; in which merit alone, and not either birth or fortune, should determine rank ; and in which government would be a simple contract, and law the creation of a numerical majority. They knew nothing of politics but what they had read in books, and in the same books ; the only difference was that one party was bent on trying a great social experiment, which must be made at the expense of the other party. But, though their interests were different, their opinions were the same : those same patricians would have made the Revolution if they had been born plebeians.

When therefore they suddenly found themselves attacked, they were singularly embarrassed in their defence. Not one of them had ever considered by what means an aristocracy may justify its privileges in the eyes of the people. They knew not what to say in order to show how it is that an aristocracy can alone preserve the people from oppression of the Crown and the calamities of revolution, insomuch that the privileges apparently established in the sole interest of those who possess them do constitute the best security that can be found for the tranquillity and prosperity even of those who are without them. All these arguments which are so familiar to those who have a long experience of public affairs, and who have acquired the science of government, were to those nobles of France novel and unknown.

Instead of this, they spoke of the services which their fore-fathers had rendered six hundred years ago ; of the superstitious veneration due to a past, which was now detested ; of the necessity of a nobility to uphold the honour of arms and the traditions of military valour. In opposition to a proposal to admit the peasantry to the franchise in the provincial assemblies, and even to preside over those bodies, M. de Bazancourt, a Councillor of State, declared that the kingdom of France was based upon honour and prerogative: so great was the ignorance and so deep the obscurity in which absolute power had concealed the real laws of society, even from the eyes of those to whom it was most interested in making them known.

The language of the nobles was often arrogant, because they were accustomed to be the first; but it was irresolute, because they doubted of their own right. Who can depict the endless divisions in the bosom of the assailed parties ? The spirit of rivalry and contention raged amongst those who were thus isolated themselves —the nobles against the priests (the first voice raised to demand the confiscation of the property of the clergy was that of a noble[1]), the priests against the nobles, the lesser nobility against the great lords, the parish priests against the bishops.[2]

The discussion roused by the King's Edicts, after having run round a vast circumference of institutions and laws, always ended at the two following points, which practically expressed the objects of the contest.

1. In the States-General, then about to meet, were the com-mons to have a greater number of representatives than each of the

[1] The Marquis de Gouy d'Arcy in a ' Mémoire au Roi en faveur de la no-blesse Française, par un patricien ami du peuple,' 1788.

[2] This appears from a correspond-ence of M—— with M. Necker, ex-amined by me in the archives.

two other Orders, so that the total number of its deputies should be equal to those of the nobility and clergy combined?

2. Were the Orders to deliberate together or separately?

This reduplication of the commons and the fusion of the three Orders in one assembly appeared, at the time, to be things less novel and less important than they were in reality. Some minor circumstances which had long existed, or were then in existence, concealed their novelty and their magnitude. For ages the provincial Estates of Languedoc had been composed and had sat in this manner, with no other result than that of giving to the middle class a larger share of public business, and of creating common interests and greater facility of intercourse between that class and the two higher Orders. This example had been copied, subsequently, in the two or three provincial assemblies which were held in 1779 : instead of dividing the classes, it had been found to draw them together.

The King himself appeared to have declared in favour of this system; for he had just applied it to the provincial assemblies, which the last edict had called into being in all the provinces having previously no Estates of their own (1788). It was still imperfectly seen, without a clear perception of the fact, that an institution which had only modified the ancient constitution of the country, when established in a single province, could not fail to bring about its total and violent overthrow the moment it was applied to the whole State. It was evident that the commons, if equal in number to the two other Orders in the General Assembly of the nation, must instantly preponderate there ;—not as participating in their business, but as the supreme master of it. For the commons would stand united between two bodies, not only divided against each other, but divided against themselves—the commons having the same interests, the same passions, the same object : the two other Orders having different interests, different objects, and frequently different passions : these having the current of public opinion in their favour, those having it against them. This preference from without could not fail to drive a certain number of nobles and priests to join the commons; so that whilst it banded all the commons together, it detached from the nobility and the clergy all those who were aiming at popularity or seeking to track out a new road to power.

In the States of Languedoc it was common to see the commons forsake their own body to vote with the nobles and the bishops, because the established influence of aristocracy, still prevailing in their opinions and manners, weighed upon them. But here, the reverse necessarily occurred ; and the commons necessarily found themselves in a majority, although the number of their own representatives was the same.

The action of such a party in the Assembly could not fail to be, not only preponderating, but violent ; for it was sure to encounter there all that could excite the passions of man.   To bring parties to live together in a conflict of opposite opinions is no easy task. But to enclose in the same arena political bodies, already formed, completely organised, each having its proper origin, its past, its traditions, its peculiar usages, its spirit of union—to plant them apart, always in presence of each other, and to compel them to carry on an incessant debate, with no medium between them, is not to provoke discussion but war.

Moreover, this majority, inflamed by its own passions and the passions of its antagonists, was all powerful. Nothing could, I will not say arrest, but retard its movements ; for nothing remained to check it but the power of the Crown, already disarmed, and inevitably destined to yield to the strain of a single Assembly concentrated against itself.

This was not to transpose gradually the balance of power, but to upset it.   It was not to impart to the commons a share in the exorbitant rights of the aristocracy, but suddenly to transfer unbounded power to other hands—to abandon the guidance of affairs to a single passion, a single idea, a single interest.   This was not a reform, but a revolution.   Mounier, who, alone among the reformers of that time, seems to have settled in his own mind what it was he wished to effect, and what were the conditions of a regular and free government,—Mounier, who in his plan of government had divided the three Orders, was nevertheless favourable to this union of them, and for this reason : that what was wanted before all things was an assembly to destroy the remains of the old constitution, all special privileges, and all local privileges, which could never be done with an Upper House composed of the nobles and the clergy.

It would seem at any rate that the reduplication of the votes of the commons and the fusion of the three Orders in one body must have been questions inseparable from each other ; for to what end should the number of representatives of the commons be augmented, if that branch of the Assembly was to debate and vote apart from the other two ?

M. Necker thought proper to separate these questions.   No doubt he desired both the reduplication of the commons, and that the three Orders should vote together.   It is very probable that the King leaned in the same direction. By the aristocracy he had just been conquered. It was the aristocracy which pressed him hardest, which had roused the other classes against the royal authority, and had led them to victory. These blows had been felt, and the King had not sufficient penetration to perceive that his adversaries would soon be compelled to defend him, and that his friends would become his masters. Louis XVI. therefore, like his minister, was inclined to constitute the States-General in the manner which the commons desired. But they were afraid to go so far. They stopped half-way, not from any clear perception of their danger, but confused by the inarticulate clamour around them. What man or what class has ever had the penetration to see when it became necessary to come down from a lofty pinnacle, in order to avoid being hurled down from it?

It was then decided that the commons should return twice as many members as each of the other Orders, but the question of the vote in common was left unsettled. Of all courses of action, this was certainly the most dangerous.

Nothing contributes more to the maintenance of despotism than the division and mutual rivalry of classes. Absolute power lives on them: on condition, however, that these divisions are confined to a pacific bitterness, that men envy their neighbours without excessive hatred, and that these classes, though separated, are not in arms. But every Government must perish in the midst of a violent collision of classes, when once they have begun to make war on each other.

No doubt, it was very late in the day to seek to maintain the old constitution of the States-General, even if it were reformed. But this resolution, however rash, was supported by the law of the land, which had still some authority. The Government had tradition in its favour, and still had its hand upon the instrument of the law. If the double number of the commons and the vote of the three Orders in common had been conceded at once, no doubt a revolution would have been made, but it would have been made by the Crown, which by pulling down these old institutions itself might have deadened their fall. The upper classes must have submitted to an inevitable necessity. Borne in by the pressure of the Crown, simultaneously with that of the commons, they would at once have acknowledged their inability to resist. Despairing of their own ascendency, they would only have contended for equal rights, and would have learnt the lesson of fighting to save something, instead of fighting to retain everything.

Would it not have been possible to do throughout France what was actually done by the Three Orders in Dauphiny ? In that province the Provincial Estates chose, by a general vote, the representatives of the Three Orders to the States-General. Each Order in the provincial State had been elected separately and stood for itself alone ; but all the Orders combined to name the deputies to the States-General, so that every noble had commoners among his constituents, and every commoner nobles. The three representations, though remaining distinct, thus acquired a certain resemblance. Could not the same thing have been done elsewhere than in Dauphiny ? If the Orders had been constituted in this manner, might they not have co-existed in a single Assembly without coming to a violent collision ?

Too much weight must not be given to these legislative expedients. The ideas and the passions of man, not the mechanism of law, are the motive force of human affairs. Doubtless whatever steps had at that time been taken to form and regulate the Assemblies of the nation, it may be thought that war would have broken forth in all its violence between classes. Their animosities were perhaps already too fierce for them to have worked in harmony, and the power of the King was already too weak to compel them to agree. But it must be admitted that nothing could have been done more calculated than what was done to render the conflict between them instantaneous and mortal. Could the utmost art, skill, and deliberate design have brought all this to pass more surely than was actually done by inexperience and temerity ? An opportunity had been afforded to the commons to take courage, to prepare for the encounter, and to count their numbers. Their moral ardour had immoderately increased, and had doubled the weight of their party. They had been allured by every hope ; they were intimidated by every fear. Victory had been flaunted before their eyes, not given, but they were invited to seize it. After having left the two classes for five months to exasperate their old hatreds, and repeat the long story of their grievances, until they were inflamed against each other with furious resentment, they were arrayed face to face, and the first question they had to decide was one which included all other questions ; on that issue alone they might have settled at once, and in a single day, all their quarrels.

What strikes one most in the affairs of the world is not so much the genius of those who made the Revolution, because they desired it, as the singular imbecility of those who made it without desiring it,—not so much the part played by great men as the influence frequently exercised by the smallest personages in history. When I survey the French Revolution I am amazed at the immense magnitude of the event, at the glare it has cast to the extremities of the earth, at the power of it, which has more or less been felt by all nations.   If I turn to the Court, which had so great a share in the Revolution, I perceive there some of the most trivial scenes in history—a king, who had no greatness save that of his virtues, and those not the virtues of a king; hairbrained or narrow-minded ministers, dissolute priests, rash or money-seeking courtiers, futile women, who held in their hands the destinies of the human race. Yet these paltry personages set going, push on, precipitate prodigious events.   They themselves have little share in them.   They themselves are mere accidents.   They might almost pass for primal causes.   And I marvel at the Almighty Power which, with levers as short as these, can set rolling the mass of human society.

CHAPTER VI.

THE PREPARATION OF THE INSTRUCTIONS TO THE MEMBERS OF THE STATES-GENERAL DROVE THE CONCEPTION OF A RADICAL REVOLUTION HOME TO THE MIND OF THE PEOPLE.

ALMOST all the institutions of the Middle Ages had a stamp of boldness and truth. Those laws were imperfect, but they were sincere. They had little art, but they had less cunning. They always gave all the rights they seemed to promise. When the commons were convoked to form part of the assemblies of the nation, they were at the same time invested with unbounded freedom in making known their complaints and in sending up their requests. In the cities which were to send deputies to the States-General, the whole people was called upon to say what it thought of the abuses to be corrected and the demands to be made. None were excluded from the right of complaint, and any man might express his grievance in his own way. The means were as simple as the political device was bold. Down to the States-General of 1614, in all the towns, and even in Paris, a large box was placed in the market-place, with a slit in it, to receive the papers and opinions of all men, which a committee sitting at the Hôtel de Ville was empowered to sift and examine. Out of all these diverse remonstrances a bill was drawn up, which expressed the public grievances and the complaint of each individual.

The physical and social constitution of that time was based on such deep and solid foundations, that this sort of public inquest could take place without shaking it. There was no question of changing the principle of the laws, but simply of putting them straight. Moreover, what were then styled the commons were the burgesses of certain towns. The people of the towns might enjoy an entire liberty in the expression of their wrongs, because they were not in a condition to enforce redress: they exercised without inconvenience that amount of democratic freedom, because in all other respects the aristocracy reigned supreme. The communities of the Middle Ages were aristocratic bodies, which merely contained (and this contributed to their greatness) some small fragments of democracy.

In 1789, the commons who were to be represented in the States-General no longer consisted of the burgesses of the towns alone, as was the case in 1614, but of twenty millions of peasants scattered over the whole area of the kingdom. These had till then never taken any part in public affairs. Political life was not to them even the casual reminiscence of another age : it was, in all respects, a novelty. Nevertheless, on a given day, the inhabitants of each of the rural parishes of France, collected by the sound of the church bells on the market-place in front of the church, proceeded, for the first time since the commencement of the monarchy, to confer together in order to draw up what was called the *cahier* of their representatives.[1]

In all the countries in which political assemblies are chosen by universal suffrage, no general election takes place which does not deeply agitate the people, unless the freedom of voting be a lie. Here it was not only a universal voting ; it was a universal deliberation and inquest. The matter in discussion was not some particular custom or local interest ; each member of one of the greatest nations in the world was asked what he had to say against all the laws and all the customs of his country. I think no such spectacle had been seen before upon the earth. All the peasants of France set to work therefore, at the same time, to consider among themselves and recapitulate all that they had suffered, all they had to complain of. The spirit of the Revolution which excited the citizens of the towns, rushed therefore through a thousand rills, penetrated the rural population, which was thus agitated in all its parts, and sunk to its very depths; but the form it assumed was not entirely the same ; its shape became peculiar and appropriate to those just affected by it. In the cities, it was a cry for rights to be acquired. In the country, men thought principally of wants to be satisfied. All the large, general, and abstract theories which filled the minds of the middle classes here took a concrete and definite form.

When the peasants came to ask each other what they had to complain of, they cared not for the balance of powers, the guarantees of political freedom, the abstract rights of man or of citizens. They dwelt at once on objects more special and nearer to themselves, which each of them had had to endure. One thought of the feudal dues which had taken half his last year's crop ; another

---

[1] For a fuller account of these Instructions, and a specimen of them, see Note XLIV. in the Appendix.

of the days of forced labour on which he had been compelled to work without wages. One spoke of the lord's pigeons, which had picked his seed from the ground before it sprouted ; another of the rabbits which had nibbled his green corn. As their excitement grew by the mutual relation of their wretchedness, all these different evils seemed to them to proceed, not so much from institutions, as from that single person, who still called them his subjects, though he had long ceased to govern them—who was the creature of privileges without obligations, and retained none of his political rights but that of living at their cost; and they more and more agreed in considering *him* as their common enemy.

Providence, which had resolved that the spectacle of our passions and our calamities should be the lesson of the world, permitted the commencement of the Revolution to coincide with a great scarcity and an extraordinary winter. The harvest of 1788 was short, and the first months of the winter of 1789 were marked by cold of unparalleled severity—a frost, like that which is felt in the northern extremity of Europe, hardened the earth to a great depth. For two months the whole of France lay hidden under a thick fall of snow, like the steppes of Siberia. The atmosphere was congealed, the sky dull and sad ; and this accident of nature gave a gloomier and fiercer tone to the passions of man. All the grievances which might be urged against the institutions of the country, and those who ruled by those institutions, were felt more bitterly amidst the cold and want that prevailed; and when the peasant left his scarcely burning hearth and his chill and naked abode, with a famished and frozen family, to meet his fellows and discuss their common condition of life, it cost him no effort to discover the cause of all his calamities, and he fancied that he could easily, if he dared, put his finger on the source of all his wrongs.

CHAPTER VII.

HOW, ON THE EVE OF THE CONVOCATION OF THE NATIONAL ASSEMBLY, THE MIND OF THE NATION WAS MORE ENLARGED, AND ITS SPIRIT RAISED.

Two questions had thus far divided all classes—that of the reduplication of the commons, and that of the voting of the Orders in one body : the first was settled, the second was postponed. That great Assembly which every man had regarded in his own heart as the fulfilment of his hopes, and which all had demanded with equal fervour, was about to meet. The event had long been anticipated. To the last it seemed doubtful. It came at length. Preparation was passing into reality, speech into action. At that solemn moment all paused to consider the greatness of the undertaking— near enough to discern the bearing of what was to be done, and to measure the effort which the work required. Nobles, clergy, and citizens alike distinctly perceived that the object was not to modify this or that law, but to remodel all laws, to breathe a new spirit into them, to impart to all of them new purposes and a new course. No one knew as yet exactly what would be destroyed, or what would be created ; but all felt that immense ruins would be made, and immense structures raised. Nor was this the limit of public confidence. None doubted that the destiny of mankind was engaged in the work about to be accomplished.

Nowadays when the calamity of revolutions has rendered us so humble that we scarcely believe ourselves worthy of the freedom enjoyed by other nations, it is difficult to form a conception of the proud anticipations of our sires. The literature of the time shows to our amazement the vast opinions which the French of all ranks had at that time conceived of their country and of their race. Amongst the schemes of reform just brought to light, hardly any were formed on the model of foreign imitation. They were not received as lessons from the British constitution, or borrowed from the experience of American democracy. Nothing was to be copied ; nothing was to be done that was not new. Everything was to be different and more perfect than had been seen before. The confidence of the French in themselves and in the superiority of their own reason was unbounded—a great cause of their mistakes, but also of their inimitable energy. What was applicable to themselves alone would be equally applicable to all men. Not a Frenchman but was convinced that not only was the government of France to be changed, but new principles of government were to be introduced into the world, applicable to all the nations of the earth, and destined to regenerate the sum of human affairs. Every man imagined that he held in his hand not only the fate of his country, but that of his species. All believed that there existed for mankind, whatever might be their condition, but one sovereign method of government, dictated by reason. The same institutions were held to be good for all countries and for any people. Whatever government was not approved by the human reason was to be destroyed and superseded by the logical institutions to be adopted, first by the French, and afterwards by the human race.

The magnitude, the beauty, and the risks of such an enterprise captivated and ravished the imagination of the whole French people. In presence of this immense design, each individual completely forgot himself. The illusion lasted but for a moment, but that moment was perhaps unexampled in the existence of any people. The educated classes had nothing of the timorous and servile spirit which they have since learnt from revolutions. For some time past they had ceased to fear the power of the Crown ; they had not yet learned to dread the power of the people. The grandeur of their design rendered them intrepid. Reforms already accomplished had caused a certain amount of private suffering ; to this they were resigned. The reforms which were inevitable must alter the condition of thousands of human beings : that was not thought of. The uncertainty of the future had already checked the course of trade and paralysed the exertions of industry : neither privations nor suffering extinguished their ardour. All these private calamities disappeared, in the eyes even of those who suffered by them, in the splendour of the common enterprise. The love of well-being, which was one day to reign supreme over all other passions, was then but a subordinate and feeble predilection. Men aimed at loftier pleasures. Every man was resolved, in his heart, to sacrifice himself for so great a cause, and to grudge neither his time, nor his property, nor his life. I hasten to record these virtues of our forefathers, for the present age, which is already incapable of imitating them, will soon be incapable of understanding them.

At that time, the nation, in every rank, sought to be free. To doubt its ability for self-government would have seemed a strange impertinence, and no phrase-maker of that day would have dared to tell the people that, for their own happiness and safety, their hands must be tied and their authority placed in leading-strings. Ere they can listen to such language, nations must be reduced to think more humbly of themselves.

The passions which had just been so violently excited between the various classes of society seemed of themselves to cool down at the moment when for the first time in two centuries these classes were about to act together. All had demanded with equal fervour the restoration of the great Assembly then new born. Each of them saw in that event the means of realising its fondest hopes. The States-General were to meet at last! A common gladness filled those divided hearts, and knit them together for an instant before they separated for ever.

All minds were struck by the peril of disunion. A sovereign effort was made to agree. Instead of dwelling on the causes of difference, men applied themselves to consider what all alike desired : the destruction of arbitrary power, the self-government of the nation, the recognition of the rights of every citizen, liberty of the press, personal freedom, the mitigation of the law, a stronger administration of justice, religious toleration, the abolition of restraint on labour and human industry—these were all things demanded by all. This, at least, was remembered : this was a ground of common rejoicing.

I think no epoch of history has seen, on any spot on the globe, so large a number of men so passionately devoted to the public good, so honestly forgetful of themselves, so absorbed in the contemplation of the common interest, so resolved to risk all they cherished in life to secure it. This it is which gave to the opening of the year 1789 an incomparable grandeur. This was the general source of passion, courage, and patriotism, from which all the great deeds of the Revolution took their rise. The scene was a short one ; but it will never depart from the memory of mankind. The distance from which we look back to it is not the only cause of its apparent greatness ; it seemed as great to all those who lived in it. All foreign nations saw it, hailed it, were moved by it. There is no corner of Europe so secluded that the glow of admiration and of hope did not reach it. In the vast series of memoirs left to us by the contemporaries of the Revolution, I have met with none in which the recollection of the first days of 1789 has not left imperishable traces ; everywhere it kindled the freshness, clearness, and vivacity of the impressions of youth.

I venture to add that there is but one people on the earth which could have played this part. I know my country—I know but too well its mistakes, its faults, its foibles, and its sins. But I know, too, of what it is capable. There are undertakings which the French nation can alone accomplish; there are magnanimous resolutions which this nation can alone conceive. France alone may, on some given day, take in hand the common cause and stand up in defence of it; and if she be subject to awful reverses, she has also moments of sublime enthusiasm which bear her aloft to heights which no other people will ever reach.

NOTES AND ILLUSTRATIONS.[1]

—◆—

NOTE (I.)—Page 12, line 18.

THE POWER OF THE ROMAN LAW IN GERMANY.—THE MANNER IN WHICH IT
HAD SUPERSEDED THE GERMANIC LAW.

TOWARDS the end of the Middle Ages the Roman law became the principal and almost the sole study of the German legists; indeed, at this time, most of them pursued their education out of Germany in the Italian universities. These legists, though not the masters of political society, were charged with the explanation and application of its laws; and though they could not abolish the Germanic law, they altered and disfigured it so as to fit into the frame of the Roman law. They applied the Roman law to everything in the German institutions that seemed to have the most remote analogy with the legislation of Justinian; and they thus introduced a new spirit and new usage into the national legislation; by degrees it was so completely transformed that it was no longer recognisable, and in the seventeenth century, for instance, it was almost unknown. It had been replaced by a nondescript something, which was German indeed in name, but Roman in fact.

I find reason to believe that owing to these efforts of the legists, the condition of ancient Germanic society deteriorated in many respects, especially so far as the peasants were concerned; many of those who had succeeded until then in preserving the whole or part of their liberties or of their possessions, lost them at this period by learned assimilations of their condition to that of the Roman bondsmen or emphyteotes.

This gradual transformation of the national law, and the vain efforts which were made to oppose it, may be clearly traced in the history of Würtemberg.

From the origin of the county of that name in 1250, until the creation of the duchy in 1495, the legislation was purely indigenous; it was composed of customs and local laws made by the towns or by the Courts of Seignory, and of statutes promulgated by the Estates; ecclesiastical affairs alone were regulated by a foreign code, the canon law.

From 1495 the character of the legislation was changed: the Roman law began to penetrate; the *doctors*, as they were called, those who had studied law in the foreign schools, entered the Government and possessed themselves of the direction of the superior courts. During the whole of the first half of the sixteenth century political society maintained the same struggle against them that was going on in England at the same time, but with very different success. At the diet of Tübingen in 1514, and at those which succeeded it, the representatives of feudalism and the deputies of the towns made all kinds of representations against that which was taking place; they attacked the legists who were invading all the courts, and changing the spirit or the letter of all customs and laws. The advantage at first seemed on their side; they obtained from the Government the promise that henceforth the high courts should be composed of honourable and enlightened

---

[1] These Notes and Illustrations were translated by the late Lady Duff Gordon.

men chosen from among the nobility and the Estates of the Duchy, and not of doctors, and that a commission composed of agents of the Government, and of representatives of the estates, should draw up the project of a code which might serve as a rule throughout the country. These efforts were vain. The Roman law soon drove the national law out of a great portion of the legislation, and even took root in the very ground on which it still suffered this legislation to subsist.

This victory of a foreign over the indigenous law is ascribed by many German historians to two causes :—
1. To the movement which at that period attracted all minds towards the languages and literature of antiquity, and the contempt which this inspired for the intellectual productions of the national genius. 2. To the idea which had always possessed the whole of the Middle Ages in Germany, and which displays itself even in the legislation of that period, that the Holy Empire was the continuation of the Roman Empire, and that the legislation of the former was an inheritance derived from the latter.

· These causes, however, are not sufficient to explain why the same law should at the same period have been introduced into the whole continent of Europe. I believe that this arose from the fact that at this time the absolute power of the sovereigns was everywhere established on the ruins of the ancient liberties of Europe, and that the Roman law, a law of servitude, was admirably fitted to second their views.

The Roman law which everywhere perfected civil society tended everywhere to degrade political society, inasmuch as it was chiefly the production of a highly civilised but much enslaved people. The kings of Europe accordingly adopted it with eagerness, and established it wherever they were the masters. Throughout Europe the interpreters of this law became their ministers or their chief agents. When called on to do so the legists even gave them the support of the law against the law itself, and they have frequently done so since. Wherever there was a sovereign who violated the laws we shall generally find at his side a legist who assured him that nothing was more lawful, and who proved most learnedly that his violence was just, and that the oppressed party was in the wrong.

NOTE (II.)—Page 13, line 37.

THE TRANSITION FROM FEUDAL TO DEMOCRATIC MONARCHY.

As all monarchies had become absolute about the same period, it is scarcely probable that this change of constitution was owing to any particular circumstance which accidentally occurred at the same time in every State, and we are led to the belief that all these similar and contemporary events must have been produced by some general cause, which simultaneously acted everywhere in the same manner.

This general cause was the transition from one state of society to another, from feudal inequality to democratic equality. The nobility was already depressed, and the people were not yet raised; the former were brought too low, and the latter were not sufficiently high to restrain the action of the ruling power. For a hundred and fifty years kings and princes enjoyed a sort of golden age, during which they possessed at once stability and unlimited power, two things which are usually incompatible; they were as sacred as the hereditary chiefs of a feudal monarchy, and as absolute as the rulers of a democratic society.

NOTE (III.)—Page 14, line 25.

DECAY OF THE FREE TOWNS OF GERMANY.—IMPERIAL TOWNS (REICHSTÄDTE).

According to the German historians the period of the greatest splendour of these towns was during the fourteenth and fifteenth centuries. They were then the abode of wealth, of the arts and sciences—masters of the commerce of Europe—the most powerful centres of civilisation. In the north and in the south of Germany especially, they had ended by forming independent confederations with the surrounding nobles, as the towns in Switzerland had done with the peasants.

In the sixteenth century they still enjoyed the same prosperity, but the period of their decay was come. Tho Thirty-years' War hastened their fall, and scarcely one of them escaped destruction and ruin during that period.

Nevertheless, the Treaty of Westphalia mentions them positively, and asserts their position as immediate States, that is to say, States which depended immediately upon the Emperor; but the neighbouring Sovereigns, on the one hand, and on the other the Emperor himself, the exercise of whose power, since the Thirty-years' War, was limited to the lesser vassals of the empire, restricted their sovereignty within narrower and narrower limits. In the eighteenth century fifty-one of them were still in existence, they filled two benches at the Diet, and had an independent vote there; but, in fact, they no longer exercised any influence upon the direction of general affairs.

At home they were all heavily burdened with debts, partly because they continued to be charged for the Imperial taxes at a rate suited to their former splendour, and partly because their own administration was extremely bad. It is very remarkable that this bad administration seemed to be the result of some secret disease which was common to them all, whatever might be the form of their constitution; whether aristocratic or democratic it equally gave rise to complaints, which, if not precisely similar, were equally violent; if aristocratic, the Government was said to have become a coterie composed of a few families: everything was done by favour and private interest; if democratic, popular intrigue and venality appeared on every side. In either case there were complaints of the want of honesty and disinterestedness on the part of the Governments. The Emperor was continually forced to interpose in their affairs, and to try to restore order in them. Their population decreased, and distress prevailed in them. They were no longer the abodes of German civilisation; the arts left them, and went to shine in the new towns created by the sovereigns, and representing modern society. Trade forsook them—their ancient energy and patriotic vigour disappeared. Hamburg almost alone still remained a great centre of wealth and intelligence, but this was owing to causes quite peculiar to herself.

NOTE (IV.)—Page 19, line 14.

DATE OF THE ABOLITION OF SERFDOM IN GERMANY.

The following table will show that the abolition of serfdom in most parts of Germany has taken place very recently. Serfdom was abolished—

1. In Baden, in 1783.

2. In Hohenzollern, in 1804.

3. In Schleswig and Holstein, in 1804.

4. In Nassau, in 1808.

5. In Prussia, Frederick William I. had done away with serfdom in his

own domains so early as 1717. The code of the Great Frederick, as we have already seen, was intended to abolish it throughout the kingdom, but in reality it only got rid of it in its hardest form, the *leibeigenschaft*, and retained it in the mitigated shape of *erbunterthänigkeit*. It was not till 1809 that it disappeared altogether.

6. In Bavaria serfdom disappeared in 1808.

7. A decree of Napoleon, dated from Madrid in 1808, abolished it in the Grand-duchy of Berg, and in several other small territories, such as Erfurt, Baireuth, &c.

8. In the kingdom of Westphalia, its destruction dates from 1808 and 1809.

9. In the principality of Lippe Detmold, from 1809.

10. In Schomburg Lippe, from 1810.

11. In Swedish Pomerania, from 1810 also.

12. In Hessen Darmstadt, from 1809 and 1811.

13. Würtemberg, from 1817.

14. In Mecklenburg, from 1820.

15. In Oldenburg, from 1814.

16. In Saxony for Lusatia, from 1832.

17. In Hohenzollern-Sigmaringen, only from 1833.

18. In Austria, from 1811. So early as in 1782 Joseph II. had destroyed *leibeigenschaft*; but serfage in its mitigated form of *erbunterthänigkeit* lasted till 1811.

Note (V.)—Page 19, line 17.

A part of the countries which are now German, such as Brandenburg, Prussia proper, and Silesia, were originally inhabited by a Slavonic race, and were conquered and partially occupied by Germans. In those countries serfdom had a far harsher aspect than in Germany itself, and left far stronger traces at the end of the eighteenth century.

Note (VI.)—Page 20, line 11.

CODE OF FREDERICK THE GREAT.

Amongst the works of Frederick the Great the least known, even in his own country, and the least brilliant, is the Code drawn up under his directions and promulgated by his successor. I do not know, however, whether any of them throws more light upon the man himself and on his time, or which more fully displays their reciprocal influence on each other.

This code is a real constitution, in the sense usually attached to the word; it undertakes to define not only the relations of the citizens to one another, but also the relations between the citizens and the State: it is at once a civil code, a criminal code, and a charter.

It rests, or appears to rest, on a certain number of general principles expressed in a very philosophical and abstract form, and resembling in many respects those which abound in the Declaration of the Rights of Man in the French Constitution of 1791.

It proclaims that the good of the State and of its inhabitants is the object of society and the limit of the law; that the laws cannot restrict the liberty or the rights of citizens except for the sake of public utility; that every member of the State is bound to labour for the public good, according to his position and fortune; and that the rights of individuals must give way to the interests of the public.

There is no mention of the hereditary right of the Sovereign and his family, nor even of any private rights distinct from the rights of the State. The name of the State is the only one used to designate royal power.

On the other hand, much is said about the general rights of man : these general rights of man are based on the natural liberty of each to pursue his advantage, provided it be done without injury to the rights of others. All actions not forbidden by the natural law, or by the positive laws of the State, are permitted. Every inhabitant of the State may demand from it protection for his person and property, and has the right to defend himself by force if the State does not come to his assistance.

After laying down these first great principles, the legislator, instead of deducing from them, as in the code of 1791, the doctrine of the sovereignty of the people and the organisation of a popular government in a free state of society, turns shortly round and arrives at another result equally democratic but by no means liberal ; he looks upon the sovereign as the sole representative of the State, and invests him with all the rights that have been recognised as belonging to society. In this code the sovereign is no longer the representative of God, he is the representative of society, its agent and its servant, to use Frederick's own words printed in his works ; but he alone represents it, he alone wields its whole power. The head of the State, says the Introduction, whose duty it is to bring forth the general good, which is the sole object of society, is authorised to govern and direct all the actions of individuals towards that end.

Among the chief duties of this all-powerful agent of society we find the following : to preserve peace and public security at home, and to protect every one against violence. Abroad it is for him to make peace or war ; he only is to make laws and enact general police regulations ; he alone possesses the right to pronounce pardons and to stop criminal proceedings.

All associations that may exist in the State, and all public establishments, are subject to his inspection and direction for the sake of general peace and security. In order that the head of the State may be enabled to fulfil these obligations, he must possess certain revenues and profitable rights ; accordingly he has the power of taxing private fortunes and persons, their professions, their trades, their produce, or their consumption. The orders given by the public functionaries who act in his name are to be obeyed, like his own, in all matters within the limits of their functions.

Beneath this perfectly modern head we shall presently see a thoroughly Gothic body ; Frederick only removed from it whatever stood in the way of the action of his own power, and the result was a monster which looked like a transition from one order of creation to another. In this strange production Frederick exhibited as much contempt for logic as care for his own power and anxiety not to place needless difficulties in his own way by attacking that which was still strong enough to defend itself.

The inhabitants of the rural districts, with the exception of a few districts and a few places, were in a state of hereditary servitude, which was not confined to the forced labour and services inherent to the possession of certain estates, but which extended, as we have seen, to the person of the possessor.

Most of the privileges of the owners of the soil were confirmed afresh by the code ; it may even be said that they were confirmed in opposition to the code, since it states that where the local customs and the new legislation differed the former were to be followed. It formally declares that the State cannot destroy any of these privileges except by purchasing them and the following forms of justice.

The code asserted, it is true, that serfage, properly so called (*leibeigenschaft*), inasmuch as it established personal servitude, was abolished, but the hereditary subjection which replaced it (*erbunterthänigkeit*) was still a kind of servitude, as may be seen by reading the text.

In the same code the burgher remained carefully separated from the peasant ; between the burghers and the nobility a sort of intermediate class was recognised, composed of high functionaries who were not noble, ecclesiastics, professors of learned schools, gymnasia and universities.

Though apart from the rest of the burghers, these men were by no means confounded with the nobles; they remained in a position of inferiority towards them. They could not in general purchase noble estates (*rittergüter*), or fill the highest places in the civil service. Moreover, they were not *hoffähig*, that is to say, they could not be presented at court except in very rare cases, and never with their families. As in France, this inferiority was the more irksome, because every day this class became more enlightened and influential, and the burgher functionaries of the State, though they did not occupy the most brilliant posts, already filled those in which the work was the hardest and the most important. The irritation against the privileges of the nobility, which was about to contribute so largely to the French Revolution, prepared the way for the approbation with which it was at first received in Germany. The principal author of the code, nevertheless, was a burgher; but he doubtless followed the directions of his master.

The ancient constitution of Europe was not sufficiently destroyed in this part of Germany to make Frederick believe that, in spite of the contempt with which he regarded it, the time was yet come for sweeping away its remains. He mostly confined himself to depriving the nobles of the right of assembling and governing collectively, and left each individual in possession of his privileges, only restricting and regulating their application. Thus it happened that this code, drawn up under the direction of a disciple of our philosophers, and put in force after the French Revolution had broken out, is the most authentic and the most recent legislative document that gives a legal basis to those very feudal inequalities which the Revolution was about to abolish throughout Europe.

In it the nobility was declared to be the principal body in the State; the nobles were to be appointed by preference, it says, to all posts of honour which they might be competent to fill. They alone might possess noble estates, create entails, enjoy the privileges of sporting and of the administration of justice inherent in noble estates, as well as the rights of patronage over the Church; they alone might take the name of the estates they possessed. The burghers who were authorised by express exemption to own noble estates could only enjoy the rights and honours attached to their ownership, within the precise limits of this permission. A burgher possessed of a noble estate could not bequeath it to an heir of his own class unless he was within the first degree of consanguinity. If there was no such heir, or any heir of noble birth, the estate was to be sold by public auction.

One of the most characteristic parts of Frederick's code is the penal law for political offences, which is appended to it.

The successor of the Great Frederick, Frederick William II., who, in spite of the feudal and absolutist portion of the legislation, of which I have given a sketch, thought he perceived a revolutionary tendency in his uncle's production, and accordingly delayed its publication until 1794, was only reassured, it is said, by the excellent penal regulations by means of which this code corrected the bad principles which it contained. Never, indeed, has anything been contrived, even since that time, more perfect in its kind; not only were revolts and conspiracies to be punished with the greatest severity, but even disrespectful criticisms of the acts of the Government were likewise to be most severely repressed. The purchase and dissemination of dangerous works was carefully prohibited; the printer, the publisher, and the disseminator were made responsible for the sins of the author. Ridottos, masquerades, and other amusements, were declared to be public assemblages, and must be authorised by the police; the same thing held good with respect to dinners in public places. The liberty of the press and of speech was completely subjected to an arbitrary surveillance; the carrying of fire-arms was also prohibited.

In the midst of this production, of which half was borrowed from the Middle Ages, there appear regulations, which, by their extreme spirit of centralisation, actually bordered on socialism. Thus, it is laid down that it is incumbent on the State to provide food, work, and wages for all who are unable to maintain themselves, and who are not entitled to assistance either from the lord or from the parish: for such as these work was to be provided, according to their strength and capacity. The State was to form establishments for the relief of the poverty of its citizens; the State, moreover, was authorised to destroy foundations which tended to encourage idleness, and to distribute amongst the poor the money under their control.

The novelty and boldness of the theories, and the timidity in practice which characterises this work of the Great Frederick, may be found in every part of it. On the one hand, it proclaimed the great principle of modern society, that all ought to be alike subject to taxation; on the other, it suffered the provincial laws, which contain exemptions from this rule, to subsist. It ordained that all lawsuits between a subject and the sovereign shall be judged according to the forms and precedents laid down for all other litigation; but, in fact, this rule was never obeyed when the interests or the passions of the King were opposed to it. The Mill of Sans-Souci was ostentatiously exhibited, while on many other occasions justice was quietly suppressed.

The best proof of how little real innovation was contained in this apparently innovating code, and which, therefore, renders it a most curious study for those who desire to know the true state of society in that part of Germany at the end of the eighteenth century, is that the Prussian nation scarcely seemed to be conscious of its publication. The legists alone studied it, and at the present day a great number of educated men have never read it.

NOTE (VII.)—Page 21, last line.

LANDS OF THE PEASANTS IN GERMANY.

Amongst the peasantry there were many families who were not only freemen and owners of land, but whose estates formed a perpetual entail. The estate they possessed could not be divided, and was inherited by only one of the sons, usually the youngest, as is the case in certain English customs. This son was only bound to pay a certain portion to his brothers and sisters.

These *Erbgüter* of the peasantry were more or less common throughout Germany; for in no part of it was the whole of the soil swallowed up by the feudal system. In Silesia, where the nobility still retain immense domains, of which most of the villages formed a part, there were nevertheless villages owned entirely by their inhabitants, and entirely free. In certain parts of Germany, such as the Tyrol and Friesland, the predominant state of things was that the peasants owned the soil as *Erbgüter*.

But in the greater part of Germany this kind of possession was but a more or less frequent exception. In the villages where it existed the small proprietors of this kind formed a sort of aristocracy among the peasantry.

Note (VIII.)—Page 22, line 3.

POSITION OF THE NOBILITY AND DIVISION OF LANDS ALONG THE BANKS OF
THE RHINE.

From information gathered on the spot, and from persons who lived under the old state of things, I gather that in the Electorate of Cologne, for instance, there was a great number of villages without lords, governed by the agents of the Prince; that in those places where the nobility existed, its administrative powers were much restricted; that its position was rather brilliant than powerful (at least individually); that they enjoyed many honours, and formed part of the council of the Prince, but exercised no real and immediate power over the people. I have ascertained from other sources that in the same electorate property was much divided, and that a great number of the peasants were landowners; this was mainly attributable to the state of embarrassment and almost distress in which so many of the noble families had long lived, and which compelled them constantly to alienate small portions of their land which were bought by the peasants, either for ready money or at a fixed rent-charge. I have read a census of the population of the Bishopric of Cologne at the beginning of the eighteenth century, which gives the state of landed property at that time, and I find that even then one-third of the soil belonged to the peasants. From this fact arose a combination of feelings and ideas which brought the population of this part of Germany far nearer to a state of revolution than that of other districts in which these peculiarities had not yet shown themselves.

Note (IX.)—Page 22, line 27.

HOW THE USURY LAWS HAD ACCELERATED THE SUBDIVISION OF THE SOIL.

A law prohibiting usury at whatever rate of interest was still in force at the end of the eighteenth century. We learn from Turgot that even so late as 1769 it was still observed in many places. The law subsists, says he, though it is often violated. The consular judges allow interest stipulated without alienation of the capital, while the ordinary tribunals condemn it. We may still see fraudulent debtors bring criminal actions against their creditors for lending them money without alienation of the capital.

Independently of the effects which this legislation could not fail to produce upon commerce, and upon the industrial habits of the nation generally, it likewise had a very marked influence on the division and tenure of the land. It had multiplied, *ad infinitum*, perpetual rent-charges, both on real and other property. It had led the ancient owners of the soil instead of borrowing when they wanted money to sell small portions of their estates for payments partly in capital and partly in perpetual annuities; this had contributed greatly on the one hand to the subdivision of the soil, and on the other to burdening the small proprietors with a multitude of perpetual services.

NOTE (X.)—Page 25, line 9.

EXAMPLE OF THE PASSIONS EXCITED BY THE TITHES TEN YEARS BEFORE THE
REVOLUTION.

In 1779 an obscure lawyer of Lucé complained in very bitter language, which already had a flavour of the revolution, that the curés and other great titheholders sold to the farmers, at an exorbitant price, the straw they had received in tithe, which was indispensable to the latter for making manure.

NOTE (XI.)—Page 25, line 15.

EXAMPLE OF THE MANNER IN WHICH THE CLERGY ALIENATED THE PEOPLE
BY THE EXERCISE OF ITS PRIVILEGES.

In 1780 the prior and the canons of the priory of Laval complained of an attempt to subject them to the payment of the tariff duties on articles of consumption, and on the materials needed for the repairs of their buildings. They pleaded that as the tariff duties represented the *taille*, and as they were exempt from the *taille*, they therefore owed nothing. The minister referred them to a decision at the election, with the right of appeal to the *Cour des Aides*.

NOTE (XII.)—Page 25, line 23.

FEUDAL RIGHTS POSSESSED BY PRIESTS.—ONE EXAMPLE FROM AMONGST A
THOUSAND.

Abbey of Cherbourg (1753).—This abbey possessed at this period the seignorial rent-charges, payable in money or in kind in almost every parish round Cherbourg ; one single village owed it three hundred and six bushels of wheat. It owned the barony of Ste. Geneviève, the barony and the seignorial mill of Bas-du-Roule, and the barony of Neuville-au-Plein, situated at a distance of at least ten leagues. It received moreover the tithes of twelve parishes in the peninsula, of which several were very distant from it.

NOTE (XIII.)—Page 27, line 21.

IRRITATION AMONG THE PEASANTS CAUSED BY FEUDAL RIGHTS, AND ESPE-
CIALLY BY THE FEUDAL RIGHTS OF THE PRIESTS.

The following letter was written shortly before the Revolution by a farmer to the Intendant himself. It cannot be quoted as an authority for the truth of the facts which it alleges, but it is a perfect indication of the state of feeling among the class to which its writer belonged.

'Although we have few nobles in this part of the country,' says he, ' you must not suppose that the land is any the less burdened with rent-charges; far from it, almost all the fiefs belong to the cathedral, to the archbishopric, to the College of St. Martin, to the Benedictines of Noir-moutiers, of Saint Julien, and other ecclesiastics, who never suffer them to lapse from disuse, but perpetually hatch fresh ones out of musty old parchments which are manufactured God only knows how !

'The whole country is infected with rent-charges. The greater part of the land owes annually a seventh of wheat per half acre, others owe wine; one has to send a quarter of his fruit to the seigneurie, another the fifth, &c., the tithe being always previously deducted; this man a twelfth, that a thirteenth. All these rights are so strange that I know them of all amounts, from a fourth to a fortieth of the fruit.

' What is to be said of the dues payable in all kinds of grain, vegetables, money, poultry, labour, wood, fruit, candles ?

'I know strange dues in bread, wax, eggs, pigs without the head, wreaths of roses, bunches of violets, gilt spurs, &c. There is also a countless multitude of other seignorial rights. Why has not France been released from all these absurd dues ? At last men's eyes are beginning to be opened, and everything may be hoped from the wisdom of the present Government : it will stretch forth a helping hand to the poor victims of the exactions of the old fiscal laws called seignorial rights, which ought never to be alienated or sold.

' Again, what shall we think of the tyranny of fines (*lods et ventes*)? A purchaser exhausts his means to buy some land, and is then compelled to pay heavy expenses for adjudication and contract, entering upon possession, *procès-verbaux* (*contrôle*), verification and registration (*insinuation*), hundredth *denier*, eight sous in the livre, &c. : and besides all this, he has to submit his contract to his seigneur, who makes him pay the fines (*lods et ventes*) on the principal of his purchase; some exact a twelfth, others a tenth : some demand a fifteenth, others a fifteenth and the fifth of that again. In short they are to be found of all prices; and I even know some who exact a third of

the purchase money. No, the fiercest and most barbarous nations in the universe never invented exactions so great and so numerous as those of which our tyrants have heaped upon the heads of our forefathers.' (This philosophical and literary tirade is misspelt throughout.)

' How ! can the late king have authorised the redemption of rent-charges on property in towns and not have included those in the country ? The latter ought to have come first : why should the poor farmers not be allowed to burst their fetters, to redeem and free themselves from the multitude of seignorial rent-charges which cause so much injury to the vassals and so little profit to their lords ? There ought to be no distinction as to the power of redemption between town and country and between the lords and private persons.

' The Intendants of the incumbents of ecclesiastical property pillage and mulct all their farmers every time the property changes hands. We have a recent example of this. The intendant of our new archbishop on his arrival gave notice to quit to all the farmers of his predecessor M. de Fleury, declared all the leases which they had taken under him to be void, and turned out all who would not double their leases and give over again heavy "pots de vin," which they had already paid to the intendant of M. de Fleury. They were thus deprived, in the most notorious manner, of seven or eight years of their leases which had still to run, and were forced to leave their homes suddenly just before Christmas, the most critical time of the year on account of the difficulty of procuring food for cattle, without knowing where to go for shelter. The King of Prussia could have done no worse.'

It seems, indeed, that on ecclesiastical property the leases of the preceding incumbent were not legally binding on his successor. The author of the above letter is quite correct in his statement that the feudal rent-charges were redeemable in the towns and not in the country. It is a fresh proof of the neglect shown towards the peasantry, and of the way in which all those placed above them found means to forward their own interests.

NOTE (XIV.)—Page 27, line 27.

EFFECTS OF FEUDALISM.

Every institution that has long been dominant, after establishing itself firmly in its proper sphere, penetrates beyond it, and ends by exerting considerable influence even over that part of the legislation which it does not govern; thus feudalism, although it belonged above all to political law, had transformed the whole civil law as well, and deeply modified the state of property and of persons in all the relations of private life. It had affected the law of inheritance by the inequality of partition, a principle which had even reached down to the middle classes in certain provinces, for instance, Normandy. Its influence had extended over all real property, for no landed estates were entirely excluded from its action, or of which the owners did not in some way feel its effects. It affected not only the property of individuals but even that of the communes; it reacted on manufactures by the duties which it levied upon them; it reacted on private incomes by the inequality of public employments, and on pecuniary interests generally in every man's business; on landowners by dues, rent-charges, and the corvée; on the tenant in a thousand different ways, amongst others by the *banalités* (the right of the seigneur to compel his vassals to grind their corn at his mill, &c.), seignorial monopolies, perpetual rent-charges, fines, &c.; on tradesmen, by the market dues; on merchants by the transport dues, &c. By putting the final stroke to the feudal system the Revolution made itself seen and felt, so to speak, at all the most sensitive points of private interest.

NOTE (XV.)—Page 35, line 8.

PUBLIC CHARITY DISTRIBUTED BY THE STATE.—FAVOURITISM.

In 1748 the King granted 20,000 lbs. of rice (it was a year of great want and scarcity, like so many in the eighteenth century). The Archbishop of Tours asserted that this relief was obtained by him, and ought therefore to be distributed by him alone and in his own diocese. The Intendant declared that the succour was granted to the whole *généralité*, and ought therefore to be distributed by him to all the different parishes. After a protracted struggle, the King, by way of conciliating both, doubled the quantity of rice intended for the *généralité*, so that the Archbishop and the Intendant might each distribute half. Both were agreed that the distribution should be made by the curés. There was no question of entrusting it to the seigneurs or to the syndics. We see, from the correspondence between the Intendant and the Comptroller-General, that in the opinion of the former the Archbishop wanted to give the rice entirely to his own protégés, and especially to cause the greater part of it to be distributed in the parishes belonging to the Duchess of Rochechouart. On the other hand, we find among these papers letters from great noblemen asking relief for their own parishes in particular, and letters from the Comptroller-General recommending the parishes belonging to particular persons.

Legal charity gives scope for abuses, whatever be the system pursued; but it is perfectly impracticable when exercised from a distance and without publicity by the Central Government.

No   (XVI.)—Page 35, line 8.

We find in the report made to the provincial assembly of Upper Guienne in 1780: 'Out of the sum of 385,000 livres, the amount of the funds granted by his Majesty to this *généralité* from 1773, when the *travaux de charité* were first established, until 1779 inclusively, the elective district of Montauban, which is the chef-lieu and residence of the Intendant, has received for its own share above 240,000 livres, the greater part of which sum was actually paid to the communauté of Montauban.

NOTE (XVII.)—Page 35, line 12.

POWERS OF THE INTENDANT FOR THE REGULATION OF TRADES AND MANUFACTURES.

The archives of the Intendancies are full of documents relating to this regulation of trades and manufactures.

Not only was industry subjected to the restrictions placed upon it by the *corps d'état*, *maîtrises*, &c., but it was abandoned to all the caprices of the Government, usually represented by the King's council, as far as general regulations went, and by the intendants in their special application. We find the latter constantly interfering as to the length of which the pieces of cloth are to be woven, the pattern to be chosen, the method to be followed, and the defects to be avoided in the manufacture. They had under their orders, independently of the sub-delegates, local inspectors of manufactures. In this respect centralisation was pushed even further than at the present time; it was more capricious and more arbitrary: it raised up swarms of public functionaries, and created all manner of habits of submission and dependence.

It must be remembered that these habits were engrafted above all upon the manufacturing and commercial middle classes whose triumph was at hand, far more than upon those which were doomed to defeat. Accordingly the Revolution, instead of destroying these habits, could not fail to make them spread and predominate.

All the preceding remarks have been suggested by the perusal of a voluminous correspondence and other documents, entitled 'Manufactures and Fabrics, Drapery, Dry-goods,' which are to be found among the remaining papers belonging to the archives of the Intendancy of the Isle of France. They likewise contain frequent and detailed reports from the inspectors to the Intendant of the visits they have made to the various manufactures, in order to ascertain whether the regulations laid down for the methods of fabrication are observed. There are, moreover, sundry orders in council, given by the advice of the Intendant, prohibiting or permitting the manufacture, either in certain places, of certain stuffs, or according to certain methods.

The predominant idea in the remarks of these inspectors, who treat the manufacturers with great disdain, is that it is the duty and the right of the State to compel them to do their very best, not only for the sake of the public interest, but for their own. Accordingly they thought themselves bound to force them to adopt the best methods, and to enter carefully into every detail of their art, accompanying this kind interest with countless prohibitions and enormous fines.

NOTE (XVIII.)—Page 36, last line.

SPIRIT OF THE GOVERNMENT OF LOUIS XI.

No document better enables us to estimate the true spirit of the government of Louis XI. than the numerous constitutions granted by him to the towns. I have had occasion to study very carefully those which he conferred on most of the towns of Anjou, of Maine, and of Touraine.

All these constitutions are formed on the same model, and the same designs are manifest in them all. The figure of Louis XI., which they reveal to us, is rather different from the one which we are familiar with. We are accustomed to consider him as the enemy of the nobility, but at the same time as the sincere though somewhat stern friend of the people. Here, however, he shows the same hatred towards the political rights of the people and of the nobility. He makes use of the middle classes to pull down those above them, and to keep down those below : he is equally anti-aristocratic and anti-democratic ; he is essentially the citizen-king. He heaps privileges upon the principal persons of the towns, whose importance he desires to increase ; he profusely confers nobility on them, thus lowering its value, and at the same time he destroys the whole popular and democratic character of the administration of the towns, and restricts the government of them to a small number of families attached to his reforms, and bound to his authority by immense advantages.

NOTE (XIX.)—Page 37, line 30.

ADMINISTRATION OF A TOWN IN THE EIGHTEENTH CENTURY.

I extract from the inquiry made in 1764 into the administration of towns, the document relating to Angers ; in it we shall find the constitution of the town analysed, attacked, and defended by turns by the Présidial, the Corporation, the Sub-delegate, and the Intendant. As the same facts were repeated in a great number of other places, this must not be looked upon merely as an individual picture.

'*Report of the Présidial on the actual state of the Municipal Corporation of Angers, and on the Reforms to be made in it.*'

'The corporation of Angers,' says the Présidial, ' never consults the inhabitants generally, even on the most important subjects, except in cases in which it is obliged by special orders to do so. This system of administration is, therefore, unknown to all those who do not belong to the corporation, even to the échevins amovibles, who have but a very superficial idea of it.'

(The tendency of all these small civic oligarchies was, indeed, to consult what are here called the inhabitants generally as little as possible.)

The corporation was composed, according to an arrêt de règlement of 29th March, 1681, of twenty-one officers :—

A mayor, who becomes noble, and whose functions continue for four years.

Four échevins amovibles, who remain in office two years.

Twelve échevins conseillers, who, when once elected, remain for life.

Two procureurs de ville.

One procureur in reversion.

One greffier.

They possessed various privileges, amongst others the following : their capitation tax was fixed and moderate ; they were exempt from having soldiers billeted upon them and from providing ustensiles, fournitures, and contributions ; from the franchise des droits, the cloison double and triple, the old and new octroi and accessoire on all articles of consumption, even from the don gratuit, from which, says the Présidial, they chose to exempt themselves on their own private authority; they receive moreover allowances for wax-lights, and some of them salaries and apartments.

We see by these details that it was a very pleasant thing to be perpetual échevins of Angers in those days. Always and everywhere we find the system which makes the exemption from taxation fall on the richest classes. In a subsequent part of the same report we read: 'These places are sought by the richest inhabitants, who aspire to them in order to obtain a considerable reduction of capitation, the surcharge of which falls on the others. There are at present several municipal officers, whose fixed capitation is 30 livres, whereas they ought to be taxed 250 or 800 livres; there is one especially among them, who, considering his fortune, might pay, at least, 1000 livres of capitation tax.' We find in another part of the same report, that 'amongst the richest inhabitants there are upwards of forty officers, or widows of officers (men holding office), whose places confer on them the privilege of not contributing to the heavy capitation levied on the town; the burden of this capitation accordingly falls on a vast number of poor artisans, who think themselves overtaxed, and constantly appeal against the excessive charges upon them, though almost always unjustly, inasmuch as there is no inequality in the distribution of the amount, which remains to be paid by the town.'

The General Assembly consisted of seventy-six persons :—

The Mayor;
Two deputies from the Chapter;
One Syndic of the clerks;
Two deputies from the Présidial;
One deputy from the University;
One Lieutenant-general of Police;
Four Échevins;
Twelve Conseillers-échevins;

One Procureur du Roi au Présidial;
One Procureur de Ville;
Two deputies from the Eaux et Forêts;
Two from the Élection (elective district ?);
Two from the Grenier à sel;
Two from the Traites;
Two from the Mint;
Two from the body of Avocats and Procureurs;
Two from the Juges Consuls;
Two from the Notaries;
Two from the body of Merchants; and, lastly,
Two sent by each of the sixteen parishes.

These last were supposed to represent the people, properly so called, especially the industrial corporations. We see that care had been taken to keep them in a constant minority.

When the places in the town corporation fell vacant, the general assembly selected three persons to fill each vacancy.

Most of the offices belonging to the Hôtel de Ville were not exclusively given to members of corporations, as was the case in several municipal constitutions, that is to say, the electors were not obliged to choose from among them their magistrates, advocates, &c. This was highly disapproved by the members of the Présidial.

According to this Présidial, which appears to have been filled with the most violent jealousy against the corporation of the town, and which I strongly suspect objected to nothing so much in the municipal constitution as that it did not enjoy as many privileges in it as it desired, 'the General Assembly, which is too numerous, and consists, in part, of persons of very little intelligence, ought only to be consulted in cases of sale of the communal domains, loans, establishment of octrois, and elections of municipal officers. All other business matters might be discussed in a smaller assembly, composed only of the *notables*. This assembly should consist only of the Lieutenant-General of the Sénéchaussée, the Procureur du Roi, and twelve other notables, chosen from amongst the six bodies of clergy, magistracy, nobility, university, trade, and bourgeois, and others not belonging to the above-named bodies. The choice of the notables should at first be confined to the General Assembly, and subsequently to the Assembly of *Notables*, or to the body from which each *notable* is to be selected.'

All these functionaries of the State, who thus entered in virtue of their office or as *notables* into the municipal corporations of the ancien régime, frequently resembled those of the present day as to the name of the office which they held, and sometimes even as to the nature of that office; but they differed from them completely as to the position which they held, which must be carefully borne in mind, unless we wish to arrive at false conclusions. Almost all these functionaries were *notables* of the town previous to being invested with public functions, or they had striven to obtain public functions in order to become notables; they had no thought of leaving their own town and no hope of any higher promotion, which alone is sufficient to distinguish them completely from anything with which we are acquainted at the present day.

Report of the Municipal Officers. —We see by this that the corporation of the town was created in 1474, by Louis XI., on the ruins of the ancient democratic constitution of the town, on the system which we have already described of restricting political rights to the middle classes only, of setting aside or weakening the popular influence, of creating a great number of municipal officers in order to interest a greater number of persons in his reform, of a prodigal grant of hereditary nobility, and of all sorts of privileges, to that part of the middle classes in whose hands the administration was placed.

We find in the same report letters patent from the successors of Louis XI. which acknowledge this new constitution, while they still further restrict the power of the people. We learn that in 1485 the letters patent issued to this effect by Charles VIII. were attacked before the parliament by the inhabitants of Angers, just as in England a lawsuit, arising out of the charter of a town, would have been brought before a court of justice.

In 1601 a decision of the parliament determined the political rights created by the Royal Charter. From that time forward nothing appears but the *conseil du Roi.*

We gather from the same report that, not only for the office of mayor, but for all other offices belonging to the corporation of the town, the General Assembly proposed three candidates, from amongst whom the King selects one, in virtue of a decree of the council of 22nd June, 1708. It appears, moreover, that in virtue of decisions of the council of 1733 and 1741, the merchants had the right of claiming one place of *échevin* or *conseiller* (the perpetual échevins). Lastly, we find that at that period the corporation of the town was entrusted with the distribution of the sums levied for the capitation, the *ustensile*, the barracks, the support of the poor, the soldiery, coast-guard, and foundlings.

There follows a long enumeration of the labours to be undergone by the municipal officers, which fully justified, in their opinion, the privileges and the perpetual tenure of office, which they were evidently greatly afraid of losing. Many of the reasons which they assign for their exertions are curious; amongst others, the following: 'Their most important avocations,' they say, 'consist in the examination of financial affairs, which continually increased, owing to the constant extension of the *droits d'aides*, the *gabelle*, the *contrôle*, the *insinuation des actes*, *perception illicite des droits d'enrégistrement et de francs fiefs*. The opposition which was incessantly offered by the financial companies to these various taxes compelled them to defend actions in behalf of the town before the various jurisdictions, either the parliament or the *conseil du Roi*, in order to resist the oppression under which they suffered. The experience and practice of thirty years had taught them that the term of a man's life scarcely suffices to guard against all the snares and pitfalls which the clerks of all the departments of the *fermes* continually set for the citizens in order to keep their own commissions.'

The most curious circumstance is,

that all this is addressed to the Comptroller-General himself, in order to dispose him favourably towards the privileges of those who make the statement, so inveterate had the habit become of looking upon the companies charged with the collection of the taxes as an enemy who might be attacked on every side without blame or opposition. This habit grew stronger and more universal every day, until all taxation came to be looked upon as an unfair and hateful tyranny; not as the agent of all men, but as the common enemy.

'The union of all the offices,' the report goes on to say, 'was effected for the first time by an order in council of the 4th September, 1694, for a sum of 22,000 livres;' that is to say, that the offices were redeemed in that year for the above-named sum. By an order of 26th April, 1723, the municipal offices created by the edict of 24th May, 1722, were united to the corporation of the town, or, in other words, the town was authorised to purchase them. By another order of 24th May, 1723, the town was permitted to borrow 120,000 livres for the purchase of the said offices. Another order of 26th July, 1728, allowed it to borrow 50,000 livres for the purchase of the office of *greffier* secretary of the Hôtel de Ville. 'The town,' says the report, 'has paid these moneys in order to maintain the freedom of its elections, and to secure to the officers elected—some for two years and others for life—the various prerogatives belonging to their offices.' A part of the municipal offices having been re-established by the edict of November, 1733, an order in council intervened, dated 11th January, 1751, at the request of the mayor and échevins, fixing the rate of redemption at 170,000 livres, for the payment of which a prorogation of the octrois was granted for fifteen years.

This is a good specimen of the administration of the monarchy, as far as the towns were concerned. They were forced to contract debts, and then authorised to impose extraordinary and temporary taxes in order to pay them. Moreover, I find that these temporary taxes were frequently rendered perpetual after some time, and then the Government took its share of them.

The report continues thus: 'The municipal officers were only deprived of the important judicial powers with which Louis XI. had invested them by the establishment of royal jurisdictions. Until 1669 they took cognisance of all disputes between masters and workmen. The accounts of the octrois are rendered to the Intendant, as directed in all the decrees for the creation or prorogation of the said octrois.'

We likewise find in this report that the deputies of the sixteen parishes, who were mentioned above, and who appeared at the General Assembly, were chosen by the companies, corporations, or *communautés*, and that they were strictly the envoys of the small bodies by which they were deputed. They were bound by exact instructions on every point of business.

Lastly, this report proves that at Angers, as everywhere else, every kind of expenditure was to be authorised by the Intendant and the Council; and, it must be admitted, that when the administration of a town is given over completely into the hands of a certain number of men, to whom, instead of fixed salaries, are conceded privileges which place them personally beyond the reach of the consequences which their administration may produce upon the private fortunes of their fellow-citizens, this administrative superintendence may appear necessary.

The whole of the report, which is very ill drawn up, betrays extraordinary dread, on the part of the official men, of any change in the existing order of things. All manner of arguments, good and bad, are brought forward by them in favour of maintaining the *status quo*.

Report of the Sub-delegate.—The Intendant having received these two reports of opposite tendency, desires to have the opinion of his Sub-delegate, who gives it as follows:—

'The report of the municipal councillors,' says he, 'does not deserve a moment's attention; it is merely intended to defend the privileges of those officers. That of the *présidial* may be consulted with advantage; but there is no reason for granting all the prerogatives claimed by those magistrates.'

According to the Sub-delegate, the constitution of the Hôtel de Ville has long stood in need of reform. Besides the immunities already mentioned, which were enjoyed by the municipal officers of Angers, he informs us that the Mayor, during his tenure of office, had a dwelling which was worth, at least, 600 francs rent, a salary of 50 francs, and 100 francs for *frais de poste*, besides the *jetons*. The *procureur syndic* was also lodged, and the *greffier* as well. In order to procure their own exemption from the *droits d'aides* and the *octroi*, the municipal officers had fixed an assumed standard of consumption for each of them. Each of them had the right of importing into the town, free of duty, so many barrels of wine yearly, and the same with all other provisions.

The Sub-delegate does not propose to deprive the municipal councillors of their immunities from taxation, but he desires that their capitation, instead of being fixed and very inadequate, should be taxed every year by the Intendant. He desires that they should also be subject, like every one else, to the *don gratuit*, which they had dispensed themselves from paying, on what precedent no one can tell.

The municipal officers, the report says further, are charged with the duty of drawing up the *rôles de capitation* for all the inhabitants—a duty which they perform in a negligent and arbitrary manner; accordingly a vast number of complaints and memorials are sent in to the Intendant every year. It is much to be desired that henceforth the division should be made in the interest of each company or *communauté* by its own members, according to stated and general rules; the municipal officers would have to make out only the *rôles de capitation*. for the burghers and others who belong to no corporation, such as some of the artisans and the servants of all privileged persons.

The report of the Sub-delegate confirms what has already been said of the municipal officers—that the municipal offices had been redeemed by the town in 1735 for the sum of 170,000 livres.

Letter of the Intendant to the Comptroller-General.—Supported by all these documents, the Intendant writes to the Minister: ' It is important, for the sake of the inhabitants and of the public good, to reduce the corporation of the town, the members of which are too numerous and extremely burdensome to the public, on account of the privileges they enjoy.' ' I am struck,' continues the Intendant, ' with the enormous sums which have been paid at all periods for the redemption of the municipal offices at Angers. The amount of these sums, if employed on useful purposes, would have been profitable to the town, which, on the contrary, has gained nothing but an increased burden in the authority and privileges enjoyed by these officers.'

' The interior abuses of this administration deserve the whole attention of the council,' says the Intendant further. ' Independently of the *jetons* and the wax-lights, which consume an annual sum of 2127 livres (the amount fixed for expenses of this kind by the normal budget, which from time to time was prescribed for the towns by the King), the public moneys are squandered and misapplied at the will of these officers to clandestine purposes, and the *procureur du Roi*, who has been in possession of his place for thirty or forty years, has made himself so completely master of the administration, with the secret springs of which he alone is acquainted, that the inhabitants have at all times found it impossible to obtain the smallest information as to the employment of the communal revenues.' The result of all this is, that the Intendant requests the Minister to reduce the corporation of the town to a mayor appointed for four years, a *procureur du Roi* appointed for eight, and a *greffier* and *receveur* appointed for life.

Altogether the constitution which he proposes for this corporation is exactly the same as that which he elsewhere suggested for towns. In his opinion it would be desirable—

1st. To maintain the General Assembly, but only as an electoral body for the election of municipal officers.

2nd. To create an extraordinary

Conseil de Notables, which should perform all the functions which the edict of 1764 had apparently entrusted to the General Assembly; the said council to consist of twelve members, whose tenure of office should be for six years, and who should be elected, not by the General Assembly but by the twelve corporations considered as *notable* (each corporation·electing its own). He enumerates the *corps notables* as follows :—

The Présidial.
The University.
The Election.
The Officers of Woods and Forests.
The Grenier à sel.
The Traites.
The Mint.
The Avocats and Procureurs.
The Juges Consuls.
The Notaires.
The Tradesmen.
The Burghers.

It appears that nearly all these *notables* were public functionaries, and nearly all the public functionaries were notables ; hence we may conclude, as from a thousand other passages in these documents, that the middle classes were as greedy of place and as little inclined to seek a sphere of activity removed from Government employment. The only difference, as I have said in the text, was that formerly men purchased the trifling importance which office gave them, and that now the claimants beg and entreat some one to be so charitable as to get it for them gratis.

We see that, according to the project we have described, the whole municipal power was to rest with the extraordinary council, which would completely restrict the administration to a very small middle-class coterie, while the only assembly in which the people still made their appearance at all was to have no privilege beyond that of electing the municipal officers, without any right to advise or control them. It must also be observed that the Intendant was more in favour of restriction and more opposed to popular influence than the King, whose edict seemed intended to place most of the power in the hands of the General Assembly, and that the Intendant again is far more liberal and democratic than the middle classes, judging at least by the report I have quoted in the text, by which it appears that the *notables* of another town were desirous of excluding the people even from the election of municipal officers, a right which the King and the Intendant had left to them.

My readers will have observed that the Intendant uses the words burghers and tradesmen to designate two distinct categories of notables. It will not be amiss to give an exact definition of these words, in order to show into how many small fractions the middle classes were divided, and by how many petty vanities they were agitated.

The word *burgher* had a general and a restricted sense ; it was used to designate those belonging to the middle class, and also to specify a certain number of persons included within that class. 'The burghers are those whose birth and fortune enable them to live decently, without the exercise of any gainful pursuit,' says one of the reports produced on occasion of the inquiry in 1764. We see by the rest of the report that the word burgher was not to be used to designate those who belonged either to the companies or the industrial corporations ; but it is more difficult to define exactly to whom it should be applied. 'For,' the report goes on to say, ' amongst those who arrogate to themselves the title of burgher, there are many persons who have no other claim to it but their idleness, who have no fortune, and lead an obscure and uncultivated life. The burghers ought properly to be distinguished by fortune, birth, talent, morality, and a handsome way of living. The artisans, who compose the *communautés*, have never been admitted to the rank of *notables*.'

After the burghers, the mercantile men formed a second class, which belong to no company or corporation ; but the limits of this small class were hard to define. 'Are,' says the report, ' the petty tradesmen of low birth to be confounded with the great wholesale dealers ?' In order to resolve these difficulties, the report proposes to have a list of the *notable* tradesmen drawn up by the *échevins*, and given to their head or syndic, in order that he may summon to the deliberations at the Hôtel de Ville none but those set down in it. In this list none were to be inscribed who had been sérvants, porters, drivers, or who had filled any other mean offices.

NOTE (XX.)—Page 39, line 33.

One of the most salient characteristics of the eighteenth century, as regards the administration of the towns, was not so much the abolition of all representation and intervention of the public in their affairs as the extreme variation of the rules by which the administration was guided, rights were incessantly granted, recalled, restored, increased, diminished, and modified in a thousand different ways. Nothing more fully shows into what contempt these local liberties had fallen as this continual change in their laws, which seemed to excite no attention. This variation alone would have been sufficient to destroy beforehand all peculiar ideas, all love of old recollections, all local patriotism in those very institutions which afford the greatest scope for them. This it was which prepared the way for the great destruction of the past, which the Revolution was about to effect.

NOTE (XXI.)—Page 41, line 6.

ADMINISTRATION OF A VILLAGE IN THE EIGHTEENTH CENTURY. FROM THE PAPERS OF THE INTENDANCY OF THE ÎLE-DE-FRANCE.

I have selected the transaction which I am about to describe from amongst a number of others, in order to give an example of some of the forms followed by the parochial administration, to show how dilatory they were, and to give a picture of the General Assembly of a parish during the eighteenth century.

The matter in hand was the repairs to be done to the parsonage and steeple of a rural parish, that of Ivry, in the Île-de-France. The question was, to whom to apply to get these repairs done, how to determine on whom the expense should fall, and how to procure the sum which was needed.

1. Memorial from the curé to the Intendant, setting forth that the steeple and the parsonage are in urgent need of repairs; that his predecessor had added useless buildings to the parsonage, and thus entirely altered and spoiled it; that the inhabitants, having allowed this to be done, were bound to bear the expense of restoring it to a proper condition, and, if they chose, to claim the money from the heirs of the last curé.

2. Ordonnance of the Intendant (29th August, 1747), directing that the syndic shall make it his business to convoke a meeting to deliberate on the necessity of the operations demanded.

3. Memorial from the inhabitants, setting forth that they consent to the repairs of the parsonage but oppose those of the steeple, seeing that the steeple is built over the chancel, and that the curé, who is the great-tithe-owner, is liable for the repairs of the chancel. [By a decree in council of the end of the preceding century (April, 1695) the person in receipt of the great tithes was bound to repair the chancel, the parishioners being charged only with keeping up the nave.]

4. Fresh ordonnance of the Intendant, who, in consequence of the contradictory statements he has received, sends an architect, the Sieur Cordier, to inspect and report upon the parsonage and the steeple, to draw up a statement of the works and to make an inquiry.

5. *Procès-verbal* of all these operations, by which it appears that at the inquiry a certain number of landowners of Ivry appeared before the commissioner sent by the Intendant, which persons appeared to be nobles, burghers, and peasants of the place, and inscribed their declarations for or against the claim set up by the curé.

7. Fresh ordonnance of the Intendant, to the effect that the statements drawn up by the architect whom he had sent shall be communicated to the landowners and inhabitants of the parish at a fresh general meeting to be convoked by the syndic.

8. Fresh Parochial Assembly in consequence of this ordonnance, at which the inhabitants declare that they persist in their declarations.

9. Ordonnance of the Intendant, who directs, 1st, That the adjudication of the works set forth in the architect's statement shall be proceeded with before his Sub-delegate at Corbeil, in the dwelling of the latter; and that the said adjudication shall be made in the presence of the curé, the syndic, and the chief inhabitants of the parish. 2nd, That inasmuch as delay would be dangerous, the whole sum shall be raised by a rate on all the inhabitants, leaving those who persist in thinking that the steeple forms part of the choir, and ought therefore to be repaired by the large titheowners, to appeal to the ordinary courts of justice.

10. Summons issued to all the parties concerned to appear at the house of the Sub-delegate at Corbeil, where the proclamations and adjudication are to be made.

11. Memorial from the curé and several of the inhabitants, requesting that the expenses of the administrative proceeding should not be charged, as was usually the case, to the adjudicator, seeing that the said expenses were very heavy, and would prevent any one from undertaking the office of adjudicator.

12. Ordonnance of the Intendant, to the effect that the expenses incurred in the matter of the adjudication shall be fixed by the Sub-delegate, and that their amount shall form a portion of the said adjudication and rate.

13. Powers given by certain *notable*

inhabitants to the Sieur X. to be present at the said adjudication, and to assent to it, according to the statement of the architect.

14. Certificate of the syndic, to the effect that the usual notices and advertisements have been published.

15. *Procès-verbal* of the adjudication—

	liv.	s.	d.
Estimate of repairs	487	0	0
Expenses of adjudication	237	18	6
	724	18	6

16. Lastly, an order in council (23rd July, 1748) authorising the imposition of a rate to raise the above sum.

We see that in this procedure the convocation of the Parochial Assembly was alluded to several times.

The following *procès-verbal* of the meeting of one of these assemblies will show the reader how business was conducted on such occasions :—

Acte notarié.—' This day, after the parochial mass at the usual and accustomed place, when the bell had been rung, there appeared at the Assembly held before . the undersigned X., notary at Corbeil, and the witnesses hereafter named, the Sieur Michaud, vine-dresser, syndic of the said parish, who presented the ordonnance of the Inte idant permitting the Assembly to be held, caused it to be read, and demanded that note should be taken of his diligence.

' Immediately an inhabitant of the said parish appeared, who stated that the steeple was above the chancel, and that consequently the repairs belonged to the curé; there also appeared [here follow the names of some other persons, who, on the other hand, were willing to admit the claim of the curé]. . . . Next appeared fifteen peasants, labourers, masons, and vine-dressers, who declared their adhesion to what the preceding persons had said. There likewise appeared the Sieur Raimbaud, vine-grower, who said that he is ready to agree to whatever Monseigneur the Intendant may decide. There also appeared the Sieur X., doctor of the Sorbonne, the curé, who persists in the declarations and purposes of the memorial. Those who appeared demanded that all the above should be taken down in the Act. Done at the said place of Ivry, in front of the churchyard of the said parish, in the presence of the undersigned ; and the drawing up of the present report occupied from 11 o'clock in the morning until 2 o'clock.'

We see that this Parochial Assembly was a mere administrative inquiry, with the forms and the cost of judicial inquiries ; that it never ended in a vote, and consequently in the manifestation of the will of the parish ; that it contained only individual opinions, and had no influence on the determination of the Government. Indeed we learn from a number of other documents that the Parochial Assemblies were intended to assist the decision of the Intendant, and not to hinder it even where nothing but the interests of the parish were concerned.

We also find in the same documents that this affair gave rise to three inquiries: one before the notary,

a second before the architect, and lastly a third, before two notaries, in order to ascertain whether the parishioners persisted in their previous declarations.

The rate of 524 liv. 10s., imposed by the decree of the 13th July, 1748, fell upon all the landowners, privileged or otherwise, as was almost always the case with respect to expenses of this kind ; but the principle on which the shares were apportioned to the various persons was different. The *taillables* were taxed in proportion to their *taille*, and the privileged persons according to their supposed fortunes, which gave a great advantage to the latter over the former.

Lastly, we find that on this same occasion the division of the sum of 523 liv. 10s. was made by two collectors, who were inhabitants of the village ; these were not elected, nor did they fill the post by turns, as was commonly the case, but they were chosen and appointed officially by the Sub-delegate of the Intendant.

Note (XXII.)—Page 46, line 21.

The pretext taken by Louis XIV. to destroy the municipal liberties of the towns was the bad administration of their finances. Nevertheless the same evil, as Turgot truly says, continued and increased since the reform introduced by that sovereign. Most of the towns, he adds, are greatly in debt at the present time, partly owing to the sums which they have lent to

the Government, and partly owing to the expenses and decorations which the municipal officers, who have the disposal of other people's money and have no account to render to the inhabitants, or instructions to receive from them, multiply with a view of distinguishing and sometimes of enriching themselves.

Note (XXIII.)—Page 46, line 82.

THE STATE WAS THE GUARDIAN OF THE CONVENTS AS WELL AS OF THE COMMUNES.—EXAMPLE OF THIS GUARDIANSHIP.

The Comptroller-General, on authorising the Intendant to pay 15,000 livres to the convent of Carmelites, to which indemnities were owing, desires the Intendant to assure him-

self that this money, which represents a capital, is advantageously re-invested. Analogous facts were constantly recurring.

NOTE (XXIV.)—Page 50, line 22.

SHOWING THAT THE ADMINISTRATIVE CENTRALISATION OF THE OLD MONARCHY
COULD BE BEST JUDGED OF IN CANADA.

The physiognomy of the metropolitan government can be most fully appreciated in the colonies, because at that distance all its characteristic features are exaggerated and become more visible. When we wish to judge of the spirit of the Administration of Louis XIV. and its vices, it is to Canada we must look. There we shall see the deformity of the object of our investigation, as through a microscope.

In Canada a host of obstacles, which anterior circumstances or the ancient state of society opposed either in secret or openly to the spirit of the Government, did not exist. The nobility was scarcely seen there, or, at all events, it had no root in the soil; the Church had lost its dominant position; feudal traditions were lost or obscured; judicial authority was no longer rooted in ancient institutions and manners. There was nothing to hinder the central power from following its natural bent and from fashioning all the laws according to its own spirit. In Canada accordingly we find not a trace of any municipal or provincial institutions; no authorised collective force; no individual initiative allowed. The Intendant occupied a position infinitely more preponderant than that of his fellows in France; the Administration interfered in many more matters than in the metropolis, and chose to direct everything from Paris, spite of the eighteen hundred leagues by which they were divided. It adopted none of the great principles by which a colony is rendered populous and prosperous, but, on the other hand, it had recourse to all kinds of trifling artificial processes and petty tyrannical regulations in order to increase and extend the population; compulsory cultivation, all lawsuits arising out of the grants of land withdrawn from the tribunals and referred to the sole decision of the Administration, obligation to pursue particular methods of cultivation, to settle in certain places rather than

others, &c. All these regulations were in force under Louis XIV., and the edicts are countersigned by Colbert. One might imagine oneself in the very thick of modern centralisation and in Algeria. Indeed Canada presents an exact counterpart of all we have seen in Algeria. In both we find ourselves face to face with an administration almost as numerous as the population, preponderant, interfering, regulating, restricting, insisting upon foreseeing everything, controlling everything, and understanding the interests of those under its control better than they do themselves; in short, in a constant state of barren activity.

In the United States, on the other hand, the decentralisation of the English is exaggerated; the townships have become nearly independent municipalities, small democratic republics. The republican element, which forms the basis of the English constitution and manners, shows itself in the United States without disguise or hindrance, and becomes still further developed. The Government, properly so called, does but little in England, and private persons do a great deal; in America, the Government really takes no part in affairs, and individuals unite to do everything. The absence of any higher class, which rendered the inhabitants of Canada more submissive to the Government than even those of France at the same period, makes the population of the English provinces more and more independent of authority.

Both colonies resulted in the formation of a completely democratic state of society; but in one, so long at least as Canada still belonged to France, equality was united with absolutism; in the other it was combined with liberty. As far as the material consequences of the two colonial systems were concerned, we know that in 1763, the period of the Conquest, the population of Canada consisted of 60,000 souls, and that of the English provinces of 3,000,000.

NOTE (XXV.)—Page 52, line 10.

ONE EXAMPLE, AMONG MANY, OF THE GENERAL REGULATIONS CONTINUALLY MADE BY THE COUNCIL OF STATE, WHICH HAD THE FORCE OF LAWS THROUGHOUT FRANCE, AND CREATED SPECIAL OFFENCES, OF WHICH THE ADMINISTRATIVE TRIBUNALS WERE THE SOLE JUDGES.

I take the first which comes to hand : an order in council of the 29th April, 1779, which directs that throughout the kingdom the breeders and sellers of sheep shall mark their flocks in a particular manner, under a penalty of 300 livres. His Majesty, it declares, enjoins upon the Intendants the duty of enforcing the execution of the present order, which infers that the Intendant is to pronounce the penalty on its infraction. Another example : an order in council, 21st December, 1778, prohibiting the carriers and drivers to warehouse the goods entrusted to them, under a penalty of 300 livres. His Majesty enjoins upon the Lieutenant-General of Police and the Intendants to enforce this order.

NOTE (XXVI.)—Page 60, line 39.

RURAL POLICE.

The provincial assembly of Upper Guienne urgently demanded the creation of fresh brigades of the maréchaussée, just as now-a-days the general council of Aveyron or Lot doubtless requests the formation of fresh brigades of gendarmerie. The same idea always prevails—the gendarmerie is the symbol of order, and order can only be sent by Government through the gendarme. The report continues : ' Complaints are made every day that there is no police in the rural districts ' (how should there be ? the nobles took no part in affairs, the burghers were all in the towns, and the townships, represented by a vulgar peasant, had no power), ' and it must be admitted that with the exception of a few cantons in which just and benevolent seigneurs make use of the influence which their position gives them over their vassals in order to prevent those acts of violence to which the country people are naturally inclined, by the coarseness of their manners and the asperity of their character, there nowhere exists any means of restraining these ignorant, rude, and violent men.'

Such were the terms in which the nobles of the Provincial Assembly allowed themselves to be spoken of, and in which the members of the *Tiers-Etat*, who made up half the assembly, spoke of the people in public documents !

NOTE (XXVII.)—Page 61, line 24.

Licences for the sale of tobacco were as much sought for under the old monarchy as they are now. The greatest people begged for them for their creatures. I find that some were given on the recommendation of great ladies, and one at the request of some archbishops.

Note (XXVIII.)—Page 62, line 22.

The extinction of all local public life surpassed all power of belief. One of the roads from Maine into Normandy was impracticable. Who do our readers imagine requested to have it repaired? the *généralité* of Touraine, which it traversed? the provinces of Normandy or Maine, so deeply interested in the cattle trade which followed this road? or even some particular canton especially inconvenienced by its impassable condition? The *généralité*, the provinces, and the cantons had no voice in the matter. The dealers who travelled on this road and stuck fast in the ruts were obliged to call the attention of the Central Government to its state, and to write to Paris to the Comptroller-General for assistance.

Note (XXIX.)—Page 69, line 8.

MORE OR LESS IMPORTANCE OF THE SEIGNORIAL DUES OR RENT-CHARGES, ACCORDING TO THE PROVINCE.

Turgot says in his works, ‘I ought to point out the fact that these dues are far more important in most of the rich provinces, such as Normandy, Picardy, and the environs of Paris. In the last named the chief wealth consists in the actual produce of the land, which is held in large farms, from which the owners derive heavy rents. The payments in respect of the lord’s rights, in the case even of the largest estates, form but an inconsiderable part of the income arising from these properties, and such payments are little more than nominal.

In the poorer provinces, where cultivation is managed on different principles, the lords and nobles have scarcely any land in their own hands; properties, which are extremely divided, are charged with heavy corn-rents, for payment of which all the co-tenants are jointly and severally liable. These rents, in many instances, absorb the bulk of the produce, and the lord’s income is almost entirely derived from them.

Note (XXX.)—Page 74, line 34.

INFLUENCE OF SELF-GOVERNMENT UNFAVOURABLE TO CASTE.

The unimportant labours of the agricultural societies of the eighteenth century show the adverse influence which the common discussion of general interests exercised on *caste*. Though the meetings of these societies date from thirty years before the Revolution, when the *ancien régime* was still in full force, and though they dealt with theories only—by the very fact of their discussions turning on questions in which the different classes of society felt themselves interested, and, therefore, took common part in—we may at once perceive how they brought men together, and how by means of them—limited as they were to conversations on agriculture—ideas of reasonable reform spread alike among the privileged and unprivileged classes.

I am convinced that no Government could have kept up the absurd and mad inequality which existed in France at the moment of the Revolution, but one which, like the Government of the old monarchy, aimed at finding all its strength in its own ranks, continually recruited by remarkable men. The slightest contact with *self-government* would have materially modified such inequality, and soon transformed or destroyed it.

Note (XXXI.)—Page 75, line 8.

Provincial liberties may exist for a while without national liberty, when they are ancient, entwined with habits, manners, and early recollections, and while despotism, on the contrary, is recent. But it is against reason to suppose that local liberties may be created at will, or even long maintained, when general liberty is crushed.

Note (XXXII.)—Page 75, line 19.

Turgot, in a report to the King, sums up in the following terms, which appear to me singularly exact, the real privileges of the noble class in regard to taxation :—

' 1. Persons of the privileged class have a claim to exemption from all taxation in money to the extent of a four-plough farm, equivalent in the neighbourhood of Paris to an assessment of 2,000 francs.

' 2. The same persons are entirely exempt from taxation in respect of woods, meadows, vineyards, fishponds, and for enclosed lands appurtenant to their castles, whatever their extent. In some cantons the principal culture is of meadows or vineyards : in these the noble proprietor escapes from all taxation whatever, the whole weight of which falls on the tax-paying class; another immense advantage for the privileged.'

Note (XXXIII.)—Page 76, line 7.

INDIRECT PRIVILEGES IN RESPECT OF TAXATION : DIFFERENCE IN ASSESSMENT EVEN WHEN THE TAX IS GENERAL.

Turgot has given a description of this also, which, judging by the documents, I have reason to believe exact.

' The indirect advantages of the privileged classes in regard to the poll-tax are very great. The poll-tax is in its very nature an arbitrary impost; it cannot be distributed among the community otherwise than at random. It has been found most convenient to assess it on the tax-collector's books, which are ready prepared. It is true that a separate list has been made out for those whose names do not appear in these books but as they resist payment, while the tax-paying classes have no organ, the poll-tax paid by the former in the provinces has gradually dwindled to an insignificant amount, while the poll-tax on the latter is almost equal in amount to the whole tax-paying capital.

Note (XXXIV.)—Page 76, line 14.

ANOTHER INSTANCE OF INEQUALITY OF ASSESSMENT IN THE CASE OF A GENERAL TAX.

It is well known that local rates were general : ' which sums,' say the orders in council authorising the levy of such rates, ' shall be levied on all liable, exempt or non-exempt, privileged or non-privileged, without any exception, together with the poll-tax, or in the proportion of a mark to every franc payable as poll-tax.'

Observe that, as the tax-payer's poll-tax, assessed according to the assessment for other taxes, was always higher in comparison than the poll-tax of the privileged class, inequality re-appeared even under the form which seemed most to exclude it.

Note (XXXV.)—Page 76, line 14.

ON THE SAME SUBJECT.

I find in a draft edict of 1764, the aim of which is to equalise taxation, all sorts of provisions, the object of which is to preserve exceptional advantages to the privileged classes, in the mode of levy : among these I find that all steps for the purpose of determining, in their case, the value of the assessable property, must be taken in their presence or that of their proxies.

Note (XXXVI.)—Page 76, line 27.

ADMISSION BY THE GOVERNMENT OF THE ADVANTAGES ENJOYED BY THE PRIVILEGED CLASSES IN THE ASSESSMENT EVEN OF GENERAL TAXES.

'I see,' writes the Minister, in 1766, 'that the portion of the taxes most difficult to levy is always that due from the noble and privileged classes, from the consideration the tax-collectors feel themselves bound to show such persons; in consequence of which long-standing arrears of far too great an amount will be found due on their poll-tax and their "twentieths"' (the tax which they paid in common with the rest of the community).

Note (XXXVII.)—Page 85, line 7.

In Arthur Young's Travels, in 1789, is a little picture in which the contrast of the systems of the two countries is so well painted, and so happily introduced, that I cannot resist the temptation of citing it.

Young, travelling through France during the first excitement caused by the taking of the Bastille, is arrested in a certain village by a crowd, who, seeing him without a cockade, wish to put him in prison. Young contrives to extricate himself by this speech :—

'It has been announced, gentlemen, that the taxes are to be paid as they have been hitherto. Certainly, the taxes ought to be paid, but *not* as they have been hitherto. They ought to be paid as they are in England. We have many taxes there which you are free from; but the *Tiers-État*—the people—does not pay them : they fall entirely on the rich. Thus, in England, every window is taxed; but the man with only six windows to his house does not pay anything for them. A nobleman pays his twentieths[1] and his King's-taxes, but the poor proprietor pays

[1] See last note.

nothing on his little garden. The rich man pays for his horses, carriages and servants—he pays even for a licence to shoot his own partridges; the poor man is free from all these burdens. Nay, more, in England we have a tax paid by the rich to help the poor! So that, I say, if taxes are still to be paid, they should be paid differently. The English plan is far the better one.'

'As my bad French,' adds Young, ' was much on a par with their patois, they understood me perfectly.'

Note (XXXVIII.)—Page 86, line 24.

The church at X., in the electoral district of Chollet, was going to ruin : it was to be repaired in the manner provided by the order of 1684 (16th December), viz., by a rate levied on all the inhabitants. When the collectors came to levy this rate, the Marquis de X., seigneur of the parish, refused to pay his proportion of the rate, as he meant to take on himself the entire repair of the chancel ; the other inhabitants reply, very reasonably, that as lord of the manor and holder of the great tithes, he is *bound* to repair the chancel, and cannot, on the plea of this obligation, claim to escape his proportion of the common rate. This produces an order of the Intendant declaring the Marquis's liability, and authorising the collector's proceedings. Among the papers on the subject are more than ten letters from the Marquis, one more urgent than the other, begging hard that the rest of the parish may pay instead of himself, and, to obtain his prayer, stooping to address the Intendant as ' Monseigneur,' and even ' *le supplier.*'

Note (XXXIX.)—Page 87, line 35.

AN INSTANCE OF THE WAY IN WHICH THE GOVERNMENT OF THE OLD MONARCHY RESPECTED VESTED RIGHTS, FORMAL CONTRACTS, AND THE FRANCHISES OF TOWNS OR CORPORATIONS.

A royal declaration ' suspending in time of war repayment of all loans contracted by towns, villages, colleges, communities, hospitals, charitable houses, trade-corporations,[1] and others, repayable out of town dues by us conceded, though the instrument securing the said loans stipulates for the payment of interest in the case of non-payment at the stipulated terms.'

Thus not only is the obligation to repayment at the stipulated terms suspended, but the security itself is impaired. Such proceedings, which abounded under the old monarchy, would have been impracticable under a Government acting under the check of publicity or representative assemblies. Compare the above with the respect always shown for such rights in England, and even in America. The contempt of right in this instance is as flagrant as that of local franchises.

Note (XL.)—Page 89, line 21.

The case cited in the text is far from a solitary instance of an admission by the privileged class that the feudal burdens which weighed down the peasant reached even to themselves. The following is the lan-

---

[1] *I.e.* not corporations for trading purposes, but bodies like our livery companies.

guage of an agricultural society, exclusively composed of this class, thirty years before the Revolution :—

'Perpetual rent-charges, whether due to the State or to the lord, if at all considerable in amount, become so burdensome to the tenant that they cause first his ruin, and then that of the land liable to them ; the tenant is forced to neglect it, being neither able to borrow on the security of an estate already too heavily burdened, nor to find purchasers if he wish to sell. If then payments were commutable, the tenant would readily be able to raise the means of commuting them by borrowing, or to find purchasers at a price that would cover the value both of the land and the payments with which it might be charged. A man always feels pleasure in keeping up and improving a property of which he believes himself to be in peaceable possession. It would be rendering a great service to agriculture to discover means of commutation for this class of payments. Many lords of manors, convinced of this, would readily give their aid to such arrangements. It would, therefore, be very interesting to discover and point out practicable means for thus ridding land from permanent burdens.'

Note (XLI.)—Page 90, line 38.

All public functionaries, even the agents of farmers of the revenue, were paid by exemptions from taxes—a privilege granted by the order of 1681. A letter from an Intendant to the minister in 1782 states, 'Among the privileged orders the most numerous class is that of clerks in the Excise of salt, the public domain, the post-office, and other royal monopolies of all kinds. There are few parishes which do not include one ; in many, two or three may be found.'

The object of this letter is to dissuade the minister from proposing an extension of exemption from taxation to the clerks and servants of these privileged agents; which extension, says the Intendant, is unceasingly backed by the Farmers-General, that they may thus get rid of the necessity of paying salaries.

Note (XLII.)—Page 91, line 1.

The sale of public employments, which were called *offices*, was not quite unknown elsewhere. In Germany some of the petty princes had introduced the practice to a small extent and in insignificant departments of administration. Nowhere but in France was the system followed out on a grand scale.

Note (XLIII.)—Page 95, line 17.

We must not be surprised, strange as it may appear and is, to find, under the old monarchy, public functionaries—many of them belonging to the public service, properly so called—pleading before the Parliaments to ascertain the limits of their own powers. The explanation of this is to be found in the fact that all these questions were questions of private property as well as of public administration. What is here viewed as an encroachment of the judicial power was a mere consequence of the error which the Government had committed in attaching public functions to certain offices. These offices being bought and sold, and their holders' income being regulated by the work done and paid for, it was impossible to change the functions of an office without impairing some right for which money had been paid to a predecessor in the office.

To quote an instance out of a thousand :—At Mans the Lieutenant-General of Police carries on a prolonged suit with the *Bureau de Finance* of the town, to prove, that being charged with the duty of street-watching, he has a right to execute all legal instruments relative to the paving of the streets, and to the fees for such instruments.

The *Bureau* replies, that the paving is a duty thrown upon him by the nature of his office.

The question in this case is not decided by the king in council; the parliament gives judgment, as the principal matter in dispute is the interest of the capital devoted to the purchase of the office. The administrative question becomes a civil action.

NOTE (XLIV.)—Page 96, line 23.

ANALYSIS OF THE INSTRUCTIONS OF THE ORDER OF NOBILITY IN 1789.

The French Revolution is, I believe, the only one, at the beginning of which the different classes were able separately to bear authentic witness to the ideas they had conceived, and to display the sentiments by which they were moved before the Revolution had altered and defaced these ideas and feelings. This authentic testimony was recorded, as we all know, in the *cahiers* drawn up by the three Orders in 1789. These *cahiers*, or Instructions, were drawn up under circumstances of complete freedom and publicity, by each of the Orders concerned; they underwent a long discussion from those interested, and were carefully considered by their authors; for the Government of that period did not, whenever it addressed the nation, undertake both to put the question and to give the answer. At the time when the Instructions were drawn up, the most important parts of them were collected in three printed volumes, which are to be found in every library. The originals are deposited in the national archives, and with them the *procès-verbaux* of the assemblies by which they were drawn up, together with a part of the correspondence which passed between M. Necker and his agents on the subject of these assemblies. This collection forms a long series of folio volumes. It is the most precious document that remains to us from ancient France, and one which should be constantly consulted by those who wish to know the state of feeling amongst our forefathers at the time when the Revolution broke out.

I at first imagined that the abridgment printed in three volumes, which I mentioned above, might perhaps be the work of one party, and not a true representation of the character of this immense inquiry; but on comparing one with the other, I found the strongest resemblance between the large original picture and the reduced copy.

The extract from the *cahiers* of the nobility, which I am about to give, contains a true picture of the sentiments of the great majority of that Order. It clearly shows how many of their ancient privileges they were obstinately determined to maintain, how many they were not disinclined to give up, and how many they offered to renounce of their own accord. Above all, we see in full the spirit which animated them with regard to political liberty. The picture is a strange and sad one!

Individual Rights.—The nobles demand, first of all, that an explicit declaration should be made of the rights which belong to all men, and that this declaration should confirm their liberties and secure their safety.

Liberty of the Person.—They desire that the servitude to the glebe should be abolished wherever it still exists, and that means should be formed to destroy the slave trade and to emancipate the negroes; that every man should be free to travel or to reside wherever he may please, whether within or without the limits of the kingdom, without being liable to arbitrary arrest; that the abuses of police regulations shall be reformed, and that henceforth the police shall be under the control of the judges, even in cases of revolt; that no one shall be liable to be arrested or tried except by his natural judges; that, consequently, the state prisons and other illegal places of detention shall be suppressed. Some of them require the demolition of the Bastille. The nobility of Paris is especially urgent upon this point.

Are 'Lettres Closes,' or 'Lettres de Cachet,' to be prohibited?—If any danger of the State renders the arrest of a citizen necessary, without his being immediately brought before the ordinary courts of justice, measures should be taken to prevent any abuses, either by giving notice of the imprisonment to the *Conseil d'État*, or by some other proceeding.

The nobility demands the abolition of all special commissions, all courts of attribution or exemption, all privileges of *committimus*, all dilatory judgments, &c., &c., and requires that the severest punishment should be awarded to all those who should issue or execute an arbitrary order; that in common jurisdiction (the only one that ought to be maintained) the necessary measures should be taken for securing individual liberty, especially as regards the criminal; that justice should be dispensed gratuitously; and that useless jurisdictions should be suppressed. 'The magistrates are instituted for the people, and not the people for the magistrates,' says one of the memorials. A demand is even made that a council and gratuitous advocates for the poor should be established in each bailiwick; that the proceedings should be public, and permission granted to the litigants to plead for themselves; that in criminal matters the prisoner should be provided with counsel, and that in all stages of the proceedings the judge should have adjoined to him a certain number of citizens, of the same position in life as the person accused, who are to give their opinion relative to the fact of the crime or offence with which he is charged (referring on this point to the English constitution); that all punishments should be proportioned to the offence, and alike for all; that the punishment of death should be made more uncommon, and all corporal pains and tortures, &c., should be suppressed; that, in fine, the condition of the prisoner, and more especially of the simply accused, should be ameliorated.

According to these memorials, measures should be taken to protect individual liberty in the enlistment of troops for land or sea service; permission should be given to convert the obligation of military service into pecuniary contributions. The drawing of lots should only take place in the presence of a deputation of the three Orders together; in fact, that the duties of military discipline and subordination should be made to tally with the rights of the citizen and freemen, blows with the back of the sabre being altogether done away with.

Freedom and Inviolability of Property.—It is required that property should be inviolable, and placed beyond all attack, except for some reason of indispensable public utility; in which case the Government ought to give a considerable and immediate indemnity: that confiscation should be abolished.

Freedom of Trade, Handicraft and Industrial Occupation.—The freedom of trade and industry ought to be secured; and, in consequence, freedoms and other privileges of certain companies should be suppressed, and the custom-house lines all put back to the frontiers of the country.

Freedom of Religion. — The Catholic religion is to be the only dominant religion in France; but liberty of conscience is to be left to everybody: and the non-Catholics are to be restored to their civil rights and their property.

Freedom of the Press.—Inviolability of the Secrecy of the Post.— The freedom of the press is to be secured, and a law is to establish beforehand all the restrictions which may be considered necessary in the general interest. Ecclesiastical censorship to exist only for books relative to the dogmas of the Church ; and in all other cases it is considered sufficient to take the necessary precautions of knowing the authors and printers. Many of the memorials demand that offences of the press should only be tried by juries.

The memorials unanimously demand above all that the secrecy of letters entrusted to the post should be inviolably respected, so that (as they say) letters may never be made to serve as means of accusation or testimony against a man. They denounce the opening of letters, crudely enough, as the most odious espionage, inasmuch as it institutes a violation of public faith.

Instruction, Education. — The memorials of the nobility on this point require no more than that active measures should be taken to foster education, that it should be diffused throughout the country, and that it should be directed upon principles conformable to the presumed destination of the children ; and, above all, that a national education should be given to the children, by teaching them their duties and their rights of citizenship. They urge the compilation of a political catechism, in which the principal points of the constitution should be made clear to them. They do not, however, point out the means to be employed for the diffusion of instruction : they do no more than demand educational establishments for the children of the indigent nobility.

Care to be taken of the People.— A great number of the memorials lay much stress upon greater regard being shown to the people. Several denounce, as a violation of the natural liberty of man, the excesses committed in the name of the police, by which, as they say, quantities of artisans and useful citizens are arbitrarily, and without any regular examination, dragged to prison, to houses of detention, &c., frequently for slight offences, or even upon simple suspicion. All the memorials demand the definitive abolition of statute labour. The greater portion of the bailiwicks desire the permission to buy off the vassalage and toll-dues ; and several require that the receipt of many of the feudal dues should be rendered less onerous, and that those paid upon *franc-fief* should be abolished. ' It is to the advantage of the Government,' says one of the memorials, ' to facilitate the purchase and sale of estates.' This reason was precisely the one given afterwards for the abolition at one blow of all the seignorial rights, and for the sale of property in the condition of *mainmorte*. Many of the memorials desire that the *droit de colombier* (exclusive right of keeping pigeons) should be rendered less prejudicial to agriculture. Demands are made for the immediate abolition of the establishments used as royal game-preserves, and known by the name of '*capitaineries*,' as a violation of the rights of property. The substitution of taxes less onerous to the people in the mode of levying for those then existing is also desired.

The nobility demand that efforts should be made to increase the prosperity and comfort of the country districts ; that establishments for spinning and weaving coarse stuffs should be provided for the occupation of the country people during the dead season of the year; that public granaries should be established in each bailiwick, under the inspection of the provincial authorities, in order to provide against times of famine, and to maintain the price of corn at a certain rate ; that means should be studied to improve the agriculture of the country, and ameliorate the condition of the country people ; that an augmentation should be given to the public works; and that particular attention should be paid to the draining of marsh lands, the prevention of inundations, &c. ; and finally, that the prizes of encouragement to commerce and agriculture should be distributed in all the provinces.

The memorials express the desire that the hospitals should be broken up into smaller establishments, erected in each district ; that the asylums for beggars (*dépôts de mendicité*) should be suppressed, and replaced by charitable workhouses (*ateliers de charité*); that funds for the aid of the sick and needy should be established under the management of the Provincial States, and that surgeons, physicians, and midwives should be distributed among the *arrondissements* at the expense of the provinces, to give their gratuitous services to the poor; that the courts of justice should likewise be gratuitous to the people; finally, that care should be taken for the establishment of institutions for the blind, the deaf and dumb, foundling children, &c.

Generally speaking, in all these matters the order of nobles does no more than express its desire for reform, without entering into any minor details of execution. It may be easily seen that it mixed much less with the inferior classes than the lower order of clergy; and thus, having come less in contact with their wretchedness, had thought less of the means for mitigating it.

Admissibility to Public Functions; Hierarchy of Ranks; Honorary Privileges of the Nobility.—It is more especially, or rather it is solely, upon the points that concern the hierarchy of ranks and the difference of social classes, that the nobility separates itself from the general spirit of the reforms required, and that, though willing to concede some few important points, it still clings to the principles of the old system. It evidently is aware that it is now struggling for its very existence. Its memorials, consequently, urgently demanded the maintenance of the clergy and the nobility as distinct orders. They even require that efforts should be made to maintain the order of nobility in all its purity, and that to this intent it should be rendered impossible to acquire the title of noble by payment of money; that it should no longer be attached to certain places about Court, and that it should only be obtained by merit, after long and useful services rendered to the State. They express the desire that men assuming false titles of nobility should be found out and prosecuted. All these memorials, in fact, make urgent protestations in

favour of the maintenance of the noble in all his honours. Some even desire that a distinctive mark should be given to the nobles to ensure their exterior recognition. It is impossible to imagine anything more characteristic than this demand, or more indicative of the perfect similitude that must have already existed between the noble and the plebeian in spite of the difference of their social conditions. In general, in its memorials, the nobility, although it appears easily disposed enough to concede many of its more profitable rights, clings energetically to its honorary privileges. So greatly does it feel itself already hurried on by the torrent of democracy, and fear to sink in the stream, that it not only wants to preserve all the privileges it already enjoys, but is desirous of inventing others it never possessed. It is singular to remark how it has a presentiment of the impending danger without the actual perception of it.

With regard to public employments, the nobles require that the venality of offices should be done away with in all places connected with the magistracy, and that, in appointments of this kind, the citizens in general should be presented by the nation to the king, and nominated by him without any distinction, except as regards conditions of age and capacity. The majority also opines that the *Tiers-État* should not be excluded from military rank, and that every military man, who had deserved well of his country, should have the right to rise to the very highest grade. 'The order of nobility does not approve of any law that closes the portals of military rank to the order of the *Tiers-État*,' is the expression used by some of the memorials. But the nobles desire that the right of coming into a regiment as officer, without having first gone through the inferior grades, should be reserved to themselves alone. Almost all the Instructions, however, require the establishment of fixed regulations, applicable alike to all, for the bestowal of rank in the army, and demand that they should not be entirely left to favour, but be conferred, with the exception of those of superior officers, by right of seniority.

As regards the clerical functions, they require the re-establishment of the elective system in the bestowal of benefices, or at least the appointment by the King of a committee that may enlighten him in the distribution of these benefices.

Lastly, they express the opinion that, for the future, pensions ought to be given away with more discernment; that they ought no longer to be exclusively lavished upon certain families; that no citizen ought to have more than one pension, or receive the salary of more than one place at a time, and that all reversions of such emoluments should be abolished.

The Church and the Clergy.—In matters which do not affect its own interests and especial constitution, the nobility is far less scrupulous. In all that regards the privileges and organisation of the Church, its eyes are opened wide enough to existing abuses.

It desires that the clergy should have no privileges in matters of taxation, and that it should pay its debts without putting the burden of them on the nation: moreover, that the monastic orders should ·undergo a complete reformation. The greater part of the Instructions declare that these monastic establishments have wholly departed from the original spirit of their institution.

The majority of the bailiwicks express their desire that the tithes should be made less prejudicial to agriculture; many demand their abolition altogether. 'The greater part of the tithes,' says one of the memorials, 'is collected by those incumbents who do the least towards giving spiritual succour to the people.' It is easy to perceive that the latter order has not much forbearance for the former in its remarks. No greater respect was shown in its treatment of the Church itself. Several bailiwicks formally admit the right of the States-General to suppress certain religious orders, and apply their revenues to some other use. Seventeen bailiwicks declare the competence of the States-General to regulate their discipline. Several complain that the holidays (*jours de fête*) are too frequent, are prejudicial to agriculture, and are favourable to drunkenness, and suggest that, in consequence, a great number of them ought to be suppressed and kept only on the Sundays.

Political Rights.—As regards political rights, the Instructions establish the right of every Frenchman to take his part in the government, either directly or indirectly; that is to say, the right to elect or be elected, but without disturbing the gradation of social ranks; so that no one may nominate or be nominated otherwise than in his own Order. This principle once established, it is considered that the representative system ought to be established in such wise, that the power of taking a serious part in the direction of affairs may be guaranteed to each Order of the nation.

With regard to the manner of voting in the Assembly of the States-General the opinions differ. Most desire a separate vote for each Order; others think that an exception ought to be made to this rule in the votes upon taxation; whilst others again consider that it should always be so. 'The votes ought to be counted by individuals and not by Orders,' say the latter. 'Such a manner of proceeding being the only sensible one, and the only one tending to remove and destroy that egotism of caste, which is the source of all our evils — to bring men together and lead them to that result, which the nation has the right to expect from an Assembly, whose patriotism and great moral qualities should be strengthened by its united intelligence.' As an immediate adoption of this innovation, however, might prove dangerous in the existing state of general feeling, many of the Instructions provide that it should be only decided upon with caution, and that the assembly had better decide whether it were not more prudent to put off the system of individual voting to the following States-General. The nobility demands that, in any case, each Order should be allowed to preserve that dignity which is due to every Frenchman, and consequently that the humiliating ceremonies, to which the *Tiers-État* was subjected under the old system, should be abolished, as, for instance, that of being obliged to kneel—'inasmuch,' says one of these documents, 'as the spectacle of one man kneeling before another is offensive to the dignity of man, and emblematic of an inferiority between creatures equal by nature, incompatible with their essential rights.'

The System to be established in the Form of Government, and the Principles of the Constitution.—With regard to the form of government, the nobility desired the maintenance of the monarchical constitution, the preservation of the legislative, judicial, and executive powers in the person of the King, but, at the same time, the establishment of fundamental laws for the purpose of guaranteeing the rights of the nation in the exercise of these powers.

All the Instructions, consequently, declare that the nation has the right to assemble in States-General, composed of a sufficient number of members to ensure the independence of the Assembly; and they express the desire that, for the future, these States should assemble at fixed periodical seasons, as well as upon every fresh succession to the throne, without the issue of any writs of convocation. Many of the bailiwicks even advise the permanence of this Assembly. If the convocation of the States-General were not to take place within the period prescribed by the law, they should have the right of refusing the payment of taxes. Some few of the Instructions desire that, during the intervals between the sittings of the States, an intermediary commission should be appointed to watch over the administration of the kingdom; but most of them formally oppose the appointment of any such commission, as being unconstitutional. The reason given for this objection is curious enough. They feared lest so small an Assembly, left to itself in the presence of the Government, might be seduced by it.

The nobility desires that the Ministers should not possess the right of dissolving the Assembly, and should be punished by law for disturbing it by their cabals; that no public functionary, no one dependent in any way upon the Government, should be a deputy; that the person of the deputies should be inviolable, and that they should not be able (according to the terms of the memorials) to be prosecuted for any opinions they may emit; finally, that the sittings of the Assembly should be public, and that, in order that the nation might more generally take part in them, they should be made known by printed reports.

The nobility unanimously demands that the principles destined to regulate the government of the State should be applied to the administration of the different parts of the kingdom, and that, consequently, Assemblies made up of members freely elected, and for a limited period of time, should be formed in each district and each parish.

Many of the Instructions recommend that the functions of *Intendants* and *Receveurs-Généraux* ought to be done away with; all are of opinion that, in future, the Provincial Assemblies should alone take in hand the assessment of the taxes, and see to the special interests of the province. The same ought to be the case, they consider, with the Assemblies of each *arrondissement* and of each parish, which ought only to be accountable for the future to the Provincial States.

Distribution of the Powers of State.—Legislative Power.—As regards the distribution of the powers of the State between the assembled nation and the King, the nobility requires that no law should be considered effective until it has been consented to by the States-General and the King and entered upon the registers of the courts empowered to maintain the execution of the laws; that the States-General should have the exclusive attribute of determining and fixing the amount of the taxes; that all subsidies agreed upon should be only for the period that may elapse between one sitting of the States and the next; that all which may be levied or ordained, without the consent of the States, should be declared illegal, and that all ministers and receivers of such subsidies, who may have ordered or levied them, should be prosecuted as public defaulters; that, in the same way, no loan should be contracted without the consent of the States-

General, but that a credit alone should be opened, fixed by the States, of which the Government might make use in case of war or any great calamity, taking care, however, that measures should be taken to convoke the States-General in the shortest possible time; that all the national treasuries should be placed under the superintendence of the States; that the expenses of each department should be fixed by them; and that the surest measures should be taken to see that the funds voted were not exceeded.

The greater part of the Instructions recommend the suppression of those vexatious taxes, known under the names of *insinuation, entérinement*, and *centième denier*, coming under the denomination of ' Administration (*Régie*) of the Royal domains,' upon the subject of which one of the memorials says : ' The denomination of *Régie* is alone sufficient to wound the feelings of the nation, inasmuch as it puts forward, as belonging to the King, matters which are in reality a part of the property of the citizens ; ' that all the domains, not alienated, should be placed under the administration of the Provincial States, and no ordinance, no edict upon financial matters, should be given without the consent of the three Orders of the nation.

It is evidently the intention of the nobility to confer upon the nation the whole of the financial administration, as well in the regulation of loans and taxes, as in the receipt of the same by the means of the General and Provincial Assemblies.

Judicial Power.—In the same way, in the judicial organisation, it has a tendency towards rendering the power of the judges, at least in a great measure, dependent upon the nation assembled. And thus many of the memorials declare ' that the magistrates should be responsible for the fact of their appointments to the nation assembled ; ' that they should not be dismissed from their functions without the consent of the States-General ; that no court of justice, under any pretext whatever, should be disturbed in the exercise of its functions without the consent of these States ; that the disputed mat-

ters in the Appeal Court, as well as those before the Parliament, should be decided upon by the States-General. The majority of the Instructions add that the judges ought only to be nominated by the King, upon presentation to him by the people.

Executive Power.—The executive power is exclusively reserved to the King; but necessary limits are proposed, in order to prevent its abuse.

For instance, in the administration, the Instructions require that the state of the accounts of the different departments should be rendered public by being printed ; likewise, that before employing the troops in the defence of the country from without, the King should make known his precise intention to the States-General ; that, in the country itself, the troops should never be employed against the citizens, except upon the requisition of the States-General ; that the number of the troops should be limited, and that two-thirds of them alone should remain, in common times, upon the second effective list ; and that the Government ought to keep away all the foreign troops it may have in its pay from the centre of the kingdom, and send them to the frontiers.

In perusing the Instructions of the nobility, the reader cannot fail to be struck, more than all, with the conviction that the nobles are so essentially of their own time. They have all the feelings of the day, and employ its language with perfect fluency ; they talk of ' the inalienable rights of man ' and ' the principles inherent to the social compact.' In matters appertaining to the individual, they generally look to his rights—in those appertaining to society, to its duties. The principles of their political opinions appear to them *as absolute as those of morality, both one and the other being based upon reason.* In expressing their desire to abolish the last remnants of serfdom, they talk of *effacing the last traces of the degradation of the human race.* They sometimes denominate Louis XVI. the ' Citizen-King,' and frequently speak of that crime of *lèse-nation* (treason to the nation), which afterwards was so frequently imputed to themselves.

In their opinion, as in that of every one else, everything was to be expected from the results of public education, which the States were to direct. ' *The States-General*,' says one of the *Cahiers*, ' *must take care to inspire a national character by alterations in the education of children.*' Like the rest of their contemporaries, they show a. lively and constant desire for uniformity in the legislation, excepting, however, in all that affected the existence of ranks. They are as desirous as the *Tiers-État* of administrative uniformity—uniformity of measures, &c. They point out all kinds of reforms, and expect that these reforms should be radical. According to their suggestions, all the taxes, without exception, should be abolished or transferred, and the whole judicial system changed, except in the case of the Seignorial Courts of Justice, which they considered only to need improvement. They, as well as all the other French, looked upon France as a field for experiment—a sort of political model-farm, in which every portion was to be turned up and every experiment tried, except in one special little corner, where their own privileges blossomed. It must be said to their honour, however, that even this was but little spared by them. In short, as may be seen by reading their memorials, all the nobles wanted in order to make the Revolution was that they should be plebeians.

NOTE (XLV.)—Page 97, line 2.

SPECIMEN OF THE RELIGIOUS GOVERNMENT OF AN ECCLESIASTICAL PROVINCE IN THE MIDDLE OF THE EIGHTEENTH CENTURY.

1. The Archbishop.
2. Seven Vicars-General.
3. Two Ecclesiastical Courts, denominated *Officialités*. One, called the Metropolitan *Officialité*, took cognisance of the judgments of the suffragans. The other, called the *Officialité* of the Diocess, took cognisance (1) of personal affairs between clerical men; (2) of the validity of marriages, as regarded the performance of the ceremony.

This latter court was composed of three judges, to whom were adjoined notaries and attorneys.

4. Two Fiscal Courts. The one, called the office of the Diocess (*Bureau Diocésain*), took cognisance, in the first instance, of all matters having reference to the dues levied on the clergy of the diocess. (As is well known, they were fixed by the clergy themselves.) This court was presided over by the Archbishop, and made up of six other priests. The other court gave judgment in appeals on causes, which had been brought before the other *Bureaux Diocésains*, of the ecclesiastical province.

All these courts admitted counsel and heard pleadings.

NOTE (XLVI.)—Page 97, line 10.

GENERAL FEELING OF THE CLERGY IN THE STATES AND PROVINCIAL ASSEMBLIES.

What has been said in the text respecting the States of Languedoc is applicable just as well to the Provincial Assemblies that met in 1779 and 1787, for instance, in Haute-Guienne. The members of the clergy, in this Provincial Assembly, were among the most enlightened, the most active, and the most liberal. It was the Bishop of Rhodez who proposed to publish the minutes of the Assembly.

NOTE (XLVII.)—Page 98, line 26.

This liberal disposition on the part of the priests in political matters, which displayed itself in 1789, was not only produced by the excitement of the moment, evidence of it had already appeared at a much earlier period. It exhibited itself, for instance, in the province of Berri as early as 1779, when the clergy offered to make voluntary donations to the amount of 68,000 livres, upon the sole condition that the provincial administration should be preserved.

NOTE (XLVIII.)—Page 100, line 11.

It must be carefully remarked that, if the political conditions of society were without any ties, the civil state of society still had many. Within the circle of the different classes men were bound to each other; something even still remained of that close tie which had once existed between the class of the *Seigneurs* and the people; and although all this only existed in civil society, its consequence was indirectly felt in political society. The men, bound by these ties, formed masses that were irregular and unorganised, but refractory beneath the hand of authority. The Revolution, by breaking all social ties, without establishing any political ties in their place, prepared the way at the same time for equality and servitude.

NOTE (XLIX.)—Page 101, line 5.

EXAMPLE OF THE MANNER IN WHICH THE COURTS EXPRESSED THEMSELVES UPON THE OCCASION OF CERTAIN ARBITRARY ACTS.

It appears, from a memorial laid before the *Contrôleur-Général* in 1781, by the *Intendant* of the *Généralité* of Paris, that it was one of the customs of that *Généralité* that the parishes should have two syndics— the one elected by the inhabitants in an Assembly presided over by the *Subdélégué*, the other chosen by the *Intendant*, and considered the overseer of the former. A quarrel took place between the two syndics in the parish of Rueil, the elected syndic not choosing to obey the chosen syndic. The *Intendant*, by means of M. de Breteuil, had the elected syndic put into the prison of La Force for a fortnight; he was arrested, then dismissed from his post, and another was put in his place. Thereupon the Parliament, upon the requisition of the imprisoned syndic, commenced proceedings at law, the issue of which I have not been able to find, but during which it declared that the imprisonment of the plaintiff and the nullification of his election could only be considered as *arbitrary and despotic acts*. The judicial authorities, it seems, were then sometimes rather hard in the mouth.

NOTE (L.)—Page 103, line 30.

So far from being the case that the enlightened and wealthy classes were oppressed and enslaved under the *ancien régime*, it may be said, on the contrary, that all, including the *bourgeoisie*, were frequently far too free to do all they liked; since the Royal authority did not dare to prevent members of these classes from constantly creating themselves an exceptional position, to the detriment of the people; and almost always considered it necessary to sacrifice the latter to them, in order to obtain their good will, or put a stop to their ill humour. It may be said that, in the eighteenth century, a Frenchman belonging to these classes could more easily resist the Government, and force it to use conciliatory measures with him, than an Englishman of the same position in life could have done at that time. The authorities often considered themselves obliged to use towards such a man a far more temporising and timid policy than the English Government would ever have thought itself bound to employ towards an English subject in the same category —so wrong is it to confound independence with liberty. Nothing is less independent than a free citizen.

Note (LI.)—Page 103, line 37.

REASON THAT FREQUENTLY OBLIGED THE ABSOLUTE GOVERNMENT IN THE ANCIENT STATE OF SOCIETY TO RESTRAIN ITSELF.

In ordinary times the augmentation of old taxes, and more especially the imposition of new taxes, are the only subjects likely to cause trouble to a Government, or excite a people. Under the old financial constitution of Europe, when any Prince had expensive desires, or plunged into an adventurous line of policy, or allowed his finances to become disordered, or (to take another instance) needed money for the purpose of sustaining himself by winning partisans by means of enormous gains or heavy salaries that they had never earned, or by keeping up numerous armies, by undertaking great public works, &c. &c., he was obliged at once to have recourse to taxation; a proceeding that immediately roused and excited every class, especially that class which creates revolutions— the people. Nowadays, in similar positions, loans are contracted, the immediate effect of which passes almost unperceived, and the final result of which is only felt by the succeeding generation.

Note (LII.)—Page 105, line 29.

As one example, among many others, the fact may be cited, that the principal domains in the jurisdiction of Mayenne were farmed out to *Fermiers-Généraux*, who took as *Sous-Fermiers* little miserable tillers of land, who had nothing of their own, and for whom they were obliged to furnish the most necessary farming utensils. It may be well conceived that *Fermiers-Généraux* of this kind had no great consideration for the farmers or due-paying tenants of the old feudal *Seigneur*, who had put them in his place, and that the exercise of feudalism in such hands as these was often more hard to bear than in the Middle Ages.

Note (LIII.)—Page 105, line 29.

ANOTHER EXAMPLE.

The inhabitants of Mantbazon had put upon the *taille* the Stewards of the Duchy, which was in possession of the Prince de Rohan, although these Stewards only farmed in his name. This Prince (who must have been extremely wealthy) not only caused this 'abuse,' as he termed it, to be put a stop to, but obtained the reimbursement of 5844 livres 15 sous, which he had been improperly made to pay, and which was charged upon the inhabitants.

Note (LIV.)—Page 108, line 7.

EXAMPLE OF THE MANNER IN WHICH THE PECUNIARY CLAIMS OF THE CLERGY ALIENATED FROM THEM THE HEARTS OF THOSE WHOSE ISOLATED POSITION OUGHT TO HAVE CONCILIATED THEM.

The Curé of Noisai asserted that the inhabitants were obliged to undertake the repairs of his barn and winepress, and asked for the imposition of a local tax for that purpose. The *Intendant* gave answer that the inhabitants were only obliged to repair the parsonage-house, and that the barn and wine-press were to be at the expense of this pastor, who was evidently more busied about the affairs of his farm than his spiritual flock (1767).

Note (LV.)—Page 110, line 4.

In one of the memorials sent up in 1788 by the peasants—a memorial written with much clearness and in a moderate tone, in answer to an inquiry instituted by a Provincial Assembly—the following passages occur :—' In addition to the abuses occasioned by the mode of levying the *taille*, there exists that of the *garnissaires*. These men generally arrive five times during the collection of the *taille*. They are commonly *invalides*, or Swiss soldiers. They remain every time four or five days in the parish, and are taxed at 36 sous a day by the tax-receipt office. As to the assessment of the *taille*, we will forbear to point out the too well-known abuses occasioned by the arbitrary measures employed and the bad effects produced by the officious parts played by officers who are frequently incapable and almost always partial and vindictive. They have been the cause, however, of many disturbances and quarrels, and have occasioned proceedings at law, extremely expensive for the parties pleading, and very advantageous to the courts.'

Note (LVI.)—Page 110, line 39.

THE SUPERIORITY OF THE METHODS ADOPTED IN THE PROVINCES POSSESSING ASSEMBLIES (PAYS D'ÉTAT) RECOGNISED BY THE GOVERNMENT FUNCTIONARIES THEMSELVES.

A confidential letter, written by the Director of the Taxes to the *Intendant*, on June 3rd, 1772, has the following :—' In the *Pays d'États*, the tax being a fixed *tantième* (percentage), every taxpayer is subject to it, and really pays it. An augmentation upon this *tantième* is made in the assessment, in proportion to the augmentation required by the King upon the total supplied—for instance, a million instead of 900,000 livres. This is a simple operation; whilst in the *Généralité* the assessment is personal, and, so to say, arbitrary ; some pay their due, others only the half, others the third, the quarter, or nothing at all. How, in this case, subject the amount of taxation to the augmentation of one-ninth ? '

Note (LVII.)—Page 112, line 37.

THE MANNER IN WHICH THE PRIVILEGED CLASSES UNDERSTOOD AT FIRST THE PROGRESS OF CIVILISATION IN ROAD-MAKING.

Count X., in a letter to the *Intendant*, complains of the very little zeal shown in the establishment of a road in his neighbourhood. He says it is the fault of the *Subdélégué* who does not use sufficient energy in the exercise of his functions, and will not compel the peasants to do their forced labour (*corvées*).

Note (LVIII.)—Page 112, line 42.

ARBITRARY IMPRISONMENT FOR THE CORVÉE.

An example is given in a letter of a *Grand Prévôt*, in 1768:—'I ordered yesterday,' it says, 'the imprisonment of three men (at the demand of M. C., Sub-Engineer), for not having done their *corvée*. Upon which there was a considerable agitation among the women of the village, who exclaimed, "The poor people are thought of quite enough when the *corvée* is to be done; but nobody takes care to see they have enough to live upon."'

Note (LIX.)—Page 113, line 20.

The resources for the making of roads were of two kinds. The greater was the *corvée*, for all the great works that required only labour; the smaller was derived from the general taxation, the amount of which was placed at the disposition of the *Ponts et Chaussées* for the expenses of works requiring science. The privileged classes—that is to say, the principal landowners—though more interested than all in the construction of roads, contributed nothing to the *corvée* and, moreover, were still exempt otherwise, inasmuch as the taxation for the *Ponts et Chaussées* was annexed to the *taille*, and levied in the same manner.

Note (LX.)—Page 113, line 29.

EXAMPLE OF FORCED LABOUR IN THE TRANSPORT OF CONVICTS.

It may be seen by a letter, addressed by a Commissary at the head of the police department of convict-gangs, to the *Intendant*, in 1761, that the peasants were compelled to cart the galley-slaves on their way; that they executed this task with very ill will; and that they were frequently maltreated by the convict-guards, 'inasmuch,' says the Commissary, 'as the guards are coarse and brutal fellows, and the peasants who undertake this work by compulsion are often insolent.'

Turgot has given descriptions of the inconvenience and hardship of forced labour for the transport of military baggage, which, after a perusal of the office papers, appear not to have been exaggerated. Among other things, he says that its chief hardship consisted in the unequal distribution of a very heavy burden, inasmuch as it fell entirely upon a small number of parishes, which had the misfortune of being placed on the high road. The distance to be done was often one of five, six, or sometimes ten and fifteen leagues. In which case three days were necessary for the journey out and home again. The compensation given to the landowners only amounted to one-fifth of the expense that fell upon them. The period when forced labour was required was generally the summer, the time of harvest. The oxen were almost always over-driven, and frequently fell ill after having been employed at the work—so much so that a great number of landowners preferred giving a sum of 15 to 20 livres rather than supply a waggon and four oxen. The consequent confusion which took place was unavoidable. The peasants were constantly exposed to violence of treatment from the military. The officers almost always demanded more than was their due; and sometimes they obliged the drivers, by force, to harness saddle-horses to the vehicles at the risk of doing them a serious injury. Sometimes the soldiers insisted upon riding upon carts already overloaded; at other times, impatient at the slow progress of the oxen, they goaded them with their swords, and when the peasants remonstrated they were maltreated.

EXAMPLE OF THE MANNER IN WHICH FORCED LABOUR WAS APPLIED TO EVERYTHING.

A correspondence arising, upon a complaint made by the Intendant of the Naval department at Rochefort, concerning the difficulties made by the peasants who were obliged by the *corvée* to cart the wood purchased by the navy contractors in the different provinces for the purposes of shipbuilding, shows that the peasants were in truth still (1775) obliged to do this forced labour, the price of which the Intendant himself fixed. The Minister of the Navy transferred the complaint to the Intendant of Tours, with the order that he must see to the supply of the carriages required. The Intendant, M. Ducluzel, refused to authorise this species of forced labour, whereupon the Minister wrote him a threatening letter, telling him that he would have to answer for his refusal to the King. The Intendant, to this, replied at once (December 11th, 1775) with firmness, that, during the ten years he had been Intendant at Tours, he never had chosen to authorise these *corvées*, on account of the inevitable abuses resulting from them, for which the price fixed for the use of the vehicles was no compensation. 'For frequently,' says his letter, 'the animals are crippled by the weight of the enormous masses they are obliged to drag through roads as bad as the time of year when they are ordered out.' What encouraged the Intendant in his resistance seems to have been a letter of M. Turgot, which is annexed to the papers on this matter. It is dated on July 30th, 1774, shortly after his becoming Minister; and it says that he himself never authorised these *corvées* at Limoges, and approves of M. Ducluzel for not authorising them at Tours.

It is proved by some portions of this correspondence that the timber contractors frequently exacted this forced labour even when they were not authorised to do so by the contracts made between themselves and the State, inasmuch as they thus profited at least one-third in the economy of their transport expenses. An example of the profit thus obtained is given by a *Subdélégué* in the following computation : ' Distance of the transport of the wood from the spot where it is cut to the river, by almost impracticable cross-roads, six leagues; time employed in going and coming back, two days; reckoning (as an indemnity to the *corvéables*) the square foot at the rate of six liards a league, the whole amounts to 13 francs 10 sous for the journey —a sum scarcely sufficient to pay the actual expenses of the small landowner, of his assistant, and of the oxen or horses harnessed to his cart.

His own time and trouble, and the work of his beasts, are dead losses to him.' On May 17th, 1776, the Intendant was served by the Minister with a positive order from the King to have this *corvée* executed. M. Ducluzel being then dead, his successor, M. l'Escalopier, very readily obeyed, and published an ordinance declaring that the *Subdélégué* had to make the assessment of the amount of labour to be levied upon each parish, in consequence of which the different persons obliged to statute labour in the said parishes were constrained to go, according to the time and place set forth by the syndics, to the spot where the wood might happen to be, and cart it at the price regulated by the *Subdélégué*.

NOTE (LXIII.)—Page 115, line 22.

EXAMPLE OF THE MANNER IN WHICH THE PEASANTS WERE OFTEN TREATED.

In 1768 the King allowed a remittance of 2000 francs to be made upon the *taille* in the parish of Chapelle-Blanche, near Saumur. The *curé* wanted to appropriate a part of this sum to the construction of a belfry, in order to get rid of the sound of the bells that annoyed him, as he said, in his parsonage-house. The inhabitants complained and resisted. The *Subdélégué* took part with the *curé*, and had three of the principal inhabitants arrested during the night and put into prison.

Further examples may be found in a Royal order to imprison for a fortnight a woman who had insulted two of the mounted rural police; and another order for the imprisonment for a fortnight of a stocking-weaver who had spoken ill of the same police. In this latter case the Intendant replied to the Minister, that he had already put the man in prison— a proceeding that met with the approval of the Minister. This abuse of the *maréchaussée* had arisen from the fact of the violent arrest of several beggars, that seems to have greatly shocked the population. The *Subdélégué*, it appears, in arresting the

weaver, made publicly known that all who should continue to insult the *maréchaussée* should be even still more severely punished.

It appears by the correspondence between the *Subdélégué* and their Intendant (1760-1770) that orders were given by him to them to have all ill-doing persons arrested—not to be tried, but to be punished forthwith by imprisonment. In one instance the *Subdélégué* asks leave of the Intendant to condemn to perpetual imprisonment two dangerous beggars whom he had arrested ; in another we find the protest of a father against the arrest of his son as a vagabond, because he was travelling without his passport. Again, a householder of X. demands the arrest of a man, one of his neighbours, who had come to establish himself in the parish, to whom he had been of service, but who had behaved ill, and was disagreeable to him ; and the Intendant of Paris writes to request the Intendant of Rouen to be kind enough to render this service to the householder, who is one of his friends.

In another case an Intendant replies to a person who wants to have some beggars set at liberty, saying that the *Dépôt des Mendicants* was not to be considered as a prison, but only as a house intended for the detention of beggars and vagabonds, as an 'administrative correction.' This idea has come down to the French Penal Code, so much have the traditions of the old monarchy, in these matters, maintained themselves.

Note (LXIV.)—Page 121, line 7.

It has been said that the character of the philosophy of the eighteenth century was a sort of adoration of human reason—a boundless confidence in its almighty power to transform at its will laws, institutions, and morals. But, upon examination, we shall see that, in truth, it was more their own reason that some of these philosophers adored than human reason. None ever showed less confidence in the wisdom of mankind than these men. I could name many who had almost as much contempt for the masses as for the Divinity. The latter they treated with the arrogance of rivals, the former with the arrogance of upstarts. A real and respectful submission to the will of the majority was as far from their minds as submission to the Divine will. Almost all the revolutionists of after days have displayed this double character. There is a wide distance between their disposition and the respect shown by the English and Americans to the opinion of the majority of their fellow-citizens. Individual reason in those countries has its own pride and confidence in itself, but is never insolent; it has thus led the way to freedom, whilst in France it has done nothing but invent new forms of servitude.

Note (LXV.)—Page 132, line 15.

Frederick the Great, in his Memoirs, has said: 'Your great men, such as Fontenelle, Voltaire, Hobbes, Collins, Shaftesbury, Bolingbroke, have struck a mortal blow at religion. Men began to look into that which they had blindly adored; reason overthrew superstition; disgust for all the fables they had believed succeeded. Deism acquired many followers. As Epicureanism became fatal to the idolatrous worship of the heathen, so did Deism in our days to the Judaical visions adopted by our forefathers. The freedom of opinion prevalent in England contributed greatly to the progress of philosophy.'

It may be seen by the above passage that Frederick the Great, at the time he wrote those lines, that is to say, in the middle of the eighteenth century, still at that time looked upon England as the seat of irreligious doctrines. But a still more striking fact may be gathered from it, namely, that one of the sovereigns, the most experienced in the knowledge of man, and of affairs in general, does not appear to have the slightest idea of the political utility of religion. The errors of judgment in the mind of his instructors had evidently disordered the natural qualities of his own.

Note (LXVI.)—Page 150, line 1.

The spirit of progress which showed itself in France at the end of the eighteenth century appeared at the same time throughout all Germany, and was everywhere accompanied by the same desire to change the institutions of the time. A German historian gives the following picture of what was then going on in his own country:—

'In the second half of the eighteenth century the new spirit of the age gradually introduced itself even into the ecclesiastical territories. Reforms were begun in them; industry and tolerance made their way in them on every side; and that enlightened absolutism, which had already taken possession of the large states, penetrated even there. It must be said at the same time, that at no period of the eighteenth century had these ecclesiastical territories possessed such remarkable and estimable Princes as during the last ten years preceding the French Revolution.'

The resemblance of this picture to that which France then offered is remarkable. In France, the movement in favour of amelioration and progress began at the same epoch; and the men the most able to govern appeared on the stage just at the time when the Revolution was about to swallow up everything.

It must be observed also how much all that portion of Germany was visibly hurried on by the movement of civilisation and political progress in France.

NOTE (LXVII.)—Page 151, line 1.

THE LAWS OF ENGLAND PROVE THAT IT IS POSSIBLE FOR INSTITUTIONS TO BE FULL OF DEFECTS AND YET NOT PREVENT THE ACCOMPLISHMENT OF THE PRINCIPAL END AND AIM FOR WHICH THEY WERE ESTABLISHED.

The power, which nations possess, of prospering in spite of the imperfections to be met with in secondary portions of their institutions, as long as the general principles and the actual spirit which animate those institutions are full of life and vigour, is a phenomenon which manifests itself with peculiar distinctness when the judicial constitution of England in the last century, as described by Blackstone, is looked into.

The attention is immediately arrested by two great diversities, that are very striking:—

First. The diversity of the laws.

Secondly. The diversity of the Courts that administer them.

I.—*Diversity of the Laws.*—(1.) The laws are different for England (properly so called), for Scotland, for Ireland, for the different European dependencies of Great Britain, such as the Isle of Man, the Channel Islands, &c., and, finally, for the British Colonies.

(2.) In England itself may be found four kinds of laws—the common law, statute law, canon law, and equity. The common law is itself divided into general customs adopted throughout the whole kingdom, and customs specially belonging to certain manors or certain towns, or sometimes only to certain classes, such as the trades. These customs sometimes differ greatly from each other; as those, for instance, which, in opposition to the general tendency of the English laws require an equal distribution of property among all the children (gavelkind), and, what is still more singular, give a right of primogeniture to the youngest child (borough-English).

II.—*Diversity of the Courts.*— Blackstone informs us that the law has instituted a prodigious variety of different courts. Some idea of this may be obtained from the following extremely summary analysis:—

(1.) In the first place there were the Courts established without the limits of England, properly so called; such as the Scotch and Irish courts, which never were dependencies of the superior courts in England, although an appeal lies from these several jurisdictions to the House of Lords.

(2.) In England itself, if I am correct in my memory, among the classifications of Blackstone are to be found the following:

1. Eleven kinds of Courts of Common Law, four of which, it is true,

seem to have already fallen into disuse.

2. Three kinds of courts, the jurisdiction of which extends to the whole country, but which take cognisance only of certain matters.

3. Ten kinds of courts, having a special character of their own. One of these kinds consists of Local Courts, established by different Acts of Parliament, and existing by tradition, either in London itself or in towns and boroughs in the counties. These Courts were so numerous, and were so extremely various in their constitution and in their regulations, that it would be out of the question to attempt to give a detailed account of them.

Thus, in England (properly so called) alone, if Blackstone is to be believed, there existed, at the period when he wrote, that is to say, in the second half of the eighteenth century, twenty-four kinds of Courts, several of which were subdivided into a great number of individual courts, each of which had its special peculiarities. If we set aside those kinds, which appear at that time to have almost fallen into disuse, we shall then find eighteen or twenty.

If now the judicial system in itself be examined it will be found to contain all sorts of imperfections.

In spite of the multiplicity of the courts there was frequently a want of smaller courts, of primary instance, placed within the reach of those concerned, and empowered to judge on the spot, and at little expense, all minor matters. This want rendered such legal proceedings perplexing and expensive. The same matters came under the jurisdiction of several courts; and thus an embarrassing uncertainty hung over the commencements of legal proceedings. Some of the Appeal Courts were also Courts of original jurisdiction—sometimes the Courts of Common Law, at other times the Courts of Equity. There was a great diversity of Appeal Courts. The only central point was that of the House of Lords. The administrative litigant was not separated from the ordinary litigant—a fact which, in the eyes of most French legal men, would appear a monstrous anomaly. All these courts, moreover,

looked for the grounds of their judgments in four different kinds of legislation; that of the Courts of Equity was established upon practice and tradition, since its very object was most frequently to go against custom and statute, and to correct, by the rules of the system framed by the Judges in Equity, all that was antiquated or too harsh in statute and custom.

These blemishes were very great; and if the enormous old machine of the English judicial system be compared with the modern construction of that of France, and the simplicity, consistence, and natural connexity to be observed in the latter, with the remarkable complication and incoherence of the former, the errors of the English jurisprudence will appear greater still. Yet there is not a country in the world in which, in the days of Blackstone, the great ends of justice are more completely attained than in England; that is to say, no country in which every man, whatever his condition of life—whether he appeared in court as a common individual or a Prince—was more sure of being heard, or found in the tribunals of his country better guarantees for the defence of his property, his liberty, and his life.

It is not meant by this that the defects of the English judicial system were of any service to what I have here called the great ends of justice: it proves only that in every judicial organisation there are secondary defects that are only partially injurious to these ends of justice; and other principal ones, that not only prove injurious to them, but destroy them altogether, although joined to many secondary perfections. The first mentioned are the most easily perceived; they are the defects that generally first strike common minds: they stare one in the face, as the saying goes. The others are often more concealed; and it is not always the men the most learned in the law, and other men in the profession, who discover them and point them out.

It must be observed, moreover, that the same qualities may be either secondary or principal, according to the period of history or the political organisation of a country. In periods of aristocratic predominance and inequality everything that tends to lessen any privilege of any individual before the face of justice,·to afford guarantees to the weak against the strong, and to give a predominance to the action of the state—which is naturally impartial in differences only occurring between subjects—becomes a principal quality; whereas it diminishes in importance in proportion to the inclination of the social state and political constitution towards democracy.

In studying the English judicial system upon these principles it will be found that, although it permitted the existence of every defect that could contribute to render justice in that country obscure, hampered, slow, expensive, and inconvenient, it had taken infinite precautions to prevent the strong from ever being favoured at the expense of the weak, or the State at the expense of the private individual. The more the observer penetrates into the details of the English legislation the more he will see that every citizen was

provided with all sorts of weapons for his defence, and that matters were so arranged as to afford to every one the greatest number of guarantees possible against partiality, actual venality, and that sort of venality which is more common, and especially more dangerous in democratic times—the venality consisting of the servility of the courts towards the Government.

In this point of view the English judicial system, in spite of the numerous secondary errors that may still be found in it, appears to me superior to the French, which, although almost entirely untainted, it is true, by any one of these defects, does not at the same time offer in like degree the principal qualities that are to be found in it, which, although excellent in the guarantees it affords to every citizen in all disputes between individuals, fails precisely in that point that ought always to be strengthened in a democratic state of society like the French, namely, in the guarantees afforded to individuals against the State.

NOTE (LXVIII.)—Page 151, line 19.

ADVANTAGES ENJOYED BY THE GÉNÉRALITÉ OF PARIS.

This *Généralité* was as much favoured in charities bestowed by the Government as it was in the levying of taxes. An example may be found in a letter of the *Contrôleur-Général* to the *Intendant* of the *Généralité* of the Île-de-France (dated May 22nd, 1787), in which he informs the latter that the King had fixed the sum, which was to be employed upon works of charity during the year, in the *Généralité* of Paris, at 172,800 livres; and 100,000 livres,

moreover, were destined for the purchase of cows, to be given to different husbandmen. It may be seen by this letter that the sum of 172,000 livres was to be distributed by the *Intendant* alone, with the proviso that he was to conform himself to the general rules already made known to him by the Government, and that he was to lay the account of the distribution before the *Contrôleur-Général* for approval.

NOTE (LXIX.)—Page 152, line 27.

The administration of the old monarchy was made up of a multitude of different powers, which had been established at different times, but generally for the purposes of the

Treasury, and not of the Administration, properly so called, and which frequently had the same field of action. It was thus impossible to avoid confusion and contention otherwise than by each party acting but little, or even doing nothing at all. As soon as they made any efforts to rise above this sort of languor, they hampered and entangled each other's movements; and thus it happened that the complaints made against the complication of the administrative machinery, and the confusion as to its different attributions, were very much more grievous during the years that immediately preceded the Revolution than thirty or forty years before. The political institutions of the country had not become worse— on the contrary, they had been greatly ameliorated; but the general political movement had become much more active.

Note (LXX.)—Page 157, line 30.

ARBITRARY AUGMENTATION OF THE TAXES.

What was here said by the King respecting the *taille* might have been said by him, with as much reason, concerning the *vingtièmes*, as may be seen by the following correspondence :—In 1772 the *Contrôleur-Général* Terray had decided upon a considerable augmentation (as much as 100,000 livres) upon the *vingtièmes* of the *Généralité* of Tours. It is evident that this measure caused M. Ducluzel, an able administrator and an honourable man, both sorrow and embarrassment; for, in a confidential letter, he says : 'It is probably the facility with which the 200,000 livres ' (a previous augmentation) 'have been given, that has encouraged the cruel interpretation and the letter of the month of June.'

In a private and confidential letter, which the Director of Contributions wrote thereupon to the *Intendant*, he says: 'If the augmentations which, have been demanded appear to you, on account of the general distress, to be as aggravating and as revolting as you give me to understand, it would be better for the province, which can have no other defence or protection than in your generous good-feeling, that you should spare it, at least, the *rôles de supplément*, a retroactive tax, that is always odious.'

It may be seen by this correspondence what a complete absence there was of any solid basis, and what arbitrary measures were exercised, each with honest intentions. Both Minister and Intendant laid the weight of the increased taxation sometimes upon the agricultural rather than the manufacturing interests, sometimes upon one kind of agriculture more than another (as the growth of vines, for instance), according as they fancied that the manufacturing or any one branch of the agricultural interest ought to be more tenderly handled.

Note (LXXI.)—Page 159, line 13.

EXPRESSIONS USED BY TURGOT RESPECTING THE COUNTRY PEOPLE IN THE PREAMBLE OF A ROYAL DECLARATION.

'The rural communities consist, throughout the greater part of the kingdom, of poor peasants, who are ignorant and brutal, and incapable of self-administration.'

NOTE (LXXII.)—Page 163, line 24.

HOW IT WAS THAT REVOLUTIONARY IDEAS NATURALLY SPRANG UP IN MEN'S MINDS, EVEN UNDER THE OLD MONARCHY.

In 1779 an *avocat* addressed a petition to the Council for a decree to establish a maximum of the price of straw throughout the whole kingdom.

NOTE (LXXIII.)—Page 163, line 32.

The Head Engineer, in a letter written to the *Intendant*, in 1781, relative to a demand for an increase of indemnification, thus expresses himself: 'The claimant does not pay heed to the fact that the indemnifications granted are an especial favour to the *Généralité* of Tours, and that people ought to consider themselves very fortunate in recovering only a part of their loss. If such compensations as the claimant requires were to be given, four millions would not suffice.'

NOTE (LXXIV.)—Page 167, line 39.

The Revolution did not break out on account of this prosperity, but that active, uneasy, intelligent, innovating, ambitious spirit, that was destined to produce the Revolution—the democratic spirit of new states of society—began to stir up everything, and, before it overthrew for a period the social state of France, was already strong enough to agitate and develop it.

NOTE (LXXV.)—Page 169, line 13.

COLLISION OF THE DIFFERENT ADMINISTRATIVE POWERS IN 1787.

The following may be taken as an example :—The intermediate commission of the Provincial Assembly of the Île-de-France claimed the administration of the *Dépôt de Mendicité*. The *Intendant* insisted upon its remaining in his own hands, 'inasmuch,' said he, 'as this establishment is not kept up by the funds of the province.' During the discussion, the intermediate commission communicated with the intermediate commissions of other provinces, in order to learn their opinions. Among other answers given to its questions, exists one from the intermediate commission of Champagne, informing that of the Île-de-France that it had met with the very same difficulties, and had offered the same resistance.

NOTE (LXXVI.)—Page 172, line 2.

In the minutes of the first Provincial Assembly of the Île-de-France, the following declaration may be found, proceeding from the mouth of the reporter of the committee :—' Up to the present time the functions of syndic, which are far more onerous than honourable, are such as to indispose from accepting them all those who unite a sufficient competency to the intelligence to be expected from their position in life.'

NOTE (LXXVII.)—Page 173, line 9.

FEUDAL RIGHTS, WHICH STILL EXISTED AT THE PERIOD OF THE REVOLUTION, ACCORDING TO THE FEUDAL LAWYERS.

It is not the intention of the author here to write a treatise upon feudal rights, and, least of all, to attempt any research into their possible origin. It is simply his desire to point out those which were still exercised in the eighteenth century. These rights played so important a part at that time, and have since retained so large a space in the imagination of the very persons who have no longer anything to suffer from them, that it was a most interesting task to find out precisely what they were when the Revolution destroyed them all. For this purpose a great number of *terriers*, or rolls of feudal manors, were studied,—those of the most recent date being selected. But this manner of proceeding led to nothing ; for the feudal rights, although regulated by a legal code, which was the same throughout the whole of feudal Europe, were infinitely various in their kinds, according to the province, or even the districts, where they existed. The only system, then, which appeared likely to lead, in an approximate manner, to the required result, was the following :—These feudal rights were continually giving rise to all sorts of disputes and litigation. In these cases it was necessary to know how these rights were acquired, how they were lost, in what they consisted exactly, which were the dues that could only be collected by virtue of a Royal patent, which those that could only be established by private title, which those on the contrary that had no need of formal titles, and might be collected upon the strength of local custom, or even in virtue of long usage. Again, when they were for sale, it was necessary to know in what manner they were to be valued, and what capital each of them represented, according to its importance. All these points, so immediately affecting a thousand pecuniary interests, were subject to litigation ; and thus was constituted a distinct class of legal men, whose only occupation it was to elucidate them. Many of these men wrote during the second half of the eighteenth century ; some even just upon the threshold of the Revolution. They were not lawyers, properly speaking, but practitioners, whose only task it was to point out to professional men the rules to be followed in this special and little attractive portion of legal science. By an attentive study of these *feudistes*, a tolerably minute and distinct idea of a subject, the size and confusion of which is at first bewildering, may be at last come at. The author gives below the most succinct summary he was able to make of his work. These notes are principally derived from the work of Edmé de Fréminville, who wrote about the year 1750, and from that of Renauldon, written in 1765, and entitled ' *Traité historique et pratique des Droits Seigneuriaux.*'

The *cens* (that is to say, the perpetual quit-rent, in kind and in money, which, by the feudal laws, was affixed to the possession of certain lands) still, in the eighteenth century, affected most deeply the position of a great number of landed proprietors. This *cens* continued to be indivisible, that is to say, the entire *cens* might be claimed of any one of the possessors of the property, subject to the *cens* at will. It was always irredeemable. No proprietor of any lands, subject to the *cens*, could sell them without being exposed to the *retrait censuel*, that is to say, without being obliged to let the property be taken back at the price of the sale; but this only took place in certain *coutumes*. The *coutume* of Paris, which was the most general, did not recognise this right.

Lods et Ventes.—It was a general rule that, in every part of the country where the *coutume* prevailed, the sale of every estate subject to the *cens* should produce what were called *lods et ventes*; in other words, the fines paid to the lords of the manor, upon the alienation of this kind of property. These dues were more or less considerable, according to the customs of the manor, but were everywhere considerable enough; they existed just as well in parts where the *droit écrit* (written law) was established. They generally consisted of one-sixth of the price, and were then named *lods*. But in these parts the lord of the manor had to establish his rights. In what was called *pays écrit*, as well as in *pays coutumier*, the *cens* gave the lord of the manor a privilege which took precedence of all other debts on the estate.

Terrage or Champart.—Agrier.— Tasque.—These dues consisted of a certain portion of the produce, which the lord of the manor levied upon lands subject to the *cens*. The amount varied according to the contracts or the customs of the place. This right is frequently to be met with in the eighteenth century. I believe that the *terrage*, even in *pays coutumier*, could only be claimed under express deed. The *terrage* was either *seigneurial* or *foncier*. It is not necessary to explain here the distinctions which existed between these two different kinds. Suffice it to say that the *terrage foncier* was fixed for thirty years, like the *rentes foncières*, whilst the *terrage seigneurial* was irredeemable. Lands subject to *terrage* could not be mortgaged without the consent of the lord of the manor.

Bordelage.—A right which only existed in the Nivernais and Bourbonnais countries, and which consisted in an annual quit-rent, paid in money, corn, and fowls, upon lands subject to the *cens*. This right entailed very rigorous consequences: non-payment of the dues during three years gave cause for the exercise of the *commise* or entry to the advantage of the lord of the manor. A tenant owing the *bordelage* was more open than any other to a variety of annoyances on his property. Sometimes the lord of the manor possessed the right of claiming his inheritance, even when he died having heirs who had legal rights to the succession. This was the most rigorous of any of the feudal rights; and the law had finally restricted it only to rural inheritances. 'For,' as our author says, 'the peasant is always the mule ready to bear every burden.'

Marciage was the name of peculiar dues levied upon the possessors of land, subject to the *cens*, in very few places, and consisting in certain payments due only upon the natural death of the lord of the manor.

Dîmes Inféodées.—There still existed in the eighteenth century a great number of tithes in fief. They were generally established by separate contract, and did not result from the mere fact of the lordship of the manor.

Parcière.—The *parcières* were dues levied upon the crops of fruit gathered on the manor-lands. They bore resemblance to the *champart* and the *dîme inféodée*, and were principally in usage in the Bourbonnais and Auvergne countries.

Carpot.—This was observed in the Bourbonnais country, and was a due levied upon the vineyards, as the *champart* was upon arable lands, that is to say, it was levied upon a portion of the crops. It amounted to a quarter of the vintage.

Servage.—The customs that still possessed traces of serfdom were called *coutumes serves*; they were very few in number. In the provinces where they were still observed there were no estates, or at least very few, where some traces of ancient serfdom were not visible. [This remark is derived from a work written in 1765.] The *Servage* (or, as the author terms it, the *Servitude*) was either personal or real.

The personal servitude was attached to the person, and followed him everywhere. Wherever the serf might go, to whatever place he might transport his substance, he might be reclaimed by the lord by right of *suite*. Our authors cite several legal verdicts that establish this right—among others, a verdict given on the 17th June, 1760, in which the court decides against a *Seigneur* of the Nivernais in respect to his right of claiming the succession of Pierre Truchet, who was the son of a serf subject to *poursuite*, according to the custom of the Nivernais, who had married a Parisian woman, and who had died in Paris, as well as his son. But this verdict seems to have been founded on the fact that Paris was a 'place of refuge' (*lieu d'asile*) in which the *suite* could not take place. If the right of *asile* alone prevented the *Seigneur* from seizing upon property possessed by his serfs in the *lieu d'asile*, it formed no opposition against his claiming to succeed to property left in his own manor.

The 'real' servitude resulted from the occupation of land, and might cease upon the land being given up or residence in a certain place changed.

Corvées.—The right possessed by the lord of the manor over his subjects, by means of which he could employ for his own profit a certain number of their days of labour, or of their oxen and horses. The *corvée à volonté*, that is to say, at the arbitrary will of the *Seigneur*, had been completely abolished : forced labour had been for some time past confined to a certain number of days a year.

The *corvée* might be either personal or real. The personal *corvées* were paid by labourers and workmen, whose residence was established upon the manor, each according to his occupation. The real *corvées* were attached to the possession of certain

lands. Nobles, ecclesiastics, clerical personages, officers of justice, advocates, physicians, notaries, and bankers, and men in that position of life, were exempt from the *corvée*. A verdict, given on the 18th August, 1735, is cited by one of our authors, exempting a notary whom his *Seigneur* wanted to force to come for nothing, during three days, and draw up certain law papers concerning the *seigneurie* on which the notary resided. Another verdict, of the date of 1750, decides that, when the *corvée* is personal, it may be paid either in person or by money, the choice to be left to the person by whom it is due. Every *corvée* had to be established by written title-deeds. The *corvée seigneuriale* had become extremely rare in the eighteenth century.

Banalités. (Rights possessed by the lords of certain manors to oblige those residing on them to make use of his baking-office, mill, &c., upon payment.)—The provinces of Flanders, Artois, and Hainault were alone exempt from *banalités*. The Custom of Paris rigorously requires that this should not be exercised without written title. Every person domiciled within the circuit of the *banalité* was subject to it, and, most generally, even the nobles and priests also.

Besides the *banalité* of the winepress and baking-office there existed several others :—

(1.) *Banalités* of industrial establishments, such as for cloth, tanning, or hemp. This *banalité* is established by many *coutumes*, as for instance, by those of Anjou, the Maine, and Brittany.

(2.) *Banalités* of the wine-press. Few *coutumes* mention this. But that of Lorraine, as well as that of the Maine, establish it.

(3.) *Banalité* of the manor bull. No *coutumes* mention this; but there were title-deeds that established the right. The same may be said of the right of *banalité* for butchers' shambles.

In general these latter *banalités* of which we have just spoken were more uncommon, and looked upon with a still less favourable eye than the others. They could only be exercised by the clearest declaration of the *coutumes*, or, where that was wanting, by the most precise title.

Ban des Vendanges.—This was still practised throughout the whole of the kingdom in the eighteenth century. It was a simple right of police attached to the right of *haute justice*. In order to exercise it, the *Seigneur*, who was *Haut Justicier*, did not need to possess any other title. The *ban des vendanges* was obligatory upon everybody. The *coutumes* of Burgundy give the *Seigneur* the right of gathering in his vintage a day before any other vine proprietor.

Droit de Banvin.—This was a right still possessed by a quantity of *Seigneurs* (as our authors have it), either by custom or special title, to sell the wine grown upon their manors for a certain period of time, in general a month or forty days, before any one else. Among the *grandes coutumes* those of Tours, Anjou, the Maine, and La Marche alone established it, and had regulations for it. A verdict of the *Cour des Aides*, dated 28th August, 1751, authorises publicans (as an exception to the common rule) to sell wine during the *banvin*; but this must have referred only to the wine of the *Seigneur*, made from that year's growth. The *coutumes* that establish and regulate the right of *banvin* generally require that it should be founded upon legal title.

Droit de Blairie was a right belonging to the *Seigneur*, who was *Haut Justicier*, to grant permission to the inhabitants to have their cattle graze upon lands situated throughout his jurisdiction, or upon waste lands. This right did not exist in any parts regulated by *droit écrit*; but it was common enough in those where the *droit coutumier* was in force. It was to be found under different denominations, more particularly in the Bourbonnais, the Nivernais, Auvergne, and Burgundy. This right rested upon the supposition that the whole territory originally belonged to the *Seigneur*, in such wise that, after the distribution of the greater part into *fiefs, cencites*, and other concessions of lands upon quit-rents, there still remained portions which could only be used for waste pasture-ground, and of which he might grant the temporary use to others. The *blairie* was established in several *coutumes*; but it could only be claimed by a *Seigneur* who was *Haut Justicier*, and was maintained only by some special title, or at least by old claims supported by long possession.

Péages.—According to our authors, there originally existed a prodigious number of manorial tolls upon bridges, rivers, and roads. Louis XIV. did away with a great number of them. In 1724 a commission, nominated to examine into the titles by which the tolls were claimed, suppressed twelve hundred of them; and, in 1765, they were still being constantly suppressed. 'The principle observed in this respect,' says Renauldon, 'was that, inasmuch as the toll was a tax, it was necessary to be founded not only upon legal title, but upon one emanating from the sovereign.' The toll was levied '*De par le Roi*.' One of the conditions of the toll was that it should be established by *tarif* regulating the dues, which each kind of merchandise had to pay. It was necessary that this *tarif* should be approved by a decree of the Council. 'The title of concession,' says one author, 'had to be followed by uninterrupted possession.' In spite of these precautions legally taken, it appears that the value of the tolls had greatly increased in later times. 'I know one toll,' says the same author, 'that was farmed out, a century ago, at 100 livres, and now brings in 1400; and another, farmed at 39,000 livres, that brings in 90,000.' The principal ordinances or principal decrees that regulated the right of toll, were paragraph 29 of the Ordinance of 1669, and the Decrees of 1683, 1693, 1724, 1775.

The authors I have quoted, although in general favourable enough to feudal rights, acknowledge that great abuses were committed in the levying of the tolls.

Bacs.—The right of ferries differed materially from the right of toll. The latter was only levied upon merchandise; the former upon individuals, animals, and carriages. It was necessary that this right, in order to be exercised, should likewise be authorised by the King; and the dues, to be levied, had to be fixed by the same decree of Council that established and authorised it.

Droit de Leyde (to which many other names have been given in different places) was a tax levied upon merchandise brought to fairs and markets. Many lords of the manor (as appears by our *feudistes*) considered this right as one attached to the right of *haute justice*, and wholly manorial, but quite mistakenly, inasmuch as it could only be authorised by the King. At all events, this right only belonged to the *Seigneur*, who was *Haut Justicier*: he levied the police fines, to which the exercise of the right gave occasion. It appears, however, that, although by theory the *droit de leyde* could only emanate from the King, it was frequently set up solely upon the basis of feudal title or long possession.

It is very certain that fairs could not be established otherwise than by Royal authorisation.

The lords of the manor, however, had no need of any precise title, or any concession on the part of the King, for the exercise of the right of regulating the weights and measures to be used by their vassals in all fairs and markets held upon the manor. It was enough for the right to be founded upon custom and constant possession. Our authors say that all the Kings, who, one after the other, were desirous of re-establishing uniformity in the weights and measures, failed in the attempt. Matters had been allowed to remain at the same point where they were when the old *coutumes* were drawn up.

Chemins. (Rights exercised by the lords of the manor upon roads.) —The high roads, called '*Chemins du Roi*' (King's highway), belonged, in fact, to the sovereigns alone; their formation, their reparation, and the offences committed upon them, were beyond the cognisance of the *Seigneurs* or their judges. The by-roads, to be met with on any portion of a *Seigneurie*, doubtless belonged to such *Seigneurs* as were *Hauts Justiciers*. They had all the rights

of *voirie* and police upon them, and their judges took cognisance of all the offences committed upon them, except in Royal cases. At an earlier period the *Seigneurs* had been obliged to keep up the high roads passing through their *seigneurie*, and, as a compensation for the expenses incurred in these repairs, they were allowed the dues arising from tolls, settlement of boundaries, and barriers; but, at this epoch, the King had resumed the general direction of the high roads.

Eaux.—All the rivers, both navigable and floatable (admitting the passage of rafts), belonged to the King, although they flowed through the property of lords of the manor, and in spite of any title to the contrary. (See Ordinance of 1669.) If the lords of the manor levied any dues upon these rivers, it was those arising from the rights of fishing, the mills, ferry-boats, and bridge-tolls, &c., in virtue of concessions emanating only from the King. There were some lords of the manor who still arrogated to themselves the rights of jurisdiction and police upon these rivers; but this manifestly only arose from usurpation, or from concessions improperly acquired.

The smaller rivers unquestionably belonged to the *Seigneurs* through whose property they flowed. They possessed in them the same rights of property, of jurisdiction, and police, which the King possessed upon the navigable rivers. All *Seigneurs Hauts Justiciers* were universally the lords of the non-navigable rivers running through their territory. They wanted no other legal title for the exercise of their claims than that which conferred the right of *haute justice*. There were some customs, such as the *Coutume du Berri*, that authorised private individuals to erect a mill upon the seignorial river passing through the lands they occupied, without the permission of the *Seigneur*. The *Coutume de Bretagne* only granted this right to private personages who were noble. As a matter of general right, it is very certain that the *Seigneur Haut Justicier* had alone the right of erecting mills throughout every part of his jurisdiction. No one was entitled to erect barriers for the protection of his property without the permission of the judges of the *Seigneur*.

Fontaines.—Puits.—Routoirs.—Étangs.—The rain-water that fell upon the high roads belonged exclusively to the *Seigneurs Hauts Justiciers*; they alone were enabled to dispose of it. The *Seigneur Haut Justicier* possessed the right of constructing ponds in any part throughout his jurisdiction, and even upon lands in the possession of those who resided under it, upon the condition of paying them the price of the ground put under water. Private individuals were only able to make ponds upon their own soil; and, even for this, many *coutumes* require that permission should be obtained of the *Seigneur*. The *coutumes*, however, thus requiring the acquiescence of the *Seigneur*, establish that it is to be given gratuitously.

La Pêche.—The right of fishing on navigable or floatable rivers belonged only to the King, and he alone could make grants of this right. The Royal Judges alone had the right of judging offences against the right of fishery. There were many *Seigneurs*, however, who exercised the right of fishing in these streams; but they either possessed by concession made by the King, or had usurped it. No person could fish, even with the rod, in non-navigable rivers without permission from the *Seigneur Haut Justicier* within whose limits they flowed. A judgment (dated April 30th, 1749) condemns a fisherman in a similar case. Even the *Seigneurs* themselves, however, were obliged, in fishing, to observe the general regulations respecting fisheries. The *Seigneur Haut Justicier* was enabled to give the right of fishing in his river to tenants in fief, or *à cens*.

La Chasse.—The right of the chase was not allowed to be farmed out like that of fishing. It was a personal right, arising from the consideration that it belonged to the King, and that the nobles themselves could not exercise it, in the interior of their own jurisdiction, without the permission of the King. This doctrine was established in an Ordinance of 1669 (par. 30). The judges of the *Seigneur* had the power of taking

cognisance of all offences against the rights of the chase, except in cases appertaining to *bêtes uresses* (signifying, it would appear, what were generally called '*grosses bêtes*'—stags, does, &c.), which were considered Royal.

The right of shooting and hunting was more interdicted to the non-noble than any other. The fee fief of the non-noble did not even bestow it. The King never granted it in his own hunt. So closely observed was this principle, and so rigorous was the right considered, that the *Seigneur* was not allowed to give any permission to hunt. But still it did constantly occur that *Seigneurs* granted such permissions not only to nobles but to non-nobles. The *Seigneur Haut Justicier* possessed the faculty of hunting and shooting on any part of his own jurisdiction, but alone. He was allowed to make regulations and establish prohibitions upon matters appertaining to the chase throughout its extent. Every *Seigneur de Fief*, although not having the feudal power of judicial courts, was allowed to hunt and shoot in any part of his fief. Nobles who possessed neither fief nor jurisdiction were allowed to do so upon the lands belonging to them in the immediate neighbourhood of their dwelling-houses. It was decided that the non-noble possessing a park upon the territory of a *Seigneur Haut Justicier* was obliged to leave it open for the diversion of the lord. But this judgment was given as long ago as 1668.

Garennes.—Rabbit-warrens could not be established without title-right. Non-nobles, as well as nobles, were allowed to have rabbit-warrens; but the nobles alone were allowed to keep ferrets.

Colombiers. — Certain *coutumes* only give the right of *colombiers à pied* (dovecots standing apart from a building) to the *Seigneurs Hauts Justiciers*; others grant it to all holders of fiefs. In Dauphiny, Brittany, and Normandy, no non-noble was allowed to possess dovecot, pigeon-house, or aviary; the nobles alone were allowed to keep pigeons. The penalties pronounced against those who killed the pigeons were extremely severe: the most afflictive punishments were sometimes bestowed.

Such, according to the authors above cited, were the principal feudal rights still exercised and dues still levied in the second half of the eighteenth century. 'The rights here mentioned,' they add, 'are those generally established at the present time. But there are still very many others, less known and less widely practised, which only occur in certain *coutumes*, or only in certain *seigneuries*, in virtue of peculiar titles.' These rarer and more restricted feudal rights, of which our authors thus make mention, and which they enumerate, amount to the number of ninety-nine; and the greater part of them are directly prejudicial to agriculture, inasmuch as they give the *Seigneurs* certain rights over the harvests, or tolls upon the sale or transport of grain, fruit, provisions, &c. Our authors say that most of these feudal rights were out of use in their day; I have reason to believe, however, that a great number of these dues were still levied, in some places, in 1789.

After having studied, among the writers on feudal rights in the eighteenth century, the principal feudal rights still exercised, I was desirous of finding out what was their importance in the eyes of their contemporaries, at least as regarded the fortunes of those who levied them and those who had to pay them.

Renauldon, one of the authors I have mentioned, gives us an insight into this matter, by laying before us the rules that legal men had to follow in their valuation of the different feudal rights which still existed in 1765, that is to say, twenty-four years before the Revolution. According to this law writer, the rules to be observed on these matters were as follow :—

Droits de Justice.—' Some of our *coutumes*,' he says, 'estimate the value of *justice haute*, *basse*, or *moyenne* at a tenth of the revenues of the land. At that time the seignorial jurisdiction was considered of great importance. Edmé de Fréminville opines that, at the present day, the right of jurisdiction ought not to be valued at more than a twentieth of the revenues of the land; and I consider this valuation still too large.'

Droits Honorifiques.—' However inestimable these rights may be considered,' declares our author, a man of a practical turn of mind, and not easily led away by appearances, ' it would be prudent on the part of those who make valuations to fix them at a very moderate price.'

Corvées Seigneuriales.—Our author, in giving the rules for the estimation of the value of forced labour, proves that the right of enforcing it was still to be met with sometimes. He values the day's work of an ox at 20 sous, and that of the labourer at 5 sous, with his food. A tolerably good indication of the price of wages paid in 1765 may be gathered from this.

Péages.—Respecting the valuation of the tolls our author says, ' There is not one of the Seignorial rights that ought to be estimated lower than the tolls. They are very precarious. The repairs of the roads and bridges—the most useful to the commerce of the country—being now maintained by the King and the provinces, many of the tolls become useless nowadays, and they are suppressed more and more every day.

Droit de Pêche et de Chasse.—The right of fishing may be farmed out, and may thus give occasion for valuation. The right of the chase is purely personal, and cannot be farmed out; it may consequently be reckoned among the honorary rights but not among the profitable rights, and cannot, therefore, be comprehended in any valuation.

Our author then mentions more particularly the rights of *banalité*, *banvin*, *leyde*, and *blairie*, and thus proves that these rights were those most frequently exercised at that time, and that they maintained the greatest importance. He adds, ' There is a quantity of other seignorial rights, which may still be met with from time to time, but which it would be too long and indeed impossible to make mention of here. But intelligent appraisers will find sufficient rules, in the examples we have already given, for the estimation of those rights of which we do not speak.'

Estimation du Cens.—The greater number of the *coutumes* place the estimation of the *cens, au denier* 80 (8⅓ per cent.). The high valuation of the *cens* arises from the fact that it represents at the same time all such remunerative casualties as the *lods et ventes,* for instance.

Dimes inféodées.—*Terrage.*—The tithes in fief cannot be estimated at less than 4 per cent.; this sort of property calling neither for care, culture, nor expense. When the *terrage* or *champart* includes *lods et*

ventes, that is to say, when the land subject to these dues cannot be sold without paying for the right of exchange to the *Seigneur,* who has the right of tenure *in capite,* the valuation must be raised to 8⅓ per cent.; if not it must be estimated like the tithes.

Les Rentes foncières, which produced no *lods et ventes* or *droit de retenu* (that is to say, which are not seignorial revenue), ought to be estimated at 5 per cent.

ESTIMATE OF THE DIFFERENT HEREDITARY ESTATES EXISTING IN FRANCE
BEFORE THE REVOLUTION.

We recognise in France, says this writer, only three kinds of estates :—

(1.) The *Franc Alleu.*—This was a freehold estate, exempt from every kind of burden, and subject neither to seignorial duties nor dues, either profitable or honorary.

There were both noble and non-noble *francs alleux.* The noble *franc alleu* had its right of jurisdiction or fiefs dependent on it, or lands paying quit-rents : it followed all the observances of feudal law in subdivision. The non-noble *franc alleu* had neither jurisdiction, nor fief, nor *censive,* and was heritable according to the laws affecting non-nobles. The author looks upon the holders of *francs alleux* as alone possessing complete property in the land.

Valuation of Estates in Franc Alleu.—They were valued the highest of all. The *coutumes* of Auvergne and Burgundy put the valuation of them as high as 40 years' purchase. Our author opines that their valuation at 80 years' purchase would be exact. It must be observed that all non-noble *francs alleux* placed within the limits of a seignorial jurisdiction were subject to this jurisdiction. They were not in any dependence of vassalage to the *Seigneur,* but owed submission to a jurisdiction which had the position of that of the Courts of the State.

(2.) The second kind was that of estates held in fief.

(3.) The third was that of estates held on quit-rents, or, in the law language of the time, *Rotures.*

Valuation of an Estate held in Fief.—The valuation was less, according as the feudal burdens on it were greater.

(1.) In the parts of the country where written law was observed, and in many of the *coutumes,* the fiefs lay only under the obligation of what was called ' *la bouche et les mains,*' that is to say, that of doing homage.

(2.) In other *coutumes* the fiefs, besides the obligation of ' *la bouche et les mains,*' were what was called ' *de danger,*' as in Burgundy, and were subject to the *commise,* or feudal resumption, in case the holder of the property should take possession without having rendered submission or homage.

(3.) Other *coutumes,* again, as in that of Paris and many others, subject the *fiefs* not only to the obligation of doing homage, but to the *rachat,* the *quint,* and the *requint.*

(4.) By other *coutumes,* also, such as that of Poitou and a few others, they were subjected to *chambellage* dues, the *cheval de service,* &c.

Of these four all estates of the first category were valued more highly than the others.

The *coutume* of Paris laid their valuation at 20 years' purchase, which is looked upon by our author as tolerably correct.

Valuation of Estates 'en roture' and ' en censive.'—In order to come to a proper valuation, these lands have to be divided into three classes :—

(1.) Estates held simply on quit-rents.

(2.) Those which, beside the quit-rent, are subject to other kinds of feudal servitude.

(3.) Those held in mortmain, *à taille réelle, en bordelage.*

Only the first and second of these three forms of non-noble property were common in the eighteenth century ; the third was extremely rare. The valuations to be made of them, according to our author, were less on coming down to the second class, and still less on coming down to the third. Men in possession of estates of the third class were not even, strictly speaking, their owners, inasmuch as they were not able to alienate them without permission from the *Seigneur.*

Le Terrier.—The *feudistes*, whom we have cited above, point out the following rules observed in the compilation or renewal of the seignorial registers, called *' Terriers,'* mention of which has been made in many parts of the work. The *Terrier* was a single register, in which were recorded all the titles proving the rights appertaining to the *seigneurie*, whether in property or in honorary, real, personal, or mixed rights. All the declarations of the payers of the *cens*, the usages of the *seigneurie*, the leases *à cens*, &c., were inserted in it. We learn by our authors that, in the *coutume* of Paris, the *Seigneurs* were permitted to renew their registers every thirty years at the expense of their *censitaires* : they add, however, ' It may be considered a very fortunate circumstance, nevertheless, when a new one may be found once a century.' The *Terrier* could not be renewed (it was a vexatious business for all the persons dependent on the *seigneurie*) without obtaining, either from the *Grande Chancellerie* (if in cases of *seigneuries* situated within the jurisdiction of different Parliaments), or of the Parliaments (in the contrary case), an authorisation which was denominated *' Lettres à Terrier.'* The notary who drew them up was nominated by the judicial authorities. All the vassals, noble or non-noble, the payers of the *cens*, holders of long leases (*emphytéotes*), and personages subject to the jurisdiction of the *seigneurie* were bound to appear before this notary. A plan of the *seigneurie* had to be annexed to the *Terrier.*

Besides the *Terrier*, the *seigneurie* was provided with other registers, called *' lièves,'* in which the *Seigneurs* or their farmers inscribed the sums received in payment of the *cens*, with the names of those who paid and the dates of the receipts.

www.ingramcontent.com/pod-product-compliance
Lightning Source LLC
Chambersburg PA
CBHW060539030726
47498CB00004B/1251